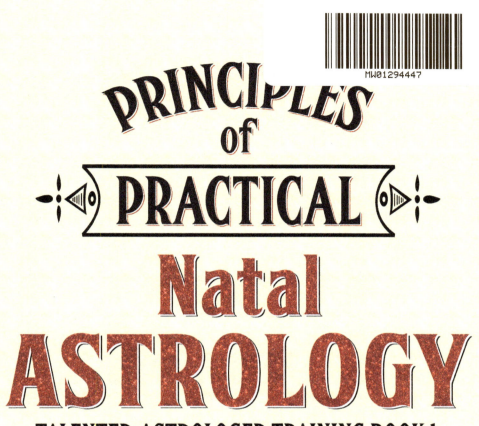

Principles of Practical Natal ASTROLOGY

TALENTED ASTROLOGER TRAINING BOOK 1

Also by Kevin B. Burk

Astrology: Understanding the Birth Chart

The Complete Node Book

The Relationship Handbook:
How to Understand and Improve Every Relationship in Your Life

The Relationship Workbook:
How to Understand and Improve Every Relationship in Your Life

Astrology Math Made Easy

The Relationship Workbook:
How to Design and Create Your Ideal Romantic Relationship

The Relationship Workbook:
The Secrets of Successful Team Building

Astrological Relationship Handbook:
How to Use Astrology to Understand Every Relationship in Your Life

Astrological Relationship Workbook:
How to Use Astrology to Understand Every Relationship in Your Life

Anger Mastery: Get Angry, Get Happy

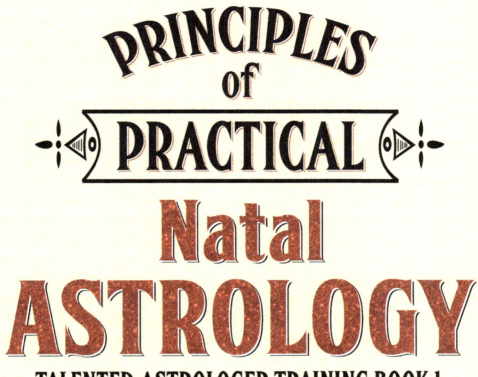

Principles of Practical Natal ASTROLOGY

TALENTED ASTROLOGER TRAINING BOOK 1

KEVIN B. BURK

Serendipity Press
La Mesa, California

ISBN 978-0-9865596-0-4

©2015 Kevin B. Burk. All rights reserved. No part of this publication may be reproduced, transmitted, transcribed, stored in a retrieval system, or translated into any language, in any form, by any means, without written permission of the author.

Printed in the United States of America.

Published by
Serendipity Press
La Mesa, California

Portions of this work appear in slightly different versions in *Anger Mastery: Get Angry, Get Happy.* ©2011 Kevin B. Burk.

All horoscope charts in this book were generated using Solar Fire™ © Astrolabe, Inc.

Celebrity birth data provided by AstroDatabank, www.AstroDatabank.com

Book design and cover design by Kevin B. Burk

For astrologers and astrology students everywhere.

Contents

PART 1
PRINCIPLES OF PRACTICAL ASTROLOGY

CHAPTER 1
What Is Practical Astrology? 3

CHAPTER 2
How to Become a Talented Astrologer 7
Deep Practice:
The Astrological Talent Code 7
   Wax On, Wax Off 8
Natal Chart Interpretation Skills 9
   Phase 1: Reading the Chart 9
   Phase 2: Drafting a Blueprint 9
   Phase 3: Building a Chair 10
How to Develop Interpretation Skills 10
The Sweet Spot: Information, Education, and Training 11

CHAPTER 3
The Art of Astrological Interpretation 13
   See What's Really There 14
   Reproduce What You See 14
   The Process of Portrait Art 15
      Begin With a Sketch 15
      Create a Context 16
      Fill in the Details 16

CHAPTER 4
Three-Dimensional Chart Interpretation 19
   The Kingdoms of Consciousness 19
   The Nature of Reality 20

The Science of Truth.. 25
The Appeal of Victim Consciousness 30
Consciousness and Astrology...................................... 31

PART 2
GRAMMAR AND SYNTAX OF THE LANGUAGE OF ASTROLOGY

CHAPTER 5
Introduction to the Grammar and Syntax of the Language of Astrology 35

The Planets: The Subject of the Sentence 35
The Predicate of the Sentence 36
    Signs: Adjectives and Adverbs 36
    Houses: Prepositions 36
    Aspects: Conjunctions 37
    House Rulers: Pronouns 37

CHAPTER 6
Meet the Planets 39

The Sun: The Hero 39
    The Sun in First Kingdom 40
    The Sun in Second Kingdom 40
    The Sun in Third Kingdom 40
    The Sun in Fourth Kingdom 41
Saturn: The Judge 41
    Saturn in First Kingdom 42
    Saturn in Second Kingdom 42
    Saturn in Third Kingdom 42
The Moon: The Reflection 43
    The Moon in First Kingdom 43
    The Moon in Second Kingdom 44
    The Moon in Third Kingdom 44

Contents

Mars: The Warrior 44
    Mars in First Kingdom 45
    Mars in Second Kingdom 45
    Mars in Third Kingdom 45
Venus: The Beloved 46
    Venus in First Kingdom 46
    Venus in Second Kingdom 47
    Venus in Third Kingdom 47
Mercury: The Storyteller 47
    Mercury in First Kingdom 48
    Mercury in Second Kingdom 48
    Mercury in Third Kingdom 48
Jupiter: The Dreamer 49
    Jupiter in First Kingdom 49
    Jupiter in Second Kingdom 49
    Jupiter in Third Kingdom 50

CHAPTER 7
Elements, Modalities, and Signs 51

The Four Elements 52
    Fire 52
    Earth 53
    Air 54
    Water 55
The Three Modalities 56
    Cardinal 56
    Fixed 57
    Mutable 58
The Twelve Signs 59
    Introduction to Essential Dignities 60
    Aries 61
    Taurus 63
    Gemini 65
    Cancer 67
    Leo 69
    Virgo 71

Libra 73
Scorpio 75
Sagittarius. 77
Capricorn 79
Aquarius 81
Pisces 83

CHAPTER 8
Simple Sentences: Planets in Signs 85
Planets in Signs Template Sentences 86
    The Sun 86
    The Moon. 87
    Mercury 87
    Venus 88
    Mars 89
    Jupiter. 89
    Saturn 90

CHAPTER 9
Houses and Angles 91
Angular, Succedent, and Cadent Houses 92
A Tour of the Houses and Angles 93
    Ascendant. 93
    1st House 93
    2nd House 94
    3rd House 95
    Imum Coeli. 96
    4th House 96
    5th House 97
    6th House 98
    Descendant 99
    7th House 100
    8th House 101
    9th House 102
    Midheaven 103
    10th House 103

- 11th House 104
- 12th House 105
- House Rulers 106
  - House Almutens 107
  - Intercepted Signs 107
- Blueprint Template Sentences for Planets in Signs and Houses 108

CHAPTER 10
Essential Dignities and the Board of Directors . . 111
- E-Z Essential Dignity™ Card 113
- The Board of Directors 115
  - Board of Directors Blueprint Templates 116
  - Sylvester Stallone's Moon in Libra 119
  - Nicolas Cage's Moon in Libra 122
  - Board of Directors Dynamic 124
  - Sting's Moon in Libra 126
  - Board of Directors Dynamic 128
- Essential Dignity and Debility 128
  - Rulership 128
  - Exaltation 128
  - Triplicity 129
  - Term 129
  - Face 129
  - Essential Debilities 129
    - Detriment 129
    - Fall 129
    - Peregrine 130
- Modern Rulership 130

CHAPTER 11
Aspects and the Outer Planets 131
- Receptions 131
- Zodiacal Aspects 132
  - Ptolemaic Aspects 132
  - Harmonic Aspects 132
  - Orbs and Moiety 133

Practical Aspects Defined 134
   Conjunction (0°) 134
   Opposition (180°) 135
   Trine (120°) 135
   Square (90°) 135
   Sextile (60°) 136
   Quincunx (150°) 136
   Semi-Square (45°) 137
   Sesquisquare (135°) 137
Spotting Aspects in the Chart 138
   Out-of-Sign Aspects 138
Aspect Patterns 139
The Outer Planets 139
   Uranus 140
   Neptune 140
   Pluto 141
   Chiron 141
Aspect Blueprint Template Sentences 142
   Outer Planet Aspects to Inner Planets 142
   Inner Planet Aspects 143

CHAPTER 12
How to Build a Chair 145
Notes: Cause, Action, and Effect 146
   Cause 146
      House Ruled 146
      Sign Carrots and Sticks 147
   Action 149
   Effect 150
      House Occupied 150
Sketch Sentences: Chairs 151
Example Sketches: Burt Reynolds' Moon 153
   Blueprint Sentence 153
   Notes 153
      Sketch Sentences 155
Deep Practice: Building Chairs 156

Contents

PART 3
SYSTEMATIC APPROACH TO SYNTHESIZED INTERPRETATION

CHAPTER 13
Introduction to Written Interpretations 159
- Synthesized Chart Interpretation Process 160

CHAPTER 14
Interpreting the Personality 163
- Elements and Modalities 163
  - Emphasis of an Element. 163
  - Lack of an Element. 164
  - Emphasis of a Modality. 164
- The Sun: The Authentic "Big S" Self 165
- The Ascendant: The Persona 165
  - Ascendant Blueprint Template Sentences 166

CHAPTER 15
Sally Ride: Personality 169
- Elements and Modalities 169
- The Sun 172
  - Board of Directors for the Sun 174
  - Aspects to the Sun. 178
- Ascendant 179
  - Ascendant's Board of Directors 179
  - Aspects to the Ascendant. 182
  - Planets in the Ascendant. 185
- Summary of Ride's Personality 185

CHAPTER 16
Interpreting Relationship Needs 187
- Relationship Needs. 187
- Need Bank Accounts 189
  - Checklists and Watchlists 190
- The Moon: Safety Needs. 191
  - Safety Checklist Languages 193
- Venus: Validation Needs 193
  - Validation Checklist Languages 194
- Can You Meet Your Needs?. 194
  - Safe Doesn't Feel Safe. 195
  - Saturn Aspects: Checklists From Hell 195
  - Uranus Aspects: Rejection, Abandonment, and Unreliability 196
  - Neptune Aspects: Bad Boundaries and Hopeless Romantics. 196
  - Pluto Aspects: Power, Control, and Manipulation 196
  - Chiron Aspects: Core Wounds 196
  - Connections Between the Moon and Venus. 197

CHAPTER 17
Sally Ride: Relationship Needs 199
- The Moon: Safety Needs. 199
  - Board of Directors for the Moon 202
  - Aspects to the Moon 206
- Summary of Sally Ride's Safety Needs. 208
- Venus: Validation Needs 209
  - Board of Directors for Venus 211
  - Aspects to Venus. 216
- Summary of Relationship Needs:
- Connection Between Moon and Venus 217

CHAPTER 18
Interpreting Relationship Wants 221
- The Descendant and the Vertex 221
- The Marriage Blueprint 222
- Friend, Lover, or Spouse?. 223
  - Aspects Between House Rulers 223

Contents

Emplacement...224
Board of Directors Connections.................................225
Blueprint Template Sentences for
Relationship Houses..225

CHAPTER 19
Sally Ride: Relationship Wants 227
Descendant in Capricorn / Vertex in Scorpio....................227
Marriage Blueprint...228
Friends, Lovers, Spouses.......................................229
    11th House: Friendships..............................229
    5th House: Love Affairs..............................230
    7th House: Marriage..................................231
    Connections Between 11th, 5th, and 7th Houses........231

CHAPTER 20
Interpreting Career, Job, and Money 233
Career, Life Path, and Public Image: 10th House................233
Job and Service: 6th House.....................................234
Money: 2nd House and Part of Fortune...........................234
Career, Job, and Money Connections.............................234
    Blueprint Template Sentences for Career, Job, and Money.......235

CHAPTER 21
Sally Ride: Career, Job, and Money 239
10th House: Career...239
    10th House Ruler (Jupiter in Aries) Board of Directors.........241
6th House: Job...243
2nd House: Money...243
    2nd House Ruler (Sun in Gemini) Board of Directors.............244
Connections Between Career Houses..............................245

PART 4
THE SPICE RACK

CHAPTER 22
A Pinch of Spice 249

CHAPTER 23
Sensitive Points in the Chart 251
- The Moon's Nodes 251
- The Part of Fortune 253
- The Vertex 254

CHAPTER 24
Dispositor Trees 257

CHAPTER 25
Dignity and Debility 265
- Power 266
  - Essential Dignity 266
    - Rulership 266
    - Exaltation 267
    - Triplicity 267
    - Term 267
    - Face 267
  - Essential Debility 268
    - Detriment 268
    - Fall 268
    - Peregrine 268
- Prominence 269
  - House Placement 269
  - At the Bendings 269
  - Proximity to the Sun 270
    - Under the Sun's Beams 270
    - Combust 270

Contents

    Cazimi 270
Performance 271
    Benefics and Malefics 271
    Retrograde Planets 271

PART 5
SYNTHESIZED NATAL CHART INTERPRETATION EXAMPLE

CHAPTER 26
George Lucas Interpretation Notes 277
  Part 1: Personality 277
    Elements and Modalities 277
    The Sun 280
    Board of Directors for the Sun 282
    Aspects to the Sun 288
    Ascendant 289
    Ascendant's Board of Directors 290
    Planets in the Ascendant 292
    Aspects to Ascendant 293
    Summary of Lucas' Personality 295
  Part 2: Relationship Needs 296
    The Moon: Safety Needs 296
    Board of Directors for the Moon 298
    Aspects to the Moon 301
    Summary George Lucas' Safety Needs 305
    Venus: Validation Needs 306
    Board of Directors for Venus 308
    Aspects to Venus 309
    Summary of Relationship Needs:
    Connection Between Moon and Venus 312
  Part 3: Relationship Wants 313
    Marriage Blueprint 314

Friends, Lovers, Spouses.. 315
    11th House: Friendships 315
    5th House: Love Affairs.. 316
    7th House: Marriage 317
    Connections Between 11th, 5th, and 7th Houses 318
Part 4: Career 318
    10th House: Career.. 318
    10th House Ruler (Saturn in Gemini) Board of Directors......... 320
    6th House: Job 321
    2nd House: Money 321
    2nd House Ruler (Mercury in Taurus) Board of Directors 322
    Connections Between Career Houses 323

CHAPTER 27
George Lucas: An Astrological Portrait 325

Part 1: Personality 325
    Sun in Taurus 326
    Ascendant in Taurus 329
Part 2: Relationship Needs 329
    Safety Needs: Moon in Aquarius 329
    Validation Needs: Venus in Taurus 331
    Summary of Relationship Needs 332
Part 3: Relationship Wants.. 333
    Marriage Blueprint 334
    Friends, Lovers, Spouses.. 334
Part 4: Career 335

Contents

PART 6
APPENDICES AND RESOURCES

APPENDIX A
Spiritual Practices A-1
- Choose the Best-Feeling Thought Currently Available to You A-2
- Present Moment Awareness Safety Meditation A-2
- Whose Business Is It? A-4
  - Does It Affect You, Personally? A-4
  - Is It Really Your Responsibility? A-5
  - Do I Have Any Power or Influence to Change It? A-6
  - How to Play *Whose Business Is It?* A-6
- The List Exercise A-6
  - Troubleshooting The List A-8
    - I'm forgetting to do The List A-8
    - This is too easy... I can't be doing it right A-8
    - I'm not getting everything done on my list A-8
- Gratitude and Core Values A-10
  - Gratitude ("I Love and Appreciate _____") A-10
  - Core Value Affirmation Meditation A-11
- Tithing A-11

APPENDIX B
Bonus Gifts B-1

APPENDIX C
The Real Astrology Academy C-1
- Online Natal Astrology Class C-3
- Natal Interpretation Training Intensive C-3
- Online Relationship Astrology Class C-5
- Online Predictive Astrology Class C-6

APPENDIX D
Glossary of Terms D-1

Contents

List of Figures

Figure 1: How to Draw an Owl 5
Figure 2: The Four Kingdoms of Consciousness 21
Figure 3: The Nature of Reality 23
Figure 4: Combined Map of Consciousness 27
Figure 5: Area Map of Consciousness 29
Figure 6: Houses and Angles in the Chart 92
Figure 7: Table of Almutens 107
Figure 8: The Board of Directors for Libra 112
Figure 9: E-Z Essential Dignity™ Card 113
Figure 10: Finding the Board of Directors with the
    E-Z Essential Dignity Card 114
Figure 11: Finding the Board of Directors with the Essential Dignities
    Table in Solar Fire 114
Figure 12: Sylvester Stallone's Natal Chart 118
Figure 13: Board of Directors for Sylvester Stallone's Moon in Libra 119
Figure 14: Nicolas Cage's Natal Chart 121
Figure 15: Board of Directors for Nicolas Cage's Moon in Libra . . . 122
Figure 16: Sting's Natal Chart 125
Figure 17: Board of Directors for Sting's Moon in Libra 126
Figure 18: Burt Reynolds' Natal Chart 152
Figure 19: Sally Ride's Natal Chart 170
Figure 20: Sally Ride's Elements and Modalities 171
Figure 21: Sally Ride's Sun 172
Figure 22: Sally Ride's Ascendant 180
Figure 23: Maslow's Pyramid of Needs 188
Figure 24: Need Bank Accounts 190

Figure 25: Attachments 192

Figure 26: Sally Ride's Moon 199

Figure 27: Sally Ride's Venus 209

Figure 28: Sally Ride's Marriage Blueprint 228

Figure 29: Sally Ride's Relationship Houses 230

Figure 30: Sally Ride's Career Houses 240

Figure 31: The Moon's Nodes 252

Figure 32: Solar and Lunar Eclipses 252

Figure 33: Calculating the Part of Fortune 254

Figure 34: Liza Minnelli's Dispositor Tree 258

Figure 35: Paul Newman's Dispositor Tree 259

Figure 36: Meryl Streep's Dispositor Tree 261

Figure 37: Sylvester Stallone's Dispositor Tree 263

Figure 38: Retrograde Planets 272

Figure 39: George Lucas' Natal Chart 278

Figure 40: George Lucas' Elements and Modalities 279

Figure 41: George Lucas' Sun 280

Figure 42: George Lucas' Ascendant 290

Figure 43: George Lucas' Moon 296

Figure 44: George Lucas' Venus 306

Figure 45: George Lucas' Marriage Blueprint 314

Figure 46: George Lucas' Relationship Houses 316

Figure 47: George Lucas' Career Houses 319

Acknowledgments

This book exists because I wanted to learn how to illustrate comic books. I used to collect comics and I used to copy the illustrations. My mother, a portrait artist, encouraged me. I took a drawing class my first year of college, and had such a frustrating experience with it that I gave it up. But I never gave up wanting to be able to create my own illustrations.

In summer 2012, Sean D'Souza, the marketing guru behind Psychotactics.com, sent out an email announcing the Da Vinci Online Cartooning course. I got the email late one night, read the sales letter, checked out the web page with the course description and testimonials from past students, and immediately registered for the program.

The course took place in an online bulletin board community. We had to post our assignments in the forums, so we could receive (and give) feedback. The students came from all over the world, and yet we very quickly formed close, supportive relationships and a tight-knit community. This was a fascinating experience for me, both as a student and as a teacher.

But the most important part of the experience was that Sean based the class on the principles defined in a book by Daniel Coyle called *The Talent Code*. The very first assignment in the Da Vinci Cartooning Course was to buy a copy of *The Talent Code* and read it.

I did, and it changed my life forever.

The cartooning course didn't take me where I wanted to go with my art, but this book—and The Real Astrology Academy—exist because of Sean D'Souza and Daniel Coyle.

The Real Astrology Academy opened its (virtual) doors in February 2013 with the official motto, *Facere Discimus per Facere*, which is Latin for "We learn to do by doing." My intention with The Real Astrology Academy was to provide a forum for astrology training and master coaching, two critical talent-building components that were missing from my online astrology classes. I launched the first Natal Interpretation Training Intensive with a group of ten intrepid cadets, who had no idea what they were getting into. To be fair, neither did I. Thanks to the faith, support, feedback, and patience of these students, I was able to develop the practical, systematic approach to natal chart interpretation you'll find here. I owe these students a debt of gratitude—and if you find this book useful, you do, too.

I also want to acknowledge my mother, Barbara Burk. Her insights about how to paint a portrait and get a good likeness of a subject were invaluable. I wasn't able to include any of her work in this book, but her portfolio is online at BarbaraBurkPortraits.com.

Finally, I want to thank my dear friend (and editor), Claudia Previn Stasny, who has witnessed, supported, and encouraged the creation of this book from the very beginning.

Principles of Practical Astrology

CHAPTER 1

What Is Practical Astrology?

This is probably not your first astrology book. If it is, you're in good hands. But chances are, you've come to this book with a reasonable amount of information about astrology. You're reading this book because you can't use that information.

Knowing about something isn't the same thing as knowing it. When you *know about* something, it lives in your head. When you *know* something, you embody it. If you want to use astrology to interpret a natal chart, you have to know it. To move from knowing about astrology to knowing it, you have to go back to the beginning and be willing to question everything.

So, the first question is: What is practical astrology?

The short answer is: **Practical astrology is astrology you can use.**

Ironically, the short answer isn't practical. It seems to answer the question, but you can't use it to determine if astrology is practical or not. For that, you need the long answer.

Practical Astrology Is Astrology You Can Use

Astrology can tell you about your soul evolution, past lives, karma, and your highest potential in this lifetime. This information is fascinating, entertaining, and even enlightening, but it's not practical. You can't apply it in your life to address challenges or become happier.

Practicality isn't a requirement for something to have value. Art isn't the least bit practical, and it's profoundly important. But if you're drawn to astrology because you hope to improve your life, you need practical astrology.

Horary astrology[1] is extremely practical. You ask a question, and the chart for the moment you asked the question contains the answer. Most of the time, the answer is "No," but you don't have to like an answer for it to be practical.

Practical **natal astrology** gives you insight into your personality. It can identify key spiritual or psychological lessons, and answer questions about your money, relationships, career, family, and life path. You can use this information to alter patterns, resolve conflict, and improve your life.

Practical Astrology Is Astrology You Can Use

In almost every astrology class, the presenter gives you information on the topic and demonstrates it by working through a few examples. And then they tell the biggest lie in all of astrology: "You can do this yourself."

To be fair, they don't know this is a lie, and neither do their students.

What makes the lie so insidious is that it's not a lie for everyone. A small percentage of astrology students operate on the same wavelength as the teacher, and they *can* do it themselves. But the rest of the students can't. The lie makes the other students feel like they've failed, but the one who really failed is the teacher.

Being a talented *astrologer* doesn't make you a talented *astrology teacher*. To teach astrology you need to understand that astrology is a language.

You can't become fluent in a language by memorizing vocabulary words and phrases. You have to understand the principles of grammar and syntax. In the language of astrology, the planets, signs, and houses represent different parts of speech, and the principles of grammar and syntax define the correct relationship between them. These allow you to assemble your thoughts into coherent sentences, and are how you become fluent in the language of astrology.

Practical Astrology Is Astrology You Can Use

Figure 1 illustrates a popular Internet meme called "How to Draw an Owl." In Step 1, you draw two circles: a small one for the head, and a larger one for the body. In Step 2, you draw the rest of the owl. This describes most approaches to natal chart interpretation. In Step 1, you refer to a list of keywords for the planets and signs, and in Step 2, you interpret the rest of the chart.

---

[1] Terms in green are defined in the Glossary in Appendix D.

What Is Practical Astrology?

When you approach a complex task, whether it's drawing an owl or interpreting a natal chart, what matters is the size of the steps, not the number of steps. If the steps on a staircase are too big, the staircase isn't practical. But if the steps are small enough for you to manage, it doesn't matter how many there are. If you follow them in sequence, you'll always reach the top.

I've developed a systematic approach to synthesized chart interpretation that breaks the process into small, manageable steps. Each step requires a particular set of skills, and you'll have to invest time and energy to master those skills. But you *can* master them.

That's the long answer to the question, "What is practical astrology?"

Of course, the long answer raises some new questions, such as "What are the skills needed to interpret a natal chart?" and "How do you master those skills?" You'll find the answers to those questions in the next chapter.

STEP 1
Draw two circles, one for the head, and the other for the body.

STEP 2
Draw the rest of the owl.

Figure 1: How to Draw an Owl

CHAPTER 2

How to Become a Talented Astrologer

Have you ever attended an astrology class and watched someone interpret a natal chart with ease? It's always impressive to watch a talented astrologer show off his or her skills.

But at the end of the class, did you find yourself thinking you could never do that yourself? You've tried to learn astrology, but you've never been able to master it. You might think you don't have the talent.

But consider this: no one is born with the ability to interpret a natal chart. The only difference between you and that talented astrologer is that the talented astrologer has mastered the skills needed to interpret a natal chart and you haven't. Talent in astrology—or in any other field—isn't something you're born with. Talent is something you develop.

Deep Practice: The Astrological Talent Code

In his thought-provoking book, *The Talent Code*, Daniel Coyle explores the nature of talent. His examples are musicians, athletes, and singers, but the principles apply to talent in every field, including astrology. No one is born talented. Talented people got that way because they developed skills. The brain doesn't distinguish between athletic skill and astrological skill. To the brain, every skill is just an impulse traveling along a neural pathway.

When you learn a new skill, you map new neural pathways in your brain, forming a new circuit. Each time you activate that circuit, the brain wraps those neurons in myelin, which insulates it. The more myelin, the faster the electrical impulse can travel. It's like upgrading from a dial-up connection to broadband Internet.[1]

Practice makes perfect, but as Coyle explains, it has to be the right kind of practice. Building skills requires **deep practice**. Deep practice is slow, focused, and tedious. But mainly, deep practice is a struggle. It's the struggle that causes your brain to create myelin. Twenty minutes of deep practice can accomplish more than weeks of casual practice.[2]

This is harder than you think. Twenty minutes of deep practice isn't the same thing as twenty minutes of clock time. What counts is the time you spend struggling in the deep practice zone. It's difficult to stay there for twenty consecutive minutes. I tell my students to budget an hour of clock time to accomplish twenty minutes of deep practice.

Wax On, Wax Off

The best example of the value of deep practice comes from the iconic 1984 film, *The Karate Kid*. In the film, Daniel asks Mr. Miyagi for lessons in self-defense. For his first lesson, Miyagi has Daniel wash and wax his cars. Miyagi demonstrates how to apply and remove the wax in a broad circular motion, and tells Daniel, "Wax on, wax off." Over the next few days, Miyagi has Daniel sand a floor, paint a fence, and paint a house, each time with specific instructions on how to perform the simple, repetitive actions.

Daniel loses his patience and confronts Miyagi. He's supposed to be learning Karate, not home improvement. Miyagi tells Daniel to demonstrate each of the movements, and Daniel realizes they're defensive blocks in karate. Miyagi spars with Daniel, and Daniel is able to deflect every attack because he had mastered the skills through deep practice.

Deep practice is the only way to develop skills. Watching *The Karate Kid* won't make you a black belt, and reading this book won't make you a talented astrologer. If you want to become a talented astrologer, you have to do the work.

---

[1] Coyle, Daniel. "The Deep Practice Cell." In *The Talent Code: Greatness Isn't Born : It's Grown, Here's How*. New York: Bantam Books, 2009.
[2] Ibid.

Natal Chart Interpretation Skills

Interpreting a natal chart isn't a simple a skill. It's not even a complex skill. Interpreting a natal chart is a process. The process consists of three phases, and each phase requires mastery of a different set of skills.

Phase 1: Reading the Chart

The skills of Phase 1 allow you to recognize the glyphs in the chart and identify the planets, signs, houses, and aspects. If you've been studying astrology for a while, you may take these skills for granted. You may not remember that you struggled to master these skills (but you did).

You will never attempt to interpret the *chart*. The chart is overwhelming because it contains too much information. You want to spend as little time as possible looking at the chart. In Phase 1, you read the chart and organize the information in a worksheet. The **Chart Interpretation Worksheet,** one of the bonus gifts bundled with this book, simplifies the process of chart interpretation by helping you focus on what's relevant. Each time you fill out the Chart Interpretation Worksheet, you strengthen your Phase 1 chart-reading skills.

Phase 2: Drafting a Blueprint

In Phase 2, you use the Chart Interpretation Worksheet to assemble the planets, signs, and houses into coherent sentences that follow the rules of grammar and syntax of the language of astrology. I provide you with examples of fill-in-the-blank blueprint template sentences, and you fill in the blanks with appropriate keywords for the planet, sign, and houses. The templates keep everything organized in the correct relationships. These are not your final interpretations. They're the blueprint of a chair, not the chair itself. But every time you complete a blueprint template sentence, you strengthen key interpretation skills.

You master a complex skill by breaking it down into small components. You practice each component individually, and then "chunk" them together. When you learned to read, you first had to learn the letters of the alphabet. With practice, you learned to chunk groups of letters and recognize words, and now you're able to chunk groups of words together and comprehend sentences. You have to go through the same process as you learn the language of astrology.

A typical sentence in the language of astrology is, "Mars in Cancer in the 3rd house." When you begin to learn the language of astrology, you have to parse the sentence one word at a time. You start with Mars, and then consider Cancer, and then you consider Mars *in* Cancer; next, you might consider the 3rd house, and then Mars *in* the 3rd house, and so on. Every time you complete a blueprint sentence, you strengthen the neural network that makes it possible for you to chunk it together and understand Mars in Cancer in the 3rd house as a single, integrated concept.

Phase 3: Building a Chair

In Phase 3, you take the two-dimensional blueprints and transform them into something three-dimensional, like a chair. Each of the sections of a natal chart interpretation—Personality, Relationship Needs, Relationship Wants, and Career—contains multiple blueprint sentences. You organize them in a hierarchy, so you can know which blueprints build the structure, and which add decoration.

How to Develop Interpretation Skills

The approach you take to *developing* skills is different from how you will *use* those skills. When you *use* your interpretation skills, you communicate directly with a client, in person, by video chat, or by phone. But the way to *develop* interpretation skills is to write your interpretations.

Communicating a general sense of the chart is easy when you're in front of a client, because the words aren't that important. Most of what you communicate comes through your tone of voice (38%) and nonverbal expression, such as body language (55%). Content, the actual words you say, makes up only 7% of communication.[3] If you have a general feel for Venus in Capricorn, you can convey that to a client with ease. But writing even a simple interpretation of Venus in Capricorn is surprisingly difficult.

---

[3] Mehrabian, Albert. *Silent Messages*. 1st ed. Belmont, Calif.: Wadsworth Pub., 1971.

This is an example of the gap between what you *know about* astrology and what you *know*. You have a lot of information, but you need to develop the skills, infrastructure, and neural pathways that let you communicate it. You do this by writing interpretations.

Developing interpretation skills is hard work. It requires an investment of money, energy, and time. And whether or not that investment is worth it depends on your sweet spot.

The Sweet Spot: Information, Education, and Training

You care about astrology for the same reason you care about anything: happiness. Astrology gives you pleasure. You study astrology because you believe the better you understand astrology, the more you'll enjoy it.

You're on a path that begins with this book and ends with your becoming a talented astrologer. However, you don't need to walk the whole path. You just need to follow the path until you find your sweet spot: the point where your investment of money, energy, and time returns the greatest amount of enjoyment. Your sweet spot may be the point where you know enough astrology to enjoy reading articles in astrology magazines. Or your sweet spot may be the point where you are fluent in the language of astrology and can interpret a chart on your own. To navigate the path and find your sweet spot, you need to understand the difference among information, education, and training.

Information, usually in the form of astrology books and articles, helps you *know about* astrology. Information requires the smallest investment of money, energy, and time, and for many people, it's sufficient. With astrology information, you can enjoy reading astrology books and attending lectures and workshops. You may not grasp the finer points, but because you *know about* astrology, you'll be able to keep up.

Information can take you only so far along the path. After a certain point, the more information you acquire, the less you understand. That's when you need education.

Astrology education helps you to organize and understand the information you've acquired. Reading is passive, but taking a class is active. It engages your brain on multiple levels, which is why you can understand a concept better when it's taught than when you read it in a book. In terms of your investment, education requires a greater amount of money than information does, but about the same amount of time and energy.

Education leads to understanding, but not to ability. For many people, understanding is the sweet spot. But if you want to be able to use what you understand and interpret charts on your own, you need training.

Training involves consistent, focused struggle, and delayed gratification. It requires the greatest investment of time and energy. Before you begin astrology training, you need to consider if it will be worth it. Will the pleasure you get from having astrological interpretation skills be greater than the struggle you'll experience to develop them?

If the answer to that question is yes, and you're serious about becoming a talented astrologer, you need to work with a coach. A coach keeps you motivated, holds you accountable, and supports you to overcome your resistance and reach your goals. A master coach provides feedback and guidance, and identifies your mistakes so you can correct them, improve, and get the most benefit from your deep practice.

The Real Astrology Academy provides astrological information, education, and training to astrologers and astrology students around the world. If you're interested in education, **The Real Astrology Academy's Online Natal Astrology Class** will deepen your understanding of the information in this book. And I offer training and master coaching through the **Natal Interpretation Training Intensive**. You can learn more about these programs in Appendix C.

Wherever your sweet spot may be, your journey to find it begins with this book. And the next step is to explore the art of astrological interpretation.

CHAPTER 3
The Art of Astrological Interpretation

Astrology is often described as an art. This is a true and precise description of astrology, but it may not mean what you think it does. All forms of art combine objective standards with subjective expression. The objective standards are not always obvious; often, they require training to understand. You may not be able to tell the difference between a paint spill and a Jackson Pollock worth millions of dollars, but that doesn't change the fact that one of them is art, and the other is a clean up on aisle five.

Creating art requires dedication, focus, and hard work. Many people assume that inspiration strikes, and after a flurry of activity, you end up with art. The only people who don't believe this are artists. Everyone appreciates when a creation appears elegant and effortless, but only artists appreciate how hard it is to make something look easy. Artists, including astrologers, must develop skills to channel their personal inspiration into creations that speak to others.

Interpreting a natal chart is like painting a portrait. A portrait doesn't describe everything about the subject. A portrait captures a moment and conveys an attitude. It doesn't matter if it's a pen-and-ink caricature or a formal oil painting; the objective of a portrait is to capture a likeness of the subject. This is also the objective of a natal chart interpretation. To capture a likeness of your subject, you need to see what's really there, and reproduce what you see.

See What's Really There

If I gave you a box of crayons and asked you to draw a tree, you would probably use a green crayon to draw the leaves and a brown crayon to draw the trunk. Everyone knows that trees have green leaves and brown trunks.

Except they don't.

Look closely at a tree and see what's really there. Not all tree trunks are brown. Some are tan, or grey, or white. And even if you find a tree with a brown trunk, when you see what's really there, you notice dozens of colors. If a green leaf is in direct sunlight, it may appear yellow, and if it's in the shade, it may appear gray.

When most astrologers look at a chart, they see a brown trunk and green leaves. The Moon in Libra is "balanced emotions," Jupiter in Leo is "a big ego," and Venus in Scorpio is "a potential restraining order." A talented astrologer can look beyond these expectations and see what's really there.

Reproduce What You See

Seeing what's really there is the easy part; reproducing what you see is difficult. You have to translate your perceptions into a different medium without losing the essence. An artist has to depict a three-dimensional subject in a two-dimensional medium and retain the sense of depth. An astrologer has to translate between the language of astrology and English[1] and retain the meaning.

Artists create the illusion of depth by following the rules of linear perspective. Converging lines meet at a single vanishing point, and as shapes recede into the distance, they get smaller. The artists of ancient Greece understood these rules, but after the fall of Rome, the rules were lost. Paintings from the Middle Ages look so odd because they're flat and lack perspective. Artists in the Middle Ages knew it was possible to create the illusion of depth on a canvas, but until the principles of linear perspective were rediscovered and defined in the 15th century, they didn't know how to do it.

The art of astrology has faced a similar challenge.

---

[1] Or whatever language you speak.

The Art of Astrological Interpretation

For thousands of years, astrologers observed a specific relationship between planets, signs, and houses. When you read the works of traditional astrologers from **Ptolemy** through **William Lilly**, you find an internal consistency to their interpretations. The rules of grammar and syntax clearly exist, but modern astrologers don't understand how to follow them. The order of the words matters. "John ate the cake" uses the same words as "The cake ate John," but they don't mean the same thing. Not knowing the rules of perspective made paintings in the Middle Ages flat, and not knowing the rules of grammar and syntax fills astrology with carnivorous desserts.

When I created **The Real Astrology Academy** in 2013, my first priority was to discover and define the grammar and syntax of the language of astrology. You will be amazed at how much depth these principles create when you apply them to an astrological portrait.

The Process of Portrait Art

Portrait art is a process. The details vary with the artist and the medium, but the sequence never changes. You begin with a sketch, you establish a context, and you fill in the details. This process also applies to natal chart interpretation.

Begin With a Sketch

A portrait artist begins with a sketch. Sketching is loose and messy. It's about putting lines on the paper and getting a sense of the shapes, structures, and proportions. The lines of a sketch are usually quite faint, but while sketching, the artist restates lines and shapes by drawing over them. The important lines gain depth and intensity, and the less important ones fade by contrast. When sketching a person, artists rely on their knowledge of the human skeleton. The underlying structure of the bones supports the surface details. Without it, you won't capture a likeness of your subject.

When painting an astrological portrait, you also begin with a sketch. You take a keyword-based blueprint sentence, and imagine the ways that sentence could express. You consider the cause (a disruption in one of the houses ruled by the planet), the action (the expression of the planet, modified by the sign), and the effect (the house occupied by the planet). Some elements will remain constant across different permutations. Like the restated lines in an artist's sketch, these repeated themes help define the final portrait.

Create a Context

A portrait artist begins by sketching the ideal proportions of the face and figure. The artist then selects a reference point and evaluates how the actual features differ from the ideal proportions. This reference point establishes the context. Next, the artist looks at the shapes of the shadows, mid-tones, and highlights. These help create the illusion of depth. The artist chooses a color palette, and defines the range of values for the shadows and highlights. Color and contrast help establish the mood of the portrait and convey the artist's point of view.

Repeated themes from the blueprints and sketches become the references that define the context of your interpretation. For example, **Liza Minnelli** has six out of seven personal planets in Cardinal signs. Planets in Cardinal signs like to start new projects, but lose interest the moment something becomes routine. This establishes a context that shapes every part of the interpretation of Minnelli's chart.[2]

Astrologers must choose a color palette just as a portrait artist does, but instead of tints and hues, astrologers choose from levels of consciousness. Each color has a range of values from dark to bright, and each planet–sign combination has a range of expression from negative to positive. At lower levels of consciousness, Mars in Aries might express as aggressive, brutal, and violent behavior, but at higher levels of consciousness, it might be innovating, dynamic, and inspiring. Astrologers must establish the dominant levels of consciousness for the interpretation, and the degree of contrast between the high-consciousness highlights and the low-consciousness shadows.

Fill in the Details

You don't need a lot of detail to capture a likeness of your subject. Adding detail to a portrait gives it depth and richness, but you have to be careful. The more detail you add to a feature, the more important it becomes. This is one way that artists establish the focus of a portrait, because the viewer's eye will be drawn

---

[2] See Figure 34 on page 258.

The Art of Astrological Interpretation

to the areas with the most detail. If you include too much detail, the portrait will lose focus. The viewer will be overwhelmed, and won't know where to look.

When you interpret a natal chart, you need to choose a focus. If you choose to focus on the personality, you would include the greatest amount of detail when interpreting the Sun, Moon, and Ascendant. But if you choose to focus on career and life path, you would include the most detail when exploring the 10th house (career), the 6th house (job), and the 2nd house (money).

More detail doesn't give you more depth. Paintings in the Middle Ages were full of intricate detail, but they were still flat. To create a three-dimensional astrological portrait, you need to understand the levels of consciousness.

CHAPTER 4

Three-Dimensional Chart Interpretation

For thousands of years, astrology was predictive. Astrologers gazed into the future to get practical answers to important questions. A 21st century merchant who wants to know if his ship has come in uses GPS, but an 18th century merchant asked an astrologer.

You approach predictive astrology with a question, and you want a clear, unambiguous, definitive answer. This requires a two-dimensional approach to astrological interpretation that considers planets and signs. In this system, planets are "good" or "bad," and they can be "strong" or "weak" based on their dignity or debility. In the context of predictive astrology, this two-dimensional approach is practical, but in the context of natal astrology, it's limiting, judgmental, and disempowering.

You are free to choose how you live your life — and how you experience your birth chart. Astrology does not predict behavior. It's not possible to look at a planet–sign combination in a natal chart and know how it will express. Each astrological signature can express along a broad spectrum from the "negative" to the "positive." To interpret a natal chart, you need to work in three dimensions: planets, signs, and consciousness.

The Kingdoms of Consciousness

A simple definition of **consciousness** is the vibrational frequency of your thoughts. Your thoughts determine how you perceive and experience the world. When you change how you think about an experience, it changes the experience.

Rev. Dr. Michael Beckwith (whom you might know from the movie, *The Secret*) popularized a model of consciousness developed by his mentor, the late Dr. Homer Johnson. This model divides human consciousness into four "kingdoms." Each Kingdom of Consciousness represents a unique experience of reality (Figure 2).

First Kingdom is **Victim Consciousness**, and it's where you, and almost everyone else in the world, spend the bulk of your time. When you're in First Kingdom, things are done *to* you.

Second Kingdom is where you take back your power and manifest things using reason, logic, and the linear mind. In Second Kingdom, things are done *by* you.

Third Kingdom represents higher spiritual states. They are nonlinear, and beyond both the world of form and the Law of Cause and Effect. In Third Kingdom, things are done *through* you.

Fourth Kingdom includes the enlightened and transcendent states. Beckwith says in Fourth Kingdom, things are done *as* you.[1]

At any given moment, your experience of the world — and more importantly, how happy you are with it — depends on which Kingdom of Consciousness you're in. Think about a time when you were depressed, and remember how the world looked to you then. Now, think about a time when you were in love, and remember how the world looked.

The world didn't just *look* different based on how you were feeling; the world actually *was* different. To understand why this is true, we need to explore the nature of reality itself.

The Nature of Reality

I'd like you to consider that there are two different kinds of reality: the "Big R" Reality and the "little r" reality. The "Big R" Reality is infinite. It contains everything in the world. Your "little r" reality is finite. It contains everything in *your* world. Your "little r" reality is a very small part of the "Big R" Reality (Figure 3).

---

[1] I disagree with this, because when you reach the levels of consciousness of Fourth Kingdom, there is no longer a *you* for things to be done *as*.

Three-Dimensional Chart Interpretation

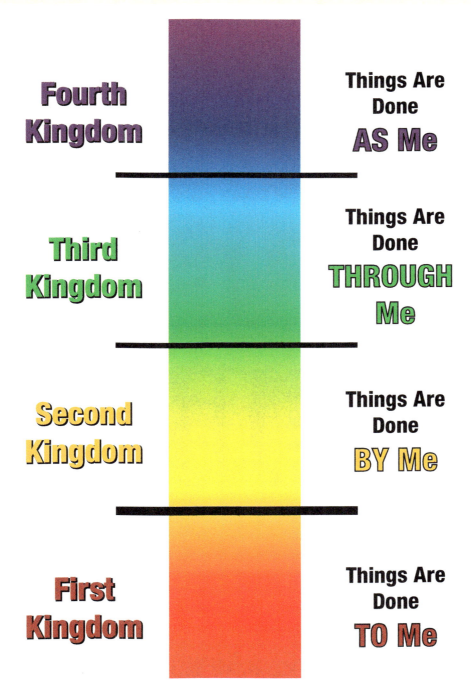

Figure 2: The Four Kingdoms of Consciousness

"little r" reality

Three-Dimensional Chart Interpretation

"Big R" Reality: Everything in the World

"little r" reality: everything in *your* world

Figure 3: The Nature of Reality

Think of it this way: the "Big R" Reality contains everything. Everything includes experiences like poverty, war, and oppression. I accept that these things exist in the world; however, they don't exist in *my* world. I don't have any personal experience of them. They're not a part of my "little r" reality, and they're probably not a part of your "little r" reality, either.

Your "little r" reality contains only the things that you experience. What you experience as real is determined by where you put your attention.

You're a lot like a radio. A radio can tune to only one frequency at a time, and that frequency determines what kind of music you hear. If you pick a rock station, your "little r" reality will be filled with rock music. As long as you stay tuned to that frequency, you will never hear any classical music.

How happy you are with this depends on whether or not you enjoy rock music. If you like rock music, you'll be happy. If you don't like rock music, and would prefer to listen to classical music, you won't be happy. Classical music exists as a part of the "Big R" Reality, but as long as you're tuned to a rock music station, it will never exist in your "little r" reality. To become happy, you would have to change your frequency and tune to a classical music station.

Consider the chair (or sofa, or bed) you're sitting on now. It's completely real. It's solid, and it supports your weight. You can see and feel it. You can hear it. You can smell it. You can even taste it, if you're into that sort of thing. But the truth is it's mostly empty space. The molecules that make up the chair don't touch each other.

The reason you don't fall through the chair to the floor (or *through* the floor, because the floor's just a lot of empty space, too) is that you *tell yourself* that the chair and the floor are solid. In fact, the reason that you believe that you can see, feel, hear, smell, and/or taste the chair is that you tell yourself you can. A voice in your head narrates and describes every single experience to you, and that's what makes the experience real.

You know something is real because you tell yourself it is. Everything you experience in your "little r" reality is a story. It's all made up of words.

This next part is a bit of a stretch. You may want to sit down.[2]

Just because something is *real* doesn't mean it's *true*.

---

[2] That is, if you still believe there's anything for you to sit down on. Or with, for that matter.

Three-Dimensional Chart Interpretation

Your "little r" reality is *subjective*. No matter what you experience, it always feels real. When you dream, it feels real. When you wake up, *that's* real, too. You can't compare two experiences and say that one was more *real* than the other.

Truth, on the other hand, is *objective*. You *can* compare two experiences (both of which feel equally real) and see that one is more *true* than the other.

Each time you step back and see the bigger picture, you expand the context of your story. When you expand the context of your story, you make your "little r" reality bigger. The bigger your "little r" reality is, the more it resembles the "Big R" Reality and the more truth it contains.

The Science of Truth

Dr. David R. Hawkins was a pioneer researcher in the field of human consciousness. All of Dr. Hawkins' research is based on the science of Applied Kinesiology, also known as muscle testing. It's been extensively documented that the body's acupuncture system has the ability to tell if something is beneficial or harmful. When in the presence of something that supports the body, the acupuncture system gives a positive response, and the muscle tests strong. When in the presence of something that is harmful to the body, the acupuncture system gives a nonresponse, and the muscle tests weak.

The breakthrough that formed the basis of Dr. Hawkins' research was the discovery that muscle testing could be used to differentiate between truth and falsehood in any context. The acupuncture system gives a strong response in the presence of truth, but does not respond in the presence of falsehood (i.e., the absence of truth).

Dr. Hawkins' findings have been documented and repeated hundreds of thousands of times, in a variety of situations. The results are consistent both when testing the arm strength of a naive subject, and when measuring an involuntary reaction in the human eye (the pupil dilates for a fraction of a second in the presence of falsehood).

Using applied kinesiology, Dr. Hawkins developed a Map of Human Consciousness™. This map includes a full range of "little r" realities that can be experienced by humans. The calibrations on the scale of consciousness go from 1 (the lowest amount of energy needed for something to be alive) to 1,000 (the highest possible consciousness that can be experienced in human form; this is the level of consciousness of Christ, Krishna, and Buddha, and only a few individuals in the history of the world have attained it). The scale is logarithmic, which means that each time it moves up a point, it's actually a factor of 10. In other words, it's not 1, 2, 3, 4, 5…, it's 1, 10, 100, 1,000, 10,000, 100,000, etc. Even a one-point increase represents a massive increase in energy.

I've combined this map with the model of the Four Kingdoms of Consciousness, as you can see in Figure 4.

Each point on the map represents its own "little r" reality, defined by the amount of available energy. Dr. Hawkins discovered that the critical point on the scale calibrates at 200. Anything that calibrates below 200 causes the acupuncture system to go weak. Anything that calibrates above 200 causes the acupuncture system to go strong. Notice that everything that calibrates below 200 falls within First Kingdom or Victim Consciousness. In Victim Consciousness, you encounter Pride, Anger, Desire, Fear, Grief, Apathy, Guilt, and Shame.

Everything that calibrates below 200 represents **force**, while everything that calibrates above 200 represents increasing levels of **power**.

Force is inherently weak. Force does not have enough energy to sustain itself, so it consumes energy. Force looks outside of itself for survival. Force moves in a negative (downward) direction. It is destructive, and does not support life. Force creates a counter-force; something is always working against it. For example, when you act from Anger (calibration [cal.] 150) you use force, which is why you're never happy with the outcome.

Power, on the other hand, is strong. Power has enough energy to sustain itself. Power is self-sufficient. In fact, Power creates energy. Power moves in a positive (upward) direction. Power is creative, and nurtures and supports life. Power has no opposite. Power is free to grow and expand because there is nothing that can work against it.

Your level of consciousness determines your level of happiness. The more energy (i.e., power) you have, the better you feel, and the happier you are. Dr. Hawkins calibrated the rate of happiness at each of the levels of consciousness. The level of Shame (cal. 20) has only a 1% rate of happiness; Guilt (cal. 30) has

Three-Dimensional Chart Interpretation

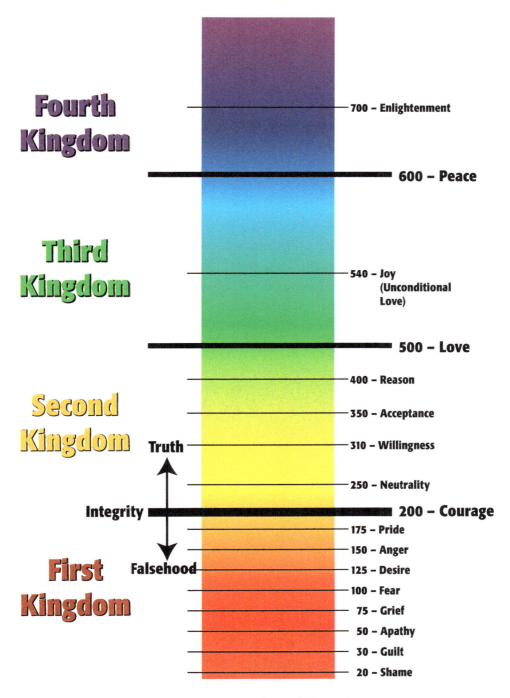

Figure 4: Combined Map of Consciousness

a 4% rate; Apathy (cal. 50) has a 5% rate; Grief (cal. 75) has a 9% rate; both Fear (cal. 100) and Desire (cal. 125) have a 10% rate; Anger (cal. 150) has a 12% rate; and Pride (cal. 175) has a 22% rate of happiness.[3] As soon as you step out of Victim Consciousness and move into integrity in Second Kingdom at the level of Courage (cal. 200), **the rate of happiness more than doubles to 55%.** When you begin to feel truly safe and reach the level of Neutrality (cal. 250), the rate of happiness is 60%, five times greater than it is at the level of Anger. Willingness (cal. 310) has a 68% rate; Acceptance (cal. 350) has a 71% rate; and Reason (cal. 400) has a 79% rate of happiness. When you cross into Third Kingdom at Love (cal. 500), the rate of happiness jumps to 89%, and at Joy (cal. 540), the rate of happiness is 96%. In Fourth Kingdom, at the level of Peace (cal. 600) and above, there is a 100% rate of happiness.[4]

The Map of Human Consciousness and the model of the Four Kingdoms of Consciousness are valuable tools. All you need to do is identify where you are on the map based on how you're feeling. You can then **choose the best-feeling thought currently available to you**, and move up the scale one level at a time.

Anger is a part of Victim Consciousness. It represents force and it's inherently negative. But Anger doesn't always feel bad. Anger has more energy (and feels better) than Grief, Fear, or Desire. If you're coming from one of those "little r" realities, Anger feels good. On the other hand, Anger has less energy than Pride, Courage, or Neutrality, and by comparison with them, Anger feels bad.

The challenge with the linear model consciousness is that it makes it look like you can escape the negative energies of Victim Consciousness by moving up the scale. This is not accurate. When you step into integrity in Second Kingdom, you are no longer limited by the ego and the negativity of Victim Consciousness, but you can still experience those energies. A more accurate representation of the levels of consciousness might look like Figure 5. This model illustrates that each increased level of consciousness is an expanded context that includes all of the lower vibrations. It also illustrates how a slight increase in vibration results in a significant increase in power.

---

[3] And a 78% chance of a fall.
[4] Hawkins, David R. *Transcending the Levels of Consciousness: The Stairway to Enlgihtenment*. W. Sedona, AZ .: Veritas Publishing, 2006. 30.

Three-Dimensional Chart Interpretation

You have a dominant vibration—a level of consciousness that defines your "little r" reality. However, you can operate from almost any location on the map, depending on where you put your attention. When you go to school to learn new skills to get a promotion at work, you use your linear, rational mind, and operate from Second Kingdom. When you meditate or experience spiritual community, your heart opens and you experience the energy of Third Kingdom. And when the holidays roll around, you get together with your family in the middle of First Kingdom.

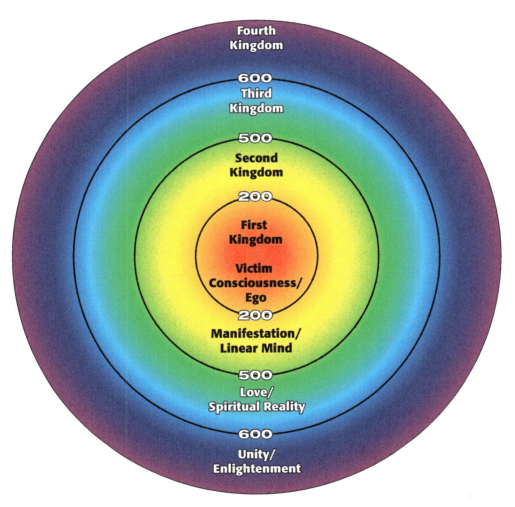

Figure 5: Area Map of Consciousness

The Appeal of Victim Consciousness

Let's take a moment to address any judgments you may have about First Kingdom and Victim Consciousness. **There is nothing wrong with being in Victim Consciousness.** Approximately 85% of the world lives there full time (55% of the population of the United States), and everyone else has a vacation home there.[5] What you need to know about First Kingdom is that happiness is a rare commodity there. If your goal is happiness, you need to look for it somewhere else.

So why would you choose to spend any time in Victim Consciousness? When you step into Victim Consciousness, you get to make yourself the center of the universe. You're entitled to complain. You're entitled to special treatment. You're entitled to sympathy and attention. You get to be self-righteous. You get to be right—and even better, you get to prove that everyone else is wrong. And the best part of it is that nothing is ever your fault. As soon as you step into Victim Consciousness, you are no longer responsible for anything.

Doesn't that sound wonderful?

First Kingdom seems like the ideal place to live until you read the fine print. Giving up responsibility means giving up power. The levels of consciousness in First Kingdom all represent force. They lack sufficient energy to manifest or sustain anything. Everything you create in First Kingdom requires effort, and when you stop pouring energy into it, it falls apart. Life in First Kingdom is a constant struggle, because force creates a counter-force. You thought things would be easier in Victim Consciousness because other people would have to do things for you, but you discover that it's less work and less stressful to be accountable and take care of yourself. First Kingdom isn't a shortcut to happiness: it's a wrong turn.

It's easy to get to First Kingdom, but hard to leave. Everything in First Kingdom is backward. It's like a hall of mirrors. The levels of consciousness in First Kingdom move in a negative direction. Dr. Hawkins discovered that in Victim Consciousness, even the body's acupuncture system is inverted: positive, truthful influences make the body go weak, while negative, false influences make the body go strong. Once you are in Victim Consciousness, any action

---

[5] Hawkins, David R. *Reality, Spirituality, and Modern Man.* Toronto, Ont.: Axial Pub., 2008. 35.

you take to try to leave will draw you further in. When you are in First Kingdom, you quite literally don't know what's good for you.[6]

Consciousness and Astrology

So what does all of this have to do with astrology? Consciousness is how you create a three-dimensional interpretation of a natal chart, and capture a good likeness when you paint an astrological portrait.

Each astrological signature is unique, and yet it also has an infinite range of expression. It's not possible to look at a chart and predict how a person will experience it. How you experience your chart changes from moment to moment. Incorporating the levels of consciousness as the third dimension of chart interpretation, in addition to the planets and signs, gives you the flexibility to engage with the chart in powerful, dynamic ways.

You'll develop these skills by choosing from a mixture of high-consciousness and low-consciousness keywords when you create the blueprint sentences for each planet-sign combination. This will expand your understanding of the potential of each astrological signature by giving you a range of references. At the more advanced phases of interpretation, you will consider behavior patterns from different levels of consciousness. This allows you to shift the vibrations and experience greater levels of happiness.

An understanding of the levels of consciousness is one of the principles that makes natal astrology practical.

---

[6] The spiritual practices in Appendix A will help you get out of Victim Consciousness.

PART 2

Grammar and Syntax of the Language of Astrology

CHAPTER 5

Introduction to the Grammar and Syntax of the Language of Astrology

Astrology is a language. This is probably not news to you. I've mentioned this several times before, and I'm not the only astrologer who views astrology this way.

Language communicates through content and context. The words make up the content, but the meaning of those words comes from the context. This is why you can't translate between languages using only a dictionary.

The rules of grammar and syntax in the language of astrology help you to translate between the language of astrology and English[1] without changing the meaning of the sentence. The relationship between planets, signs, and houses is specific and objective, and the order of the words matters. Remember, the sentence "John ate the cake" uses the same words as the sentence "The cake ate John," but they don't mean the same thing. The correct use of grammar and syntax can help you avoid carnivorous desserts.

The Planets: The Subject of the Sentence

Every sentence has two parts: the **subject** and the **predicate**. The subject is what the sentence is talking about. The predicate tells you something about the subject.

---

[1] Or whatever language you speak.

In the language of astrology, the subject of a sentence always will be a planet. **Every sentence in the language of astrology must contain a planet as the subject.** More specifically, every sentence in the language of astrology must contain one of the seven personal, or inner planets, as the subject. The outer planets are important, but they will never be the subject of a sentence in natal astrology.[2]

In the language of astrology, the personal planets are the nouns and verbs: they tell you *who* and *what*.

The Predicate of the Sentence

The signs, houses, and aspects are all parts of the predicate of the sentence. Each tells you something about the subject of the sentence.

Signs: Adjectives and Adverbs

Signs function as adjectives and adverbs in the language of astrology. The planets tell you *who* and *what*, and the signs modify the expression of the planets and tell you *how* and *why*. **The signs do not change the fundamental nature of the planet.**

When you combine a planet and a sign, you have a complete sentence in the language of astrology. It's a simple sentence, and it doesn't include much detail, but it's the basic building block of the language of astrology.

Houses: Prepositions

In the language of astrology, houses relate to different areas of life. They act as prepositions, telling you *where* and *with what* the planet (the subject of the sentence) expresses. When a planet rules a house, it is responsible for all of the affairs of that house. It expresses *with* those affairs. A disruption in the affairs of that house will cause the planet to take action. However, the planet takes action *in* the house it occupies. The *cause* of a behavior comes from the houses a planet *rules*, but the *effect* is experienced in the house it *occupies*.

---

[2] They can be the subject of a sentence in mundane astrology, which considers world events.

Aspects: Conjunctions

In the grammar of astrology, aspects are the conjunctions: they connect two phrases or clauses, linking the planets in some kind of relationship.[3] Aspects are complicated. Not only do they define a relationship between two planets, but they also define a relationship between the houses ruled by those planets. Each planet experiences the effect of the relationship in the house it occupies.

House Rulers: Pronouns

Every sentence in the language of astrology must have a planet as the subject, but which planet to choose may not be obvious. If you want to know about your authentic Self, you would look at the Sun, but what if you have a question about your money?

The system of rulerships helps you to find the specific planet in charge. You consider the house of the question (money belongs in the 2nd house) and then look at the sign on the **cusp** of that house. The ruler of that sign is the planet that is in charge of the affairs of the 2nd house, and that planet will be the subject of any sentence exploring a question about money. You can use the planet as a virtual pronoun—a proxy that represents the affairs of the house.

---

[3] This is unintentionally confusing. In grammar, a conjunction is a connecting word, such as "and," "but," "yet," and "or." In astrology, a conjunction is a type of aspect formed when two planets occupy the same degree of a sign.

CHAPTER 6

Meet the Planets

In my counseling practice, I've developed an approach to natal astrology that I call **Archetypal Astrology**. In this model, the seven personal planets are the **Astrological Archetypes**. They're the seven voices in your head. You can move into right relationship with each of the planets through targeted spiritual practices. This raises your vibration, expands your consciousness, and creates greater levels of happiness. I've included the spiritual practices associated with each planet in Appendix A.

The personal planets live inside you, so you already *know* them. When you meet the planets in the different Kingdoms of Consciousness, you create objective references that connect to your subjective experiences. This deepens your understanding of the planets.

The Sun: The Hero

The Sun is the Archetype of the Hero, and the process of moving into right relationship with the Sun is the Hero's Journey. The Hero's Journey is a story—in fact, it's *the* Story. The Hero's Journey is a quest to find the answer to the question, "Who am I?" You answer this question by connecting with the Sun, your authentic "Big S" Self.

The Sun is who you truly are; it's not who you think you are. You *think* you are your "little s" self (Mars), which represents your ego/body. As you move into right relationship with the Sun,

you become aware of your "Big S" Self, and recognize the truth that you are one with All That Is.

On a practical level, you experience the Sun when you encounter your Personal Standards of Integrity. Your Personal Standards of Integrity are personal, so they don't matter to anyone else. These qualities and values define and shape your identity. They represent subtle and specific distinctions that other people rarely appreciate.

The Sun in First Kingdom

In First Kingdom, the answer to the question "Who am I?" is, "I am a victim."

Technically, it's not possible to experience the Sun from First Kingdom. The Sun is the essence of integrity, and integrity doesn't exist in Victim Consciousness. In First Kingdom, you can't experience the "Big S" Self. You identify with your ego/body and your "little s" self.

The idea that you yourself could be a hero is unthinkable in First Kingdom. You look outside of yourself for a hero to rescue you.

The Sun in Second Kingdom

Once you step into Second Kingdom, you can connect with the Sun. When you ask, "Who am I?" in Second Kingdom, the answer is, "I am the master of my fate and the captain of my soul."

Second Kingdom is where the Hero's Journey begins. You admire other people as heroes, and you strive to embody their best qualities. This is how you discover your Personal Standards of Integrity. As you advance through Second Kingdom, you look for recognition from other people for your accomplishments and integrity.

The Sun in Third Kingdom

The transformation when you move into Third Kingdom is subtle, yet profound. How you do things doesn't change, but why you do things does. In Third Kingdom, you realize that the source of your happiness is within you. Your values shift, and you find that you are less interested in the external world and more interested in the internal one.

When you experience the Sun from Third Kingdom, you live in the present moment, and you effortlessly **choose the best-feeling thought currently available to you**. You identify with your "Big S" Self. The answer to the question "Who am I?" is "I am a multidimensional, eternal being having a human experience."

The Sun in Fourth Kingdom

The Sun is the only planet that can be said to exist in Fourth Kingdom, although the Sun that is experienced from Fourth Kingdom is the integrated Self. When you reach Fourth Kingdom, the individual Astrological Archetypes merge into the Sun, and all sense of "little s" self vanishes. Only the "Big S" Self exists. There is no longer a sense of separation from the Divine.

Fourth Kingdom marks the beginning of the Enlightened and Transcendent states of consciousness. It's the ultimate goal of the Hero's Journey.

Saturn: The Judge

Saturn is the Archetype of the Judge. Saturn enforces the law in your "little r" reality. In First and Second Kingdom, the highest law is the **Law of Cause and Effect**, but in Third Kingdom, the highest law is the **Law of Attraction**. Saturn represents limits, boundaries, and restrictions, including your perception of time.

Without Saturn, you would not be able to connect with the Sun and discover your Personal Standards of Integrity. After all, your Personal Standards of Integrity are limitations. Saturn creates the feeling of discomfort you experience when you cross a boundary and step out of integrity.

While the other Archetypes express by saying "Yes," Saturn is the Archetype that says "No." This can be unpleasant, especially when you experience Saturn from First Kingdom. But the truth is, Saturn supports you in your pursuit of happiness. Saturn closes doors because those doors don't lead to your happiness. Every time Saturn says "No," you're one step closer to discovering your authentic "Big S" Self and becoming completely happy.

Saturn in First Kingdom

The experience of Saturn from First Kingdom can be summed up as, "I fought the law and the law won." When you experience Saturn from First Kingdom, you give your power away to external authority figures. You avoid accountability because you fear being punished for your mistakes. When you encounter Saturn in First Kingdom, the punishment is death for a first offense.

To move out of First Kingdom, you must be willing to be accountable. You literally have to throw yourself on the mercy of the court.

Saturn in Second Kingdom

When you experience Saturn from Second Kingdom, you accept accountability for your actions and for your intentions. Because you experience Saturn from a place of integrity, the dynamic of the relationship transforms. You learn to respect the Law of Cause and Effect. In First Kingdom, punishment seemed random, but in Second Kingdom, you understand that you won't get punished if you don't break the law. Ironically, the more you respect the limits and boundaries of Saturn, the freer you feel.

Saturn in Third Kingdom

When you experience Saturn from Third Kingdom, you follow the Law of Attraction rather than the Law of Cause and Effect. In Third Kingdom, you recognize the truth that everything you experience in your "little r" reality is *effect*. The *cause* is your level of consciousness. The Law of Attraction creates experiences in your "little r" reality that match the vibration of your thoughts.

The laws that limit the world of form in Second Kingdom no longer apply. What is impossible from Second Kingdom becomes effortless from Third Kingdom. When you experience Saturn from Third Kingdom, you appreciate that Saturn works for you.

The Moon: The Reflection

The Moon is the Archetype of the Reflection. The Moon reflects the light of the Sun, and like all reflections, it distorts and filters the essence of the source. The Moon is your **Emotional Guidance System**. This allows you to navigate the levels of consciousness by turning away from the "little r" realities that feel unpleasant, and turning toward the "little r" realities that feel good.

The difference between feelings and emotions is important. Feelings are the *cause* of your experiences, not the *effect* of them. Feelings arise spontaneously because you have tuned to a specific level of consciousness. The Law of Attraction fills your "little r" reality with experiences that match that vibration. If you don't like how you feel, you can tune to a different level of consciousness: just **choose the best-feeling thought currently available to you,** and your "little r" reality will change automatically.

However, you may distance yourself from the pain of an unpleasant feeling by creating a story about it. When you combine a feeling with a story, you get an emotion. Emotions turn down the volume, so you don't notice the feeling, but they also keep you stuck at the same "little r" reality.

When you move into right relationship with the Moon, you repair your Emotional Guidance System, drop the stories, and feel your feelings. This allows you to navigate the levels of consciousness and become truly happy.

The Moon in First Kingdom

When you experience the Moon from First Kingdom, you feel unsafe. Your Emotional Guidance System is shut down. You're conscious only of fear, anxiety, and stress.

In First Kingdom all feelings are emotions. When you experience an emotion, you react automatically, which reinforces the story and keeps you trapped in Victim Consciousness.

The Moon in Second Kingdom

When you experience the Moon from Second Kingdom, you feel safe. When your **Safety Needs** are met, you step out of Victim Consciousness and into integrity. But the moment the balance in your Safety Need Account drops below the minimum level, you dive back into Victim Consciousness.

In Second Kingdom, your Emotional Guidance System begins to function. You experience more feelings than emotions, and learn to *respond* rather than to *react*. This allows you to stay in integrity for longer periods of time.

The Moon in Third Kingdom

When you experience the Moon from Third Kingdom, you feel surrendered. You have a functional Emotional Guidance System. You allow your feelings to flow through you. You turn away from unpleasant feelings and turn toward good ones, and the Law of Attraction responds by creating more enjoyable experiences in your "little r" reality.

Mars: The Warrior

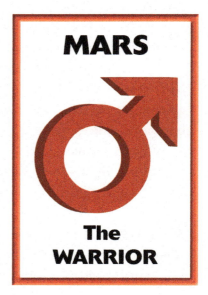

Mars is the Archetype of the Warrior. The Warrior sees the world in black and white. The Warrior chooses an objective and then follows the most direct path to reach it, overcoming obstacles with single-minded focus and utter disregard for the consequences. Mars, the Warrior, is the part of you that wants things and that goes after the things that you want. What Mars lacks is perspective.

Mars cares about power, but Mars must learn what power is. True power exists only at higher levels of consciousness.

Although the Sun is the "Big S" Self, who you *truly* are, Mars is the "little s" self, who you *think* you are. Mars is in charge of your ego/body, the vehicle you operate while you're having your human experience. Mars is responsible for protecting your physical body by meeting your **Physiological Needs** (air, food, water, shelter and sleep). To protect the body, the ego must be exquisitely sensitive to any vibration that is detrimental to life, which is why Mars always maintains a presence in First Kingdom. Private Mars operates your physical body, but ideally his orders come from higher up the chain of command.

Mars in First Kingdom

When you experience Mars from First Kingdom, the power is without, and you're without power. The Warrior fights to control the outside world and the ego seeks survival.

In First Kingdom, Private Mars fights alone, trying to survive the dangers of your "little r" reality without perspective or guidance. You act from force, rather than from power. Mars in First Kingdom worries about the future, but the future Mars fears is actually a projection of the past.

Mars in Second Kingdom

When you experience Mars from Second Kingdom, the power is within you. The Warrior fights to control the "little s" self, and the ego seeks actualization.

In the lower levels of Second Kingdom, you connect with Sergeant Mars. Sergeant Mars trains Private Mars to take the energy of anger and use it in positive ways. Sergeant Mars excels at crisis management. As you advance to the higher levels of Second Kingdom, you encounter Lieutenant Mars. Lieutenant Mars has even greater perspective than Sergeant Mars, and helps you set long-term goals. The best way to manage a crisis is to prevent it in the first place.

Mars in Third Kingdom

When you experience Mars from Third Kingdom, the power is in the present moment. Mars in Third Kingdom is the Peaceful Warrior: there is nothing to fight. In Third Kingdom, the ego seeks transcendence.

In Third Kingdom, you meet Captain Mars and the Top Brass. They give the orders that Private Mars carries out. The actions don't change, but the intentions behind them do. You no longer pursue the things that you want, because you lack nothing. You act to align with your Core Values and your Personal Standards of Integrity.

Venus: The Beloved

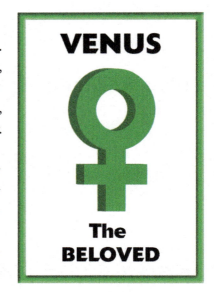

Venus is the Archetype of the Beloved. Wherever you experience love or appreciation, you find Venus. Venus is the archetype who determines your values. Values give meaning, purpose and direction to the Hero's Journey. Venus motivates you to embark on the Hero's Journey in the first place. You set out on your own, face challenges, pass tests, and claim your greatness because doing so will bring you into closer relationship with the Beloved.

Venus represents your **Core Values**. These are eternal qualities of the Divine. They're abstract concepts that include Abundance, Balance, Beauty, Freedom, Harmony, Joy, Love, Order, Peace, Power, Unity, and Wisdom. These qualities are present at all times in all things. You just have to notice them.

Although the Core Values represent the highest and most direct experience of Venus and the Beloved, they're not how you encounter Venus on a daily basis. Core Values operate from Third Kingdom, which is nonlinear and beyond form. This means they're true, but they're not necessarily real.

Venus is in charge of your **Validation Needs**. When you receive a deposit in your Validation Need Account, you feel loved and appreciated. Until you experience Venus from Third Kingdom, the love and appreciation are conditional, and can be lost.

Venus in First Kingdom

When you experience Venus from First Kingdom, Venus is in service to Mars. You value what Mars wants, which is control over conditions in your "little r"

Meet the Planets

reality. You value things like money, sex, fame, and the envy of others because these things represent power to you.

Venus in Second Kingdom

When you experience Venus from Second Kingdom, you value status. Meeting your Validation Needs in relationships becomes important. You care what other people think of you. You value intangibles like respect, success, and approval, but you still look for these in other people. The experience of love in Second Kingdom is conditional, and limited to "special" relationships, such as romantic partners, close friends, and family.

Venus in Third Kingdom

When you experience Venus from Third Kingdom, you value Love. The transformation in your life is both subtle and profound. Your Core Values motivate you, and alter how you engage with your life. At the higher levels of consciousness in Third Kingdom, Love becomes unconditional.

Mercury: The Storyteller

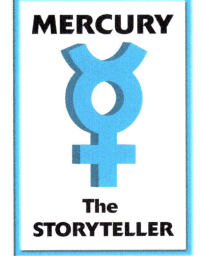

Mercury is the archetype of the Storyteller. Most people underestimate the power and importance of story. Your life—your "little r" reality—is a story. The story seems real, and it engrosses and transports you. But no matter how real it appears, it's still a story.

Mercury is the part of you that tells the story. Mercury convinces you that everything you experience is real. Mercury is the part of you that lies, and then convinces you to believe the lies.

Everything in your story is *real*, but it's not necessarily *true*. If you don't like how your story unfolds, you have the power to change it. You need only remember that you are both the story and the Storyteller. When you question your story and move into right relationship with Mercury, you choose better-feeling thoughts. Raising the vibration of your thoughts expands your consciousness, which in turn shifts the context of your story. When you experience your story from an expanded context, it feels better.

Mercury in First Kingdom

When you experience Mercury from First Kingdom, the story you tell is a tragedy. You experience only the "little s" story, which keeps you small. You gather evidence to prove "I'm right," and "It's not my fault." This keeps you trapped in Victim Consciousness. Your thoughts and the story you tell feel stressful.

Mercury in Second Kingdom

When you experience Mercury from Second Kingdom, the story you tell is an adventure. You catch glimpses of your "Big S" Story, which inspires you to move beyond the limitations of your "little s" story. In Second Kingdom, you're willing to learn, and more importantly, you're willing to be wrong. When you experience Mercury from Second Kingdom, your thoughts and the story you tell feel empowering.

Mercury in Third Kingdom

When you experience Mercury from Third Kingdom, the story you tell is an epic. You pursue your "Big S" Story and release the "little s" story. In Third Kingdom, you recognize and appreciate the game of the Hero's Journey. You become the author of your own story. When you change the words, you change the world.

Jupiter: The Dreamer

Jupiter is the archetype of the Dreamer. In traditional astrology, Jupiter symbolizes growth and expansion, but all growth and expansion begin with dreams. In dreams, you escape the illusion of your "little s" self and enter the realm of infinite possibility. Don't expect all of your dreams to be enjoyable. Sometimes you have to confront your fears to grow. Jupiter supports you by expanding the context and allowing you to move from the "little s" self to the "Big S" Self.

Mercury provides the *content* of your story, but Jupiter provides the *context* that gives the story meaning.

To move into right relationship with Jupiter, you must appreciate the difference between fantasy and imagination. Imagination is creative, but fantasy is not. When you imagine, you activate the Law of Attraction. When you fantasize, you push your dream away. The difference between fantasy and imagination is faith, which is also the domain of Jupiter.

Jupiter in First Kingdom

When you experience Jupiter from First Kingdom, the dream is either a fantasy or a nightmare. You fantasize about escape from the pain of Victim Consciousness, but you lack the faith to move out of it on your own. Jupiter makes everything bigger, and in First Kingdom, what you experience is big lack. There are endless possibilities of how things could go wrong.

Jupiter in Second Kingdom

When you experience Jupiter from Second Kingdom, you dream of the possibilities of your "Big S" Story. You have faith in your authentic "Big S" Self, and this helps you grow as an individual. As you deepen your faith, you expand your consciousness, and access the creative power of imagination.

Jupiter in Third Kingdom

When you experience Jupiter from Third Kingdom, you surrender to the creative process. In Third Kingdom, you have faith in (and of) whatever name or concept you have of God. You appreciate the truth that you are infinite, and that your thoughts create your reality.

CHAPTER 7

Elements, Modalities, and Signs

The **planets** are the most important part of speech in the language of astrology. This is unfamiliar to most astrologers. The popular perception of astrology is that it's all about the signs. When people say, "I'm a Scorpio," or "I'm a Gemini," what they're really saying is, "My Sun is in Scorpio," or "My Sun is in Gemini."

In the language of astrology, the planets are the nouns and the verbs: they tell you *who* and *what*. In natal astrology, every sentence must have one of the seven personal planets as the subject.

Signs are part of the predicate of the sentence, so they tell you something about the planet that is the subject of the sentence. The signs are the adjectives and adverbs in the language of astrology. The signs modify the expression of a planet, and tell you *how* and *why* the planet expresses.

Signs do not change the fundamental nature of the planet! Planets in Pisces lose their ability to recognize boundaries or operate in the world of form, but Saturn is always Saturn. Saturn in Pisces doesn't stop caring about enforcing rules, boundaries, limits, and structures; Saturn in Pisces just isn't very good at it. Saturn in Pisces cares about emotional and spiritual boundaries instead of physical and material boundaries.

Each of the twelve signs represents a unique combination of one of the four **elements** and one of the three **modalities**. When considering a planet in a sign, consider the element and the modality before you explore the specific associations of the sign. The element and the modality establish the context, and any other qualities associated with the sign itself have to be considered within this context. Aquarius has a reputation for making planets revolutionary and erratic; however, Aquarius is a Fixed sign. Planets in Aquarius care as much about stability as they do about freedom. Once you understand the nature of the elements and the modalities, you can easily combine them to interpret how a sign modifies the expression of a planet.

You'll use the keywords for the elements, modalities, and signs with the blueprint template sentences, which you'll learn about in Chapter 8.

The Four Elements

The four elements in astrology are **Fire**, **Earth**, **Air**, and **Water**. The elements represent different realms of reality. They define the primary arena where a planet will express.

The elements belong to one of two **polarities**. Fire and Air are expressive, and belong to the masculine or yang polarity, while Earth and Water are receptive, and belong to the feminine or yin polarity.

Fire

The Fire signs are **Aries**, **Leo**, and **Sagittarius**. The element of Fire represents the energy of life and spirit. Fire rises, seeking higher levels of expression. Planets in Fire signs act because they need to express and affirm life. They are concerned with the question of identity.

> Planets in Fire signs gain focus, intensity, passion, and energy.
>
> Planets in Fire signs lose perspective, moderation, and awareness of others.

The element of Fire is outgoing, energizing, and transforming, and it's the most self-motivated of the elements. Planets in Fire signs are very intense: they radiate great warmth and light, but in close quarters, they can burn.

Planets in Fire signs are extremely honest; they express their true nature and have little tolerance for dishonesty in others. Planets in Fire signs can experience the full range of emotions, but they prefer intense emotions, especially joy and anger.

Fire depends on a fuel source. Planets in Fire signs express fully until they burn out. The most important lesson for planets in Fire signs is moderation.

Lower-Consciousness Keywords for Fire

aggressive	belligerent	forceful	hotheaded
angry	egotistical	headstrong	overenthusiastic
arrogant	explosive	hostile	self-centered

Higher-Consciousness Keywords for Fire

active	courageous	individual	self-assured
assertive	decisive	outgoing	straightforward
confident	honest	passionate	zealous

Earth

The Earth signs are **Taurus**, **Virgo**, and **Capricorn**. The element of Earth represents substance and physical form. Earth does not move; it stays in one place. Earth is practical, substantial, and material. Earth is passive and receptive: it must be acted on and formed by external energies. Earth is the most stable of the elements. Planets in Earth signs are concerned with the material realm and with issues of worth and value.

> Planets in Earth signs gain stability, form, structure, and practicality.
>
> Planets in Earth signs lose speed, fluidity, and expressiveness.

Planets in Earth signs become practical. They operate on the physical, tangible level, and may struggle with abstract concepts. They rely on direct sensual experiences and disregard information received on the mental, intellectual, or verbal level.

Planets in Earth signs may become addicted to the illusions of the physical plane. They can become so grounded in the reality of the world of form that they can't accept the truth of the nonlinear Spiritual Realities. Planets in Earth must discover the truth of the spiritual within the world of form.

Lower-Consciousness Keywords for Earth

dull	heavy	numb	sluggish
envious	indulgent	sedate	stiff
greedy	materialistic	slow	stodgy

Higher-Consciousness Keywords for Earth

calm	enduring	practical	solid
dependable	grounded	productive	stable
efficient	industrious	sensual	tactile

Air

The Air signs are **Gemini**, **Libra**, and **Aquarius**. The element of Air represents the mental and social realms. Air moves horizontally, and forms connections with great speed. The Air signs are double signs, rooted in duality. Planets in Air signs are able to appreciate all sides of an issue simultaneously. They are concerned with relationships: to the environment (Gemini), to other individuals (Libra), and to society (Aquarius).

> Planets in Air signs gain perspective, logic, reason, speed, and objectivity.
>
> Planets in Air signs lose focus, practicality, and empathy.

Planets in Air signs become logical and rational. They prefer to operate on the mental and social planes, and they are not comfortable with intense emotions. Planets in Air signs form connections along the surface. They care about appearances, but do not care about what lies beneath.

Planets in Air signs often struggle with the material realm. They excel at theory, but find practical application challenging. They prefer to leave that to planets in Earth signs.

Elements, Modalities, and Signs

Lower-Consciousness Keywords for Air

aloof	distracted	shallow	thoughtless
condescending	duplicitous	superficial	uncaring
detached	heartless	talkative	vacuous

Higher-Consciousness Keywords for Air

analytical	communicative	logical	reasonable
articulate	impartial	objective	sociable
associative	intellectual	rational	strategic

Water

The Water signs are **Cancer**, **Scorpio**, and **Pisces**. The element of Water represents the emotional and spiritual plane. Water relates to the deepest, most primal emotions, and to the needs and longings of the soul. Water sinks, seeking the lowest point, and water will continue to flow until it is contained. Water has no shape or structure of its own, and instead takes on the characteristics and form of its container. The element of Water is irrational, instinctive, emotional, and right-brained.

> Planets in Water signs gain compassion, depth, fluidity, and empathy.
>
> Planets in Water signs lose perspective, practicality, structure, and boundaries.

Planets in Water signs are retentive: they remember every emotional experience, no matter how painful. They may not be able to communicate the depth of their feelings because words do not come easily. Some things can be communicated only through direct emotional experiences.

Planets in Water signs have difficulty accepting and respecting interpersonal boundaries—particularly emotional ones. Planets in Water signs expect to know your soul and your deepest feelings before they know your name.

Lower-Consciousness Keywords for Water

emotional	moody	over-concerned	reactive
hidden	needy	overprotective	retentive
instinctive	no boundaries	oversensitive	unconscious

Higher-Consciousness Keywords for Water

caring	emotive	intuitive	receptive
compassionate	imaginative	persistent	resilient
deep	inspired	responsive	spiritual

The Three Modalities

The three modalities in astrology are **Cardinal**, **Fixed**, and **Mutable**. The modalities define how a planet expresses. Each modality also relates to a core false belief that fuels the Hero's Journey process.

Cardinal

The Cardinal signs are Aries, Cancer, Libra, and Capricorn, and in the **Tropical Zodiac**, they correspond to the beginnings of the seasons of spring, summer, fall, and winter in the Northern Hemisphere. Cardinal signs are initiating, and focused on new beginnings.

> Planets in Cardinal signs gain initiative, self-motivation, and the ability to overcome inertia.
>
> Planets in Cardinal signs lose tolerance for routine, and the desire to complete what was initiated.

Planets in Cardinal signs suffer a crisis of identity. The core false belief of planets in Cardinal signs is, "The Divine does not love me because there is something fundamentally wrong with who I am," or more succinctly, "I'm bad."

Planets in Cardinal signs focus on the past. They appear to act in anticipation of future events, but in fact, they react to old information.

Elements, Modalities, and Signs

Planets in Cardinal signs always look for what's new; the moment something becomes routine, they lose interest. Planets in Cardinal signs must learn the art of impulse control. They act the moment they get a new idea, and rarely, if ever, think things through or create an organized plan.

When pressured, a planet in a Cardinal sign will defend itself by counter-attacking. Planets in Cardinal signs embody the phrase, "Shoot first, ask questions later."

Lower-Consciousness Keywords for Cardinal

challenging	egotistical	impulsive	quarrelsome
competitive	forceful	peremptory	self-centered
defiant	headstrong	pushy	self-interested

Higher-Consciousness Keywords for Cardinal

active	groundbreaking	innovating	pioneering
assertive	individual	leading	self-directed
audacious	initiating	originating	trailblazing

Fixed

The Fixed signs are Taurus, Leo, Scorpio, and Aquarius. The Fixed signs correspond to the middle of each season, when the changes in the weather are well established, and the steady rhythm of life has reasserted itself. Fixed signs follow the Cardinal signs, and planets in Fixed signs sustain and maintain what planets in Cardinal signs initiated.

Planets in Fixed signs gain stamina, stability, strength, and inertia.

Planets in Fixed signs lose flexibility, speed, and the ability to change or adapt.

Planets in Fixed signs suffer a crisis of self-worth. The core false belief of planets in Fixed signs is, "The love of the Divine is conditional and must be earned." This creates a general belief that "I'm not enough," which in turn creates an endless series of specific beliefs of

"I'm not _____ enough," where you fill in the blank with a random quality (e.g., attractive, wealthy, intelligent, successful).

Planets in Fixed signs focus on the future. They anticipate future lack, so they can't appreciate their present sufficiency.

Planets in Fixed signs care about stability and structure, and they want things to last. They possess tremendous stamina and reserves. Planets in Fixed signs do not like change. They will always try to follow their original course of action, even when the context has shifted.

When confronted, a planet in a Fixed sign digs in its heels and resists. Planets in Fixed signs are willing to change, but the impetus to change has to come from within.

Lower-Consciousness Keywords for Fixed

adamant	inexorable	relentless	routine
callous	inflexible	resentful	sedate
hidebound	obstinate	rigid	unvarying

Higher-Consciousness Keywords for Fixed

constant	equanimous	loyal	secure
dependable	faithful	patient	stable
enduring	forbearing	persistent	steadfast

Mutable

The Mutable signs are Gemini, Virgo, Sagittarius, and Pisces. Mutable signs correspond to the end of each season, when the weather is preparing to change. Planets in Mutable signs adapt and transform. They work to complete the current cycle to prepare for the next cycle.

> Planets in Mutable signs gain flexibility, speed, creativity, and adaptability.
>
> Planets in Mutable signs lose stability and focus.

Elements, Modalities, and Signs

Planets in Mutable signs suffer a crisis of completion. The core false belief of planets in Mutable signs is, "I must change who I am to be loved by the Divine," although the more general sense is, "I'm incomplete." It seems to combine the "I'm bad" belief of Cardinal signs with the "I'm not enough" belief of Fixed signs.

Planets in Mutable signs are focused in time, and operate in the present moment; however, they are often scattered in space.

Planets in Mutable signs become flexible and agile; they adapt to keep things moving. They can become too flexible, however, and attempt to change their nature to avoid confrontation. Planets in Mutable signs must learn focus. They often take on too much, which scatters their energy and makes them ineffective.

Lower-Consciousness Keywords for Mutable

distracted	inconsistent	scattered	unpredictable
erratic	inconstant	undependable	unsettled
fickle	restless	unfocused	variable

Higher-Consciousness Keywords for Mutable

adaptable	deft	flexible	responsive
agile	dexterous	healing	skillful
completing	diverse	nimble	versatile

The Twelve Signs

Each of the twelve signs represents a unique combination of an element and a modality. The element tells you which realm planets in that sign prefer, and the modality tells you the core concern of the planet and how it will express. The planets that have **Essential Dignity** for the sign give you information about the specific agenda of any planets in the sign.

Introduction to Essential Dignities

Essential Dignities are an ancient system of evaluating the relative "strength" of a planet at a particular degree of a sign. They are the heart and soul of classical astrology, but modern astrology ignores them completely.

Think of a sign as a corporation. A corporation is involved in a particular type of business. The element and modality of the sign determine the type of business. For example, Libra is a Cardinal Air sign. Because it's a Cardinal sign, planets in Libra are concerned with the question of individual identity. Because it's an Air sign, planets in Libra operate in the mental, intellectual, abstract, and social realms, and are motivated to make connections.

A corporation's Chief Executive Officer (CEO) is the public face of the company. A corporation also has a **Board of Directors**. The planets that have Essential Dignity for the specific degree of a sign make up the members of the Board of Directors for that degree. The board members operate behind the scenes, influencing the policies that the CEO shares with the public.

Each member of the Board of Directors has a specific number of votes, based on the Essential Dignity. The planet with **Rulership** functions as the CEO and gets 5 votes; the planet with **Exaltation** gets 4 votes; the planet with **Triplicity** gets 3 votes; the planet with **Term** gets 2 votes; and the planet with **Face** gets 1 vote.

Rulership and Exaltation are sign-based dignities, so the planets that have the most influence over the Board of Directors for each sign never change. Triplicity is also a sign-based dignity, but it's based on the **sect** of the chart. If it's a **diurnal**, or day chart (Sun above the horizon), one planet has Triplicity; but if it's a **nocturnal**, or night chart (Sun below the horizon) a different planet has Triplicity. Term and Face vary based on the specific degree of the sign. For each of the twelve signs, we'll consider the planets with Rulership, Exaltation, and Triplicity, and note how those planets shape the agenda for planets in the sign. You'll also find an illustration from the **EZ Essential Dignity Card™** for each sign, for easy reference. See Figure 10 on page 114 for instructions on how to read the EZ Essential Dignity Card.

Aries

Aries is a Cardinal Fire sign. As a Cardinal sign, planets in Aries are involved in the initial creative process. They initiate and take action, and are concerned with the question of identity. Because Aries is a Fire sign, planets in Aries operate on the plane of life and spirit, affirming identity. Planets in Aries seek to initiate and express individual identity, freely, impulsively, and without limitation.

Planets in Aries are so focused on expressing their own identity that they rarely notice other individuals. Planets in Aries are unable to perceive how their actions affect others. These planets can be experienced as aggressive and combative, but only because they always take the shortest path to a goal, regardless of what (or who) might be in the way. Aries is the most impulsive energy in the zodiac. Planets in Aries act without a plan or any concern for the consequences.

Planets in Aries become action-oriented and single-minded in their manifestation. They are direct and honest, but they lack perspective. Planets in Aries lose stamina and burn out quickly.

Mars is the Ruler of Aries, and always has at least 5 votes. The Sun is Exalted in Aries, and always has at least 4 votes. In a day chart, the Sun also has Triplicity, giving the Sun a minimum of 7 votes; in a night chart, Jupiter

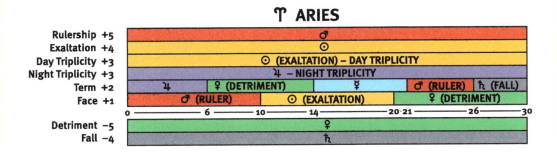

has 3 votes for Triplicity. The challenge for planets in Aries is to maintain a balance between the "little s" self (Mars) and the "Big S" Self (Sun).

Lower-Consciousness Keywords for Aries

aggressive	autocratic	combative	foolhardy
angry	challenging	defiant	impatient
arrogant	cocky	egotistical	impulsive

Higher-Consciousness Keywords for Aries

assertive	courageous	inspiring	self-assured
audacious	daring	outgoing	spontaneous
confident	enterprising	pioneering	trailblazing

Elements, Modalities, and Signs

Taurus

Taurus is a Fixed Earth sign. As a Fixed sign, planets in Taurus seek to sustain and maintain. They are concerned with the question of self-worth. Because Taurus is an Earth sign, planets in Taurus operate on the physical and the material plane. Planets in Taurus seek to express physical and material self-worth.

Planets in Taurus are sensual, and want nothing more than slow, steady, progressive growth. The challenge for these planets is to let go of the attachment to the physical. They may identify with the material plane instead of the authentic "Big S" Self, and acquire things to bolster self-worth. Planets in Taurus must learn that worth has nothing to do with appearances in the physical realm.

Planets in Taurus become slow and deliberate. They look for tangible, practical ways to express. They also become stubborn and resistant to change. They must learn to become flexible and welcome change as a natural part of life.

Venus is the Ruler of Taurus, and always has at least 5 votes. The Moon is Exalted in Taurus, and always has at least 4 votes. During the day, Venus has Triplicity, and picks up an additional 3 votes; at night, the Moon gets those votes. The challenge for planets in Taurus is to stay aligned with your Core

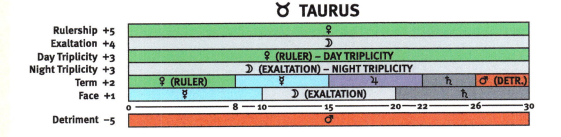

Values and meet your Validation Needs (Venus) without creating attachments and feeling unsafe (Moon).

Lower-Consciousness Keywords for Taurus

adamant	grasping	materialistic	possessive
callous	greedy	obstinate	resentful
covetous	hidebound	overindulgent	tedious

Higher-Consciousness Keywords for Taurus

affectionate	dependable	grounded	patient
artistic	diligent	introspective	practical
calm	generous	loyal	steadfast

Gemini

Gemini is a Mutable Air sign. Because Gemini is a Mutable sign, planets in Gemini adapt and change. They are concerned with healing, completion, and becoming whole. Because Gemini is an Air sign, planets in Gemini operate on the mental plane, and are most comfortable with abstract ideas, notions, and symbols. Planets in Gemini seek to heal and complete the mental and intellectual plane.

Gemini is the fastest of the mutable signs. Planets in Gemini express the fundamental nature of duality. They move quickly across the surface and map the terrain. Planets in Gemini are profoundly curious and interested in everything, which makes them charming in social situations. However, this insatiable curiosity is often accompanied by the attention span of a fruit fly. Planets in Gemini must learn to slow down, focus, and explore beneath the surface.

Planets in Gemini become quicker, more flexible, and more playful. They lose empathy, and the ability to operate in the emotional or spiritual realm. Planets in Gemini are perhaps the most uncomfortable with deep, sustained emotions.

Mercury is the Ruler of Gemini and always has at least 5 votes. During the day, Saturn receives 3 votes for Triplicity, but at night, those votes go to Mercury. Planets in Gemini seek to communicate, gather information, and understand.

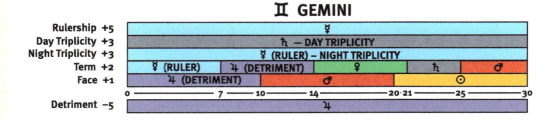

Principles of Practical Natal Astrology

They are actively involved in telling your "little s" story. However, you must always question the story to determine if you're telling it with integrity from within My Business.[1]

Lower-Consciousness Keywords for Gemini

contradictory	duplicitous	heartless	nervous
cunning	erratic	inconsiderate	scattered
deceitful	flighty	inconstant	shallow

Higher-Consciousness Keywords for Gemini

adaptable	clever	informative	objective
articulate	curious	intelligent	quick-witted
charming	friendly	logical	responsive

---

[1] See the spiritual practices in Appendix A for details.

Cancer

Cancer is a Cardinal Water sign. Because Cancer is a Cardinal sign, planets in Cancer are involved in the initial creative process. They initiate and take action, and are concerned with the question of identity. Because Cancer is a Water sign, planets in Cancer operate on the emotional and spiritual plane. Planets in Cancer seek to initiate and express emotional and spiritual identity.

Planets in Cancer become sensitive to feelings and to subtle energies. When these planets feel threatened, they can be needy, clinging, possessive, and helpless. They may look for emotional security in the physical world, and often use food as a substitute for love. Planets in Cancer must learn to be more self-reliant and self-sufficient. They must develop the strength and courage to face the world as an individual, while maintaining supportive connections with others.

Planets in Cancer gain empathy, compassion, and intuition. However, they lose perspective, structure, and awareness of appropriate boundaries.

The Moon is the Ruler of Cancer, and always has at least 5 votes. Jupiter is Exalted in Cancer, and always has at least 4 votes. Mars has Triplicity in Cancer (both day and night) and always has at least 3 votes. The challenge for planets in Cancer is to feel safe (Moon) so that the ego/body and the "little s" self

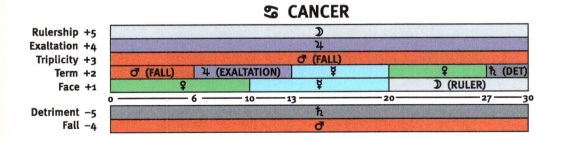

(Mars) doesn't take control and pull you into Victim Consciousness. The key to this is developing faith (Jupiter) in the abundance of the universe.

Lower-Consciousness Keywords for Cancer

addicted	codependent	manipulative	needy
attached	demanding	moody	oversensitive
clinging	emotional	mothering	temperamental

Higher-Consciousness Keywords for Cancer

attentive	considerate	imaginative	nurturing
caring	emotive	intuitive	protective
compassionate	gracious	maternal	secure

Leo

Leo is a Fixed Fire sign. Because Leo is a Fixed sign, planets in Leo seek to sustain and maintain. They are concerned with the question of self-worth. Because Leo is a Fire sign, planets in Leo operate on the plane of life and spirit, affirming identity. Planets in Leo seek to demonstrate your individual self-worth.

Planets in Leo want to shine; but above all, they want to be the center of attention. When these planets express from integrity, they are warm, generous, creative, and courageous. They demonstrate their worth by coming from the heart. When planets in Leo express from Victim Consciousness, they act out and demand attention, whether they deserve it or not. Planets in Leo must learn that your sense of self-worth comes from within, and does not require external validation.

Planets in Leo become more open, generous, expressive and creative. Everything they do is an expression of the authentic "Big S" Self. Although planets in Leo gain strength, courage, passion, and stamina, they lose perspective, especially where other individuals are concerned. They must accept that other individuals are their co-stars, not their audience.

The Sun is the Ruler of Leo and always has at least 5 votes. During the day, the Sun picks up an additional 3 votes for Triplicity; at night, Jupiter receives those votes. Planets in Leo need to maintain a conscious connection to the

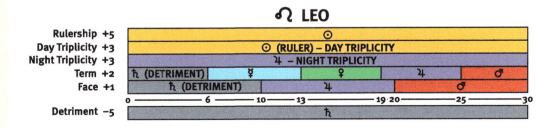

"Big S" Self (Sun). The challenge is that when you operate from First Kingdom, you lose your connection to the "Big S" Self.

Lower-Consciousness Keywords for Leo

arrogant	condescending	haughty	overblown
cocksure	domineering	indignant	pompous
childish	egotistical	infantile	self-important

Higher-Consciousness Keywords for Leo

assertive	charitable	dramatic	heroic
benevolent	courageous	expansive	honorable
charismatic	dignified	forthright	magnanimous

Virgo

Virgo is a Mutable Earth sign. Because Virgo is a Mutable Sign, planets in Virgo adapt and change. They are concerned with healing, completion, and becoming whole. Because Virgo is an Earth sign, planets in Virgo operate on the physical and the material planes. Planets in Virgo seek to heal and complete the world of form.

Perfectionism is the biggest challenge for planets in Virgo. Planets in Virgo want to analyze and improve the material world, but they must learn that perfection is a journey, not a destination. When a planet in Virgo notices something that could be improved, it's not criticism; it's an inspiration to create something new. The lesson for planets in Virgo is to appreciate the inherent perfection of what currently exists.

Planets in Virgo become precise, efficient, analytical, and practical. Virgo is an Earth sign, so planets in Virgo prefer to express on the physical and material plane. Mercury has so much influence over planets in Virgo that these planets are also comfortable expressing on the mental and intellectual plane. Planets in Virgo gain structure, but lose some of their empathy and compassion. They become more left-brained, and process information in a logical, linear manner. They find it challenging to access the creative, non-linear, and spiritual perspective of the right brain.

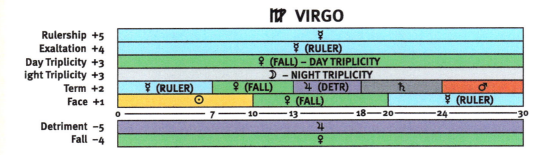

Mercury receives 5 votes for Rulership and 4 votes for Exaltation, so Mercury always has at least 9 votes on the Board of Directors for a planet in Virgo. During the day, Venus has 3 votes for Triplicity; at night, the Moon gets those votes. Planets in Virgo seek to communicate, gather information, and understand. They are actively involved in telling your "little s" story. However, you must always question the story to determine if you're telling it with integrity from within My Business.

Lower-Consciousness Keywords for Virgo

compulsive	fussy	pedantic	rigid
conniving	hypercritical	perfectionistic	scheming
finicky	insensitive	prissy	self-conscious

Higher-Consciousness Keywords for Virgo

analytical	conscientious	hardworking	judicial
careful	efficient	incisive	observant
competent	flexible	intelligent	practical

Libra

Libra is a Cardinal Air sign. Because Libra is a Cardinal sign, planets in Libra are involved in the initial creative process. They initiate and take action, and are concerned with the question of identity. Because Libra is an Air sign, planets in Libra operate on the mental plane, and are comfortable with abstract ideas, notions, and symbols. Planets in Libra seek to initiate and express a mental and social identity.

Planets in Libra want to create a greater sense of beauty and harmony in the universe by acting in relationship with other individuals. This need for relationship can lead to dependence on others, especially when experienced from First Kingdom. Saturn's influence forces planets in Libra to be accountable for their choices, and emphasizes the need for healthy, appropriate boundaries. Planets in Libra may feel incomplete without a relationship, but they must learn that they do not need other people to be whole.

Planets in Libra become objective, diplomatic, and impartial. They see both sides of every issue and can find the common ground. Because Libra is an Air sign, planets in Libra lose empathy and practicality. They care about appearances, and don't like to dive beneath the surface or deal with emotions.

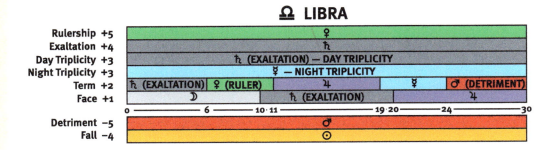

Principles of Practical Natal Astrology

Venus is the Ruler of Libra and always has at least 5 votes. Saturn always has at least 4 votes for Exaltation, but during the day, Saturn picks up 3 additional votes for Triplicity, giving Saturn as much or more influence than Venus. In a night chart, Mercury has 3 votes for Triplicity. Planets in Libra need to connect with your Core Values and Validation Needs (Venus), to be aware of boundaries and be willing to accept accountability for your actions (Saturn), and to stay within the limits of My Business (Mercury).

Lower-Consciousness Keywords for Libra

aloof	fatuous	indecisive	people-pleasing
dependent	fickle	meddling	superficial
detached	heartless	pacifying	sycophantic

Higher-Consciousness Keywords for Libra

affectionate	charming	diplomatic	impartial
artistic	civilized	elegant	peaceful
balanced	cooperative	harmonious	respectful

Elements, Modalities, and Signs

Scorpio

Scorpio is a Fixed Water sign. Because Scorpio is a Fixed sign, planets in Scorpio seek to sustain and maintain, and they are concerned with the question of self-worth. Because Scorpio is a Water sign, planets in Scorpio operate on the emotional and spiritual planes. Planets in Scorpio seek to sustain and maintain emotional and spiritual self-worth.

Planets in Scorpio experience emotions with greater depth and intensity than in any other sign. They are prepared to explore the underworld of the unconscious to confront hidden fears, wounds, and desires. These planets care nothing for surface appearances; they want to uncover the longings of the soul. Planets in Scorpio can become obsessed with transformation. They must learn to let go. After ruthlessly destroying the old to make way for the new, they must allow time and space for the new to manifest.

Planets in Scorpio gain depth, empathy, and intensity, and become agents of change. They become more perceptive, and are able to see into the hidden, spiritual truth of the matter. They lose objectivity, flexibility, and the ability to operate on the mental plane. Planets in Scorpio find it difficult to communicate with words. They operate on a powerful, emotional level; they're not built for small talk.

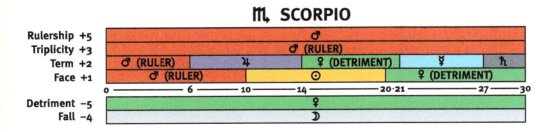

Mars has absolute control over Scorpio with a minimum of 8 votes for Rulership and Triplicity. This is why planets in Scorpio are such fierce fighters: when they are provoked, they retaliate with deadly accuracy. Being in right relationship with Mars determines if planets in Scorpio act from integrity using power, or from Victim Consciousness using force.

Lower-Consciousness Keywords for Scorpio

acrimonious	controlling	emotional	obsessed
compulsive	destructive	explosive	paranoid
conniving	devious	inhibited	spiteful

Higher-Consciousness Keywords for Scorpio

audacious	fearless	intuitive	penetrating
compelling	incisive	keen	profound
dedicated	intense	loyal	resourceful

Elements, Modalities, and Signs

Sagittarius

Sagittarius is a Mutable Fire sign. Because Sagittarius is a Mutable sign, planets in Sagittarius adapt and change. They are concerned with healing, completion, and becoming whole. Because Sagittarius is a Fire sign, planets in Sagittarius operate on the plane of life and spirit, affirming identity. Planets in Sagittarius seek to heal and complete individual identity.

Planets in Sagittarius care about the big picture; they pursue a personal connection to the Truth. They have an expansive, adventurous nature, and are willing to follow their beliefs wherever they lead. Even though Sagittarius is a Mutable sign, planets in Sagittarius can become rigid in their beliefs, and may overlook or ignore information that calls their beliefs into question. They want the freedom to run away and be alone with their beliefs, but they must learn to stay present and entertain other points of view.

Planets in Sagittarius become independent and flexible (just not about their beliefs). They gain honesty and authenticity, but lose empathy and tact. They find it difficult to have compassion for anyone who does not share their beliefs.

Jupiter is the Ruler of Sagittarius, and always has at least 5 votes. During the day, the Sun has 3 votes for Triplicity; at night, those votes go to Jupiter. Planets in Sagittarius need to develop faith and expand the context of the story (Jupiter). The lesson is to align with what is *true*, even when it doesn't appear *real*.

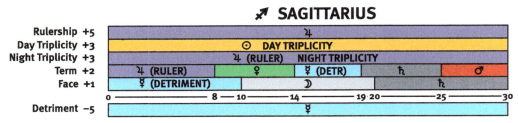

Lower-Consciousness Keywords for Sagittarius

arrogant	clumsy	haphazard	irresponsible
belligerent	dogmatic	imprudent	moralizing
blunt	foolish	inept	tactless

Higher-Consciousness Keywords for Sagittarius

adventurous	forthcoming	independent	sincere
assertive	genuine	outgoing	straightforward
enthusiastic	honorable	philosophical	truthful

Elements, Modalities, and Signs

Capricorn

Capricorn is a Cardinal Earth sign. Because Capricorn is a Cardinal sign, planets in Capricorn are involved in the initial creative process. They initiate and take action, and are concerned with the question of identity. Because Capricorn is an Earth sign, planets in Capricorn operate on the physical and the material plane. Planets in Capricorn seek to initiate and create physical, material, and tangible expressions of identity.

Planets in Capricorn work harder than planets in any other sign. Saturn's influence tells these planets that everything must be earned, and Mars' influence gives the planets the energy to pursue a goal with single-minded focus. If you combine this with the creative drive of Cardinal energy and the practicality of Earth, you get a planet determined to master the world of form. From higher levels of consciousness, this is powerful; from lower levels of consciousness, it's ruthless, selfish, and materialistic. Planets in Capricorn become attached to rules, boundaries, structure, and tradition.

Planets in Capricorn gain focus, ambition, independence, and practicality. They are conscious of their responsibilities, and strive to embody their highest potential. However, they may find it difficult to connect with others, or to accept help when needed. Planets in Capricorn experience empathy and compassion,

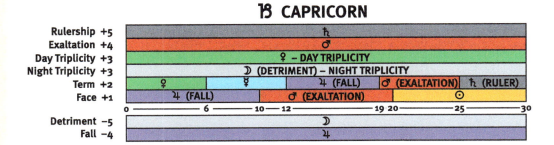

but they lose the ability to express or act on it. Compassion doesn't exempt you from the consequences of breaking the rules.

Saturn is the Ruler of Capricorn and always has at least 5 votes. Mars is Exalted in Capricorn, and always has at least 4 votes. During the day, Venus has 3 votes for Triplicity; at night, those votes go to the Moon. Planets in Capricorn need you to be accountable for your actions (Saturn and Mars), while staying connected to your Core Values (Venus) and managing your Safety Needs (Moon).

Lower-Consciousness Keywords for Capricorn

acquisitive	despotic	inflexible	miserly
autocratic	distant	insensitive	pessimistic
demanding	dour	materialistic	ruthless

Higher-Consciousness Keywords for Capricorn

ambitious	determined	industrious	practical
competent	dignified	mature	responsible
dependable	earnest	methodical	steadfast

Elements, Modalities, and Signs

Aquarius

Aquarius is a Fixed Air sign. Because Aquarius is a Fixed sign, planets in Aquarius seek to sustain and maintain, and they are concerned with the question of self-worth. Because Aquarius is an Air sign, planets in Aquarius operate on the mental plane, and are most comfortable with abstract ideas, notions, and symbols. Planets in Aquarius seek to sustain and maintain a sense of intellectual and social self-worth.

Planets in Aquarius care about freedom, particularly the freedom to explore ideas, and to express one's individual value to society. Freedom is not anarchy. Freedom requires law, boundaries, rules, and structures. Planets in Aquarius will question the established rules. If a rule no longer serves the group, a planet in Aquarius will rebel and tear down the law—and then replace it with a law that serves the group. Planets in Aquarius think only in terms of the group. The groups they identify with determine their social self-worth. A group for a planet in Aquarius is an abstract concept; an Aquarius group can have only one member.

Planets in Aquarius gain objectivity and perspective. Because they care about the greater good of society, they can be altruistic and selfless. The challenge for planets in Aquarius is that they have great compassion for humanity (which comes from the head), but difficulty feeling compassion for individual humans (which comes from the heart). Planets in Aquarius lose

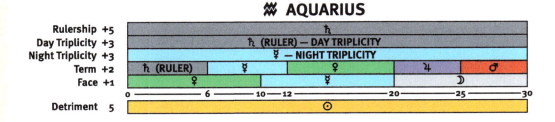

empathy, practicality, and flexibility. Aquarius is a Fixed sign, and planets in Aquarius do not like change.

Saturn is the Ruler of Aquarius and always has at least 5 votes. During the day, Saturn picks up an additional 3 votes for Triplicity; at night, those votes go to Mercury. Planets in Aquarius need to be held accountable for their actions (Saturn) while questioning the story and staying within the confines of "My Business" (Mercury).

Lower-Consciousness Keywords for Aquarius

aloof	eccentric	inflexible	obstinate
anarchic	elitist	insubordinate	rebellious
defiant	idealistic	malcontent	uncaring

Higher-Consciousness Keywords for Aquarius

altruistic	egalitarian	humanitarian	original
collaborative	freedom-loving	innovative	progressive
democratic	gregarious	liberal	unique

Elements, Modalities, and Signs

Pisces

Pisces is a Mutable Water sign. Because Pisces is a Mutable sign, planets in Pisces adapt and change. They are concerned with healing, completion, and becoming whole. Because Pisces is a Water sign, planets in Pisces operate on the emotional and spiritual planes. Planets in Pisces seek to heal and complete the emotional and spiritual planes.

Planets in Pisces value the higher spiritual vibrations, and on some level they understand the truth that there is no separation from the Source. Ironically, planets in Pisces must learn that there is also no separation between spirit and matter. They often seek to escape the limitations of the physical realm because it's painful and uncomfortable, but they must learn to exist in the world of form while knowing the truth of Spirit in all things.

Planets in Pisces gain sensitivity, compassion, empathy, and intuition. They easily adapt and go with the flow, and attune to the emotional environment. They lose the ability to take direct, focused action, and to notice boundaries, especially emotional ones. Planets in Pisces have difficulty separating their own feelings from the feelings of people around them.

Jupiter is the ruler of Pisces and always has at least 5 votes. Venus is Exalted in Pisces, and always has at least 4 votes. Mars has Triplicity in Pisces (day and

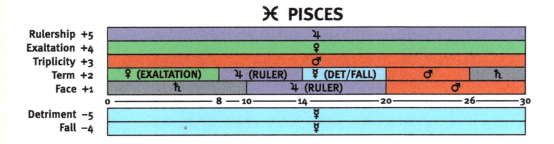

night) and always has at least 3 votes. Planets in Pisces must learn to balance what is true (Jupiter) and what you truly value (Venus) with what is real (Mars). The challenge is to balance body (Mars), mind (Jupiter), and spirit (Venus).

Lower-Consciousness Keywords for Pisces

addicted	disoriented	helpless	nebulous
codependent	emotional	hypersensitive	needy
confused	escapist	masochistic	vague

Higher-Consciousness Keywords for Pisces

adaptable	emotive	imaginative	openhearted
compassionate	empathetic	intuitive	selfless
creative	healing	merciful	understanding

CHAPTER 8
Simple Sentences: Planets in Signs

In *The Little Book of Talent*, Daniel Coyle explains the difference between hard, high-precision skills and soft, high-flexibility skills. Hard skills have specific, objective targets. You either perform them correctly or incorrectly. Your goal is consistent, repeatable precision. Soft skills don't follow a single path to a result. They involve being adaptable and flexible, recognizing patterns, and responding in the moment. Interpreting a natal chart relies on a combination of hard and soft skills. But as Coyle points out, the hard skills are the most important. They're the foundation of everything else.[1]

You develop the hard skills of the language of astrology with interpretation drills that use blueprint template sentences. The drills emphasize the correct relationship between a planet and a sign, and they help you to "chunk" a planet and a sign together and view it as a single unit. The drills also expand your references for how planets in each sign can express. When you explore the contrast between the high-consciousness and low-consciousness expressions of each planet–sign combination, you build a foundation for a three-dimensional chart interpretation.

The fill-in-the-blank blueprint template sentences eliminate any distraction, so when you use them for deep practice, you target the right circuits. The template sentences establish the context. All you have to do is choose the keywords.

To use these templates for deep practice and interpretation drills, you must write or type the entire sentence and fill in the relevant keywords as you go.

---

[1] Coyle, Daniel. *The Little Book of Talent: 52 Tips for Improving Skills*. New York, NY: Bantam Books, 2012. 17-28.

Reading the template sentences and filling in keywords in your head may help you to understand the information, but it won't develop interpretation skills.

Planets in Signs Template Sentences

You can use these templates to write a total of 336 different blueprint sentences. I've provided you with four different templates for each of the seven planets, and you can use each template with all twelve signs. You'll find starter lists of high-consciousness and low-consciousness keywords for the elements, modalities, and signs in Chapter 7, but you're not limited to these keywords. The students in **The Real Astrology Academy's Online Natal Astrology Class** receive an expanded selection of keywords—more than 120 for each sign.

It's important that you develop the habit of citing your interpretations. Every time you introduce a concept or make a statement, you need to indicate how it ties back to the astrology. I've indicated where to include these citations in the blueprint template sentences in the red brackets, and I'll demonstrate this approach throughout the book in my examples.

The Sun

He/she wants to be a hero (Sun) by being [HIGH-CONSCIOUSNESS KEYWORD] **and** [HIGH-CONSCIOUSNESS KEYWORD] ([SIGN]), **but sometimes appears to be** [LOW-CONSCIOUSNESS KEYWORD] **and** [LOW-CONSCIOUSNESS KEYWORD] ([SIGN]).

He/she seeks to express his/her authentic "Big S" Self (Sun) by being [HIGH-CONSCIOUSNESS KEYWORD] **and** [HIGH-CONSCIOUSNESS KEYWORD] ([SIGN]), **but sometimes appears to be** [LOW-CONSCIOUSNESS KEYWORD] **and** [LOW-CONSCIOUSNESS KEYWORD] ([SIGN]).

His/her Personal Standards of Integrity (Sun) call him/her to be more [HIGH-CONSCIOUSNESS KEYWORD] **and** [HIGH-CONSCIOUSNESS KEYWORD] ([SIGN]), **but sometimes he/she can appear to be** [LOW-CONSCIOUSNESS KEYWORD] **and** [LOW-CONSCIOUSNESS KEYWORD] ([SIGN]).

Simple Sentences: Planets in Signs

To live a happy, energized and vital life (Sun), he/she needs to have experiences that make him/her feel [HIGH-CONSCIOUSNESS KEYWORD] and [HIGH-CONSCIOUSNESS KEYWORD] ([SIGN]).

The Moon

To feel Safe (Moon), he/she needs to feel [HIGH-CONSCIOUSNESS KEYWORD] and [HIGH-CONSCIOUSNESS KEYWORD] ([SIGN]), and when he/she feels unsafe, he/she may become [LOW-CONSCIOUSNESS KEYWORD] and [LOW-CONSCIOUSNESS KEYWORD] ([SIGN]).

When he/she expresses his/her feelings and emotions (Moon), he/she hopes to be [HIGH-CONSCIOUSNESS KEYWORD] and [HIGH-CONSCIOUSNESS KEYWORD] ([SIGN]), but sometimes appears to be [LOW-CONSCIOUSNESS KEYWORD] and [LOW-CONSCIOUSNESS KEYWORD] ([SIGN]).

When he/she nurtures and protects others (Moon), he/she hopes to be [HIGH-CONSCIOUSNESS KEYWORD] and [HIGH-CONSCIOUSNESS KEYWORD] ([SIGN]), but sometimes he/she can appear to be [LOW-CONSCIOUSNESS KEYWORD] and [LOW-CONSCIOUSNESS KEYWORD] ([SIGN]).

He/she is the most comfortable experiencing feelings and emotions (Moon) that are [HIGH-CONSCIOUSNESS KEYWORD] and [HIGH-CONSCIOUSNESS KEYWORD] ([SIGN]).

Mercury

When he/she communicates (Mercury), he/she hopes to be seen as [HIGH-CONSCIOUSNESS KEYWORD] and [HIGH-CONSCIOUSNESS KEYWORD] ([SIGN]), but sometimes appears to be [LOW-CONSCIOUSNESS KEYWORD] and [LOW-CONSCIOUSNESS KEYWORD] ([SIGN]).

He/she intends to form connections (Mercury) that are [HIGH-CONSCIOUSNESS KEYWORD] and [HIGH-CONSCIOUSNESS KEYWORD] ([SIGN]), but sometimes are experienced as [LOW-CONSCIOUSNESS KEYWORD] and [LOW-CONSCIOUSNESS KEYWORD] ([SIGN]).

He/she expects his/her "little r" reality (Mercury) to be filled with experiences that are [HIGH-CONSCIOUSNESS KEYWORD] and [HIGH-CONSCIOUSNESS KEYWORD] ([SIGN]), but sometimes perceives it to be [LOW-CONSCIOUSNESS KEYWORD] and [LOW-CONSCIOUSNESS KEYWORD] ([SIGN]).

The way he/she processes information (Mercury) is [HIGH-CONSCIOUSNESS KEYWORD] and [HIGH-CONSCIOUSNESS KEYWORD] ([SIGN]).

Venus

He/she loves, appreciates, and values (Venus) individuals who are [HIGH-CONSCIOUSNESS KEYWORD] and [HIGH-CONSCIOUSNESS KEYWORD] ([SIGN]), but may attract individuals who are [LOW-CONSCIOUSNESS KEYWORD] and [LOW-CONSCIOUSNESS KEYWORD] ([SIGN]).

When he/she expresses affection and appreciation (Venus), he/she hopes to be [HIGH-CONSCIOUSNESS KEYWORD] and [HIGH-CONSCIOUSNESS KEYWORD] ([SIGN]), but when feeling unappreciated, he/she may become [LOW-CONSCIOUSNESS KEYWORD] and [LOW-CONSCIOUSNESS KEYWORD] ([SIGN]).

He/she hopes to attract (Venus) experiences that are [HIGH-CONSCIOUSNESS KEYWORD] and [HIGH-CONSCIOUSNESS KEYWORD] ([SIGN]), but sometimes settles for experiences that are [LOW-CONSCIOUSNESS KEYWORD] and [LOW-CONSCIOUSNESS KEYWORD] ([SIGN]).

He/she wants to be validated and appreciated (Venus) for being [HIGH-CONSCIOUSNESS KEYWORD] and [HIGH-CONSCIOUSNESS KEYWORD] ([SIGN]).

Simple Sentences: Planets in Signs

Mars
When he/she takes action (Mars) he/she intends to be [HIGH-CONSCIOUSNESS KEYWORD] and [HIGH-CONSCIOUSNESS KEYWORD] ([SIGN]), but may appear to be [LOW-CONSCIOUSNESS KEYWORD] and [LOW-CONSCIOUSNESS KEYWORD] ([SIGN]).

To be happy, he/she wants (Mars) to be [HIGH-CONSCIOUSNESS KEYWORD] and [HIGH-CONSCIOUSNESS KEYWORD] ([SIGN]), but while pursuing these goals, he/she may become [LOW-CONSCIOUSNESS KEYWORD] and [LOW-CONSCIOUSNESS KEYWORD] ([SIGN]).

He/she will take action in order to protect and defend (Mars) that which is [HIGH-CONSCIOUSNESS KEYWORD] and [HIGH-CONSCIOUSNESS KEYWORD] ([SIGN]), but when challenged, his/her "little s" self (Mars) may behave in a manner that is [LOW-CONSCIOUSNESS KEYWORD] and [LOW-CONSCIOUSNESS KEYWORD] ([SIGN]).

As a warrior (Mars), he/she wants to be seen as [HIGH-CONSCIOUSNESS KEYWORD] and [HIGH-CONSCIOUSNESS KEYWORD] ([SIGN]).

Jupiter
He/she hopes to grow and expand (Jupiter) by being [HIGH-CONSCIOUSNESS KEYWORD] and [HIGH-CONSCIOUSNESS KEYWORD] ([SIGN]), but may appear to be [LOW-CONSCIOUSNESS KEYWORD] and [LOW-CONSCIOUSNESS KEYWORD] ([SIGN]).

He/she experiences faith (Jupiter) as [HIGH-CONSCIOUSNESS KEYWORD] and [HIGH-CONSCIOUSNESS KEYWORD] ([SIGN]), and builds faith by being [HIGH-CONSCIOUSNESS KEYWORD] and [HIGH-CONSCIOUSNESS KEYWORD] ([SIGN]).

He/she fears a lack of experiences (Jupiter) that are [HIGH-CONSCIOUSNESS KEYWORD] and [HIGH-CONSCIOUSNESS KEYWORD] ([SIGN]), and overcompensates by becoming [LOW-CONSCIOUSNESS KEYWORD] and [LOW-CONSCIOUSNESS KEYWORD] ([SIGN]).

He/she has an abundance (Jupiter) of experiences that are [HIGH-CONSCIOUSNESS KEYWORD] and [HIGH-CONSCIOUSNESS KEYWORD] ([SIGN]).

Saturn

He/she hopes to encounter boundaries (Saturn) that are [HIGH-CONSCIOUSNESS KEYWORD] and [HIGH-CONSCIOUSNESS KEYWORD] ([SIGN]), but often experiences them as being [LOW-CONSCIOUSNESS KEYWORD] and [LOW-CONSCIOUSNESS KEYWORD] ([SIGN]).

He/she expects authority figures (Saturn) to be [HIGH-CONSCIOUSNESS KEYWORD] and [HIGH-CONSCIOUSNESS KEYWORD] ([SIGN]), but often experiences them as [LOW-CONSCIOUSNESS KEYWORD] and [LOW-CONSCIOUSNESS KEYWORD] ([SIGN]).

When he/she is in a position of authority (Saturn), he/she intends to be [HIGH-CONSCIOUSNESS KEYWORD] and [HIGH-CONSCIOUSNESS KEYWORD] ([SIGN]), but is often experienced as being [LOW-CONSCIOUSNESS KEYWORD] and [LOW-CONSCIOUSNESS KEYWORD] ([SIGN]).

He/she is happy to be held accountable (Saturn) for being [HIGH-CONSCIOUSNESS KEYWORD] and [HIGH-CONSCIOUSNESS KEYWORD] ([SIGN]), but does not want to be held accountable for being [LOW-CONSCIOUSNESS KEYWORD] and [LOW-CONSCIOUSNESS KEYWORD] ([SIGN]).

CHAPTER 9

Houses and Angles

The houses represent areas of life and experience. Each house as a different "room" in your life. The 6th house is your office—it's where you go to work. When you want to have fun, you visit the 5th house. You meet up with friends in the 11th house, and with family in the 4th house.

In the grammar and syntax of the language of astrology, the houses are **prepositions** that tell you *where*, and **prepositional phrases** that tell you *with what*.

Modern astrology focuses primarily on the house a planet *occupies*. This gives you the effect, by telling you where a planet will act; however, it ignores the cause. For that, you look to the houses a planet *rules*.

The dividing line that marks the start of one house and the end of another is called the cusp. The ruler of the house is the planet that rules the sign on the cusp of the house. When a planet rules a house, it becomes the manager of that house. When there's a problem in the affairs of that house, the manager's job is to fix it. This can be challenging if the planet doesn't occupy the house it rules. A planet can take action only in the house it occupies.

For example, **Burt Reynolds'** Moon in Libra *rules* his 2nd house, but *occupies* his 5th house.[1] When he experiences disruptions in his 2nd house money, resources, and finances, it triggers his Moon, and makes him feel unsafe (Moon). His Moon takes action to address the problem, but his Moon occupies his 5th house, so he can act only in the realm of the 5th house, which includes love affairs, casual romantic partners, and gambling. When he feels unsafe (Moon) because of disruptions in his finances (Moon rules 2nd), he will either blame it on whomever he's dating at the moment (Moon in 5th house),

---

[1] See Figure 18 on page 152.

or decide to make risky investments (Moon in 5th house). These actions in his 5th house may not address the issues in his 2nd house.

Angular, Succedent, and Cadent Houses

Houses can be **angular**, **succedent**, or **cadent**. The angular houses (1st, 4th, 7th, and 10th) begin with the **angles** in the chart (**Ascendant**, **Imum Coeli**, **Descendant**, and **Midheaven**). Because the angles of the chart are the virtual "doors" to the outside world, planets that occupy angular houses are prominent and their actions are visible to the outside world. The succedent houses (2nd, 5th, 8th, and 11th) follow (or succeed) the angular houses. The cadent houses (3rd, 6th, 9th, and 12th) are the least prominent houses in the chart. Planets in cadent houses have a difficult time being seen.

The prominence of a planet is important in predictive astrology, but it does not play a major role in natal chart interpretation. It's an optional "pinch of spice."

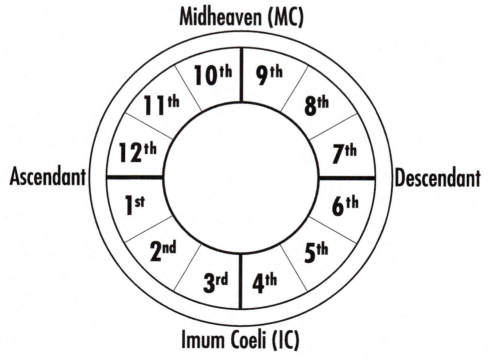

Figure 6: Houses and Angles in the Chart

A Tour of the Houses and Angles

I've included a list of keywords for each house that you can use when you complete the blueprint template sentences. The WHERE keywords make sense when describing the house a planet occupies. When describing a house a planet rules, you can choose from the WHERE keywords and any additional WHAT keywords.

Ascendant

The Ascendant is the front door of the chart. It's how you, as an individual, go forth to engage with the outside world. The Ascendant is a key component of your personality. The Sun is your authentic, "Big S" Self: who you truly are. Mars is your ego/body and "little s" self: who you think you are. The Ascendant is the mask that you wear and how you appear: who other people think you are.

The Ascendant is more than a mask. The sign of the Ascendant, known as your **rising sign**, colors your expectations of the world. If you have Gemini rising, you expect the world to be fascinating, and want to explore it. If you have Cancer rising, you expect the world to be scary and lonely, and want to connect with other people for emotional protection.

1st House

The 1st house is all about you. If you can say, "That's me," about something, it belongs in your 1st house. It's an angular house, and describes your relationship with yourself. The 1st house contains your identity, your outward personality, and your appearance. It also relates to your physical body, and your overall health, vitality, and happiness.

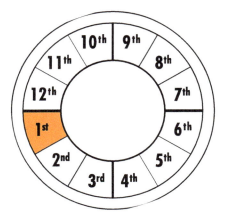

You identify with planets that occupy your 1st house. They express as part of your personality and shape your sense of self. However, you may lack perspective on these planets because you're so close to them.

The planet that rules the 1st house shows how you engage with the world in general, and with other individuals in particular. The house it occupies indicates where you express yourself and want to be recognized as an individual.

WHERE Keywords

personality	personal appearance	personal power
self-expression	self-opinion	personal interests
self-image	sense of self	relationship with self

Additional WHAT Keywords

happiness	health	vitality
physical strength	selfhood	individual identity
appearance	physical body	

2nd House

If the 1st house is "me" the 2nd house is "mine." It contains everything that belongs to you. It's a succedent house, and it describes your relationship to money, possessions, and movable property.[2] The 2nd house has come to include intangible concepts such as your skills, your talents, your values, and your opinions.

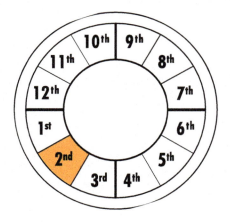

Any planets that occupy your 2nd house relate to your finances. Your money comes from the houses ruled by these planets.

The planet that rules the 2nd house describes your money, resources, and how you manage them. The house it occupies shows where you engage with money, both by earning it and spending it.

---

[2] "Movable property" is anything you own that you can pick up and move yourself. Vehicles belong in the 3rd house, and real estate belongs in the 4th house.

Houses and Angles

WHERE Keywords

money	finances	personal resources
movable property	values and opinions	talents
skills	attachments (to things)	attitude toward money
salary	income	possessions

3rd House

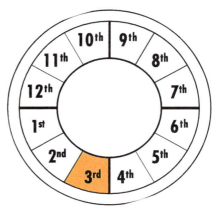

The 3rd house is your familiar environment. It's a cadent house, and it describes your relationship to siblings, neighbors, cousins, and acquaintances whom you encounter in your daily routine. The 3rd house contains an odd collection of concepts: short journeys, writing and communication, habits and routines, early education, and childhood experiences. I've found it practical to emphasize the "near" and "familiar" qualities of the 3rd house.

Planets that occupy your 3rd house are a part of your daily routine. They influence how you communicate. These planets act from habit in your familiar environment.

The planet that rules your 3rd house describes your habitual behavior patterns and how you interact with your immediate environment. The house it occupies is where you express these patterns.

WHERE Keywords

relationships with siblings	relationships with neighbors	habits and behavior patterns
childhood	communication	lower (rational) mind
writing	personal spirituality	neighborhood
familiar environment	routine interactions	early education

Additional WHAT Keywords

- changes
- news and rumors
- acquaintances
- fluctuations
- gossip
- language
- accidents
- siblings and cousins

Imum Coeli

The *Imum Coeli* (Latin for "bottom of the sky"), or IC as it is usually known, is the most private and hidden point in the chart. It's a secret door used only by close friends and family. The IC is the least visible point in the chart, but it's also the point of the greatest connection to the universe. The IC connects you to your past, your ancestors, your heritage, and ultimately to your soul's memory of what it was like to be one with all of creation. The IC symbolizes beginnings and endings, and it's the point where the soul enters the body.

4th House

The 4th house is your private life. It's an angular house, and it describes your relationship to your father,[3] your family, your ancestors, and your home, as well as to your land, property, and real estate. The 4th house is, quite literally, your foundation. In predictive astrology, the 4th house is associated with endings, but in natal astrology, it relates to your private life, home environment, and family relationships, especially in contrast to the 10th house, which relates to your public life, reputation, and career.

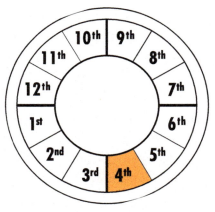

Planets that occupy your 4th house are private and personal. You encounter them at home, and express them with your family. On some level, behavior patterns associated with planets in the 4th house involve your relationship to your father.

---

[3] Modern astrology associates the 4th house with the mother and the 10th with the father. The origins of this switch date back to 1894 in the British publication *Astrologer's Magazine*, and seem to be influenced by the attribution of the 4th house to the mother in Hindu (Vedic) astrology. Many thanks to Philip Graves for this research.

Houses and Angles

The planet that rules the 4th house represents your perceptions and experience of your father. In the context of career or money questions, the ruler of the 4th house represents real estate and property.

WHERE Keywords

home	home environment	family
relationship with father	experience of father	private/personal life
past	family relationships	

Additional WHAT Keywords

ancestors	father	foundation
real estate/property	traditions	gardening/landscaping
native land/country	end of life	

5th House

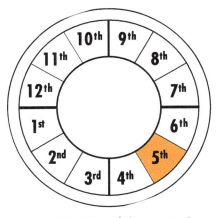

The 5th house is the house of fun. It's a succedent house, and it describes your relationship to lovers, romantic partners, and children. Everything associated with the 5th house provides you with pleasure, enjoyment, excitement, and makes you feel special. The 5th house is the house of sex, and specifically contains casual romantic and sexual partners (once you get married or move in together, it becomes a 7th house relationship). The 5th house is the house of children, and by extension, it's associated with personal creativity and self-expression. It's the house of sports, games, and entertainment—both as a performer and as an audience member. It's also the house of risk, and includes all forms of gambling, speculation, and investment.

Planets that occupy your 5th house want to have fun. They're more interested in play than in work, and will take center stage during games or competitions.

The planet that rules your 5th house describes what you look for in a casual romantic partner, and the house it occupies indicates where you're likely to meet these partners.

WHERE Keywords

love affairs	social mobility	pursuit of fun
personal creativity	investments	self-expression
casual romantic relationships	relationships with children	

Additional WHAT Keywords

casual dating	sex	risk and excitement
gambling	games	sports
recreation and pleasure	amusement and fun	children

6th House

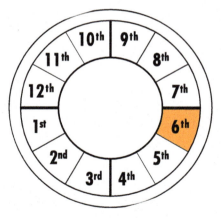

The 6th house is your job. It's a cadent house, and it describes your relationship to co-workers, employees, and servants. The 6th house is all work and no play. In modern usage, it's the house of service, but that glosses over the deeper themes. It's more accurate to call the 6th house the house of *indentured* service, because fundamentally, it's the house of slavery. The 6th house represents hard work you're obligated to perform, and for which you receive no recognition, prestige, or advancement. In other words, the 6th house describes your job.

Houses and Angles

The 6th house is the house of illness and disease (in contrast to the 1st house, which represents health). This is an important consideration in predictive astrology, but it has little practical value in a natal chart interpretation.

Planets that occupy the 6th house are, in a sense, your servants and employees. They express out of necessity, and they're used to hard work and little appreciation.

The planet that rules your 6th house describes your attitude toward work and service. The house it occupies describes the type of work you do, or the areas of life where you serve.

WHERE Keywords

job	workplace	service
relationships with employees	relationships with co-workers	daily physical routine

Additional WHAT Keywords

co-workers	employees	sickness
small animals	service	servants
nutrition	diet	illness and disease

Descendant

The Descendant is the back door to your chart. It's where you attract and interact with other individuals. Just as the Ascendant is a mask that changes how others see you and how you view the world, the Descendant filters what you expect to see in others, and what you find attractive in other people. The Ascendant is where you go out to interact with the world, but the Descendant is where other people come in to interact with you. The Descendant always involves one-to-one relationships, especially your spouse or significant other.

7th House

The 7th house is your guest room. The 1st house represents "me" and the 7th house, which opposes it, represents "you." It's an angular house, and describes your relationship to other individuals, including your spouse, contractual partners, and open enemies. Even though the 7th house is the guest room, and therefore used by other people, it's still a part of your house.

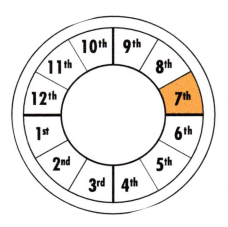

You encounter planets in your 7th house in one-to-one relationships. Your partners in relationship are mirrors that reflect your own issues back to you. You must recognize that what you see in other people is a projection of what exists inside you. Until you own these qualities, you will project them on your partners in relationship.

The planet that rules your 7th house describes your expectations of other individuals, and the qualities you seek in a partner. These are also the qualities you believe you lack, which is why you find them so attractive in other people. The house it occupies indicates the area of life where you seek partnership and relationship.

WHERE Keywords

marriage	partnership	romantic relationships
contractual relationships	perception of other people	one-to-one relationships

Additional WHAT Keywords

other people	open enemies	the public
social contracts	promises	negotiation/cooperation

8th House

The 8th house contains other people's resources. It's a succedent house, and it describes your relationship to other people's money, values, and opinions. In traditional predictive astrology, the 8th house relates to the manner of death, inheritances, and taxes. It's associated with the occult, private affairs, and hidden things. It's not associated with sex. Sex belongs in the 5th house of recreation, fun, and children. The only sex you'll find in the 8th house requires a leather wardrobe and safe words.[4]

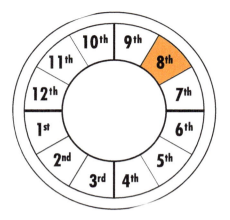

Always consider the financial perspective of the 8th house first. The 8th house relates to debts, financial obligations, loans, credit, investors, financial backers, and responsibility for managing other people's money. I've gone out on a limb and proposed that the 8th house also relates to other people's values and opinions (because the 2nd house relates to *your* values and opinions).

You experience planets in the 8th house in relationships with other individuals. Planets that occupy the 8th house look for support from other people. They operate on credit, and may incur debt and other obligations. These planets may also care too much about other people's opinions.

The planet that rules your 8th house describes your attitude toward debt, and the house it occupies suggests the area of life where you look for financial support from other people.

WHERE Keywords

| shared resources | other people's money | other people's values |
| other people's opinions | other people's resources | debts/financial obligations |

---

[4] The first association of sex with the 8th house appeared as a single sentence in a book by Alan Leo published in 1927. The notion didn't gain popularity until the 1950s in the work of C.E.O. Carter.

Additional WHAT Keywords

taxes	inheritances	wills
the occult	manner of death	insurance
private affairs	credit (i.e., debt)	hidden things

9th House

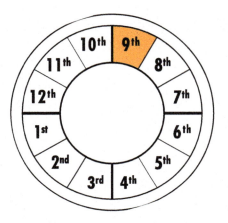

The 9th house represents foreign, unfamiliar environments. It's a cadent house, and describes your relationship to foreigners, teachers, religious leaders, beliefs, and philosophies. The 9th house opposes the 3rd house, and where the 3rd house represents "near," the 9th house represents "far." The 9th house relates to long journeys, especially to foreign lands, higher (secondary) education, the law, organized religion, beliefs, and philosophies. The "unfamiliar environment" aspect of the 9th house has practical value. Anything that takes you out of your familiar routine and your habitual behaviors and expands your world view is a part of the 9th house.

Planets that occupy the 9th house seek new and unfamiliar experiences. They operate outside of your comfort zone, and force you to move beyond your perceived limits.

The planet that rules your 9th house describes your attitude toward new experiences, beliefs, and ideas. The house it occupies shows where you seek inspiration.

WHERE Keywords

foreign travel	higher education	religion
philosophies	beliefs	abstract (higher) mind
prophetic dreams	cross-cultural experiences	unfamiliar experiences

Houses and Angles

Additional WHAT Keywords

publishing	advertising	law
foreigners	racial/cultural issues	long-distance travel
teachers	imports and exports	universities

Midheaven

The Midheaven is the door to the roof. It's where you stand out, and where you're the most visible. The Midheaven relates to career and life path because this is how you want to be recognized by society. Although the Midheaven is the most public and prominent point in the chart, it is also the most isolated. The roof is big enough for only one person at a time. The Midheaven is opposite the IC, where you are the least visible, but the most connected. The Midheaven is your crowning achievement as an individual, your most public face, and the way that you take responsibility for your role in society.

10th House

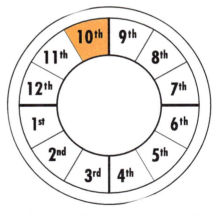

The 10th house is your public life. It's an angular house, and describes your relationship to your mother, to authority figures, to the public, and to the government. In today's world, the 10th house relates to your career and your life path, which is often quite different from your job. The 10th house and the Midheaven are associated with awards, honors, preferment, and recognition—none of which are connected with the service or work performed in the 6th house. It's possible for the 6th and 10th houses to be linked so that your job is also your career and serves your public image and reputation, but it's not automatic.

Planets that occupy the 10th house act in public ways. This is an important practical consideration. Instead of fixing a problem, a planet in the 10th house may just complain about it on Facebook.

The planet that rules the 10th house describes how you want to be known by the world. The house it occupies suggests where you will pursue your life path and seek public and professional recognition.

WHERE Keywords

career	life path	public life
relationship to mother	relationship to authority	reputation

Additional What Keywords

government	authority figures (boss)	honor
awards	fame	professional ambition
social status	public image	

11th House

The 11th house is where you socialize in groups. It's a succedent house, and describes your relationship to friends, peers, teammates, social clubs, and organizations. In traditional astrology, the 11th house relates to hopes, wishes, and aspirations—what you might call your dreams. But more importantly, the 11th house is the house of acquisition: it's where you pursue your ambitions. The 11th house also relates to collaboration and shared creativity.

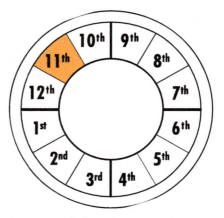

Planets that occupy the 11th house serve your ambitions and your aspirations. They want to help you become happy. They play well with others, and prefer to collaborate or work as a part of a team.

The planet that rules the 11th house describes how you pursue your goals, and your attitude toward your friends and peers. The house it occupies suggests the area of life where you meet your friends.

Houses and Angles

WHERE Keywords

hopes, wishes, aspirations	organizations and social groups	relationship with friends
teams	relationship with peers	shared creativity
social circle	personal ambition	shared beliefs

Additional WHAT Keywords

| acquisition | the money you make | pursuit of happiness |

12th House

The 12th house is your shadow. It's a cadent house, and it describes your relationship to your unconscious and your subconscious. What makes the 12th house so challenging is that it's hidden only from *you*. It's above the horizon, so it's visible to everyone else. The unconscious and subconscious qualities of the 12th house give it such a bad reputation. The 12th house relates to sorrow, adversity, and self-sabotage.

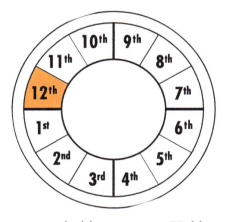

The 12th house also contains your hidden enemies. Hidden enemies include friends who secretly resent you, and who will happily betray you if they can. You created these hidden enemies yourself, because you were not conscious of your behavior.

Planets that occupy the 12th house operate in your unconscious. You're not aware of how these planets express, although they're obvious to other people.

The planet that rules the 12th house is of greater importance, because this planet is the vehicle of your self-sabotage. The house it occupies indicates the area of life where you are the most likely to sabotage yourself, experience unnecessary suffering, cause resentments, and create hidden enemies.

WHERE Keywords

| personal unconscious | shadow self | relationship with hidden enemies |

Additional WHAT Keywords

prisons	institutions	hospitals
large animals	sorrows	affliction
self-sabotage	scandal	meditation
repressed/hidden energies	cloisters and spiritual retreats	psychic manipulation ("witchcraft")

House Rulers

The planets are the most important component of the language of astrology. Every sentence in the language of astrology must have a personal planet as the subject. Finding the correct planet is easy if you have a question about identity (Sun), or safety (Moon), but what if you have a question about your job or your marriage? These questions relate to houses, not to planets. You can't have a house as the subject of a sentence in the language of astrology, so you turn to the planet that rules the house. That planet can become the subject of a sentence and answer questions about the affairs of the house. In terms of grammar, the house ruler is a pronoun that takes the place of the house.

When you consider a house ruler, you set aside the nature of the planet. If you have a question about money and Capricorn is on the cusp of your 2nd house, then Saturn is the ruler of the 2nd house. Instead of representing boundaries, limitations, responsibility or authority, in this context, Saturn represents your money. When a house ruler occupies a house, it shows a connection between the two houses.

For example, if the ruler of your 2nd house is in the 4th house, your money may come from your family, or perhaps from involvement in real estate. If the ruler of your 2nd is in the 5th house, you might encounter your money through your creativity, or through investments, which are a form of gambling. If the ruler of the 2nd is in the 7th house, your money comes from partnerships and one-to-one relationships, so you may want to marry someone rich.

House Almutens

A planet always expresses *with* the affairs of the house or houses that it rules. But it's possible for more than one planet to have influence over the same house. The **almuten** of a house is the planet that has the most Essential Dignity (the most votes on the Board of Directors) for the sign and degree on the cusp of the house. Most of the time, the almuten is the ruler of the sign, but occasionally one of the other planets on the Board of Directors will have more influence. We'll cover this in the next chapter.

When interpreting a planet, you will always consider the houses it rules. You have the option to include houses where the planet is the almuten, as well.

Solar Fire, the astrology program I use to calculate all of my charts, allows you to include a table of the almutens of the houses (Figure 7). I include this on all of the example charts. When two planets have the same number of votes, they will show up in this table as co-almutens, as the Sun and Mars do for the 4th house.

Hs	Alm.
1	♃
2	♄
3	♀
4	☉ ♂
5	♀
6	☿
7	☿
8	☽
9	☿
10	♄
11	♂
12	♃

Figure 7: Table of Almutens

Intercepted Signs

It doesn't matter which **house system** you choose, but once you choose one, you need to stick with it. I use the Koch house system for natal chart interpretation, because I find it gives me the most accurate results. The Koch house system is a quadrant system, so the angles are the cusps of the angular houses.

When you use a quadrant-based house system, like Koch or Placidus, the houses vary in size. It's possible for a house to take up more than 30° and contain an entire sign. This is called an interception. Because an **intercepted**

sign is contained within a house, that sign won't appear on the cusp of a house. The planet that rules the intercepted sign will influence fewer houses in the chart. This is only a challenge if Leo or Cancer is intercepted, because it can result in either the Sun or the Moon not ruling any houses.

If the Sun or Moon doesn't rule at least one house you're left with two options. First, see if the Sun or Moon is the almuten of a house. The Sun is often the almuten of Aries, and the Moon is often the almuten of Taurus. You can use the almuten in the blueprint template sentence in place of the ruler.

In very rare cases, when the Sun or Moon doesn't rule any houses, and isn't the almuten of any houses, you can consider the **whole-sign houses** used in traditional Hellenistic astrology. This is an equal house system, where each sign is a house. The sign of the Ascendant is the 1st house, but the angles do not define the house cusps. You can use the whole sign house ruled by the Sun or Moon in the blueprint sentence.

Count the signs from the Ascendant until you reach Cancer (for the Moon) or Leo (for the Sun). For example, in George Lucas' chart (Figure 39 on page 278), Taurus is on the Ascendant and Leo is intercepted. Using whole sign houses, Taurus is the 1st house, Gemini is the 2nd house, Cancer is the 3rd house, and Leo is the 4th house, so Lucas' Sun is the ruler of his whole sign 4th house.

Blueprint Template Sentences for Planets in Signs and Houses

Adding the houses to the blueprint template sentences is simple. The planet expresses WITH the keywords of the house or houses it rules, and the planet takes action IN the house it occupies. When working with these blueprint template sentences, I recommend choosing a mixture of high- and low-consciousness keywords for reference.

I've provided examples of the most useful blueprint template sentences for each planet, but you can append the houses to any of the planet-sign blueprint template sentences included in Chapter 8.

Houses and Angles

The Sun in [SIGN] in [HOUSE]; Sun Rules [HOUSE(s)]
He/she wants to be hero (Sun) by being [SIGN/ELEMENT/MODALITY KEYWORD], and [SIGN/ELEMENT/MODALITY KEYWORD] ([SIGN/ELEMENT/MODALITY]), WITH [HOUSE KEYWORD] and [HOUSE KEYWORD] (Sun rules [HOUSE(s)]). He/she encounters these needs particularly IN [HOUSE WHERE KEYWORD] (Sun in [HOUSE]).

The Moon in [SIGN] in [HOUSE]; Moon Rules [HOUSE(s)]
To feel Safe (Moon), he/she needs to feel [SIGN/ELEMENT/MODALITY KEYWORD], and [SIGN/ELEMENT/MODALITY KEYWORD] ([SIGN/ELEMENT/MODALITY]), WITH [HOUSE KEYWORD] and [HOUSE KEYWORD] (Moon rules [HOUSE(s)]). He/she encounters these needs particularly IN [HOUSE WHERE KEYWORD] (Moon in [HOUSE]).

Mercury in [SIGN] in [HOUSE]; Mercury Rules [HOUSE(s)]
When he/she communicates (Mercury), he/she hopes to be seen as [SIGN/ELEMENT/MODALITY KEYWORD], [SIGN/ELEMENT/MODALITY KEYWORD], and [SIGN/ELEMENT/MODALITY KEYWORD] ([SIGN/ELEMENT/MODALITY]), WITH [HOUSE KEYWORD] and [HOUSE KEYWORD] (Mercury rules [HOUSE(s)]). He/she encounters these needs particularly IN [HOUSE WHERE KEYWORD] (Mercury in [HOUSE]).

Venus in [SIGN] in [HOUSE]; Venus Rules [HOUSE(s)]
He/she loves, appreciates, and values (Venus) individuals who are [SIGN/ELEMENT/MODALITY KEYWORDS] ([SIGN/ELEMENT/MODALITY]), WITH [HOUSE KEYWORD] and [HOUSE KEYWORD] (Venus rules [HOUSE(s)]). He/she encounters these needs particularly IN [HOUSE WHERE KEYWORD] (Venus in [HOUSE]).

Mars in [SIGN] in [HOUSE]; Mars Rules [HOUSE(s)]
When he/she takes action (Mars), he/she intends to be [SIGN/ELEMENT/MODALITY KEYWORDS] ([SIGN/ELEMENT/MODALITY]), WITH [HOUSE KEYWORD] and [HOUSE KEYWORD] (Mars rules [HOUSE(s)]). He/she encounters these needs particularly IN [HOUSE WHERE KEYWORD] (Mars in [HOUSE]).

Jupiter in [SIGN] in [HOUSE]; Jupiter Rules [HOUSE(s)]
He/she hopes to grow, expand, and experience faith (Jupiter) by being [SIGN/ELEMENT/MODALITY KEYWORDS] ([SIGN/ELEMENT/MODALITY]), WITH [HOUSE KEYWORD] and [HOUSE KEYWORD] (Jupiter rules [HOUSE(s)]). He/she encounters these needs particularly IN [HOUSE WHERE KEYWORD] (Jupiter in [HOUSE]).

Saturn in [SIGN] in [HOUSE]; Saturn Rules [HOUSE(s)]
He/she hopes to encounter boundaries and limitations (Saturn) that are [SIGN/ELEMENT/MODALITY KEYWORDS] ([SIGN/ELEMENT/MODALITY]), WITH [HOUSE KEYWORD] and [HOUSE KEYWORD] (Saturn rules [HOUSE(s)]). He/she encounters these needs particularly IN [HOUSE WHERE KEYWORD] (Saturn in [HOUSE]).

CHAPTER 10

Essential Dignities and the Board of Directors

Essential Dignities are an ancient system of evaluating the relative "strength" of a planet at a particular degree of a sign. They are the heart and soul of classical astrology, but modern astrology ignores them. The Essential Dignities make it possible for you to create detailed, specific, and practical interpretations.

How you work with the Essential Dignities depends on the context of the chart. In predictive astrology, you use the Essential Dignities to evaluate the condition of a planet, and terms like "dignified" and "debilitated" have specific, practical value. In natal astrology, the relative dignity of a planet is not important; what matters is the **Board of Directors**.

Think of a sign as a corporation. A corporation is involved in a particular type of business. The element and modality of the sign determine the type of business. For example, Libra is a Cardinal Air sign. Because it's a Cardinal sign, planets in Libra are concerned with the question of individual identity. Because it's an Air sign, planets in Libra operate in the mental, intellectual, abstract, and social realms, and are motivated to make connections.

A corporation has a CEO, who is the public face of the company. A corporation also has a Board of Directors. The planets that have Essential Dignity for the specific degree of a sign make up the members of the Board of Directors for that degree. The board members operate behind the scenes, influencing the policies that the CEO shares with the public (Figure 8).

Each member of the Board of Directors has a fixed number of votes, depending on which Essential Dignity it represents. The planet with **Rulership** functions as the CEO and gets 5 votes; the planet with **Exaltation** gets 4 votes; the planet with **Triplicity** gets 3 votes; the planet with **Term** gets 2 votes; and the planet with **Face** gets 1 vote.

It's common for a planet to hold multiple seats on a Board of Directors, which gives it additional votes. For example, Saturn is Exalted in Libra, which gives Saturn a minimum of 4 votes on the Board of Directors. In a day chart, Saturn also has Triplicity, giving Saturn an additional 3 votes for a total of 7 votes. Venus, the ruler of Libra, has only 5 votes on the Board of Directors, which means Saturn can overrule Venus. The planet that has the most votes on a Board of Directors is called the **almuten**.

Figure 8: The Board of Directors for Libra

Essential Dignities and the Board of Directors

E-Z Essential Dignity™ Card

Determining the Essential Dignity and the Board of Directors for a planet used to be complicated. Ptolemy's table of Essential Dignity and Debility is compact and efficient, but it's also difficult to understand. That's why I created the **E-Z Essential Dignity™ Card** (Figure 9). This simple, visual reference allows you to determine the members of the Board of Directors for any degree of any sign at a glance (Figure 10).

The degree numbers that mark the boundaries of Term and Face represent the last degree where a planet holds that dignity. When you read the positions in the chart, you always **round up to the next whole degree**. For example, you would read a planet at 9°24 Libra as being at 10° Libra, which would still be in the first decanate, and the Moon would be the planet with Face. However, you would read a planet at 10°01 Libra as being at 11° Libra, which would put it in the second decanate, and Saturn would have Face. If a planet is at exactly 10°00 Libra, you would not round up; the Moon would still have Face.

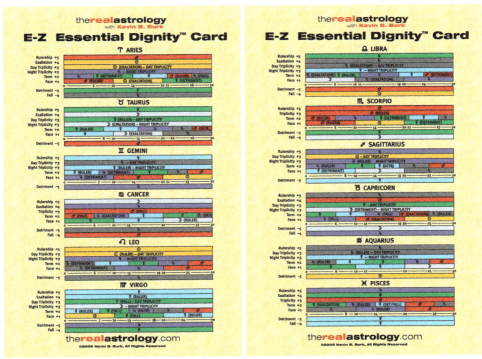

Figure 9: E-Z Essential Dignity™ Card

Principles of Practical Natal Astrology

Round up to the next whole degree and locate the degree on the table. Read down to identify the members of the Board of Directors for that degree.

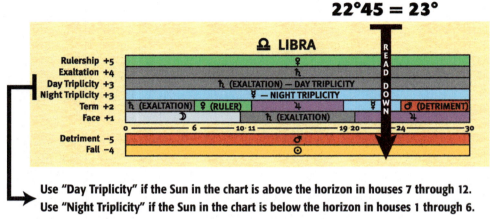

Use "Day Triplicity" if the Sun in the chart is above the horizon in houses 7 through 12.
Use "Night Triplicity" if the Sun in the chart is below the horizon in houses 1 through 6.

Figure 10: Finding the Board of Directors with the E-Z Essential Dignity Card

Solar Fire has the option to include a table of Essential Dignities for the chart itself. Figure 11 shows the Essential Dignity table for Sylvester Stallone's chart. I've highlighted the members of the Board of Directors for his Moon at 22°45 Libra.

Pt	Ruler	Exalt	Trip	Term	Face	Detri	Fall	Score
☽	♀	♄	♄	☿	♃	♂	☉	−5 p
☉	☽	♃	♂	☿	☿	♄	♂	−5 p
☿	☉	--	☉	☿ +	♃	♄	--	+2
♀	☉	--	☉	♃	♂	♄	--	−5 p
♂	☿	☿	♀	♀	☉	♃	♀	−5 p
♃	♀	♄ m	♄	♃ +	♄	♂	☉	+2
♄	☽	♃ m	♂	♀	☽	♄ −	♂	−10 p
♅	☿	☊	♄	♀	♂	♃	☋	--
♆	♀	♄	♄	♄	☽	♂	☉	--
♇	☉	--	☉	☿	♃	♄	--	--
⚷	♀	♄	♄	♃	♄	♂	☋	--
☊	♀	♄	☉	♀	☉	♂	☋	--
☋	♃	☋	☉	♄	♄	☿	☊	--
As	♃	☋	☉	♂	♄	☿	☊	--
Mc	♀	♄	♄	☿	♃	♂	☉	--
Vx	☉	--	☉	☿	♄	♄	--	--
⊗	♂	--	♀	♀	♂	♀	♄	--

Figure 11: Finding the Board of Directors with the Essential Dignities Table in Solar Fire

Essential Dignities and the Board of Directors

The Board of Directors

To illustrate the practical value of the Essential Dignities and the Board of Directors, we'll look at three different celebrity charts: **Sylvester Stallone** (Figure 12 on page 118), **Nicolas Cage** (Figure 14 on page 121), and **Sting** (Figure 16 on page 125). Each chart has the Moon in Libra, between 19° and 26° of the sign. We'll look at the Moon from the context of Safety Needs and ask the question, "What does this person need to feel safe?"

Libra is a Cardinal Air sign, so we can select any keywords associated with Libra, Cardinal, or Air. I've selected a few of the higher-consciousness Libra keywords to use in the blueprint template sentences: **harmonious**, **objective**, **gracious**, and **courteous**.[1] When you drop these keywords into a simple blueprint template sentence for the Moon in Libra, you get:

To feel safe (Moon), he needs to feel harmonious, objective, gracious, and courteous (Libra).

Libra is an Air sign, so people with the Moon in Libra look for safety in the mental, intellectual, and social realms, and they are mainly concerned with how things appear on the surface. A person with the Moon in Libra feels safe when everything appears to be balanced and harmonious. They feel unsafe when they experience deep emotions, because emotional turmoil disrupts the surface appearance of tranquility.

This isn't a bad start, but it's not specific. You can say this about Stallone, Cage, and Sting, not to mention everyone else with the Moon in Libra.

When you include the relevant houses in each chart, you get more information.

Stallone's Moon rules his 8th house, and occupies his 10th house, so this would be the blueprint sentence for Sylvester Stallone's Moon in Libra:

To feel safe (Moon), Stallone needs to feel harmonious, objective, gracious, and courteous (Libra) **WITH** his shared resources, debts, and other people's money (Moon rules 8th). He encounters these needs **IN** his career, life path, and public image (Moon in 10th).

---

[1] I've selected only high-consciousness keywords for the blueprint sentence examples in this chapter, but I recommend using both high-consciousness and low-consciousness keywords when you create your own blueprint sentences.

Nicolas Cage's Moon also rules his 8th house and occupies his 10th house, so you can say the same thing about his Moon in Libra. However, Sting's Moon rules his 12th house and occupies his 4th house, so his Moon in Libra blueprint sentence looks like this:

To feel safe (Moon), Sting needs to feel harmonious, objective, gracious, and courteous **(Libra) WITH** his shadow self and his personal unconscious (Moon rules 12th). He encounters these needs IN his home and family life (Moon in 4th).

This is as far as most astrologers can go. Sting's Moon in Libra is clearly different, but Stallone's and Cage's Moon in Libra appear identical. The top-level interpretation of the Moon in Libra creates the context, but to fill in the details, you need to consider the planets on the Board of Directors.

The planets on the Board of Directors are the *actual planets* in the chart. This means the ruler of Stallone's Moon in Libra isn't just Venus, it's Stallone's Venus in Leo. The ruler of Cage's Moon in Libra is his Venus in Aquarius. And Sting's Moon in Libra reports to his Venus in Virgo. Venus in Leo has a different agenda for the Moon in Libra than Venus in Aquarius or Venus in Virgo.

Board of Directors Blueprint Templates

When interpreting the Board of Directors, you view the needs of each board member in the context of the needs of the top-level planet. Here's an example of the Board of Directors blueprint template sentence for the Moon:

[PLANET] in [SIGN] in [HOUSE] ([#] votes on Board of Directors) [PLANET] Rules [HOUSE(s)]
To feel Safe (Moon's Board of Directors), he/she needs to [PLANET BOARD OF DIRECTORS KEYWORDS] ([PLANET]) **in a manner that is** [SIGN/ELEMENT/MODALITY KEYWORDS] ([SIGN/ELEMENT/MODALITY]), **WITH** [HOUSE KEYWORDS] ([PLANET] rules [HOUSE(s)]). **He/she encounters these needs particularly IN** [HOUSE WHERE KEYWORD] ([PLANET] in [HOUSE]).

Essential Dignities and the Board of Directors

What's different about these templates is that you need to include the planet board of directors keywords that summarize what the planet needs.

✦ **The Sun** needs to express the authentic "Big S" Self and align with his/her Personal Standards of Integrity.

✦ **The Moon** needs to feel safe, and to express emotions and feelings.

✦ **Mercury** needs to communicate and understand.

✦ **Venus** needs to feel loved and appreciated, and align with his/her Core Values.

✦ **Mars** needs to take action and expend energy.

✦ **Jupiter** needs to grow, expand, and to experience faith.

✦ **Saturn** needs to establish boundaries and limits, and to accept responsibility.

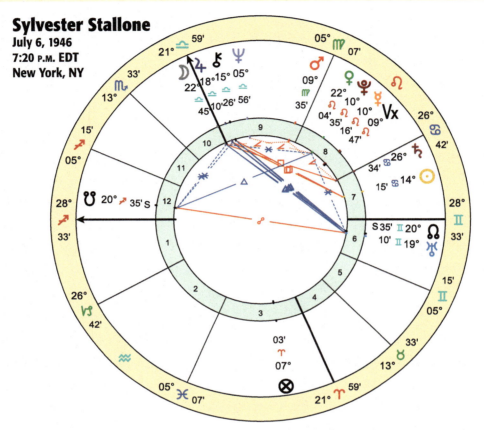

Figure 12: Sylvester Stallone's Natal Chart

Source: Astro-Databank; Rodden Rating: A, from memory.

Sylvester Stallone's Moon in Libra

The Board of Directors for Stallone's Moon in Libra (Figure 13) consists of: **Venus in Leo in the 8th** (Venus Rules 5th and 10th), 5 votes (Rulership); **Saturn in Cancer in the 7th** (Saturn Rules 2nd), 7 votes (Exaltation + Triplicity); **Mercury in Leo in the 8th** (Mercury Rules 6th, 7th, and 9th Houses), 2 votes (Term); and **Jupiter in Libra in 9th** (Jupiter Rules 1st, 3rd, and 12th Houses), 1 vote (Face).

Even though Venus is the ruler of Stallone's Moon in Libra, Saturn, with a total of 7 votes, has the most influence. What Stallone needs most to feel safe are boundaries, structures, limitations, and responsibility; all of the things that matter to Saturn. When considering the Board of Directors, you care only about planets that influence at least 3 votes. For Stallone's Moon, that's Saturn in Cancer, with 7 votes, and Venus in Leo, with 5 votes.

Saturn in Cancer in the 7th House (7 votes, Exaltation + Triplicity) Saturn Rules 2nd House

To feel safe (Moon's Board of Directors), Stallone needs to establish boundaries, limits, and structures, and to accept responsibility (Saturn) in a manner that is gentle, emotive, maternal, and tender (Cancer) **WITH** his money and resources (Saturn rules 2nd). He encounters these needs **IN** his one-to-one relationships, marriage, and partnerships (Saturn in 7th).

Planet	Ruler	Exaltation	Triplicity	Term	Face
☾ ♎	♀ ♌	♄ ♋	♄ ♋	☿ ♌	♃ ♎
	5 Votes	4 Votes	3 Votes	2 Votes	1 Vote
Condition	Total Votes	Total Votes	Total Votes	Total Votes	Total Votes
Peregrine	5	7		2	1
House Place	House Place	House Place	House Place	House Place	House Place
10th	8th	7th	7th	8th	9th
House Rule	House Rule	House Rule	House Rule	House Rule	House Rule
8th	5th, 10th	2nd	2nd	6th, 7th, 9th	1st, 3rd, 12th

Figure 13: Board of Directors for Sylvester Stallone's Moon in Libra

Notice how Saturn ties Stallone's Safety Needs to his money and resources. Because Saturn rules Stallone's 2nd house, any disruption to his finances will make a withdrawal from his Safety Need Account. Saturn in Cancer will attempt to fix the problem by creating emotional, compassionate (Cancer) boundaries (Saturn). However, Saturn occupies the 7th house, so it can act only in the context of one-to-one relationships. Stallone may expect his partner in relationship to take responsibility, fix the problem, and help Stallone to feel safe.

Venus in Leo in the 8th House (5 votes, Rulership)
Venus Rules 5th and 10th Houses

To feel safe (Moon's Board of Directors), Stallone needs to feel love and appreciation, and align with his Core Values (Venus) in a manner that is definite, loving, spectacular, and entertaining (Leo) **WITH** his personal creativity, children, love affairs, and pursuit of entertainment (Venus rules 5th) and his career, life path, and public reputation (Venus rules 10th). He encounters these needs **IN** his debts, shared resources, and other people's values and opinions (Venus in 8th).

Venus in Leo's influence means that Stallone also needs to be loved and appreciated (Venus) and be the center of attention (Leo) to feel safe. Specifically, Stallone wants validation and appreciation for his artistic and creative expression (Venus rules 5th) and for his career, public image, and reputation (Venus rules 10th). If Stallone doesn't receive enough attention for his creativity and his career, it will drain his Safety Need Account, and Venus in Leo will take action to fix the problem. Stallone's Venus is in his 8th house, so he will look for attention, approval, and validation from his fans (other people's values and opinions), or by going into debt to buy something expensive and dramatic (Venus in Leo) to make him feel better about himself.

Essential Dignities and the Board of Directors

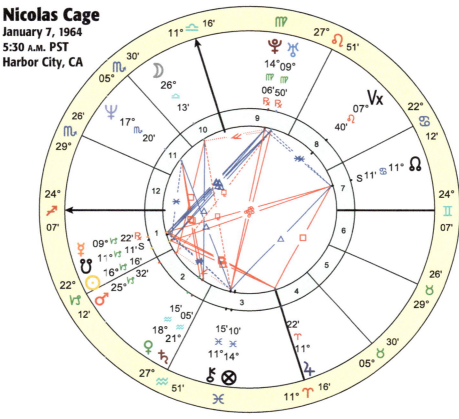

Figure 14: Nicolas Cage's Natal Chart

Source: Astro-Databank; Rodden Rating: AA, BC/BR in hand

Nicolas Cage's Moon in Libra

The Board of Directors for Cage's Moon in Libra (Figure 15) consists of: **Venus in Aquarius in the 2nd** (Venus rules 5th, 6th, and 10th), 5 votes (Rulership); **Saturn in Aquarius in the 2nd** (Saturn rules 2nd and 3rd), 4 votes (Exaltation); **Mercury in Capricorn in the 1st** (Mercury rules 7th), 3 votes (Triplicity); **Mars in Capricorn in the 2nd** (Mars Rules 4th, 11th, and 12th), 2 votes (Term); and **Jupiter in Aries in the 4th** (Jupiter Rules 1st), 1 vote (Face).

In Cage's chart, Venus, Saturn, and Mercury each have at least 3 votes on the Moon's Board of Directors, which means each of these planets has influence over what Cage needs to feel safe. First we'll consider the individual planets, and then we'll consider the broader dynamic of Cage's Board of Directors.

Venus in Aquarius in the 2nd House (5 votes, Rulership)
Venus Rules 5th, 6th, and 10th Houses

To feel safe (Moon's Board of Directors), Cage needs to feel love and appreciation, and align with his Core Values (Venus) in a manner that is liberal, inventive, articulate, and democratic (Aquarius) **WITH** his personal creativity, children, love affairs, and pursuit of entertainment (Venus rules 5th), his job, workplace relationships, and service (Venus rules 6th), and his career, life path, and public reputation (Venus rules 10th). He encounters these needs **IN** his money and resources (Venus in 2nd).

Planet	Ruler	Exaltation	Triplicity	Term	Face
☽ ♎	♀ ♒	♄ ♒	☿ ♑	♂ ♑	♃ ♈
	5 Votes	4 Votes	3 Votes	2 Votes	1 Vote
Condition	Total Votes	Total Votes	Total Votes	Total Votes	Total Votes
Peregrine	5	4	3	2	1
House Place	House Place	House Place	House Place	House Place	House Place
10th	2nd	2nd	1st	2nd	4th
House Rule	House Rule	House Rule	House Rule	House Rule	House Rule
8th	5th, 6th, 10th	2nd, 3rd	7th	4th, 11th, 12th	1st

Figure 15: Board of Directors for Nicolas Cage's Moon in Libra

Essential Dignities and the Board of Directors

Venus appears to have the most influence over Cage's Moon in Libra, with 5 votes for Rulership, so being validated and appreciated (Venus) is the most important requirement for Cage to feel safe. Cage's Venus in Aquarius is different from Stallone's Venus in Leo. Stallone needs to be in the spotlight to feel love and appreciation, while Cage's Venus in Aquarius looks for validation for the creative (Venus rules 5th) work (Venus rules 6th and 10th) he does for humanity (Aquarius). Cage's Venus is in his 2nd house, so even though he cares about the humanitarian aspects of his work, what really makes him feel validated (and by extension, safe) is a big paycheck.[2]

Saturn in Aquarius in the 2nd House (4 votes, Exaltation)
Saturn Rules 2nd and 3rd Houses

To feel safe (Moon's Board of Directors), Cage needs to establish boundaries, limits, and structures, and to accept responsibility (Saturn) in a manner that is analytical, selfless, imaginative, and independent (Aquarius) **WITH** his money and resources (Saturn rules 2nd), and his familiar environment, habits and routines, writing, and communication (Saturn rules 3rd). He encounters these needs **IN** his money and resources (Saturn in 2nd).

Saturn in Aquarius reinforces the importance of money in the context of Cage's Safety Needs. Saturn in Aquarius wants to establish and enforce rules that support freedom, and eliminate laws that no longer serve. Because Saturn both rules and occupies Cage's 2nd house, he's especially concerned with laws that allow the greatest financial freedom and security. Saturn also rules Cage's 3rd house, so the laws also need to provide freedom to move about his familiar environment. If his freedom is curtailed, it will make him feel unsafe, and Saturn will take action. Because Saturn acts from Cage's 2nd house, he'll probably respond by throwing money at the problem to get the laws changed.

Mercury in Capricorn in the 1st House (3 votes, Triplicity)
Mercury Rules 7th House

To feel safe (Moon's Board of Directors), Cage needs to understand and communicate (Mercury) in a manner that is efficient, responsible, determined, and ambitious

---

[2] Which explains his film career.

(Capricorn) **WITH** his one-to-one relationships, marriage, and partnerships (Mercury rules 7th). He encounters these needs **IN** his personality, self-image, and personal power (Mercury in 1st).

Finally, Mercury in Capricorn has 3 votes on the Moon's Board of Directors. A planet with 3 votes has enough influence that it can't be ignored, but not enough influence to change the agenda. Communication is an important part of Cage's Safety Needs, especially in the context of his one-to-one relationships (Mercury rules 7th). Given how important freedom of ideas and expression is to Cage (Venus and Saturn in Aquarius), his need for practical, direct, responsible (Capricorn) communication (Mercury) in his relationships makes sense.

Board of Directors Dynamic

In theory, Venus has the most influence over Cage's Safety Needs because Venus has the most votes on the Board of Directors. Venus rules Cage's Moon in Libra, so the Moon has to follow Venus' agenda. But Venus in Aquarius doesn't set her own agenda; she has to do what Saturn tells her to do. Because Saturn rules Venus, and Saturn also has a seat on the Board of Directors, Venus will vote however Saturn tells her to vote. Mercury in Capricorn and Mars in Capricorn both report to Saturn as well. Venus, Mercury and Mars will do whatever Saturn tells them to, which means that Saturn influences a total of 14 votes on the Moon's Board of Directors.

Essential Dignities and the Board of Directors

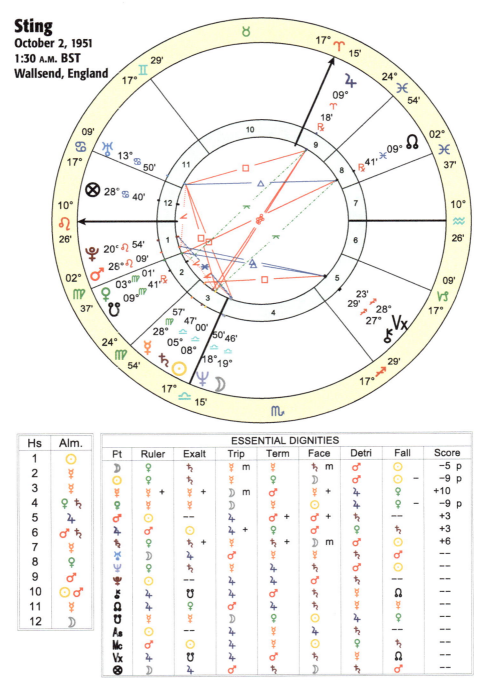

Figure 16: Sting's Natal Chart

Source: Astro-Databank; Rodden Rating: A, from memory.

Sting's Moon in Libra

The Board of Directors for Sting's Moon in Libra (Figure 17) consists of: **Venus in Virgo in the 2nd** (Venus rules 4th), 5 votes (Rulership); **Saturn in Libra in the 3rd** (Saturn Rules 6th and 7th), 5 votes (Exaltation and Face); and **Mercury in Virgo in the 3rd** (Mercury Rules 2nd, 3rd, and 11th), 5 votes (Triplicity and Term).

All three of the members of the Board of Directors of Sting's Moon have 5 votes each, so all three are important to consider.

Venus in Virgo in the 2nd House (5 votes, Rulership)
Venus Rules 4th House

To feel safe (Moon's Board of Directors), Sting needs to feel love and appreciation, and align with his Core Values (Venus) in a manner that is diligent, observant, flexible, and organized (Virgo) **WITH** his home, private life, and family relationships (Venus rules 4th). He encounters these needs **IN** his money and resources (Venus in 2nd).

Sting needs to feel loved and appreciated to feel safe, but because his Venus is in Virgo, the details matter. Sting's Venus rules the 4th house, so he wants to be appreciated for how perfectly he has arranged his home, his private life, and his family relationships. When Sting encounters a problem in these areas, his Venus will take action. Because Sting's Venus is in his 2nd house, he may rely on money to fix the problems that make him feel unsafe.

Planet	Ruler	Exaltation	Triplicity	Term	Face
☽ ♎	♀ ♍	♄ ♎	☿ ♍	☿ ♍	♄ ♎
	5 Votes	4 Votes	3 Votes	2 Votes	1 Vote
Condition	Total Votes	Total Votes	Total Votes	Total Votes	Total Votes
Peregrine	5	5	5		
House Place	House Place	House Place	House Place	House Place	House Place
4th	2nd	3rd	3rd	3rd	3rd
House Rule	House Rule	House Rule	House Rule	House Rule	House Rule
12th	4th	6th, 7th	2nd, 3rd	2nd, 3rd	6th, 7th

Figure 17: Board of Directors for Sting's Moon in Libra

Essential Dignities and the Board of Directors

Saturn in Libra in the 3rd House (5 votes, Exaltation and Face)
Saturn Rules 6th and 7th Houses

To feel safe (Moon's Board of Directors), Sting needs to establish boundaries, limits, and structures, and to accept responsibility (Saturn) in a manner that is amenable, objective, collaborative, and strategic (Libra) **WITH** his job, workplace relationships, and service (Saturn rules 6th) and his one-to-one relationships, marriage, and partnerships (Saturn rules 7th). He encounters these needs **IN** his familiar environment, daily routine, writing, and communication (Saturn in 3rd).

Sting also needs clear boundaries and expectations (Saturn), especially in his job (Saturn rules 6th) and his marriage and significant partnerships (Saturn rules 7th) to feel safe. When other people break the rules, violate agreements, or create conflict, Sting will feel unsafe. Sting's Saturn is in his 3rd house, so he will try to restore a sense of safety by enforcing the rules and agreements (Saturn) in his familiar environment and his daily routine (3rd house).

Mercury in Virgo in the 3rd House (5 votes, Triplicity + Term)
Mercury Rules 2nd, 3rd, and 11th Houses

To feel safe (Moon's Board of Directors), Sting needs to understand and communicate (Mercury) in a manner that is perceptive, adaptable, analytical, and physical (Virgo) **WITH** his money and resources (Mercury rules 2nd), his familiar environment, habits and routines, writing, and communication (Mercury rules 3rd) and his personal ambitions, friendships, and group creativity (Mercury rules 11th). He encounters these needs **IN** his familiar environment, daily routine, writing, and communication (Mercury in 3rd).

Finally, Sting needs to have clear, precise, specific (Virgo) understanding and communication (Mercury) to feel safe, especially with regard to his money and resources (Mercury rules 2nd), his familiar environment (Mercury rules 3rd), and his friendships (Mercury rules 11th). When there's a breakdown in communication, it will make Sting feel unsafe and he will attempt to fix the problem by improving communication (Mercury) in his immediate environment (Mercury in 3rd).

Board of Directors Dynamic

Sting's Safety Needs appear to be governed by a committee, because Venus, Saturn, and Mercury each have 5 votes on the Moon's Board of Directors. But closer analysis reveals a different dynamic. Venus in Virgo rules Saturn in Libra, so Saturn will always vote with Venus, which means Venus influences 10 votes. However, Venus in Virgo reports directly to Mercury in Virgo, so Mercury not only influences Venus' votes, but also Saturn's votes. This gives Mercury absolute control over Sting's Safety Needs. As long as Sting believes that he understands his environment, and the details are handled, he will feel safe.

Essential Dignity and Debility

You can also use the Essential Dignities to evaluate the relative condition of a planet. When a planet has votes **on its own Board of Directors**, it has Essential Dignity. Essential Dignity evaluates how much **power** a planet has. The more power a planet has, the greater its ability to pursue its own agenda. This has practical application when you consider the dynamic of the Board of Directors.

The descriptions of the Essential Dignities and Debilities apply when a planet holds that position on its own Board of Directors. In the context of a natal chart, having a dignified planet is not "good," and having a debilitated planet is not "bad." The dignity or debility of a planet is an optional "pinch of spice."

Rulership

A planet in a sign that it rules gets to set its own agenda. Because a planet in Rulership is its own boss, it doesn't have to play well with the other planets. A planet in Rulership is extremely persuasive. A planet in Rulership will always be allowed to argue its case, no matter how few votes it influences.

Exaltation

A planet in the sign of its Exaltation is very strong, but it doesn't get to set its own agenda. Planets in Exaltation are treated as honored guests, and other planets make an effort to do things for them on their behalf. A planet in Exaltation is very persuasive. No matter how few votes it has on a Board of Directors, the other planets will make an effort to support its agenda.

Essential Dignities and the Board of Directors

Triplicity
A planet in its own Triplicity is strong, but that strength has more to do with luck than with inherent skill or ability. Because Triplicity depends on the sect of a chart, dignity by Triplicity, like luck, is fickle. A planet with Triplicity is reasonably persuasive, but relies more on charm than on compelling arguments.

Term
A planet with dignity by Term is weak. William Lilly described planets in Term as being in declining fortunes. A planet with Term may be able to get an undecided planet to support its agenda, but it doesn't have the power to get a committed planet to change its vote.

Face
A planet that has dignity only by Face is extremely weak. The planet has no say in its own agenda, but it has a seat on its Board of Directors, so it has to witness the other planets deciding how it will express. Because a planet with dignity by Face has an interest in the matter but no ability to influence the outcome, these planets often exhibit fear.

Essential Debilities
Essential Debilities do not affect the number of votes a planet has on its own Board of Directors. It's possible for a planet to have both Essential Dignity and Essential Debility. The scoring system is a way of evaluating the overall condition of the planet, but it has no practical value in natal astrology.

Detriment
A planet in a sign opposite a sign it rules is in **Detriment**. Planets in Detriment are strong; however, they use their strength in ways that get them into trouble.

Fall
A planet in the sign opposite the sign of its Exaltation is in **Fall**. A planet in Fall, through no fault of its own, is in a situation where its skills aren't useful. The ability to knit a sweater won't save you from drowning.

Peregrine

A planet that has no Essential Dignity (i.e., no votes on its own Board of Directors) is **peregrine**. Peregrine means "wandering." A planet without Essential Dignity wanders because it has no influence over its own agenda. In the context of certain types of predictive astrology, being peregrine is a severe debility. In the context of a natal chart, a lack of Essential Dignity is of no concern.

Modern Rulership

You've probably encountered the modern system of rulership, which includes the outer planets, Uranus, Neptune, and Pluto, and assigns Uranus rulership over Aquarius, Neptune rulership over Pisces, and Pluto rulership over Scorpio. Modern rulerships have nothing to do with Essential Dignity.

In the 17th and 18th centuries, astrology fell into a serious decline. Once considered a science and taught in universities, the study and practice of astrology migrated from professional scholars to amateur enthusiasts. Without an established authority or a clear link to thousands of years of astrological history, astrologers lost touch with many important concepts. During this period, astronomers discovered two new planets: Uranus in 1781, and Neptune in 1846. Amateur astrologers proposed rulership for these new planets based on the incorrect assumption that rulerships are based on how much a sign resembles a planet. Their ideas met with scorn and resistance, and didn't gain acceptance until the 1930s, after the discovery of Pluto.

Rulership is one of five Essential Dignities. It's the most important Essential Dignity, and has the most uses, but it doesn't exist in a vacuum. Modern astrologers have shoehorned the outer planets into a system of rulership, but haven't integrated them into the rest of the Essential Dignities. This makes the "modern rulership" system incompatible with the Board of Directors. Working with the Board of Directors gives you far more information than you get from considering only the ruler. Therefore, modern rulers are not practical.

CHAPTER 11

Aspects and the Outer Planets

In the grammar and syntax of the language of astrology, aspects serve as conjunctions: they join phrases and clauses, and create connections between two planets.

You can interpret an aspect only in the context of the chart. "Mars square Jupiter" doesn't mean anything on its own. In the context of a chart, "Mars square Jupiter" shows a connection not only between Mars and Jupiter, but also between all of the houses associated with Mars and Jupiter. You consider aspects after you've interpreted the **top-level planet** and the planets on the Board of Directors. This establishes the context for the aspect.

Receptions

A **reception** is a connection between planets via the Essential Dignities and the Board of Directors. Receptions are among the oldest types of aspects. A planet that occupies a particular degree is a *guest*, and the members of the Board of Directors for that degree are the *hosts*. The energy of a reception flows in one direction, from the host to the guest. The host planet takes an interest in the affairs of the guest planet, and the guest planet must defer to the wishes of the host planet. The more votes the host planet has on the guest planet's Board of Directors, the greater its influence.

When two planets receive each other by the same dignity, it's known as a **mutual reception**. Mutual receptions can occur in any dignity, but they're the most obvious when two planets receive each other by rulership, such as Mars in Taurus and Venus in Aries. The energy of a mutual reception flows in both directions. Each planet is both a host and a guest. Planets in mutual reception are closely linked, but they do not switch places. Each planet retains its own essential dignity or debility. Mars in Taurus and Venus in Aries are in mutual reception by rulership, but both planets are still in Detriment.

Zodiacal Aspects

A **zodiacal aspect** measures the angular relationship between two points along the **ecliptic**. These include the "major" or **Ptolemaic aspects**, such as trines and oppositions, and "minor" or **harmonic aspects**, such as semi-squares.

Ptolemaic Aspects

The major aspects are the aspects included in the *Tetrabiblos*, written by **Ptolemy** in the 2nd century. These aspects are often called the Ptolemaic aspects, and include the **conjunction**, **opposition**, **trine**, **square**, and **sextile**. All of the Ptolemaic aspects are based on the relationship between the signs. Planets in signs that aspect each other can "see" or "behold" each other. Planets that are one sign apart (**semi-sextile**) or five signs apart (**quincunx**) are **inconjunct**, and can't "see" each other. The inconjunct signs have different elements, modalities, and polarities, and planets in these signs are often described as **averse**.

Harmonic Aspects

In the early 1600s, Johannes Kepler introduced a new theory of aspects, based on geometry, harmonics, and the "music of the spheres." Kepler believed that when planets move into an exact angular relationship, they vibrate at the same frequency, and this vibration triggers other planets that have a harmonic relationship to that frequency.

Kepler defined the aspects based on their harmonic signature, rather than on the relationship between the signs. The Ptolemaic aspects represent the 1st harmonic (conjunction, 360°÷1 = 360°/0°), 2nd harmonic (opposition, 360°÷2 = 180°), 3rd harmonic (trine, 360°÷3 = 120°), 4th harmonic (square, 360°÷4 = 90°), and 6th harmonic (sextile, 360°÷6 = 60°). These major aspects represent whole sign relationships. Kepler introduced the minor aspects that are independent of the signs. He invented the 5th harmonic aspects, the **quintile** (72°) and the **bi-quintile** (144°), and the 8th harmonic aspects, the **semi-square** (45°) and the **sesquisquare** or sesquiquadrate (135°).

Orbs and Moiety

Joseph Crane describes aspects in Hellenistic (Greek) astrology as "a sign to a sign, a degree to a degree."[1] Any planet in Aries is trine any planet in Leo, regardless of their relative positions within the sign. Two planets at the same whole degree form a **partile** aspect, which is powerful. Planets at different degrees form a **platick** aspect, which is less significant.

Using this system, planets at 1° Aries and 29° Aries would be conjunct even though they're 28° apart, but planets at 29° Aries and 1° Taurus would not be conjunct even though they're only 2° apart. Contemporaries of Ptolemy agreed that sometimes you have to consider degrees as well as signs.

A planet has a sphere of influence, called an **orb**. The planet occupies the center of the orb, which describes the range of the light, or influence of the planet. Each planet "looks ahead" a certain number of degrees, as its light extends forward in the zodiac, and it "hurls rays" the same number of degrees backward. An aspect between two planets is "in orb" if the planets are close enough for their light to intersect.

Each planet has a different orb, although sources differ on the size. According to William Lilly, the Sun has an orb of 15°; the Moon's orb is 12°; Mercury, Venus, and Mars each have an orb of 7°; and Jupiter and Saturn have orbs of 9°. To determine if two planets are close enough to aspect each other, you consider the **moiety**, or half-orb of each planet, and add them up. Any aspect between the Sun and Moon would be in orb as long as the aspect is within 13.5° degrees (7.5° moiety for Sun + 6° moiety for Moon); however, for an aspect between Venus and Mars, it would have to be within 7° (3.5° moiety for Venus + 3.5° moiety for Mars).

This system works if you consider only the Ptolemaic aspects; it breaks down if you include the minor aspects. Any aspect between the Moon and

---

[1] Crane, Joseph. *A Practical Guide to Traditional Astrology*. Orleans, Mass.: Archive for the Retrieval of Historical Astrological Texts, 1997. 36.

Jupiter has an orb of 13°, but if they're 125° apart, they could either be in a 120° trine or a 135° sesquisquare. This has led to the modern practice of assigning orbs to aspects rather than to planets.

A practical rule of thumb is the smaller the orb, the more important the aspect. Harmonic aspects, such as the semi-square and sesquisquare, require more precise orbs than whole-sign aspects, such as the trine or square. I consider the quincunx to be a harmonic aspect because the signs are averse.

When planets move into orb with each other, the aspect is **applying**. The aspect is **perfected** when it becomes exact, and the planets occupy the same degree of their respective signs. When the planets move away from a perfected aspect, the aspect is **separating**. Applying aspects are more important than separating aspects because they represent events that have yet to unfold. Separating aspects represent events that have already happened. The energy of the aspect is present so long as the aspect is in orb, but the power diminishes as the planets move apart.

Practical Aspects Defined

Not all aspects are practical. I use only eight aspects in my interpretations: conjunction, opposition, trine, square, sextile, quincunx, semi-square, and sesquisquare. These are the aspects that have practical value for me, in both natal interpretations and in predictive natal astrology.

Conjunction (0°)

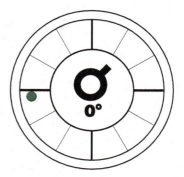

The conjunction is a 1st harmonic aspect. It perfects when two planets occupy the same degree of the same sign. The keywords for a conjunction are, "**a unity of purpose …**". However, when two planets are conjunct, they do not merge or take on each other's qualities. Conjunct planets share a unity of purpose because **they have the same Board of Directors**, so they are motivated by the same things.

Aspects and the Outer Planets

Opposition (180°)

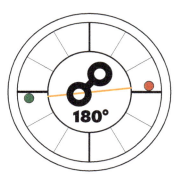

The opposition is a 2nd harmonic aspect that perfects at a 180° angle. Planets that oppose each other are six signs apart. Opposing signs have the same modality and polarity, but different elements. The keywords for an opposition are, "**a need for balance and compromise …**". Planets in opposition can "see" each other clearly across the chart. They represent opposite sides of a single issue. Oppositions play out in relationships. You "own" one of the planets, and project the other planet on your partner. Oppositions can be challenging because they suggest open warfare. However, there is always a point of balance where you can resolve the conflict.

Trine (120°)

The trine is a 3rd harmonic aspect that perfects at a 120° angle. Planets that trine each other are four signs apart, and occupy the same element. The keywords for a trine are, "**an easy, constant, effortless flow of energy …**". Trines represent a complete lack of obstacles. This is not necessarily a good thing. Trines are always active, which makes them relentless. You can't stop or even moderate the exchange of energy between the planets. This makes trines lazy. Because the energy flows so easily, there's no need to expend any effort.

Square (90°)

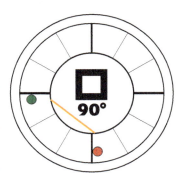

The square is a 4th harmonic aspect that perfects at a 90° angle. Planets that square each other are three signs apart. They occupy the same modality, but different elements. The keywords for a square are, "**friction, tension, stress, and conflict …**". This is not necessarily a bad thing. You resolve the tension and conflict of a square by taking action.

The 4th harmonic relates to the world of form. Squares drive manifestation and creation. The modality of the square determines how the planets act. Planets in a Cardinal square take direct action and confront obstacles head-on. Planets in a Fixed square dig trenches and prepare for a siege. Planets in a Mutable square prefer to adapt and avoid the conflict altogether.

Sextile (60°)

The sextile is a 6th harmonic aspect that perfects at a 60° angle. Planets that sextile each other are two signs apart. The signs have the same polarity, but different elements and modalities. The keywords for a sextile are "**an opportunity for support …**". Sextiles are one of the major aspects because they are a whole-sign, Ptolemaic aspect. From a practical standpoint, they're minor. Sextiles represent potential, but unlike trines, the potential of a sextile must be activated.

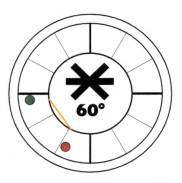

Quincunx (150°)

The quincunx is a 12th harmonic aspect that perfects at a 150° angle. Planets that quincunx each other are five signs apart. The signs are averse and have different elements, modalities, and polarities. Ptolemy made a point of calling this (and the semi-sextile, a 30° aspect) an inconjunct, to emphasize that it represented a *lack* of connection between the two planets. The planets are forced into relationship with each other by the harmonic aspect.

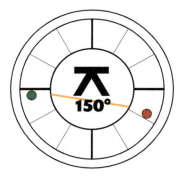

When two planets quincunx each other, they can "see" each other across the chart as they would in an opposition; however, these planets have no common ground, and unlike an opposition, there's no point of balance. The keywords for quincunxes between two inner planets are, "**a fundamental incompatibility …**". The keywords for a quincunx from an outer planet to an inner planet are, "**random, unexpected disruptions …**". Quincunxes are so challenging because they can be resolved only by raising your vibration and expanding your level of consciousness. To paraphrase Albert Einstein, you can't solve a problem at the level of consciousness that created it.

Semi-Square (45°)

A semi-square is an 8th harmonic aspect that perfects at a 45° angle. It's a minor harmonic aspect, and is not dependent on the relationship between the signs. The keywords for a semi-square are, "**a minor internal tension or friction …**". Like the square, the semi-square represents tension, friction, and conflict that can lead to action. However, the semi-square is weaker than the square. The 8th harmonic

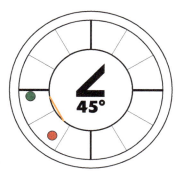

expresses in the mental realm, whereas the 4th harmonic operates in the physical and material realms. Semi-squares are internal aspects. The planets do not "see" each other. They represent inner challenges that result in decisions rather than external challenges that result in action.

Sesquisquare (135°)

A sesquisquare or sesquiquadrate is an 8th harmonic aspect that perfects at a 135° angle. It's a minor harmonic aspect, and is not dependent on the relationship between the signs. The keywords for a sesquisquare are, "**a minor annoyance or irritation …**". It represents tension, friction, and conflict that can lead to action, but it's an

8th harmonic aspect, so like the semi-square, it's more mental than physical. Sesquisquares are irritating and annoying. They often play out in relationships, where the tension expresses verbally, using humor, and may include insults, sarcasm, and put-downs.

Spotting Aspects in the Chart

It's easy to spot **whole-sign aspects** in the chart, and it's a good skill to develop. Look at the chart and pick out pairs of planets that are at similar degrees (such as a planet at 24° of a sign and another planet at 27° of a sign). These planets will be in some kind of aspect. If they're in the **same sign**, it's a **conjunction**. If they're **across the chart** from each other and in the **same modality**, it's an **opposition**. If they're in the **same element**, it's a **trine**. If they're in the **same modality** but **different polarity**, it's a **square**. If they're **two signs apart**, it's a **sextile**. If they're **five signs apart**, it's a **quincunx**. If they're **one sign apart**, it's a **semi-sextile**, which you can ignore. You determine the **orb** of the aspect by subtracting the smaller degree from the larger degree. For example, if one planet is at 27° and the other is at 24°, the orb of the aspect is 3°.

To determine if an aspect is **applying** or **separating**, you consider the faster-moving of the planets and see where it is in relationship to the slower-moving planet[2]. If the faster-moving planet is behind the slower-moving planet, and is in **direct motion**, the aspect is **applying**. If the faster-moving planet is ahead of the slower-moving planet, and is in direct motion, the aspect is **separating**. If the faster-moving planet is behind the slower-moving planet, and is in **retrograde motion**, the aspect is **separating**. And if the faster-moving planet is ahead of the slower-moving planet, and is in retrograde motion, the aspect is **applying**.

Out-of-Sign Aspects

Out-of-sign aspects occur when the angular relationship between two planets doesn't align with the sign relationship between the planets. A planet at 0° Aries and a planet at 29° Leo are 89° apart, which is a square with a 1° orb, but they're trine by sign. Much of the tension associated with a square comes from the clash of the planets being in the same modality but different elements, but in this scenario, they're in the same element and different modalities. It's an out-of-sign aspect, and must be treated with caution.

---

[2] The planets, rated from fastest to slowest in average daily motion are: Moon, Mercury, Venus, Sun, Mars, Jupiter, Saturn, Chiron, Uranus, Neptune, Pluto.

I will consider an out-of-sign aspect only if it's applying, and has a very small orb. If the aspect is separating, or has an orb greater than 2°, I ignore it. Your mileage may vary.

If I can't find a way to ignore the aspect, I weigh the sign connection (whole-sign aspect) against the angular connection (harmonic aspect) and consider how the conflicting energies might interact or express. It's hard work, and requires a great deal of effort, which is why I need to be convinced that the results will be worth it.

Aspect Patterns

An aspect pattern is a pretty picture formed when three or more planets move into a tight angular relationship with each other. Aspect patterns usually involve multiple planets in the same harmonic relationship, such as a Grand Trine (three planets trine each other), or a Grand Cross (four planets, each in the same modality, but different elements, creating a sequence of four squares), or a T-Square (a Grand Cross with one missing planet). More recently, astrologers have invented new aspect patterns with impressive-sounding names, like the Yod, or the "Finger of God," and the Mystic Rectangle.

Aspect patterns are not practical. Aspect patterns don't have an independent existence. You have to consider each individual aspect in the context of the chart. Naming the pattern doesn't provide additional information.

The Outer Planets

The outer planets are *outer*. They are impersonal and don't live inside you. This means you can't experience them directly. You experience the indirect effects of the outer planets when they make aspects to the personal planets in your chart, because they alter how you experience those planets. Each of the outer planets brings awareness of levels of consciousness beyond the Saturn-based limitations of your "little r" reality. If you are in right relationship with Saturn, these experiences can be liberating and exciting, but if you are attached to the illusions of Saturn, experiences of the outer planets can be traumatic.

Uranus

Uranus disrupts Saturn; its purpose is to make sure there's never too much order or rigidity in the world. Uranus is a flash of lightning: it's unexpected, instantaneous, and unsettling. It's also neutral in nature. Uranus brings miracles as well as accidents, and the difference between them is often a matter of perspective.

If you're in right relationship with Saturn, Uranus energy can be refreshing. It gives you the ability to think outside the box, while allowing you to sustain the illusion of the box. If you're addicted to the illusion of Saturn, Uranus energy is catastrophic. It shows you that the boundaries and rules you depend on will not keep you safe.

Uranus aspects create unexpected disruptions and interruptions. They are often associated with patterns of rejection and abandonment.

Neptune

Neptune dissolves Saturn. Neptune represents the unlimited creative possibilities of the Universe. Neptune's energy denies Saturn's structure, and blithely dissolves all boundaries. Neptune reveals where you have the weakest hold on your "little r" reality.

If you're in right relationship with Saturn, Neptune energy creates more freedom and flexibility. The rules and limits become pliable, which creates more space in your "little r" reality. If you're addicted to the illusion of Saturn, Neptune energy is disorienting. It makes navigating the world of form challenging because you don't find support or stability where you expect it.

Aspects from Neptune to personal planets create bad boundaries, deception, and the desire to escape reality through fantasy.

Pluto

Pluto destroys Saturn. Pluto represents the most destructive energy in the Universe, but it may surprise you that this energy is Unconditional Love. Unconditional Love is ruthless and unstoppable. It obliterates reality to reveal truth. Because Pluto represents the inevitable death of the ego, along with all of the associated attachments you believe make your survival possible, you probably find Pluto's energy threatening. The better your relationship with Saturn, the easier it is to surrender to Pluto, but that's not saying much.

Where Pluto contacts your personal planets, you experience issues of power, control, and manipulation.

Chiron

Chiron is a minor planet that was discovered in 1978. Chiron wounds Saturn. In mythology, Chiron is the archetype of the Wounded Healer. In astrology, Chiron represents your core spiritual wound. When you find the courage to confront and attempt to heal this unhealable wound, you expand your consciousness and discover your own healing gifts. Until then, Chiron represents where you are wounded, and shows where (and how) you wound others.

Part of what makes Chiron unique is that it's orbit crosses inside the path of Saturn, and reaches outside the path of Uranus. Chiron creates a bridge between the inner and the outer planets.

Aspects from Chiron to your personal planets show direct connections to your core wound. When you are ready to address your core wound, you will need the support of these planets.

Aspect Blueprint Template Sentences

Aspects are the last things you consider in each section of the interpretation. Aspects introduce a significant amount of detail, so you will need to decide which aspects to include. Aspects from the outer planets to inner planets are important, and they're usually worth considering. Aspects between inner planets get very complicated. Give priority to aspects a top-level planet makes to any planet on its Board of Directors, because the combination of the angular aspect and the reception makes the connection more significant. Aspects between two outer planets, such as Uranus square Pluto, represent generational influences and are not significant in natal astrology.

Outer Planet Aspects to Inner Planets

Aspects from an outer planet to an inner planet flow in one direction, from the outer planet to the inner planet. The influence of the outer planet comes from the house occupied by the outer planet, and affects the areas of life ruled by the inner planet, based on the nature of the outer planet and the aspect. The effects are experienced in the house occupied by the inner planet.

[Outer Planet] in [House] [Aspect]
[Planet] in [House] (Ruler of [House(s)])

There is a [ASPECT KEYWORDS] ([ASPECT]) **CAUSED BY** [OUTER PLANET KEYWORDS] ([OUTER PLANET]), **COMING FROM** [HOUSE KEYWORDS] ([OUTER PLANET] in [HOUSE]), and affecting his/her need to [PLANET KEYWORDS] ([PLANET]) **WITH** his/her [HOUSE KEYWORDS] ([PLANET] rules [HOUSE]) and his/her [HOUSE KEYWORDS] ([PLANET] rules [HOUSE]). He/she would experience this **IN** [house keywords] ([PLANET] in [HOUSE]).

Pluto in 5th House Square
Sun in 1st House (Ruler of 4th House)

There is friction, tension, stress, and conflict (square) **CAUSED BY** issues of power, control, and manipulation (Pluto) **COMING FROM** her personal creativity and desire to take risks (Pluto in 5th house) and affecting her need to align with her Personal Standards of Integrity and express her authentic "Big S" Self (Sun) **WITH** her home and family (Sun rules 4th house). She would experience this **IN** her personality, self-expression, and self-image (Sun in 1st house).

You can also explore an aspect from an outer planet to an inner planet as a house ruler (such as Uranus square the ruler of the 2nd house). This is a less complicated blueprint sentence because you don't need to consider the nature of the house ruler, or any other houses it rules.

[Outer Planet] in [House] [Aspect]
[Planet] in [House] (Ruler of [House])

There is a [ASPECT KEYWORDS] ([ASPECT]) **CAUSED BY** [OUTER PLANET KEYWORDS] ([OUTER PLANET]), **COMING FROM** [HOUSE KEYWORDS] ([OUTER PLANET] in [HOUSE]), and affecting his/her [HOUSE KEYWORDS] ([PLANET] rules [HOUSE]) and his/her [HOUSE KEYWORDS] ([PLANET] rules [HOUSE]). He/she would experience this **IN** [house keywords] ([PLANET] in [HOUSE]).

Uranus in the 6th House Opposite
Mercury in the 12th House (Ruler of 1st House

There is a need for balance and compromise (opposition) **CAUSED BY** disruptions and unexpected events (Uranus) **COMING FROM** his job and relationships with co-workers (Uranus in 6th house) and affecting his personality and self-expression (Mercury rules 1st house). He would experience this **IN** his personal unconscious and his shadow-self (Mercury in 12th house).

Inner Planet Aspects

Aspects between inner planets are quite involved, and you need a compelling reason to interpret them. The aspects flow in two directions, and the blueprint sentences contain a great deal of information. An aspect between a top-level planet and one of the planets on its Board of Directors is important enough to consider. However, you view it only in one direction, as it flows from the Board of Directors planet to the top-level planet, and is experienced in the house the top-level planet occupies.

[Planet A] in [House] (Ruler of [House(s)]) [Aspect]
[Planet B] in [House] (Ruler of [House(s)])
There is a [ASPECT KEYWORDS] ([ASPECT]) **BETWEEN his/her need to** [PLANET A KEYWORDS] ([PLANET A]) **WITH** [HOUSE KEYWORDS FOR HOUSES RULED BY PLANET A] ([PLANET A] **rules** [HOUSE]), **COMING FROM** [HOUSE WHERE KEYWORDS FOR PLANET A] ([PLANET A] **in** [HOUSE]) **AND his/her need to** [PLANET B KEYWORDS] ([PLANET B]), **WITH** [HOUSE KEYWORDS FOR HOUSES RULED BY PLANET B] ([PLANET B] **rules** [HOUSE]), **COMING FROM** [HOUSE WHERE KEYWORDS FOR PLANET B] ([PLANET B] **in** [HOUSE]).

Mars in 7th House (Rules 11th House, Almuten 8th House), Square Saturn in 10th House (Rules 8th and 9th Houses)
There is a conflict, challenge, or tension (square) **BETWEEN** his need to take action and expend energy (Mars) **WITH** his hopes and aspirations and his friendships (Mars rules 11th house) and his debts, financial obligations, and shared resources (Mars almuten 8th house), **COMING FROM** his one-to-one relationships (Mars in 7th house) **AND** his need to set limits and boundaries and be held accountable (Saturn) **WITH** his debts, financial obligations, and shared resources (Saturn rules 8th house) and his higher education, beliefs, and philosophies (Saturn rules 9th house), **COMING FROM** his career, public reputation, and life path (Saturn in 10th house).

CHAPTER 12
How to Build a Chair

The natal chart is not a crystal ball, and astrologers are not fortune tellers. No one can discover your most embarrassing secrets by looking at your birth chart.[1] Interpreting a natal chart is like painting a portrait: the objective is to capture a likeness. You can capture the *essence* of a person without copying their *appearance*. The events in your life, your behavior, and your choices are external, and relate to appearance. Astrology looks beneath the surface to reveal the essence.

I'd like you to picture a few images: a dining-room chair, a dentist's chair, a desk chair, and Queen Elizabeth's throne. If you judge them by their appearances, they have nothing in common. They're different sizes, different shapes, and made of different materials. And yet, as different as they appear, each has an essential quality that you recognize as "chair." The patterns in your birth chart express in different ways throughout your life. But if you view each pattern as the blueprint of a chair, you can recognize the essence of the pattern no matter how it appears.

Recognizing patterns is a soft skill. In *The Little Book of Talent*, Daniel Coyle explains the difference between hard and soft skills. Hard skills are precise and specific, while soft skills are fluid and responsive. He also emphasizes that hard skills form the foundation for soft skills.[2]

One of the most important soft skills in astrology is the ability to connect the appearance of a client to the essence of the natal chart. You develop this skill by building three-dimensional chairs from the two-dimensional blueprints. The greater variety of chairs you build from a blueprint, the more references you have

---

[1] That's what Facebook is for.
[2] Coyle, Daniel. *The Little Book of Talent: 52 Tips for Improving Skills*. New York, NY: Bantam Books, 2012. 27-28.

for the pattern, and the easier it will be to spot other chairs that use the same blueprint. As long as you maintain the correct relationships between the planets, signs, and houses, any chair you build from the blueprint will be valid.

You build chairs from a blueprint by making notes and assembling sketch sentences.

Notes: Cause, Action, and Effect

Each blueprint sentence includes a cause, an action, and an effect. The cause involves one of the houses ruled and the sign of the planet. The action involves the nature of the planet and the sign. And the effect involves the affairs of the house the planet occupies.

When you make notes, you explore each part of the blueprint sentence individually. You engage your right brain, expand on the keywords, and create specific examples from the general principles. This process is like an artist making an initial sketch. It can be rough and messy because it's about getting lines on the paper (or words on the page). The objective is to get familiar with the different parts of the chair. You'll assemble those parts later.

Use the concepts and ideas in the following sections for inspiration and guidance as you explore the cause, action, and effect. However, these are not keywords for fill-in-the-blank sentences like you used in Phase 2. This is Phase 3. Use your imagination and create your own examples.

Cause

The cause has two components, and you can consider them individually or together. The first component involves the affairs of a house where the planet is the ruler or the almuten. When someone or something messes with that house, the planet will take action to address the problem.

House Ruled
1st **House:** Don't mess with me (personally). Sense of individual identity, physical body, appearance to others, personal interests.
2nd **House:** Don't mess with my stuff. Money, resources, possessions, values, personal opinions.

3rd House: Don't mess with my environment. Neighborhood, daily routine, personal communication, relationships with siblings, neighbors, cousins.

4th House: Don't mess with my private life. Home, family, real estate, issues with father.

5th House: Don't mess with my fun. Sex, games, children, gambling, risky behavior, artistic expression, personal creativity.

6th House: Don't mess with my job. Employment, workplace environment, relationships with co-workers and employees.

7th House: Don't mess with my relationships. All one-to-one relationships, especially spouses, business partners, contractual relationships, and open enemies.

8th House: Don't mess with *our* stuff. Shared resources (everything from joint bank accounts to food in the refrigerator), debt, taxes, other people's money and possessions.

9th House: Don't mess with my beliefs. Religion, philosophy, ideals, higher education, professional authority, long-distance travel, foreign experiences.

10th House: Don't mess with my reputation. Career, profession, public image, public persona (including social media presence), issues with mother.

11th House: Don't mess with my dreams. Hopes and aspirations; the money you acquire; relationships with friends, teammates, and peers.

12th House: Don't mess with my unconscious. Shadow self, repressed desires, self-sabotage, sorrows and adversity. Behaviors that result from a 12th house trigger will often create resentment and hidden enemies.

The second component of the cause involves the sign of the planet. Each sign has a carrot (what the planet would like to experience) and a stick (experiences that are unacceptable). Any of the stick experiences qualify as "messing" with the affairs of a house.

Sign Carrots and Sticks

Aries Carrot: Action, new projects, impulsive expression, honesty, authenticity, passion.

Aries Stick: Limitations, boundaries, restrictions, delays, routine.

Taurus Carrot: Routine, stability, comfort, security, steady growth, practical expression.
Taurus Stick: Change, disruption, abstract or impractical concepts.
Gemini Carrot: Knowledge, information, connections, social and intellectual stimulation, play.
Gemini Stick: Limitations, focus, lack of options, deep emotions, restrictions.
Cancer Carrot: Emotional connections, comfort, security, nurturing, support, compassion.
Cancer Stick: Rigid boundaries, abstract concepts, emotional distance, insensitivity.
Leo Carrot: Attention, praise, passion, fun, expansiveness, time in the spotlight, creative expression.
Leo Stick: Lack of attention, being ignored or taken for granted, criticism and judgment.
Virgo Carrot: Precision, improvement, accuracy, clarity, attention to details, analysis, order.
Virgo Stick: Mistakes, imperfections, being impractical, chaos, uncontrolled emotions, disorder.
Libra Carrot: Balance, harmony, beauty, objectivity, pleasant social connections, tranquil appearance.
Libra Stick: Conflict, disagreements, deep emotions, rigidity, lack of boundaries, materialism.
Scorpio Carrot: Passion, deep emotional connections, spiritual authenticity, intensity, transformation.
Scorpio Stick: Abstract or impractical concepts, irresponsibility, superficiality.
Sagittarius Carrot: Freedom, expansion, fun, enthusiasm, big ideas, beliefs, philosophy, religion.
Sagittarius Stick: Betrayal, boundaries, limitations, rigidity, lack of trust.
Capricorn Carrot: Structure, ambition, responsibility, maturity, respect, practicality, accomplishment.
Capricorn Stick: Irreverence, irresponsibility, bad boundaries, instability, abstract, impractical.
Aquarius Carrot: Freedom, idealism, objectivity, innovation, new ideas, social justice, humanitarian.

Aquarius Stick: Individual, personal, emotional, specific, practical, concrete, obsolete, conforming.

Pisces Carrot: Compassion, empathy, emotional connections, unity, spirituality, flexibility, fluidity.

Pisces Stick: Rigid boundaries, practicality, materialism, focus, structured, linear, logical.

Action

When there is a disruption in a house, the planet that rules that house takes action to address the issue. A planet acts by getting you to behave in a particular way. Action is essence, but behavior is appearance, and the connection between them is not always obvious. Refer back to the keywords for each planet for the Board of Directors Blueprint Templates on page 117 for examples of how each planet acts and what needs it hopes to meet. Every behavior, even something as mundane as washing dishes, has a deeper significance and a hidden motivation. It depends on which planet wants you to wash dishes.

- If the **Sun** wants you to wash dishes, it's because washing dishes moves you into alignment with a Personal Standard of Integrity.

- If the **Moon** wants you to wash dishes, it's because having clean dishes will make a deposit in your Safety Need Account.

- If **Mercury** wants you to wash dishes, it's because washing dishes communicates an important message, or helps you to understand your "little r" reality.

- If **Venus** wants you to wash dishes, it could be to express appreciation or affection for someone, or it could be because you love and appreciate having a clean kitchen.

- If **Mars** wants you to wash dishes, it's a way to use up energy and maintain control over your environment.

- ✦ If **Jupiter** wants you to wash dishes, it's because it will create more space for you to grow.

- ✦ If **Saturn** wants you to wash dishes, it's because it's your responsibility to wash the dishes.

The hope is that your behavior will meet the needs of the planet. The chances of this are better when the behavior aligns with the higher-consciousness qualities of the sign than when it aligns with the lower-consciousness qualities of the sign.

Effect

A planet can act only in the house it occupies, so your behavior will involve the affairs of that house. This may not be the most effective way to address the cause in the house the planet rules. You can choose from any of the keywords associated with the house and imagine specific behaviors that relate to them. You also need to consider how the nature of the house affects the behavior.

House Occupied

1st House: The behavior is personal; it's all about you and it doesn't take other people into consideration.

2nd House: The behavior is financial; your first instinct is to fix the issue with money.

3rd House: The behavior is local; it involves your habits, your routine, and your familiar environment.

4th House: The behavior is private and personal.

5th House: The behavior is risky; you'll look for some way to have fun while fixing the problem.

6th House: The behavior involves hard work and service, and you won't be recognized for your efforts.

7th House: The behavior involves someone else; you may ask for help, or blame someone and try to get that person to fix the problem for you.

8th House: The behavior is financial; your first instinct is to fix the issue with other people's money. This often involves credit cards.

9th House: The behavior is new, unfamiliar, and outside of your usual environment. It may involve citing a higher authority or the law.

10th House: The behavior is public. Everyone knows about it (probably because you won't stop posting about it on Facebook).

11th House: The behavior involves the support of other people, including friends, peers, or teammates.

12th House: The behavior is unconscious, and has unforeseen (and undesirable) consequences.

Sketch Sentences: Chairs

Once you've explored the different options of cause, action, and effect, you can assemble them into sketch sentences and build a virtually infinite number of different chairs. When you build a chair, you're not limited to a single sentence, but you are limited to a single example of a cause, an action, and an effect.

The sketch sentences help you to understand how the cause, action, and effect fit together, which is how you learn to recognize the patterns and spot the chair. Don't limit yourself to the kinds of behavior or appearance you expect. Until you meet with a client, you won't know how they experience their chart. The more free and imaginative you are when you create your sketch sentences, the easier it will be to spot the chairs when you meet with a client, so you can connect the appearance of the client to the essence of the chart.

Principles of Practical Natal Astrology

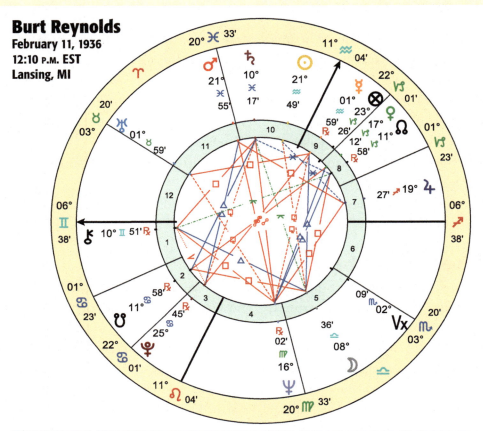

Figure 18: Burt Reynolds' Natal Chart

Source: Astro-Databank; Rodden Rating: AA, BC/BR in hand.

Example Sketches: Burt Reynolds' Moon

We'll use **Burt Reynolds**' Moon as an example (Figure 18). I'll begin with the blueprint sentence, followed by notes, which identify options for the cause, action, and effect. Finally, I'll assemble a few complete sketch sentences from the notes.

Blueprint Sentence

Moon in Libra in the 5th House
Moon Rules 2nd and 3rd Houses

To feel safe (Moon), he needs to feel diplomatic, charming, dependent, and placating (Libra) **WITH** his money and resources, values, and talents (Moon rules 2nd) and his familiar environment, daily routine, writing, and communication (Moon rules 3rd). He encounters these needs particularly **IN** his pursuit of fun, personal creativity, love affairs, and tolerance for risk (Moon in 5th).

Notes

The Moon rules both the 2nd and 3rd houses. This connects money (2nd house) and communication (3rd house). His safety depends on having enough money, but also being able to use money as a way to communicate and express himself. Money = communication = safety.

Cause in 2nd house is financial. Any drop in Reynolds' checking account will trigger a drop in his Safety Need Account (Moon). The size doesn't matter—paying a huge amount of alimony messes with his 2nd house as much as paying the electricity bill. The 2nd house relates to movable property and possessions. If someone breaks a lamp, or borrows his lawn mower and doesn't return it, that would trigger his 2nd house. The 2nd house also relates to skills and talents. If Reynolds feels like he's not getting paid well enough for his latest film project, it could trigger his 2nd house both from a financial (2nd house is your salary) and a talent perspective.

Cause in 3rd house is any disruption in his familiar environment or routine. Examples could include running errands and not finding parking; problems with Wi-Fi reception so that he can't check email; or being awakened at dawn by a garbage truck. Other 3rd house triggers include communication-related problems, such as misunderstandings, gossip, and rumors. Problems in 3rd house relationships with siblings, cousins, or neighbors will also trigger the Moon (ruler of 3rd) to act.

Cause also involves the carrot and the stick for Libra. Libra wants peace, balance, harmony, and diplomacy, or at least the surface appearance that everyone is getting along (Libra carrot). The biggest stick for Libra is interpersonal conflict. Reynolds will act to prevent or eliminate a potential confrontation.

Action is the Moon in Libra. The triggers drain the balance in Reynolds' Safety Need Account. The Moon acts to bring the balance in his Safety Need Account to the minimum level and restore a sense of safety. As noted before, he hopes to be able to regain a sense of safety by embodying the higher-consciousness qualities of Libra, but he may fall short and embody the lower-consciousness qualities. When he acts from lower levels of consciousness, his behavior will not have the intended effect of making him feel safe.

Effect is in the 5th house, so Reynolds will be willing to take risks to address the problems that come from his 2nd and/or 3rd houses. He will also look for some way to have fun fixing the problem and restoring the minimum balance in his Safety Need Account. This raises an interesting paradox because Reynolds' ability to feel safe (Moon) is heavily involved with his tolerance for risk (5th house). Reynolds may feel safe only when he's engaging in risky behavior, because risky behavior is familiar to him, and safe = familiar.

Examples of 5th house behaviors include gambling, playing games, having fun, expressing creativity, and engaging in casual sexual and romantic relationships. If the trigger is a 2nd house financial loss, responding by creating his own production company and initiating new projects (5th house) would be a good solution to the problem and help Reynolds to feel safe; making high-risk investment decisions (5th house) could make the problem worse and make Reynolds feel less safe; and behaving in a shallow, dependent, hypersensitive, and aloof (low-consciousness Libra) manner toward the person he's dating won't have any effect on his financial problems, but will probably give him new reasons to feel unsafe.

Sketch Sentences

When Reynolds experiences any kind of financial loss (Moon rules 2nd), it makes him feel unsafe (Moon). He tries to make up for this by spending time with his romantic partner (Moon in 5th house), hoping to be genial, affectionate, and flirtatious (high-consciousness Libra), but instead may appear dependent, fatuous, and unsettled (low-consciousness Libra).

A house guest in Reynolds' home breaks a beautiful (Libra) lamp (Moon rules 2nd house of possessions), which upsets Reynolds and makes him feel unsafe (Moon). Reynolds doesn't want to confront the guest directly (Libra stick), so he calls up some friends and plays basketball (Moon in 5th house) until he's able to let it go.

Reynolds' new neighbors (Moon rules 3rd house) don't take care of their lawn, park in Reynolds' driveway, and make lots of noise, which disrupts his familiar environment (3rd house) and causes him to feel unsafe (Moon). Because Reynolds wants his neighborhood to be pleasant, sociable, and friendly (Libra), and he also wants to avoid confrontation (Libra stick), he decides to throw a block party (Moon in 5th house) where all of the neighbors can socialize, in the hope that this will restore peace and harmony (Libra) to the neighborhood (Moon rules 3rd house).

Reynolds wants to nurture and protect other people (Moon) by being objective, tender, elegant, and debonair (high-consciousness Libra) in all of his communication and his routine interactions (Moon rules

3rd house). This motivates his artistic and pursuits and encourages him to take creative risks (Moon in 5th house).

Deep Practice: Building Chairs

Assembling sketch sentences and building chairs from the blueprints is a complex skill. It's also the first skill that requires the cooperation of both your left and right brain. As with any skill, you need to develop the necessary circuits in your brain through deep practice, and deep practice requires struggle. But for many people, this struggle is especially difficult.

Up to this point, you've been developing hard skills. You had clear objectives and precise instructions. Building chairs combines both hard and soft skills, and that makes it more challenging. I can give you guidance and advice, but there's no longer a single path to a correct result. You can create an infinite number of connections between the cause, action, and effect.

When you begin to assemble sketch sentences, you can use the model of the blueprint template sentences for the planets in signs. These give you four different contexts for each planet. With practice, you will develop your imagination and come up with greater variety and more specific examples of how a pattern could express.

PART 3

Systematic Approach to Synthesized Interpretation

CHAPTER 13

Introduction to Written Interpretations

This chapter contains an overview of the process of writing a synthesized interpretation of a natal chart. The remaining chapters in this section alternate between providing instruction and demonstrating the process, using Sally Ride's chart as an example.

Practice is not performance, and how you develop skills is different from how you use them. You develop chart interpretation skills by writing interpretations, but you won't provide written interpretations to your clients. From a professional standpoint, written interpretations have no practical value. A written interpretation can't help a client to change or become happier. And considering how long it takes to write an interpretation and how little you can charge for one, you'd make more money working at McDonald's.

The performance aspect of natal astrology is during an astrological consultation with a client, when you explore his or her natal chart. You may think your job is to cover the entire chart and share everything you know with the client. This couldn't be farther from the truth. Clients don't care about astrology; they care about happiness. They're looking for insight or help with a problem. Your job is to connect the appearance of the external conditions in the life of your client to the essence of his or her unique birth chart.

An astrological consultation uses soft skills. Daniel Coyle describes soft skills as "the result of super-fast brain software recognizing patterns and responding in just the right way."[1] As the client shares stories about his or her life and experiences, you spot the chairs and relate them back to the natal chart. By the end of the session, the client can see him or herself reflected in the chart.

Most of the astrology in an astrology consultation happens before you sit down with the client. You prepare for a consultation by analyzing the chart, drafting the blueprints, and creating the notes and sketch sentences. You build chairs from the blueprints and explore how the patterns could express in different contexts and from different levels of consciousness. You imagine various ways that the client might experience the chart, but you won't know the actual appearance of the client until you meet. That's when the soft skills take over, and you begin to connect the appearance to the essence.

Before you can develop the soft skills that you use in a consultation, you have to master the hard skills of reading the chart, drafting the blueprints, and creating the notes and sketch sentences. You develop these skills by writing interpretations.

Synthesized Chart Interpretation Process

The outline gives you an overview of the process of synthesized chart interpretation that I use for natal charts. You must view this process as a hierarchy. Your interpretation of the top-level planet establishes the context for how you consider all of the related sub-levels, such as planets on the Board of Directors or aspects to the top-level planet. Earlier steps are more significant, and require a greater level of detail.

Each time a planet shows up in the interpretation, you need to explore the role of the planet in the current context in your notes. You need to explore the cause, action, and effect of a planet only once; however, if a planet is important in more than one context, you may need to create multiple sets of sketch sentences.

The notes for the summary sections are very important. This is where you will identify and reiterate the important themes or patterns that have emerged in that section.

---

[1] Coyle, Daniel. *The Little Book of Talent: 52 Tips for Improving Skills*. New York, NY: Bantam Books, 2012. 24.

Introduction to Written Interpretations

This approach considers the entire chart. It emphasizes the personality and relationship needs and spends less time on relationship wants and career. It's a useful approach to develop synthesized chart interpretation skills, but it's not the only approach to natal chart interpretation. You could interpret a natal chart from the context of relationship astrology, and focus primarily on the Moon and Venus. You could explore the chart from the context of career and life path, and focus on the rulers of the 10th, 6th, and 2nd houses. I recommend that you become familiar with this approach before you explore others.

Part 1: Personality

Elements and Modalities: Notes
The Sun [Top-Level]: Blueprint, Notes, and Sketch Sentences
  Board of Directors for the Sun: Blueprint, Notes, and Sketch Sentences
  Outer Planet Aspects to the Sun: Blueprint, Notes
  Inner Planet Aspects to the Sun: Blueprint, Notes
Ascendant [Top-Level]: Blueprint, Notes
  Board of Directors for the Ascendant: Blueprint, Notes
  Aspects to the Ascendant: Blueprint, Notes
  Planets in the Ascendant: Blueprint, Notes, and Sketch Sentences
Summary of Personality: Notes

Part 2: Relationship Needs

The Moon [Top-Level]: Blueprint, Notes, and Sketch Sentences
  Board of Directors for the Moon: Blueprint, Notes, and Sketch Sentences
  Outer Planet Aspects to the Moon: Blueprint, Notes
  Inner Planet Aspects to the Moon: Blueprint, Notes
Venus [Top-Level]: Blueprint, Notes, and Sketch Sentences
  Board of Directors for Venus: Blueprint, Notes, and Sketch Sentences
  Outer Planet Aspects to Venus: Blueprint, Notes
  Inner Planet Aspects to Venus: Blueprint, Notes
Summary of Relationship Needs: Notes
  Aspect between the Moon and Venus: Blueprint, Notes

Part 3: Relationship Wants

Descendant and the Vertex: Blueprint, Notes
Elemental Balance in the Chart: Notes
The Marriage Blueprint: Notes
    Ruler of 5th House: Blueprint, Notes
    Ruler of 7th House: Blueprint, Notes
    Ruler of 11th House: Blueprint, Notes
    Connections Between Relationship Houses: Notes
Optional Summary of Relationship Needs and Wants: Notes

Part 4: Career

Ruler of 10th House (Career and Life Path) [Top-Level]: Blueprint, Notes, and Sketch Sentences
    Board of Directors for 10th House Ruler: Blueprint, Notes
Ruler of 6th House (Job) [Top-Level]: Blueprint, Notes, and Sketch Sentences
    Board of Directors for 6th House Ruler: Blueprint, Notes
Ruler of 2nd House (Money) [Top-Level]: Blueprint, Notes, and Sketch Sentences
    Board of Directors for 2nd House Ruler: Blueprint, Notes
    Part of Fortune: Blueprint, Notes
    Ruler of the Part of Fortune: Notes
Summary of Career: Notes

The blueprints, notes, and sketch sentences you create during this process are how you prepare for a consultation with a client, but they're *still* not your final interpretation. You need to summarize your conclusions and present them to a client without the astrological jargon. This is the most subjective part of the interpretation process. How you present your analysis of the chart, and how much of it you choose to share with the client, is up to you. You develop these skills by working from the blueprints, notes, and sketch sentences and creating a finished astrological portrait of a client. I demonstrate this process in Part 5.

CHAPTER 14

Interpreting the Personality

The term "personality" is imprecise, but I've yet to come up with a better description for the first part of this process of natal chart interpretation. In this context, the personality encompasses both your authentic, "Big S" Self (who you really are), and your persona (how other people see you).

Elements and Modalities

Before you dive in and consider the specific components of the chart, look for themes that show up in the distribution of the personal planets across the elements and modalities. If there's a good balance between the elements or modalities, you won't find any useful information here. But if you find an emphasis or lack in the elements or modalities, it may establish a context for the interpretation.

Emphasis of an Element

Having three or more personal planets in a single element is significant. The emphasized element represents the realm where you are the most comfortable living, and the qualities of the element will color the interpretation.

- **Three or more planets in Fire signs** gives you abundant energy, honesty, and self-expression, but you may lack moderation or middle gears.

- **Three or more planets in Earth signs** makes you stable, practical, and familiar with the material world, but you may also be literal, and lack passion, spontaneity, and faith.

- **Three or more planets in Air signs** makes you comfortable with abstract concepts, objectivity, and social connections, but you may lack practicality and emotional sensitivity.

- **Three or more planets in Water** signs means you rely on feelings and intuition, and seek deeper, spiritual understanding, but you may have poor boundaries and difficulty with objective, abstract interactions.

Lack of an Element

Having one or no personal planets in an element is also significant. You will be unfamiliar with the realm of this element, and perceive that you lack these qualities. This will cause you to value these qualities. You'll find them attractive in other people, and you will work hard to develop them yourself. This can lead to overcompensation. If you lack an element in your chart, you may need to realize that you've mastered those skills by now, and they no longer require the same level of effort or attention.

The exception to this is a lack of Fire. If you have one or no planets in Fire signs, it's important that you supplement the element of Fire through daily physical activity but good luck finding the motivation to make it to the gym.

Emphasis of a Modality

Having four or more personal planets in a single modality is significant. This suggests your dominant mode of behavior, and emphasizes the theme of your core false belief.

- **Four or more planets in Cardinal signs** suggests you will initiate action in most things, and that you always look for new challenges; the moment something becomes routine, however, you may lose interest. You're driven to express your identity, to disprove the core false belief, "I'm bad."

- **Four or more planets in Fixed signs** gives you great stamina and endurance; you crave routine, and abhor change, especially if the need to change comes from outside of you. You're driven to prove and defend your self-worth, in reaction to the core false belief, "I'm not enough."

- ◆ **Four or more planets in Mutable signs** suggests flexibility and dexterity, but also a lack of focus. Multitasking is easy, but you often take on too many projects, which scatters your energy. You're driven to adapt and to change in reaction to the core false belief, "I'm incomplete."

The Sun: The Authentic "Big S" Self

The Sun is one of the focal points of this approach to chart interpretation, so everything connected with the Sun is important: the Sun itself, all of the planets on the Sun's Board of Directors, and any planet that aspects the Sun.

When interpreting the Sun, look for repeated themes and patterns. Notice how prominent the Sun is in the chart. It may rule several houses, and have influence on the Board of Directors for many planets. It's also possible for the Sun to rule no houses in the chart (if Leo is intercepted), and to have little or no influence over how the other planets express. In these cases, you must remember that the Sun is the source of the light of the other planets. It may be difficult to know the Sun directly, but as you explore how the other planets in the chart express, you will get a deeper understanding of the authentic "Big S" Self.

The Ascendant: The Persona

The angles in the chart are the doors that connect your inner experiences with the outside world. From an individual perspective, the Ascendant, which is the front door, is the most important. It's how other people see you in one-to-one relationships.

The Ascendant is your persona: it's a mask that you wear. When other people encounter you, they base their expectations on the mask. They assume your appearance reflects your essence. If the mask resembles your authentic Self, this can be supportive. If the mask is radically different, it can create challenges. You may know yourself to be a gentle, loving person, but if you wear a scary gorilla mask, people will react as if you were a monster. If this goes on long enough, you may start to believe them.

Ascendant Blueprint Template Sentences

These blueprint template sentences will help you to explore the Ascendant and its Board of Directors, planets aspecting the Ascendant, and planets in the same sign as the Ascendant.

Ascendant Blueprint Template
Ascendant in [SIGN]
When he/she interacts with the world and other individuals (Ascendant), he/she appears to be [SIGN KEYWORD], [SIGN KEYWORD], and [SIGN KEYWORD] ([SIGN]).

Board of Directors for the Ascendant
[PLANET] in [SIGN] in [HOUSE]
([#] Votes on Ascendant Board of Directors)
[PLANET] Rules [HOUSE(s)]

Other people perceive (Ascendant's Board of Directors) his/her need to [PLANET KEYWORDS] ([PLANET]) in a manner that is [sign keywords] ([SIGN]), WITH [HOUSE KEYWORD] and [HOUSE KEYWORD] ([PLANET] rules [HOUSE]), IN [HOUSE WHERE KEYWORD] ([PLANET] in [HOUSE]).

Outer Planet Aspect to the Ascendant
[OUTER PLANET] in [HOUSE] [ASPECT] Ascendant
There is a [ASPECT KEYWORDS] ([ASPECT]) caused by [OUTER PLANET KEYWORDS] ([OUTER PLANET]) COMING FROM [HOUSE WHERE KEYWORDS] ([OUTER PLANET] in [HOUSE]) and affecting how he/she interacts with the world and appears to other individuals (Ascendant).

Interpreting the Personality

Inner Planet Aspect to the Ascendant
[PLANET] in [HOUSE] (Ruler of [HOUSE(S)]) [ASPECT] Ascendant (Note BOD Connections to Ascendant)

There is a [ASPECT KEYWORDS] ([ASPECT]) caused by [PLANET KEYWORDS] ([PLANET]), specifically involving [HOUSE WHAT KEYWORDS FOR HOUSE(S) RULED BY PLANET] ([PLANET] rules [HOUSE(S)]), **COMING FROM** [HOUSE WHERE KEYWORDS FOR PLANET] ([PLANET] in [HOUSE]) and affecting how he/she interacts with the world and appears to other individuals (Ascendant).

Inner Planet in the Same Sign as the Ascendant
[PLANET] in [SIGN] in [HOUSE]
[PLANET] Rules [HOUSE(s)]

Other people perceive (Ascendant) his/her need to [PLANET KEYWORDS] ([PLANET]) in a manner that is [SIGN/ELEMENT/MODALITY KEYWORDS] ([SIGN/ELEMENT/MODALITY]), **WITH** [HOUSE KEYWORDS] and [HOUSE KEYWORDS] ([PLANET] rules [HOUSE]).

CHAPTER 15
Sally Ride: Personality

On June 18, 1983, **Sally Ride** made history as a member of the crew of the Challenger, when she became the first woman in space. Ride was born on May 26, 1951, at 8:11 A.M., in Los Angeles, California (Figure 19).

In these chapters, I illustrate the process of creating notes, blueprints and sketch sentences. I've included my final interpretation of Sally Ride's chart, which I created based on these notes and sketches, as one of the Bonus Gifts bundled with this book in Appendix B.

Elements and Modalities

Sally Ride's Elements and Modalities are shown in Figure 20.

Notes

Three planets in Air (Sun, Moon, Mars) suggests mental, objective, social emphasis.

Two planets in Earth (Mercury and Saturn) suggests practical, grounded qualities.

One planet in Water suggests she may perceive a lack of emotional and spiritual connections and may overcompensate for this; however, the three planets in Air, including her Moon in Aquarius, are uncomfortable with emotions.

Principles of Practical Natal Astrology

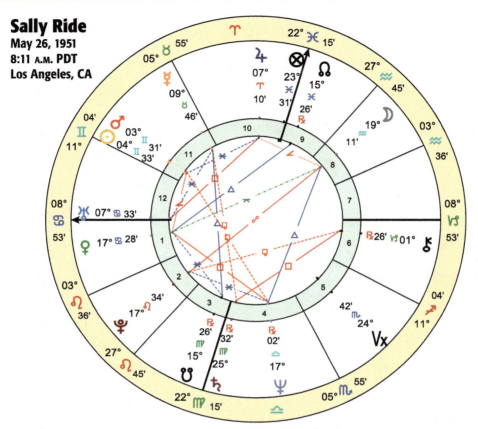

Figure 19: Sally Ride's Natal Chart
Source: Astro-Databank; Rodden Rating: AA, BC/BR in hand.

Sally Ride: Personality

Elements	INNER PLANETS	ANGLES	OUTER PLANETS
FIRE	♃		♇
EARTH	☿ ♄	☋	⚷
AIR	☉ ☽ ♂		♆
WATER	♀	AS MC ⊗ ☊ Vx	♅
Modalities	INNER PLANETS	ANGLES	OUTER PLANETS
CARDINAL	♀ ♃	AS	⚷ ♅ ♆
FIXED	☽ ☿	Vx	♇
MUTABLE	☉ ♂ ♄	MC ⊗ ☊ ☋	

Figure 20: Sally Ride's Elements and Modalities

One planet in Fire suggests she needs to supplement Fire and be physically active on a daily basis. She'll probably enjoy exercising because the Fire planet is Jupiter in Aries.

Ride has a good balance between the modalities: two planets each in Cardinal and Fixed, and three in Mutable.

The main point of interest from Ride's Elements and Modalities is the potential conflict she may have regarding emotions and feelings. She has only one planet in Water, Venus in Cancer. This suggests that Ride may overcompensate for a perceived lack of emotions by working hard to express them. It also suggests that Ride will be attracted to people who express their feelings and form emotional bonds with ease. However, Ride has three planets in Air, including her Moon in Aquarius. Emotions may be attractive, but they're also threatening. She may yearn for authentic emotional connection but feel safer living in her head.

This could end up being an important theme in Ride's chart, or it could be little more than a footnote. It's something to keep in mind while we explore the rest of the chart. If it's important, it will show up again.

The Sun

All of the considerations that apply to Sally Ride's Sun are shown below in Figure 21.

Sun in Gemini in the 11th House
Sun Rules 2nd, 3rd

Ride seeks to express her authentic "Big S" Self (Sun) by being nervous, unpredictable, articulate, and rational (Gemini) **WITH** her money and resources (Sun rules 2nd) and her writing, communication, and familiar environment (Sun rules 3rd). She encounters these needs particularly **IN** her personal aspirations, friendships, and relationships with her peers (Sun in 11th).

Planet	Ruler	Exaltation	Triplicity	Term	Face
☉ ♊	☿ ♉		♄ ♍	☿ ♉	♃ ♈
	5 Votes	4 Votes	3 Votes	2 Votes	1 Vote
Condition	Total Votes	Total Votes	Total Votes	Total Votes	Total Votes
Peregrine	7		3		1
House Place	House Place	House Place	House Place	House Place	House Place
11th	11th		4th	11th	10th
House Rule	House Rule	House Rule	House Rule	House Rule	House Rule
2nd, 3rd	4th, 12th		7th, 8th, 9th	4th, 12th	6th, 10th, 1st (alm)
Dignity Score	Aspect	Aspect	Aspect	Aspect	Aspect
-5p	☿		♄	☿	⚹ ♃
					2a37

⛢ Aspect	♆ Aspect	♇ Aspect	⚷ Aspect	Other Aspect	Other Aspect
⛢	♆	♇	⚷	∠ ♀	☌ ♂
				2a05	1s01
House Place	House Place	House Place	House Place	House Place	House Place
				1st	11th
				House Rule	House Rule
				11th	5th, 10th (alm)

Figure 21: Sally Ride's Sun

Sally Ride: Personality

Notes

Sun rules both 2nd and 3rd houses, connects her money and her environment/communication. She expresses her authentic "Big S" Self through her finances and communication. Perhaps Ride sees money as communication?

Cause comes from 2nd house money or 3rd house environment. Gemini needs things to be fast and flexible. Gemini stick would be focus, stability, routine, limitations, and practicality. Gemini emphasizes communication and connection.

Action is Sun in Gemini. She needs to be clever, skillful, intelligent, social, and adaptable. Making her own way on her own terms is what matters; she's willing to change her identity to make this possible. She doesn't need to be in the spotlight: she's willing to be a part of a team (Sun in 11th) as long as she can pull her own weight.

Effect is in 11th house of acquisition, ambition, teams, and group creativity. Ruler of 2nd (money you have) in 11th (money you make); the Sun is her money (because it rules the 2nd house), so her resources and how she acquires money are expressions of her authentic "Big S" Self. This suggests independence—she needs to be able to make her own way in the world; that's the only way she can express her identity.

Sketch Sentences

Ride's Personal Standards of Integrity (Sun) include objectivity, flexibility, curiosity, and intelligence (Gemini), especially when she manages her money and resources (Sun rules 2nd house). She shares these skills with her friends and teammates (Sun in 11th).

Ride is the happiest and most energized (Sun) when her familiar environment and daily routine (Sun rules 3rd) move at a fast and skillful pace (Gemini); but when things slow down, become too rigid, subjective, and practical (Gemini stick), she finds it difficult to pursue her dreams and ambitions (Sun in 11th).

Ride wants to express her authentic "Big S" Self (Sun) by being versatile, talented, charming, and amusing (Gemini) especially with her money (Sun rules 2nd); however, her friends (Sun in 11th) may not understand that money is an important way that Ride communicates and expresses her identity (Sun rules 2nd and 3rd), and they may experience her as inconstant, thoughtless, duplicitous, and flighty (Gemini).

Board of Directors for the Sun
Mercury in Taurus in the 11th House (7 Votes, Rulership + Term)
Mercury Rules 4th, 12th

To express her authentic "Big S" Self (Sun's Board of Directors), she needs to understand and communicate (Mercury) in a manner that is possessive, sluggish, rugged, and benevolent (Taurus), **WITH** her home environment, family relationships, and private life (Mercury rules 4th) and her personal unconscious, shadow self, and self-sabotage (Mercury rules 12th). She encounters these needs particularly **IN** her personal aspirations, friendships, and relationships with her peers (Mercury in 11th).

Notes

Right away, Mercury in Taurus changes the tone of how the Sun in Gemini expresses. The Taurus influence makes her slower, more methodical, and more practical. It makes her more concerned with the physical world, sensual pleasures, and it could also put more importance on money, although it means she might be less inclined to spend it irresponsibly.

She's far less flexible than you expect from the Sun in Gemini because Mercury is in a Fixed sign and will be stubborn.

Cause comes from the 4th house private, personal life, issues with father and family. Mercury rules 12th house, so Mercury in Taurus is the vehicle of her self-sabotage. Mercury's influence gets her into trouble, creates hidden enemies, adversity, and sorrows.

Action is Mercury in Taurus: the fastest planet in the slowest sign. Taurus is grounded, slow, practical, and kinesthetic. Learning and communicating take a lot of effort, but once she learns something, it's in her bones.

Effect is in the 11th house. This further emphasizes Ride's need for social connections, shared creativity, teamwork, and friendships. She needs other people in her life to help her achieve her dreams and ambitions.

Sketch Sentences

Ride's ability to embody her authentic "Big S" Self (Sun's Board of Directors) depends on her ability to maintain a stable, secure, grounded, steady (Taurus) understanding of her "little r" reality (Mercury). However, Ride may not be conscious (Mercury rules 12th) that her unoriginal, inflexible, grasping, and materialistic (Taurus) perceptions (Mercury) create resentment (Mercury rules 12th) among her peers and teammates (Mercury in 11th).

Ride's health and happiness (Sun's Board of Directors) are enhanced when communication and connection (Mercury) in her family relationships and personal life (Mercury rules 4th) are efficient, placid, tender, and calm (Taurus). Her friends and peers (Mercury in 11th) are like family to her (Mercury rules 4th), and these relationships support and define her authentic Self (Sun's Board of Directors).

Saturn in Virgo in the 4th House (3 Votes, Triplicity)
Saturn Rules 7th, 8th, 9th

To express her authentic "Big S" Self (Sun's Board of Directors), she needs to accept responsibility and establish boundaries and limits (Saturn) in a manner that is critical, shrewd, healing, and perceptive (Virgo), **WITH** her marriage, partnerships, and one-to-one relationships (Saturn rules 7th), her debts, shared resources, and involvement with other people's values and opinions (Saturn rules 8th), and her beliefs, higher education, religion, and foreign experiences (Saturn rules 9th). She encounters these needs particularly **IN** her home environment, family relationships, and private life (Saturn in 4th).

Notes

Yet another indication that Ride's Sun in Gemini takes life more seriously than you expect. Saturn in Virgo is ruled by Mercury in Taurus (on the Sun's Board of Directors), so not only is Saturn more stubborn and less flexible, but it also defers to Mercury in Taurus and supports whatever Mercury wants.

Saturn has 3 votes on the Sun's Board of Directors so Saturn's influence is strong enough to consider. However, Saturn's real influence in Ride's chart is on the Moon's Board of Directors.

Note some potential themes about information, education, and ideas: The Sun rules the 3rd house of communication and early education; Mercury rules the Sun and Saturn; Saturn rules the 9th house of higher education, beliefs, and philosophies. Mercury connects the 3rd and 9th houses in Ride's authentic Self.

Cause comes from partnership, relationships, and shared resources (Saturn rules 7th and 8th), and from beliefs, higher education, philosophy, or foreign experiences (Saturn rules 9th). Saturn in Virgo needs precise, specific, detailed boundaries. Virgo stick is imprecise, vague, impractical, sloppy, or subjective.

Action is Saturn in Virgo. Saturn in Virgo cares about the details of the rules: it enforces boundaries, holds other people accountable for mistakes.

Effect is in the 4th house. When there's a boundary violation, Ride will address it in a private, personal manner. Saturn seems to have a strong association with her father because it's in the 4th house, conjunct the IC, and ruled by Mercury, the planet that represents her father. Ride may have judgments (Saturn) about perfectionism (Virgo). Her "inner parent" is apt to be extremely critical, which may create challenges in her family relationships and personal life (4th house). This facet of Ride's personality is not visible to anyone but her family.

Sketch Sentences

Ride's Personal Standards of Integrity (Sun's Board of Directors) require her to maintain very precise, specific, exacting (Virgo) boundaries (Saturn) in her marriage (Saturn rules 7th). When her partner doesn't meet her expectations, Ride may become very critical (Virgo), but she will keep her judgments private (Saturn in 4th).

Ride's authentic Self (Sun's Board of Directors) relies on her ability to understand the precise nuances (Virgo) of the law (Saturn) especially with regard to her beliefs, philosophies, and higher education (Saturn rules 9th). This particular behavior pattern has strong connections to her father, and it expresses in her private affairs (Saturn in 4th).

Jupiter in Aries in the 10th House (1 Vote, Face)
Jupiter Rules 6th, 10th, Almuten 1st

To express her authentic "Big S" Self (Sun's Board of Directors), she needs to grow, expand, and experience faith (Jupiter) in a manner that is aggressive, impulsive, dynamic, and pioneering (Aries), **WITH** her job, service, and workplace relationships (Jupiter rules 6th), her career, life path, and public reputation (Jupiter rules 10th), and her personality, self-image, and pursuit of happiness (Jupiter almuten 1st). She encounters these needs particularly **IN** her career, life path, and public reputation (Jupiter in 10th).

With only one vote on the Sun's Board of Directors, it would be easy to ignore Jupiter; however, Jupiter does make an aspect to the Sun, which means it may be worth considering here.

Notes

Jupiter represents both her job (rules 6th) and her career (rules 10th), but also ties them with her identity and self-image (almuten 1st).

Cause involves her public image, career, and reputation (10th house), her job (6th house) and her personality and self-image (almuten 1st house). Aries is direct, single-minded, impulsive, and initiating. The biggest stick for Aries is accommodating (or noticing) other people.

Action is Jupiter in Aries. Big expansion of her identity. She has faith in herself, faith that she can accomplish her public and professional goals.

Effect is in the 10th house so she takes public action. She's not afraid to blow her own horn and make sure people recognize her as an individual.

Aspects to the Sun
Jupiter in the 10th House (Jupiter Rules 6th, 10th, Almuten 1st)
Sextile Sun in 11th House (Sun Rules 2nd, 3rd) [2a37][1]
Jupiter has 1 Vote (Face) on Sun's Board of Directors
Sun has 7 Votes (Exaltation, Term) on Jupiter's Board of Directors

There is an opportunity for support (sextile) **BETWEEN** her need to grow, expand, and experience faith (Jupiter) **WITH** her job, service, and workplace relationships (Jupiter rules 6th), her career, life path, and public reputation (Jupiter rules 10th), and her personality, self-image, and pursuit of happiness (Jupiter almuten 1st), **COMING FROM** her career, life path, and public reputation (Jupiter in 10th) **AND** her need to express her authentic "Big S" Self (Sun) **WITH** her money and resources (Sun rules 2nd) and her writing, communication, and familiar environment (Sun rules 3rd) **IN** her personal aspirations, friendships, and relationships with her peers (Sun in 11th).

---

[1] The numbers in brackets after an aspect show the orb of the aspect, and the letter (a or s), indicates if the aspect is applying or separating. In this example, the sextile has an orb of 2°37, and it's an applying aspect.

Sally Ride: Personality

Notes

The sextile from Jupiter in Aries to the Sun further emphasizes Ride's independent streak. The 11th house emphasis means she's willing to work in groups and teams, but Jupiter in Aries ruling the 10th and occupying the 10th means she will need to be recognized for her individual contribution to the team effort. By embracing this need to be seen (10th house) and expand her identity (Jupiter in Aries), Ride can support (sextile) her experience of her authentic Self (Sun). Even though the sextile is a relatively weak aspect, the fact that the Sun has 7 votes on Jupiter's Board of Directors strengthens this connection.

Ascendant

The considerations that apply to Sally Ride's Ascendant are shown in Figure 22.

Ascendant in Cancer

When she interacts with the world and other individuals (Ascendant), she appears to be obsessed, mothering, loyal, and receptive (Cancer).

Notes

Ride's appearance and expectations of the world embody the Cardinal Water energy of Cancer. This is somewhat at odds with her Sun in Gemini's need to be objective. Other people perceive a need to initiate emotional connections (Cancer Ascendant), but so far, this doesn't seem to connect with Ride's authentic Self.

Ascendant's Board of Directors

Moon in Aquarius in the 8th House (5 Votes, Rulership)
Moon Rules 1st House

Other people perceive (Ascendant) her need to feel safe and experience feelings and emotions (Moon) in a manner that is defiant, rebellious, liberal, and communicative (Aquarius), **WITH** her personality, self-image, and pursuit of happiness (Moon rules 1st), **IN** her shared resources, debts, and other people's values and opinions (Moon in 8th).

Notes

The Moon in Aquarius is very uncomfortable with emotions. This, at least, is more in sync with her Sun in Gemini, which is also in an Air sign, and also prefers to operate on the surface, in the mental, social, and intellectual realms.

The fact that Ride is uncomfortable with deep emotions, and prefers abstract, objective emotional concepts (Moon in Aquarius) is a big part of how she appears to others (Ascendant's Board of Directors) and also a part of her self-image (Moon rules 1st house).

Ride's Moon is in her 8th house, so she looks for safety (Moon) in other people's values and opinions and through shared resources. This is another

Planet	Ruler	Exaltation	Triplicity	Term	Face
AS ♋	☽ ♒	♃ ♈	♂ ♊	♃ ♈	♀ ♋
	5 Votes	4 Votes	3 Votes	2 Votes	1 Vote
	Total Votes	Total Votes	Total Votes	Total Votes	Total Votes
	5	6	3		1
	House Place	House Place	House Place	House Place	House Place
	8th	10th	11th	10th	1st
	House Rule	House Rule	House Rule	House Rule	House Rule
	1st	6th, 10th, 1st (alm)	5th, 10th (alm)	6th, 10th, 1st (alm)	11th
	Aspect	Aspect	Aspect	Aspect	Aspect
	☽	□ ♃	♂	♃	♂ ♀
		1s42			8a34

♅ Aspect	♆ Aspect	♇ Aspect	⚷ Aspect	Other Aspect	Other Aspect
♂ ♅	♆	♇	⚷	✶ ☿	
1s20				0a53	
House Place	House Place	House Place	House Place	House Place	House Place
1st				11th	
				House Rule	House Rule
				4th, 12th	

Figure 22: Sally Ride's Ascendant

indication of how much Ride needs connections with other people. The Moon in Aquarius needs to be free, liberal, and sometimes rebellious to feel safe, but at the same time, because the Moon expresses in the 8th house, Ride may set out to shock people by defying their values and opinions of her. Ride may need to believe that she doesn't care what other people think; however, this means she needs to be aware of what other people think, so she can prove that she doesn't care.

That the Moon rules her Ascendant means that other people are aware of Ride's Safety Needs. When Ride feels unsafe, it will be obvious.

Jupiter in Aries in the 10th House (6 Votes, Exaltation + Term)
Jupiter Rules 6th, 10th, Almuten 1st

Other people perceive (Ascendant) her need to grow, expand, and experience faith (Jupiter) in a manner that is combative, overconfident, enterprising, and confident (Aries) **WITH** her job, service, and workplace relationships (Jupiter rules 6th), her career, life path, and public reputation (Jupiter rules 10th), and her personality, self-image, and pursuit of happiness (Jupiter almuten 1st), **IN** her career, life path, and public reputation (Jupiter in 10th).

Notes

Jupiter is the almuten of Ride's Ascendant and 1st house, so Jupiter is the most dominant and visible part of Ride's personality. Jupiter in Aries has faith in her individual identity. Ride knows she can realize her dreams. Because Jupiter rules and occupies her 10th, Ride's ambition and drive for public recognition and accomplishment are obvious. She may appear competitive, aggressive, and arrogant—admirable traits in a man of her generation, but hardly encouraged in a woman growing up in the 1950s and 1960s.

Ride has dominant personality traits that may put her at odds with cultural and social norms. As mentioned earlier, her Moon is in the 8th house, so other people's values and opinions play a key role in her ability to feel safe. It may be worth considering this later in the context of Ride's Safety Needs.

Mars in Gemini in the 11th House (3 Votes, Triplicity)
Mars Rules 5th, Almuten 10th

Other people perceive (Ascendant) her need to take action and expend energy (Mars) in a manner that is two-faced, gossiping, objective, and versatile (Gemini) **WITH** her personal creativity, pursuit of entertainment, tolerance for risk, and children (Mars rules 5th), and her career, life path, and public reputation (Mars almuten 10th), **IN** her personal aspirations, friendships, and relationships with her peers (Mars in 11th).

Notes

Mars brings another iteration of the 10th and 11th houses to Ride's personality, and introduces the 5th house of risk and creativity.

Ride's Mars is **combust** the Sun, which makes it invisible[2]. This also means that Ride's "little s" self and her "Big S" Self have the exact same Board of Directors. Who she thinks she is (Mars) is virtually identical to who she truly is (Sun). This suggests a strong identity and a strong personality.

Aspects to the Ascendant
Uranus in the 12th House Conjunct Ascendant [1s20]

There is a unity of purpose (conjunction) **CAUSED BY** disruptions and unexpected events (Uranus) **COMING FROM** her personal unconscious, shadow self, self-sabotage and hidden enemies (Uranus in 12th) and affecting how she interacts with the world and appears to other individuals (Ascendant).

Notes

We've already seen indications that Ride may struggle with emotional connection. The lack of planets in Water in her chart suggests Ride isn't familiar with operating on the emotional plane, and she may feel the need to compensate for this perceived lack. The emphasis of planets in Air means she's the most comfortable on the mental, social, intellectual, and objective planes. Her Moon in Aquarius is extremely uncomfortable with

---

[2] This is a "pinch of spice." See Chapter 25.

deep, personal emotional connections. Cancer rising means Ride goes out into the world hoping to form emotional bonds, although forming these bonds is difficult.

Having Uranus rising (just over 1° above the Ascendant) is a game changer with regard to Ride's outer personality. Because Uranus is random and disruptive, Ride expects that she won't be able to sustain emotional bonds in her relationships. Because Uranus is in her 12th house, she is unconscious of her own role in these patterns.

The generation born with Uranus in Cancer disrupted the role of women in society. This generation initiated the revolution of Women's Liberation that helped women to break out of the rigid, limited roles available to them. Uranus in Cancer on Ride's Ascendant means that when people meet Ride face to face, Uranus is standing in her front door, and they're confronted with the energy of social change. Uranus is an outer planet, and this energy isn't part of Ride's essence. However, every person Ride encounters projects his or her issues with Uranus in Cancer on Ride. Ride is told time and again that she is different, unusual, radical, odd, or simply doesn't fit the mold.

Mercury in the 11th House Sextile Ascendant [0a53]
Mercury Rules 4th, 12th

There is an opportunity for support (sextile) **CAUSED BY** her need to understand and communicate (Mercury) **WITH** her home environment, family relationships, and private life (Mercury rules 4th) and her personal unconscious, shadow self, and self-sabotage (Mercury rules 12th), **COMING FROM** her personal ambitions, friendships, and relationships with peers (Mercury in 11th), and affecting how she interacts with the world and appears to other individuals (Ascendant).

Notes

Mercury sextile the Ascendant suggests that Ride's perceptions, intelligence, and need to understand show up in her outward personality. What's significant about this is that as the ruler of the 12th, Mercury is the vehicle of Ride's self-sabotage. We've noted that Mercury in Taurus is quite stubborn and intractable in its perceptions. Others may notice this in Ride, and it may create resentment and hidden enemies.

Jupiter in the 10th House Square Ascendant [1s42]
Jupiter Rules 6th, 10th, Almuten 1st

There is friction, tension, stress and conflict (square) **CAUSED BY** her need to grow, expand, and experience faith (Jupiter) **WITH** her job, service, and workplace relationships (Jupiter rules 6th), her career, life path, and public reputation (Jupiter rules 10th), and her personality, self-image, and pursuit of happiness (Jupiter almuten 1st), **COMING FROM** her career, life path, and public reputation (Jupiter in 10th), and affecting how she interacts with the world and appears to other individuals (Ascendant).

Notes

Jupiter continues to emerge as an important planet in Ride's chart. The square to her Ascendant means that her Jupiter in Aries drive to express and expand her personal and professional identity (Jupiter almuten 1st, rules 10th) is at odds with how she appears to others.

Given the social context of a woman born in America in 1951 with a strong identity and difficulty in making emotional bonds, combined with the astrological context of a woman with Cancer rising and Uranus in Cancer on the Ascendant, I think this reinforces the idea that Ride challenges other people's expectations of who she should be, especially based on her appearance. She does not fit in the mold of the docile 1950s housewife or the good little girl. She is clearly her own person.

Sally Ride: Personality

Planets in the Ascendant
Venus in Cancer in the 1st House
Venus Rules 11th House
(Venus has 1 Vote for Face on Ascendant Board of Directors)

Other people perceive (Ascendant) her need to experience love and appreciation and align with her Core Values (Venus) in a manner that is codependent, reserved, sensitive, and caring (Cancer), **WITH** her personal ambitions, friendships, and relationships with her peers (Venus rules 11th) **IN** her personality, self-image, and pursuit of happiness (Venus in 1st).

Notes

Venus in Cancer in the 1st house emphasizes the importance of authentic emotional connection for Ride. The behavior patterns that result from Ride's difficulties in meeting these needs are a key part of her personality.

Cause comes from her 11th house, which means she needs to be loved, appreciated, and validated by her friends, teammates, and peers. These are the relationships that matter the most to Ride. Venus in Cancer needs to initiate authentic emotional connections that provide nurturing and support. The biggest stick for Cancer is rigid boundaries that deny emotional connections.

Action is Venus in Cancer. Ride equates love with emotional bonds and nurturing. Note that this will be modified a bit because Venus in Cancer reports to Ride's Moon in Aquarius.

Effect happens in her 1st house, and suggests that Ride's self-image and happiness may depend on how validated she feels by her friends.

Summary of Ride's Personality
Notes

The biggest theme so far has to do with Ride's need for authentic emotional connection, and her difficulties in operating on the subjective, emotional plane. This shows up in multiple contexts. First, the lack of planets in Water and the emphasis of planets in Air show that Ride prefers to operate in the mental and intellectual realms, but that she may work hard to overcome her self-perceived lack of emotions. Next, while her Sun is in Gemini, her Ascendant is in Cancer. She appears to be emotionally available and nurturing, but her authentic Self finds sustained emotional bonds to be uncomfortable. And finally, while her Ascendant is in Cancer, her Moon, the ruler of her Ascendant, is in Aquarius, which further supports the idea that she finds deep emotional bonds to be uncomfortable.

The other big theme relates to Ride's personality and how it fits in with the expectations of society. Ride has a very strong, focused sense of self. The conjunction between her Sun (authentic, "Big S" Self) and Mars (ego/body and "little s" self) suggests that Ride really is who she thinks she is, and although both the Sun and Mars are in Gemini, a Mutable sign, they're ruled by Mercury in Taurus, a Fixed sign, which creates a solid, stubborn foundation. Other people will not influence Ride's beliefs about her identity. She also has a powerful drive for professional recognition, thanks to Jupiter in Aries, and this feeds into her identity and personality.

The challenge for Ride is that the more she embraces her authentic Self, the more she risks losing the emotional connections she seeks. Because Ride has Cancer rising, other people expect that she will conform to the accepted roles of women; however, with her strong identity, and Uranus conjunct the Ascendant, Ride will always challenge these expectations. This may create patterns of disruption and rejection when she seeks emotional connection and support in one-to-one relationships. This may drive Ride's need to be seen as an individual through her career and public reputation.

CHAPTER 16

Interpreting Relationship Needs

This chapter provides a brief introduction to human relationships and how to view them through the lens of the natal chart. You must always remember the **Universal Law of Relationships**, which states, "Your partners in relationship are mirrors: they reflect your own issues back to you."

It's *never* about the other person.

This applies to every relationship in your life, including your romantic relationships, your professional relationships, your family relationships, and even to the relationships with people you meet on the street. Relationships help you to recognize and acknowledge the parts of yourself that you have yet to accept or integrate. You project these issues onto others and experience the lessons as if they were coming from outside of you. But don't worry: your partners in relationship are doing the same thing to you.

Relationship Needs

In the 1920s, Abraham Maslow revolutionized the entire field of psychology (which, at the time, had been around only for about 30 years). Up to this point, psychology assumed that people were screwed up. The main objectives of psychology were to (a) figure out exactly how the patient is screwed up, (b) figure out how to blame it all on the patient's mother, and (c) figure out how to get the patient to pay for a full hour but get only 50 minutes of therapy.

Maslow took a radically different approach: he assumed people were fundamentally healthy. This raised some significant questions. What motivates the behavior of healthy people? And how do you get healthy people to pay for an hour but give them only 50 minutes of therapy?

Maslow proposed that humans are motivated by unmet needs; however, some needs are more important than others. Until you've met your "lower" needs, you won't be motivated to meet your "higher" needs. Maslow summed up his approach in a hierarchy of needs that's usually illustrated as a pyramid (Figure 23).

The lowest, most important needs are your **Physiological Needs**. These include everything you need to survive, such as air, food, water, sleep, and shelter. You will do anything to meet these needs, and I do mean *anything*. If these needs aren't being met, the body's instinctive, animal nature takes over. It's not pretty.

Next are your **Safety Needs**. These include everything you think you need to survive. You *could* survive without most of these things, although probably

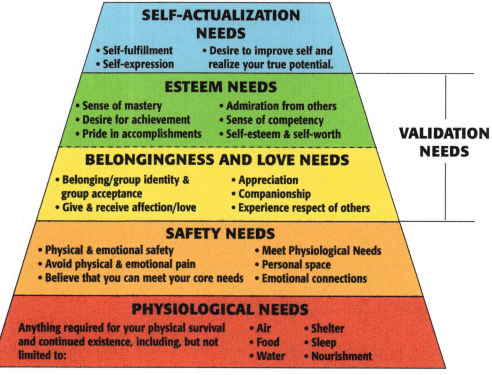

Figure 23: Maslow's Pyramid of Needs

Interpreting Relationship Needs

not without whining about it. To meet your Safety Needs, you have to believe that your Physiological Needs will be met in the future. Your Safety Needs motivate you to avoid physical and emotional pain.

The next two categories in Maslow's system, **Belongingness and Love Needs** and **Esteem Needs**, deal with being loved and appreciated in relationships. Belongingness and Love Needs involve being loved and appreciated by other people, and Esteem Needs involve loving and appreciating yourself. Since they're essentially the same thing, I've combined them into a single category, **Validation Needs**.

The highest needs in Maslow's pyramid are **Self-Actualization Needs**. These fulfill your potential as an individual.

Need Bank Accounts

In my book, *The Relationship Handbook: How to Understand and Improve Every Relationship in Your Life* (Serendipity Press, 2004), I introduced a more dynamic model to understand human needs. Rather than working with Maslow's pyramid, I suggested a series of four Need Bank Accounts (Figure 24). Mars is in charge of your Physiological Need Account, the Moon is in charge of your Safety Need Account, Venus is in charge of your Validation Need Account, and the Sun is in charge of your Self-Actualization Need Account.

Each of your Need Bank Accounts has a minimum required balance, and you are responsible for maintaining that balance on your own. When you maintain the minimum balance in a Need Bank Account, you experience that need as being met. Although you're motivated to maintain the minimum balance in all of your Need Bank Accounts, you focus on meeting your lower needs first. This model shows what Maslow's pyramid doesn't: each of your Need Bank Accounts is independent. If the balance in your Safety Need Account is below the minimum level, you can still receive deposits in your Validation Need Account and your Self-Actualization Need Account. However, you won't notice those deposits until you've met your Safety Needs.

In the context of human relationships, what matters are Safety Needs and Validation Needs because these are the only needs that can be met by other people. Once you're out of diapers (on either end of the timeline), you take care of your own Physiological Needs, and by definition, you're the only one who can meet your Self-Actualization Needs. As long as you feel safe and validated, you will be happy in any relationship. If either your Safety Needs or your Validation Needs are not being met, you will experience problems in the relationship. Regardless of what a relationship problem appears to be about, it's really about a lack of safety and/or validation.

Checklists and Watchlists

Each of your Need Bank Accounts includes a set of **checklists** and a set of **watchlists**. The checklists are unconscious expectations of experiences that will make a deposit in the account, and the watchlists are unconscious expectations of experiences that will make a withdrawal from the account. Saturn is the banker and monitors all of your Need Bank Accounts. When you meet a condition on a checklist, Saturn authorizes a deposit in the appropriate account, and when you meet a condition on a watchlist, Saturn makes a withdrawal from the account.

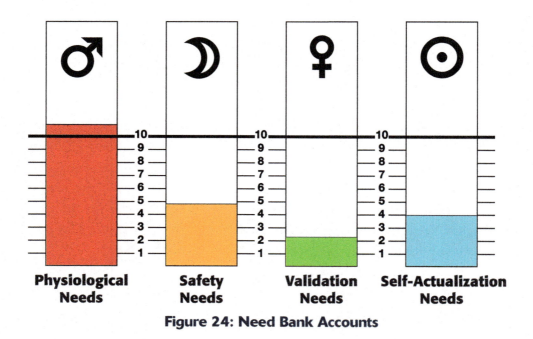

Figure 24: Need Bank Accounts

Interpreting Relationship Needs

Wants are different from needs. When you want something, it shows up as an item on a checklist. You believe that when you get the thing that you want, it will make a deposit in one or more of your Need Bank Accounts. But it's your needs that matter. You can meet all of your needs without ever getting what you want.

You speak a particular language to meet your Safety Needs, and a particular language to meet your Validation Needs. The element and sign of the Moon tells you the language you speak to meet your Safety Needs, and the element and sign of Venus tells you the language you speak to meet your Validation Needs. The carrot qualities of the sign relate to items on your checklists (things you want), and the stick qualities relate to items on your watchlists (things you don't want).

The Moon: Safety Needs

Safety Needs are extremely important, so everything associated with the Moon is significant, including the Moon itself, all of the planets on the Moon's Board of Directors, and any planets that aspect the Moon.

Once you learn how to maintain the minimum balance in your Safety Need Account, you'll find you can meet the rest of your needs with ease. The moment the balance in your Safety Need Account drops below the minimum level, you dive into Victim Consciousness. Mars, your "little s" self takes over. Any action you take uses *force*, not *power*. This means that no matter what you do, it will be counter-productive. You think you're making yourself feel more safe—and in the short term, you might be. But in the long term, the balance in your Safety Need Account will be even lower than when you started.

You spend most of your life in Victim Consciousness, feeling unsafe, and locked in a perpetual state of fight-or-flight. You call this stress.

When you feel unsafe, you create **attachments**. Attachments are the source of all suffering, and they keep you anchored in Victim Consciousness. Like everything else in Victim Consciousness, creating the attachment seemed like a good idea at the time. For example, you might receive a big bonus at work, which makes a big deposit in your checking account. It also makes a big deposit in your Safety Need Account. Your ego takes notice. The ego thinks, "Having money makes me feel safe, so having more money will make me feel more safe," and it creates an attachment.

Under normal circumstances, you receive deposits in your Safety Need Account from a variety of sources. As soon as you create an attachment, you begin to focus only on the specific channel of that attachment. This means you no longer receive deposits from the other sources. The balance in your Safety Need Account goes down instead of up. Your ego panics. You need an immediate influx of safety, so your ego directs even more attention to the attachment, because that's a reliable source of safety. This strengthens the attachment, which makes you feel even less safe (Figure 25).

The only way to feel safe is to let go of your attachments. However, you can't let go of your attachments until you feel safe. To solve this problem, you have to address it from a higher level of consciousness. Meeting your Safety Needs is quite simple, because the truth is that you're almost always safe. To experience this, you just need to become aware of the present moment. When you step into Victim Consciousness, you either dwell in the past, or worry about the future. Right here, right now, in this moment, the truth is that you are safe.

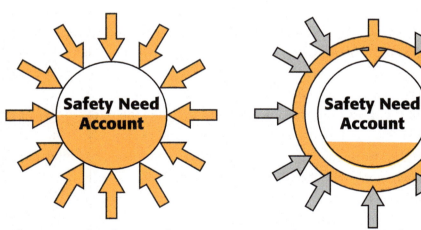

When you are free from attachments, you can receive deposits in your Safety Need Account from many different and unexpected channels.

When you create attachments, you can receive deposits in your Safety Need Account only from the channel of your attachment.

Figure 25: Attachments

I've created a powerful Spiritual Practice to help you meet your Safety Needs: the **Present Moment Awareness Safety Meditation**. You can learn about it in Appendix A.

Safety Checklist Languages

When you create your notes for the Moon, identify the main Safety Checklist Language by considering the element of the Moon's sign.

- If you have a **Fire Safety Checklist**, you need to take action and do something to meet your Safety Needs. If you're not able to take action, you will feel threatened.

- If you have an **Earth Safety Checklist**, you need to understand the rules and boundaries to feel safe, and often look to the physical and material plane for safety. When things get too abstract, you will feel threatened.

- If you have an **Air Safety Checklist**, you need to have an objective, intellectual understanding to feel safe. You find the subjective, irrational emotional realm to be threatening.

- If you have a **Water Safety Checklist**, you need emotional connections to feel safe, although you also need healthy boundaries to contain those connections. If the boundaries are too rigid, or things get too abstract, you will feel threatened.

Consider the carrot and stick for the specific sign of the Moon for more information about specific items on the Safety Checklist and the Safety Watchlist.

Venus: Validation Needs

Validation Needs are important, although they're not as important as Safety Needs. When you consider Venus, you will include Venus, any planets on

Venus' Board of Directors that influences three or more votes, and all significant aspects to Venus.

Validation Checklist Languages

When you create your notes for Venus, identify the main Validation Checklist Language by considering the element of Venus' sign.

- If you have a **Fire Validation Checklist**, you experience love and appreciation by doing things with your partners. Words, emotions, or tangible expressions of affection won't make a difference to you.

- If you have an **Earth Validation Checklist**, you experience love and appreciation through the physical and material realms. You need tangible expressions of affection (e.g., gifts); words will never be enough for you.

- If you have an **Air Validation Checklist**, you experience love and appreciation through words. Words matter more than feelings, actions, or gifts.

- If you have a **Water Validation Checklist**, you experience love and appreciation through the emotional and spiritual realms. Words won't be enough to meet your Validation Needs, and you will also feel rejected if your partners put too much emphasis on the tangible, material aspects of the relationship.

Consider the carrot and stick for the specific sign of Venus for more information about specific items on the Validation Checklist and the Validation Watchlist.

Can You Meet Your Needs?

Even though other people can make deposits in your Safety and Validation Need Accounts, you're responsible for maintaining the minimum balance in these accounts on your own. It's always possible to meet your needs, but it's not always easy. Aspects from Saturn or the outer planets to the Moon or Venus can create patterns that make it difficult to receive deposits in your Safety or Validation Need Accounts. You also have to consider the relationship between the Moon and Venus: the things that make you feel safe may not be the things that make you feel validated.

These behavior patterns will be addressed in detail in *Principles of Practical Relationship Astrology: Talented Astrologer Training Book 2*. For now, some general guidelines will suffice.

Safe Doesn't Feel Safe

On a fundamental level, safe is the same thing as familiar. Most people spend their lives living in Victim Consciousness, which objectively lacks safety. But the longer you experience fear without actually dying, the less impact it has. In time, you learn to live with it and you stop feeling unsafe. But not feeling unsafe isn't the same as being safe.

As long as you live in Victim Consciousness, you experience the physical, emotional, and spiritual cost of perpetual stress. You may not notice it because you've gotten used to it. You recognize that many of your behavior patterns are destructive, and you attempt to change them. Change is always threatening, even when the change is positive. When you encounter a situation that is objectively safe, it will feel threatening because it's unfamiliar. Safe doesn't feel safe to you.

You will have to approach change with care and awareness, and monitor the balance in your Safety Need Account. Once you become familiar with how it feels to be objectively safe, it will no longer be threatening to you.

Saturn Aspects: Checklists From Hell

The Moon is in charge of your Safety Need Account, and Venus is in charge of your Validation Need Account, but Saturn is the banker. Saturn monitors your checklists and watchlists, and authorizes deposits and withdrawals from these accounts. Saturn is also in charge of the items on the checklists and watchlists (and if you think that's a conflict of interest, you're right). When Saturn makes an aspect to the Moon or Venus, the requirements on your Safety or Validation Checklists can become so unreasonable that it's virtually impossible to receive deposits in these accounts. Not all aspects from Saturn are difficult. Trines or sextiles from Saturn to the Moon or Venus can be supportive; but conjunctions, squares, oppositions, and quincunxes from Saturn can create challenges.

Uranus Aspects: Rejection, Abandonment, and Unreliability

Uranus is disruptive, chaotic, and unpredictable. When it makes an aspect to the Moon or Venus, it creates experiences (and expectations) that those needs won't be met reliably or consistently. You project these inner issues on the outside world, and they show up as patterns of rejection, abandonment, and unreliability in your relationships.

Neptune Aspects: Bad Boundaries and Hopeless Romantics

Neptune dissolves boundaries and creates patterns that involve fantasy, deception, and disillusionment. Aspects between the Moon and Neptune relate to bad emotional, energetic, and spiritual boundaries. These are subtle, yet extremely dangerous. The fog of Neptune can make you unaware that the balance in your Safety Need Account is critically low. Aspects between Venus and Neptune are the most obvious in the context of romantic relationships, where they can create unrealistic fantasies of romantic bliss.

Pluto Aspects: Power, Control, and Manipulation

Any Pluto aspect, even an aspect between Pluto and Venus that affects your ability to feel validated, creates an underlying safety issue. Pluto aspects make you aware of the power dynamic in every situation. All reactions to Pluto, whether they involve taking control or being controlled, come from Victim Consciousness, and use force, not power.

Chiron Aspects: Core Wounds

Aspects from Chiron to the Moon or Venus mean that when you try to meet your Safety or Validation Needs, you will encounter your core wound. This wound will show up in your relationships until you are ready to transcend it.

Connections Between the Moon and Venus

If you're lucky, the language you speak to meet your Safety Needs is compatible with the language you speak to meet your Validation Needs, but this is not always the case. You've already evaluated how easy (or difficult) it will be to meet your Safety and Validation Needs independently; now you need to consider if you can meet them at the same time. The relationship between the signs of the Moon and Venus gives you the general context.

✦ If the languages are compatible (i.e., signs that are conjunct, sextile, or trine each other), it's easy to meet both needs at the same time: a deposit in one account is likely to make a deposit in the other account as well.

✦ If the languages are not compatible (i.e., signs that are square, opposite, quincunx, or semi-sextile each other), **but the Moon and Venus don't form an aspect**, the two accounts are independent of each other; you can receive a deposit in one account without having any effect on the other account.

✦ If the languages are not compatible **and the Moon and Venus aspect each other by square, opposition, or quincunx**, many of the items on your Safety Checklist will also be on your Validation Watchlist, and vice versa. A deposit in your Safety Need Account makes a withdrawal from your Validation Need Account, and a deposit in your Validation Need Account makes a withdrawal from your Safety Need Account. If you have this kind of configuration, you must learn to monitor the balance in both accounts so that neither account drops below the critical level.

You also need to consider if the Moon and Venus receive each other in any way. If the Moon has influence on Venus' Board of Directors, or Venus has influence on the Moon's Board of Directors, it complicates the connections between your Safety and Validation Needs. If the Moon is in Taurus, Libra, or Pisces, signs where Venus has at least 4 votes on the Moon's Board of Directors, you may need to feel validated (Venus) before you can feel safe (Moon). If

Venus is in Cancer or Taurus, signs where the Moon has at least 4 votes on Venus' Board of Directors, you will need to feel safe (Moon) before you can feel validated (Venus).

CHAPTER 17

Sally Ride: Relationship Needs

The Moon: Safety Needs

The considerations that apply to Sally Ride's Moon are shown in Figure 26.

Planet	Ruler	Exaltation	Triplicity	Term	Face
☽ ♒	♄ ♍		♄ ♍	♀ ♋	☿ ♉
	5 Votes	4 Votes	3 Votes	2 Votes	1 Vote
Condition	Total Votes	Total Votes	Total Votes	Total Votes	Total Votes
Peregrine	8			2	1
House Place	House Place	House Place	House Place	House Place	House Place
8th	4th		4th	1st	11th
House Rule	House Rule	House Rule	House Rule	House Rule	House Rule
1st	7th, 8th, 9th		7th, 8th, 9th	11th	4th, 12th
Dignity Score	Aspect	Aspect	Aspect	Aspect	Aspect
-5p	♄		♄	⚻ ♀	☿
				1s43	

⛢ Aspect	♆ Aspect	♇ Aspect	⚷ Aspect	Other Aspect	Other Aspect
⛢	△ ♆	☍ ♇	⚷	∠ ♃	
	2s09	1s36		2a59	
House Place	House Place	House Place	House Place	House Place	House Place
	4th	2nd		10th	
				House Rule	House Rule
				6th, 10th, 1st (alm)	

Figure 26: Sally Ride's Moon

Moon in Aquarius in the 8th House
Moon Rules 1st House

To feel safe (Moon), she needs to feel contradictory, unconventional, loyal, and social (Aquarius) **WITH** her personality, self-image, and pursuit of happiness (Moon rules 1st). She encounters these needs particularly **IN** her debts, shared resources, and other people's values and opinions (Moon in 8th).

Notes

Moon in Aquarius has an Air Safety Checklist. Ride will look for safety in the abstract, objective, social, and mental realms. She needs to have an intellectual understanding of a situation to feel safe. Words are extremely important to her. She can talk herself into feeling safe, but she can also talk herself out of feeling safe. Emotions will be unfamiliar and uncomfortable. She will feel threatened when she has to dive beneath the surface and deal with subjective and irrational experiences.

Aquarius is a Fixed Air sign, so the Moon in Aquarius needs social stability to feel safe. She needs to be accepted by the group to feel safe. Change is very threatening (Fixed). She needs consistency and routine. The Moon in Aquarius has a love of humanity, but difficulty loving individual humans. Emotional intimacy is a challenge and requires trust. Self-worth and self-esteem (Fixed) are tied to her safety; when she feels unsafe, she will question her worth.

Cause is deeply personal because the Moon rules the 1st house. Triggers can involve her physical appearance, self-image, health and vitality, desires, or personal interests. It's even more personal because Aquarius is a Fixed sign, and planets in Fixed signs take everything personally. The biggest stick for Aquarius is deep emotions, because these call attention to the individual, rather than to the group. Anything that restricts Ride's personal (1st house) freedom (Aquarius) will immediately trigger her Moon and make her feel unsafe.

Sally Ride: Relationship Needs

Action is the Moon in Aquarius. It's all about restoring the balance in her Safety Need Account by being objective, rational, logical, and abstract (Aquarius). The lower-consciousness qualities of Aquarius can be superficial, overzealous, unrealistic, and contradictory. On some level, she needs the approval and acceptance of the group to feel safe. The group is defined by certain ideals and beliefs. When Ride feels especially unsafe, she may become stubborn and inflexible as she insists that other people agree with the beliefs that define the group.

Effect is in the 8th house, which involves other individuals. Normally, the 8th house relates to shared resources, debts, and financial obligations, but given the context of the Moon in Aquarius, other people's values and opinions may become the focus. Planets in Aquarius think only in terms of the group, not in terms of the individual members of the group. Ride looks for confirmation of her group membership in the 8th house. She needs to know what other people think (often of her, because the cause is the 1st house) so she can know that she is a part of the right group. Ambiguity will be threatening. She either needs to know that other people agree with her (and are members of her group) or that they disagree with her (and are not a part of her group).

Sketch Sentences

Ride is attached (Moon) to the personal and individual (Moon rules 1st) rights and freedom that she is entitled to as a member of the group (Aquarius), and if her freedom is limited or restricted in any way (Aquarius stick), it will make her feel unsafe (Moon). She will look to other individual members of the group for support, expecting that they will share her opinion and values (Moon in 8th) and be outraged at the injustice (Aquarius).

Ride will feel unsafe (Moon) if she believes that she, personally (Moon rules 1st), is being treated unfairly (Aquarius stick), either because her rights and freedoms are being restricted or because she is being singled out for special attention over the other members of the group. In an attempt to restore the balance in her Safety Need Account (Moon), she may spend money on something that everyone can enjoy (Moon in 8th house).

Ride seeks to nurture and protect other people (Moon) by sharing her personal (Moon rules 1st) ideas, thoughts, and beliefs (Aquarius/Air), thereby inviting her partner to join her as a member of the group (Aquarius). She does this by looking for common ground with regard to her partner's values and opinions (Moon in 8th house).

Ride may spend money and even go into debt (Moon in 8th house) supporting utopian, idealistic, radical, and unconventional (Aquarius) causes and organizations to make up for a lack of safety (Moon) caused by low self-esteem and an uncertain sense of identity (Moon rules 1st).

Board of Directors for the Moon
Saturn in Virgo in the 4th House (8 Votes, Rulership, Triplicity)
Saturn Rules 7th, 8th, 9th

To feel safe (Moon's Board of Directors), she needs to accept responsibility and establish boundaries and limits (Saturn) in a manner that is critical, shrewd, healing, and perceptive (Virgo), **WITH** her marriage, partnerships, and one-to-one relationships (Saturn rules 7th), her debts, shared resources, and involvement with other people's values and opinions (Saturn rules 8th), and her beliefs, higher education, religion, and foreign experiences (Saturn rules 9th). She encounters these needs particularly **IN** her home environment, family relationships, and private life (Saturn in 4th).

Notes

The cause, action, and effect of Saturn in Virgo have already been explored because Saturn has 3 votes on the Board of Directors of Ride's Sun. The sketch sentences will consider Saturn in the context of Ride's Moon and her Safety Needs.

Sally Ride: Relationship Needs

Because Mercury rules Saturn in Virgo, Saturn will always vote in alignment with Mercury.

Sketch Sentences

To feel safe (Moon's Board of Directors), Ride needs to maintain precise, specific, practical, detailed (Virgo) boundaries (Saturn) in her one-to-one relationships (Saturn rules 7th), especially with regard to shared resources and common property in the relationship (Saturn rules 8th). When these boundaries are not respected, it will cause Ride to feel unsafe (Moon's Board of Directors), and she will respond by taking on more responsibility (Saturn) for improving and perfecting (Virgo) her private life (Saturn in 4th).

To feel safe (Moon's Board of Directors), the laws and principles (Saturn) that Ride learns in her higher education (Saturn rules 9th) need to have precise, reliable, and coherent (Virgo) application in her personal life and home environment (Saturn in 4th).

Ride may have an attachment (Moon's Board of Directors) where she expects authority figures in general (Saturn) and her teachers in particular (Saturn rules 9th) to be intelligent, flexible, perceptive, and discriminating (Virgo), and if they fall short of these ideals, it will cause Ride to feel unsafe (Moon's Board of Directors). This may cause her to become critical (Virgo) of her relationship with her father (Saturn in 4th), who may be the source of these expectations.

To feel safe, (Moon's Board of Directors), Ride needs other people to be dependable, exacting, and precise (Virgo) in their values and opinions (Saturn rules 8th). When other people are vague, imprecise, and unfocused (Virgo stick) about their opinions, it causes Ride to feel unsafe (Moon's Board of Directors). She may become introverted, critical, and sarcastic (Virgo), but she will generally keep her judgments (Saturn) private (Saturn in 4th).

Venus in Cancer in the 1ˢᵗ House (2 Votes, Term)
Venus Rules 11ᵗʰ House
Venus controls 11 votes on the Moon's Board of Directors

To feel safe (Moon's Board of Directors), she needs to experience love and appreciation and align with her Core Values (Venus) in a manner that is codependent, reserved, sensitive, and caring (Cancer) **WITH** her personal ambitions, friendships, and relationships with peers (Venus rules 11ᵗʰ). She encounters these needs particularly **IN** her personality, self-image, and pursuit of happiness (Venus in 1ˢᵗ).

Notes

Venus is in Ride's 1ˢᵗ house, and has already been explored, briefly, in the context of her personality. We'll consider Venus in detail in the context of Ride's Validation Needs in the next section. At first glance, Venus has little influence on the Moon's Board of Directors, with only 2 votes for Term. But in fact, Venus influences the entire Board of Directors.

Saturn in Virgo has the most votes on the Moon's Board of Directors, with a total of 8 votes, 5 for Rulership and 3 for Triplicity. However, Saturn in Virgo reports directly to Mercury, who has 1 vote for Face. This means that Mercury influences a total of 9 votes on the Moon's Board of Directors, because Mercury will tell Saturn how to vote. But Mercury in Taurus reports directly to Venus, which means that Venus tells Mercury how to vote (and in turn, Mercury tells Saturn how to vote), giving Venus influence over all 11 votes on the Moon's Board of Directors.

To complicate things even more, Venus in Cancer reports directly to the Moon. This is tricky, because the Moon has no direct influence on its own Board of Directors. We'll address this wrinkle when exploring the relationship between the Moon and Venus.

The most important consideration here is that Ride is likely to have an attachment to meeting her Validation Needs. For her to feel safe (Moon's Board of Directors), she needs to feel validated (Venus). A deposit in her

Sally Ride: Relationship Needs

Validation Need Account will make a deposit in her Safety Need Account, but if Ride creates an attachment to being validated, it will drain both accounts, making it difficult for her to feel either validated or safe.

Mercury in Taurus in the 11th House (1 Vote, Term)
Mercury Rules 4th, 12th
Mercury controls 9 votes on Moon's Board of Directors

To feel safe (Moon's Board of Directors), she needs to understand and communicate (Mercury) in a manner that is possessive, sluggish, rugged, and benevolent (Taurus), **WITH** her home environment, family relationships, and private life (Mercury rules 4th) and her personal unconscious, shadow self, and self-sabotage (Mercury rules 12th). She encounters these needs particularly **IN** her personal aspirations, friendships, and relationships with her peers (Mercury in 11th).

Notes

The cause, action, and effect of Mercury in Taurus have already been explored because Mercury rules Ride's Sun in Gemini. The sketch sentences will consider Mercury in the context of Ride's Moon and her Safety Needs.

Because Mercury rules Saturn in Virgo, Saturn will always vote in alignment with Mercury. In this case, however, Venus rules Mercury in Taurus, so Mercury will always vote in alignment with Venus.

Sketch Sentences

To feel safe (Moon's Board of Directors), Ride has an unconscious need (Mercury rules 12th) to experience loyal, stable, practical, and comfortable (Taurus) communication (Mercury) among her friends, peers, and teammates (Mercury in 11th house). She may not be conscious (Mercury rules 12th) that many of the disruptions in her friendships are the result of her being inflexible, materialistic, self-indulgent, and tiresome (Taurus) in her communication (Mercury).

To feel safe (Moon's Board of Directors), Ride needs to understand (Mercury) that her personal and private life and family relationships (Mercury rules 4th) are tranquil, peaceful, generous, and enduring (Taurus). When she experiences disruptions in her personal life, it will make her feel unsafe (Moon's Board of Directors), and she may try to restore a sense of safety by communicating (Mercury) with her friends and teammates (Mercury in 11th house).

Aspects to the Moon
Neptune in the 4th Trine Moon in the 8th (Moon Rules 1st) [2s09]

There is an easy, constant, effortless flow of energy (trine) caused by glamor, deception, illusion, and poor boundaries (Neptune) **COMING FROM** her home environment, family relationships, and private life (Neptune in 4th) and affecting her debts, shared resources, and involvement with other people's values and opinions (Moon in 8th). This could cause her to feel unsafe (Moon), particularly **WITH** her personality, self-image, and pursuit of happiness (Moon rules 1st).

Notes

Neptune trine the Moon can be a challenging aspect, especially when clear, precise boundaries are important for safety (as they are for Ride). The bad boundaries and unrealistic expectations (Neptune) come from her 4th house, so they originate with her family relationships and her relationship with her father, and they directly impact how Ride perceives and experiences other people's values and opinions (Moon in 8th). This aspect makes Ride more sensitive to what other people think, especially members of her 4th house family, and this can have a negative influence on Ride's self-image and self-esteem (Moon rules 1st), which may cause her to feel unsafe. Because Ride is inclined to view her friends and teammates (11th house) as family (Mercury, ruler of the 4th, is in the 11th house), Ride may also experience these patterns and issues in her relationships with her friends.

With regard to the shared resources dynamic of the 8th house, Neptune trine the Moon in the 8th suggests comfort with a communal style of living where there may be little respect for personal ownership. This may be familiar to Ride, as it comes from her 4th house family of origin, but it will drain her Safety Need Account nonetheless. Saturn in Virgo, ruling the 8th house, and ruling Ride's Moon, needs clear distinctions between *yours*, *mine*, and *ours*. The trine from Neptune to the Moon in the 8th means that Ride isn't used to having these boundaries defined or respected.

Pluto in the 2nd Opposite Moon in the 8th (Moon Rules 1st) [1s36]

There is a need for balance and compromise (opposition) caused by issues of power, control, and manipulation (Pluto) **COMING FROM** her money and resources (Pluto in 2nd) and affecting her debts, shared resources, and involvement with other people's values and opinions (Moon in 8th). This could cause her to feel unsafe (Moon), particularly **WITH** her personality, self-image, and pursuit of happiness (Moon rules 1st).

Notes

This aspect suggests issues of power, control, and manipulation that specifically involve money and financial resources. We've already noted that Ride needs to be self-reliant with her resources, because her Sun rules the 2nd house. The fact that Pluto is in her 2nd, opposing her Moon in the 8th, suggests that Ride views money as power. If she has to share her money and resources with a partner in the 8th house, it will make her feel unsafe, because it means that she's giving up her power and autonomy in the relationship. She will be sensitive to the dynamics of money and power in every situation.

Jupiter in the 10th (Jupiter Rules 6th, 10th, Almuten 1st)
Semi-Square Moon in the 8th (Moon Rules 1st) [2a59]

There is a minor internal tension or friction (semi-square) **BETWEEN** her need to grow, expand, and experience faith (Jupiter) **WITH** her job, service, and workplace relationships (Jupiter rules 6th), her career, life path, and public reputation (Jupiter rules 10th), and her personality, self-image, and pursuit of happiness (Jupiter almuten 1st), **COMING FROM** her career, life path, and public reputation (Jupiter in 10th), and her need to feel safe (Moon) **WITH** her personality, self-image, and pursuit of happiness (Moon rules 1st). This could cause her to feel unsafe **IN** her debts, shared resources, and other people's values and opinions (Moon in 8th).

Notes

Jupiter does not have any influence over the Moon (nor does the Moon have any influence over Jupiter) so this aspect is not significant. It's only worth considering because Jupiter is such an important planet in Ride's chart, and although the Moon rules the 1st house, Jupiter is the almuten of the 1st house. Ride's Jupiter in Aries is all about being recognized for her individual accomplishments. The semi-square emphasizes that Ride's Moon in Aquarius is not comfortable with being in the spotlight. When Ride receives attention for her personal and professional achievements, it may make her feel unsafe.

Summary of Sally Ride's Safety Needs

Notes

Ride has some interesting contradictions and challenges with regard to her Safety Needs. These echo the bigger themes in her personality involving the conflict between needing to remain objective and creating emotional connections. Ride's Moon in Aquarius is uncomfortable with personal emotions, and needs clear, precise boundaries (Saturn in Virgo), particularly in her one-to-one relationships (Saturn rules 7th and 8th). Because Saturn in Virgo reports to Mercury in Taurus, she can be rigid and inflexible about her judgments and expectations. When someone crosses a boundary or doesn't meet an expectation, she will feel unsafe. At the same time, she looks for safety in her 8th house shared resources and other people's values and opinions. The trine from Neptune to her Moon means that as much as she needs clear, precise, practical boundaries to feel safe, she will have a hard time creating and sustaining them.

The bigger issue with regard to Ride's safety, and the one that specifically echoes the theme of head vs. heart, involves Venus in Cancer's influence over the Moon's Board of Directors, but we'll consider this later.

Sally Ride: Relationship Needs

Venus: Validation Needs

The considerations that apply to Sally Ride's Venus are shown in Figure 27.

Venus in Cancer in the 1st House
Venus Rules 11th House

To feel validated (Venus), she needs to be inhibited, vulnerable, understanding, and imaginative (Cancer) **WITH** her personal ambitions, friendships, and relationships with peers (Venus rules 11th). She encounters these needs particularly **IN** her personality, self-image, and pursuit of happiness (Venus in 1st).

Notes

Venus in Cancer has a Water Validation Checklist. Ride needs emotional connections to experience and express love and appreciation. She feels

Planet	Ruler	Exaltation	Triplicity	Term	Face
♀ ♋	☽ ♒	♃ ♈	♂ ♊	☿ ♉	☿ ♉
	5 Votes	4 Votes	3 Votes	2 Votes	1 Vote
Condition	Total Votes	Total Votes	Total Votes	Total Votes	Total Votes
Peregrine	5	4	3	3	
House Place	House Place	House Place	House Place	House Place	House Place
1st	8th	10th	11th	11th	11th
House Rule	House Rule	House Rule	House Rule	House Rule	House Rule
11th	1st	6th, 10th, 1st (alm)	5th, 10th (alm)	4th, 12th	4th, 12th
Dignity Score	Aspect	Aspect	Aspect	Aspect	Aspect
-5p	⚹ ☽	♃	∠ ♂	☿	☿
	1s43		1a03		

♅ Aspect	♆ Aspect	♇ Aspect	⚷ Aspect	Other Aspect	Other Aspect
♅	□ ♆	♇	⚷	∠ ☉	
	0s26 [PARTILE]			2a05	
House Place	House Place	House Place	House Place	House Place	House Place
	4th			11th	
				House Rule	House Rule
				2nd, 3rd	

Figure 27: Sally Ride's Venus

loved and appreciated when other people initiate emotional bonds with her, and she feels rejected when people refuse to allow, initiate, or sustain emotional ties. Ride's idea of validation includes a distinct mothering and nurturing component (Cancer). A heart connection is essential for Ride to feel validated.

Cause comes from her 11th house relationships with friends, peers, and teammates (Venus rules 11th). These are the people from whom she seeks validation, love, and appreciation. We've already noted how important these relationships are for Ride; that Venus rules the 11th house emphasizes this even more. She also wants to be recognized and appreciated for her dreams, aspirations, and acquisitions (11th house). The carrot for Cancer is emotional connection, and in this context, Ride will feel especially validated when her friends initiate the connections. The stick for Cancer is distance, strong boundaries, and self-reliance.

Action is Venus in Cancer. If Ride isn't feeling love or appreciation, she will initiate (Cardinal) an emotional connection (Water/Cancer) to meet her Validation Needs. If she acts from lower levels of consciousness, she may become clingy, dependent, pushy, manipulative, and mothering. This will not serve her in the long term, because if she has to extract or coerce love and appreciation, it will not make her feel validated.

Effect is in the 1st house. Ride's self-image and self-esteem are tied to the balance of her Validation Need Account. She will feel good about herself when her Validation Needs are being met, and if she's not feeling loved and appreciated by other people, she will take it personally.

Sketch Sentences

It's very important that Ride experience her relationships with her friends (Venus rules 11th) as being gentle, loving, kind, and secure (Cancer). If her friends shut down the emotional connections they share with her or become distant (Cancer stick), Ride will feel invalidated (Venus), which will have a negative effect on her happiness and self-image (Venus in 1st).

Ride wants to be validated, appreciated, and recognized (Venus) by her teammates and peers (Venus rules 11th) for how warm, maternal, and intuitive (Cancer) her dreams and ambitions are (Venus rules 11th). Ride's self-image and personality (Venus in 1st) depend on this approval from her friends (Venus rules 11th).

When Ride expresses affection and appreciation (Venus), she hopes to be attentive, compassionate, and tender (Cancer), especially with her teammates and peers (Venus rules 11th). At times, however, she may appear to be clinging, mothering, and possessive (Cancer), because she believes that the emotional bonds she shares with her teammates (Venus in Cancer rules 11th) are the source of her happiness (Venus in 1st).

Board of Directors for Venus

Moon in Aquarius in the 8th House (5 Votes, Rulership)
Moon Rules 1st House

She wants to be validated (Venus' Board of Directors) **FOR** her ability to feel safe, and express her feelings and emotions (Moon) in a manner that is reforming, irritable, egalitarian, and humanistic (Aquarius), **WITH** her personality, self-image, and pursuit of happiness (Moon rules 1st). She encounters these needs particularly **IN** her debts, shared resources, and other people's values and opinions (Moon in 8th).

Notes

The cause, action, and effect of the Moon have already been explored.

The conflict between her Moon (safety) and Venus (validation) becomes even more pronounced. The kinds of deep emotional connections that Venus in Cancer needs to feel loved and appreciated are very uncomfortable for the Moon in Aquarius. Safety Needs are more important than Validation Needs in the general scheme of things, and because the Moon rules Ride's Venus, meeting her Safety Needs is a requirement to meet her Validation Needs.

Ride begins by needing distance and objectivity to feel safe, but once she feels safe, she will pursue the emotional bonds that meet her Validation Needs. The deposits in her Venus in Cancer Validation Need Account make withdrawals from her Moon in Aquarius Safety Need Account. When her Safety Need account drops below the minimum level, she will no longer notice the balance in her Validation Need Account. Her Moon will take over, she'll retreat to the objective, intellectual, social realm, and refill her Safety Need Account (which will drain her Validation Need Account). When the balance in her Safety Need Account reaches the minimum level, she will turn her attention to meeting her Validation Needs, which will start the cycle over again.

Jupiter in Aries in the 10th House (4 Votes, Exaltation)
Jupiter Rules 6th, 10th, Almuten 1st

She wants to be validated (Venus' Board of Directors) **FOR** her ability to grow, expand, and experience faith (Jupiter) in a manner that is forceful, reckless, self-aware, and truthful (Aries), **WITH** her job, service, and workplace relationships (Jupiter rules 6th), her career, life path, and public reputation (Jupiter rules 10th), and her personality, self-image, and pursuit of happiness (Jupiter almuten 1st). She encounters these needs particularly **IN** her career, life path, and public reputation (Jupiter in 10th).

Notes

Jupiter's significant influence on Venus' Board of Directors demonstrates how Ride looks for validation for her professional accomplishments, and that both the accomplishments and the validation are extremely personal (Jupiter almuten 1st, Venus in 1st).

For easy reference, the cause, action, and effect of Jupiter have been copied from Jupiter's previous appearance on the Sun's Board of Directors.

Sally Ride: Relationship Needs

Cause involves her public image, career, and reputation (10th house), her job (6th house) and her personality and self-image (almuten 1st house). Aries is direct, single-minded, impulsive, and initiating. The biggest stick for Aries is accommodating (or noticing) other people. Ride cares the most about being validated for her public, professional accomplishments and her service and hard work (Jupiter rules 10th, 6th). She takes this personal validation personally (Jupiter almuten 1st), which creates distance between how other people see her and who she truly is. Jupiter in Aries keeps the spotlight on Ride's professional, public life and away from her personal, private life.

Action is Jupiter in Aries: big expansion of her identity. She has faith in herself, faith that she can accomplish her public and professional goals.

Effect is in the 10th house so she takes public action. She's not afraid to blow her own horn and make sure people recognize her as an individual. Again, the distinction between public recognition for her professional accomplishments (and her ability to boost her self-image and self-esteem as a result of these accomplishments because Jupiter is the almuten of her 1st) and attention for her personal, private life is important. Ride's Moon in Aquarius needs strict boundaries that keep her personal life private.

Sketch Sentences

She wants to be validated for (Venus' Board of Directors) her big, expansive (Jupiter) individual and personal (Aries) professional accomplishments (Jupiter rules 10th). However, while she derives some personal satisfaction from this attention (Jupiter almuten 1st, Venus in 1st), it's very important that the public attention she receives (Jupiter in 10th) is limited to her professional accomplishments (Jupiter rules 10th, 6th), and does not focus exclusively on her personality (Jupiter almuten 1st).

She wants to be validated (Venus' Board of Directors) for the faith and optimism (Jupiter) she has in her identity (Jupiter almuten 1ˢᵗ), her work ethic (Jupiter rules 6ᵗʰ), and her professional ambition (Jupiter rules 10ᵗʰ), and especially for her ability to blaze trails, initiate, explore, inspire, and lead (Aries) in a public and visible manner (Jupiter in 10ᵗʰ).

Mars in Gemini in the 11th House (3 Votes, Triplicity)
Mars Rules 5th, Almuten 10th
Mars influences a total of 7 votes

She wants to be validated (Venus' Board of Directors) **FOR** her ability to take action and expend energy (Mars) in a manner that is two-faced, gossiping, objective, and versatile (Gemini) **WITH** her personal creativity, pursuit of entertainment, tolerance for risk, and children (Mars rules 5ᵗʰ), and her career, life path, and public reputation (Mars almuten 10ᵗʰ). She encounters these needs particularly **IN** her personal ambition, friendships, and relationships with peers (Mars in 11ᵗʰ).

Notes

Mars is combust the Sun, which means it's invisible.[1] Ride's Sun and Mars have the same Board of Directors, and as noted in the Personality section, this means that her "Big S" Self and her "little s" self have the same motivation and share a unity of purpose. This gives her tremendous focus because she really is who she thinks she is.

In the context of Ride's Validation Needs, this suggests that Ride has a deep need to be seen, loved, and appreciated for her individual identity (Sun) and how she takes action to express it (Mars). While Mars rules the 5ᵗʰ house and brings an element of personal creativity to the mix, that Mars is the almuten of the 10ᵗʰ house and the ruler of Jupiter in Aries (ruler of the 10ᵗʰ house, occupies the 10ᵗʰ house) reinforces the distinction that Ride wants to be validated for her public and professional identity.

---

[1] See Chapter 25.

Sally Ride: Relationship Needs

Mercury in Taurus in the 11th House (3 Votes, Term + Face)
Mercury Rules 4th, 12th
Mercury influences a total of 10 votes

She wants to be validated (Venus' Board of Directors) **FOR** her ability to understand and communicate (Mercury) in a manner that is possessive, sluggish, rugged, and benevolent (Taurus), **WITH** her home environment, family relationships, and private life (Mercury rules 4th) and her personal unconscious, shadow self, and self-sabotage (Mercury rules 12th). She encounters these needs particularly **IN** her personal aspirations, friendships, and relationships with her peers (Mercury in 11th).

Notes

Mercury influences the most votes on Venus' Board of Directors. In addition to its 3 votes for Term and Face, Mercury controls all of the votes influenced by Mars in Gemini, which include Mars' 3 votes for Triplicity, and the 4 votes from Jupiter in Aries.

The cause, action, and effect for Mercury have already been explored in the context of Ride's Sun.

Mercury is shaping up to be an extremely important planet in Ride's chart. Not only is Mercury the ruler of her Sun, but Mercury also has the most influence over Ride's Moon and Venus. The influence over the Moon and Venus is indirect, but it does represent substantial common ground between Ride's Safety Needs and Validation Needs (not to mention her authentic "Big S" Self). We'll explore this shortly.

Aspects to Venus
Neptune in the 4th Square
Venus in the 11th (Venus Rules 1st) [0s26, PARTILE]

There is friction, tension, stress, and conflict (square) caused by dissolving boundaries, fantasy, glamor, and illusion (Neptune) **COMING FROM** her home environment, family relationships, and private life (Neptune in 4th) and affecting her personal ambitions, friendships, and relationships with her peers (Venus in 11th). This could cause her to feel invalidated (Venus), particularly **WITH** her personality, self-image, and pursuit of happiness (Venus rules 1st).

Notes

Neptune square Venus often shows up as patterns of disillusionment and disappointment in relationships. Ride projects unrealistic expectations, illusions, and fantasies (Neptune) on her partners in relationship, which make it difficult for her to see her partners as they truly are. We've already seen how important Ride's 11th house relationships are to her, and noted more than once that she is likely to view her friends, peers, and teammates as her family. This family of choice may be more important to Ride than her family of origin, and she may try to create the experiences of intimacy, love, and appreciation in her friendships that she associated with her family relationships.

This is where the Neptune square Venus aspect may cause difficulties for her. Ride views her friends, peers, and teammates as her family. Neptune dissolves the boundaries, and Venus in Cancer needs mothering, supportive, protective (e.g., familial) emotional bonds. Ride expects that her friends will appreciate these connections and reciprocate the family dynamic, which sets her up for disappointment. When her friends put up appropriate boundaries, Ride will feel rejected, and take it personally because Venus is in her 1st house. She will believe there's something wrong (or fundamentally unlovable) about who she is.

Sally Ride: Relationship Needs

Mars in the 11th (Rules 5th, Almuten 10th) Semi-Square
Venus in the 11th (Venus rules 1st) [1a03]
Mars has 3 votes on Venus' Board of Directors (Triplicity)

There is a minor internal tension or friction (semi-square) **BETWEEN** her need to take action and expend energy (Mars) **WITH** her personal creativity, pursuit of entertainment, tolerance for risk, and children (Mars rules 5th), and her career, life path, and public reputation (Mars almuten 10th), **COMING FROM** her personal ambitions, friendships, and relationships with her peers (Mars in 11th) and her need to feel validated (Venus) **WITH** her personality, self-image, and pursuit of happiness (Venus rules 1st). This could cause her to feel invalidated **IN** her personal ambitions, friendships, and relationships with her peers (Venus in 11th).

Notes

This is a minor aspect that suggests a conflict between Ride's need to express her identity and her desire to maintain the approval and validation of her friends. On balance, Ride's need for self-expression is much stronger than her need for approval, so she will generally choose to be true to herself, and suffer the consequences if this doesn't meet with the approval of her peers.

Summary of Relationship Needs: Connection Between Moon and Venus

Moon in the 8th House (Rules 1st) Quincunx
Venus in the 1st (Rules 11th) [1s43]
Moon has 5 votes on Venus' Board of Directors;
Venus has 2 votes on Moon's Board of Directors

There is a fundamental incompatibility (quincunx) **BETWEEN** her need to feel safe (Moon) **WITH** her personality, self-image, and pursuit of happiness (Moon rules 1st), **AND** her need to feel validated (Venus) **WITH** her personal ambitions, friendships, and relationships with her peers (Venus rules 11th). This could cause her to feel unsafe **IN** her debts, shared resources, and involvement with other people's values and opinions (Moon in 8th) and invalidated **IN** her personality, self-image, and pursuit of happiness (Venus in 1st).

Notes

As I walk you through the complex dynamic between Ride's Moon and Venus, keep in mind that I'm demonstrating very advanced relationship interpretation skills. These will be covered in *Principles of Practical Relationship Astrology: Talented Astrologer Training Book 2*.

> The theme we noticed while exploring Ride's personality, where there's a conflict between her need to be objective and intellectual and her need to experience emotional connections, shows up once again when considering the relationship between Ride's Moon and Venus.
>
> Let's begin by considering that Ride's Moon and Venus are in incompatible signs. Aquarius and Cancer are averse; they have nothing in common by element, modality, or polarity. This means that Ride speaks a completely different language to meet her Safety Needs than she does to meet her Validation Needs. The items on her Safety Checklist have nothing in common with the items on her Validation Checklist. This is not unusual, and on its own it doesn't present a challenge. If there were no other factors interfering with her ability to meet her needs, Ride could manage her Safety and Validation Needs independently of each other.
>
> Ride's chart isn't so simple. Her Moon and Venus are quincunx each other with an orb of less than 2°. This forges a connection between her Safety Checklist and her Validation Checklist. They still have no common ground, but now, a deposit in her Safety Need Account makes a withdrawal from her Validation Need Account, and vice versa. Often, when someone has the Moon quincunx Venus, he or she will choose one need over the other; however, this isn't a long-term solution.
>
> Ride doesn't have this option because her Moon and Venus receive each other. The Moon in Aquarius rules Venus in Cancer, and even though Venus in Cancer has only 2 votes on the Moon's Board of Directors, it influences *all* of the votes.

Sally Ride: Relationship Needs

To feel safe, Ride has to feel validated, because Venus runs the Moon's Board of Directors, and to feel validated, Ride has to feel safe, because the Moon rules Venus. However, what makes her feel safe has no common ground with what makes her feel validated, and every time she receives a deposit in one need account, it makes a withdrawal from the other.

Neptune aspects both the Moon and Venus, which makes it difficult for Ride to get a handle on this dynamic. Ride has experienced this her entire life, and she's learned to cope with it. The lack of safety will be familiar, and objective safety—and appropriate boundaries—will feel threatening. Safe will not feel safe to Ride.

Mercury is the only common ground between Ride's Moon and Venus. Mercury has only 1 vote on the Moon's Board of Directors but it influences 9 votes (because Saturn in Virgo reports directly to Mercury in Taurus). Mercury has 3 votes on Venus' Board of Directors (Term and Face), but influences 10 votes. Mercury is the loophole. Ride would rely on Mercury to work around the conflicting programs. When Mercury is happy, it makes simultaneous deposits in her Safety and Validation Need Accounts.

Mercury links not only the Moon and Venus, but also the Sun and Mars. This suggests that Ride's best option is to stay true to herself. When she embodies and expresses her identity (both the authentic "Big S" Self and her ego/body "little s" self), she will have the best chance at feeling both safe and validated.

CHAPTER 18
Interpreting Relationship Wants

What you *need* to be happy in any relationship is safety and validation. What you *want* in relationship and the qualities you find attractive in other people don't always align with what you need to feel safe and validated. When you analyze relationship wants and the **Marriage Blueprint**, consider how well they support your ability to feel safe and validated in the relationship.

Remember that other people can meet your needs only to the degree that you can meet your own needs. If you have difficulty feeling safe or validated on your own, you can't expect your partner to meet these needs for you.

The Descendant and the Vertex

The sign of the Descendant shows the qualities you find attractive on a conscious level. The sign of the **Vertex** shows the qualities you find attractive on an unconscious level.

Begin with the Descendant. Consider how well a partner who embodies those qualities would meet your Safety Needs, and how well that partner would meet your Validation Needs. Then do the same with the Vertex. The signs of the Moon and Venus represent the languages you speak to meet your Safety and Validation Needs. How well would someone speaking the language of your Descendant or Vertex meet your Safety and Validation Needs, if they speak their language and you listen in yours?

The Marriage Blueprint

Your perceptions and experience of your parents' relationship form the basis of your Marriage Blueprint. You use this blueprint as a template when you create any romantic relationship. But there's no need to panic. You won't necessarily duplicate the appearance of your parents' relationship, but you will recreate the floor plan of it.

A **relationship blueprint** establishes the underlying structure and shape of a relationship. It's like the blueprint of a house. It defines the amount of space, the number of rooms, and where the walls are, but it's up to you to furnish and decorate. Relationship blueprints are powerful as long as they operate in your unconscious. The moment you become aware of the expectations that shape your relationships, you can change them.

A relationship blueprint works if it provides you with enough space for you to meet your Safety and Validation Needs in the relationship. You can gain some insight into the essence of the Marriage Blueprint and your perceptions of your parents' relationship by considering the dynamic between the ruler of the 4th house (father) and the ruler of the 10th house (mother).

First, consider the angular connection between the two planets. If they're in compatible signs, or form a harmonious aspect such as a trine, sextile, or conjunction, your parents' relationship appeared stable and supportive to you. If the planets are square or opposite each other, this suggests conflict and tension. And if they are quincunx or semi-sextile each other, it suggests a lack of connection or common ground.

Next, you can evaluate the relative condition of each planet. This is one of the rare instances when you will incorporate the two-dimensional approach to dignity and debility in the context of a natal chart interpretation. How do the planets compare in Essential Dignity? If they're evenly matched, either equally strong or equally weak, this suggests balance in the relationship. If one planet is more dignified than the other, it might suggests an imbalance of power. Consider any Board of Directors connections between the planets. This also reveals the dynamic of power in the relationship. If one parent has significant influence on the Board of Directors of the other parent, you may have an expectation of control in your romantic relationships. See Chapter 25 for details of how to evaluate the dignity and debility of a planet.

Finally, consider the houses each planet occupies and rules. They reveal your expectations of the responsibilities of each partner in the relationship. For example, if the ruler of the 10th is in the 2nd, you perceived your mother as being responsible for managing the money. If you take on that role in your romantic relationships, you'll expect to be in charge of the finances; if your partner takes on that role, you'll expect your partner to take responsibility for the financial aspects of your relationship. These expectations are unconscious, and they may or may not support your ability to feel safe and validated in the relationship. You have to become conscious of your expectations before you can change them.

Friend, Lover, or Spouse?

Over the course of a romantic partnership, the relationship may fall in one of three different houses: 11th house (friendship), 5th house (casual romantic relationship), or 7th house (marriage). When a relationship changes houses, it also changes blueprints, and this is significant. Friendships have the fewest expectations. A 5th house romantic relationship comes with more expectations—both conscious and unconscious—but you still have the flexibility to create your own rules. But the moment you say, "I do," or even move in together, the relationship moves to the 7th house, and the Marriage Blueprint takes effect.

When you consider the relationship houses, you look for connections between the houses and the house rulers. Look for aspects between the house rulers, **emplacement** (for example, if the ruler of the 7th house is in the 11th house), and Board of Directors connections.

Aspects Between House Rulers

If the rulers of two houses aspect each other by conjunction, sextile, or trine, it's easy to move a relationship between these two houses. If the aspect is between the ruler of the 11th (friend) and either the ruler of the 5th (lover) or the ruler of the 7th (spouse), you can stay friends with your former partners, and may become romantically involved with someone you first know as a friend. If the aspect is between the ruler of the 5th and the ruler of the 7th, a casual romantic relationship can easily turn into something serious.

If the rulers of two houses aspect each other by opposition or square, you will have a difficult time moving a relationship between the two houses. If the aspects involve the ruler of the 11th house, when the romantic relationship ends, so will the friendship. If the aspect is between the ruler of the 5th and the ruler of the 7th, casual relationships stay casual and will not evolve into something serious. If you want a 7th house relationship, you have to set that intention for the relationship from the very beginning. A semi-square or sesquisquare between the house rulers suggests minor challenges moving between the houses.

If the rulers of two houses are quincunx each other, it suggests aversion and separation. You would never move someone from one house to the other because you keep those parts of your life as far apart as possible. If the aspect involves the ruler of the 11th house, your friends rarely spend time with your 5th house romantic partners or your 7th house spouse. A quincunx between the ruler of the 5th and the ruler of the 7th often indicates a clear preference for one type of relationship: you either play the field, or you marry your high-school sweetheart. And if you decide to have an affair, you'll have the good sense to make sure that your spouse and your side dish never cross paths.

Emplacement

Aspects between house rulers flow in two directions, but a connection by emplacement flows in only one direction. The house the planet occupies is where the relationship ends up. If the ruler of the 11th is in the 5th, a friendship can become a "friends with benefits" situation; if the ruler of the 11th is in the 7th, you may be lucky enough to marry your best friend. If the ruler of the 5th is in the 11th, your casual romantic partners may end up in the "friend zone," but if the ruler of the 5th is in the 7th, you start to imagine your china pattern on the third date. If the ruler of the 7th is in the 11th, you can stay friends with your ex-spouse, and if the ruler of the 7th is in the 5th, you can stay *very* friendly with your ex-spouse.

Board of Directors Connections

Aspects and emplacement represent very strong connections between the houses; Board of Directors connections are weaker. The most significant Board of Directors connection would be if one of the house rulers rules one of the other house rulers. For example, if the ruler of the 11th house is Venus in Scorpio, and the ruler of the 5th house is Mars in Taurus, Mars would have at least 5 votes for rulership on Venus' Board of Directors, because Mars rules Scorpio. Venus (11th house) reports to Mars (5th house), so an 11th house friendship could turn into a 5th house love affair. However, this connection flows in only one direction. A relationship that starts out as a 5th house romantic flirtation will not turn into an 11th house friendship.

Blueprint Template Sentences for Relationship Houses

These blueprint template sentences will help you explore the rulers of the 5th, 7th, and 11th houses in the context of relationship wants.

Ruler of 5th House (Lovers)
[PLANET] (Ruler of 5th House) in [SIGN] in [HOUSE];
[PLANET] also Rules/Almuten [HOUSE(s)]

He/she looks for casual romantic partners (5th House) who align with his/her need to [PLANET KEYWORDS] ([PLANET]) in a manner that is [SIGN KEYWORDS] ([SIGN]), WITH [HOUSE KEYWORD FOR ADDITIONAL HOUSES RULED] ([PLANET] also rules [HOUSE]). He/she is most likely to meet these partners IN [HOUSE WHERE KEYWORD] ([PLANET] in [HOUSE]).

Ruler of 7th House (Spouse/Marriage Partner)
[PLANET] (Ruler of 7th House) in [SIGN] in [HOUSE];
[PLANET] also Rules/Almuten [HOUSE(s)]

His/her marriage and relationships with other individuals (7th House) involve being able to [PLANET KEYWORDS] ([PLANET]) in a manner that is [SIGN KEYWORDS] ([SIGN]), WITH [HOUSE KEYWORD FOR ADDITIONAL HOUSES

RULED] ([PLANET] also rules [HOUSE]). He/she is most likely to meet these partners IN [HOUSE WHERE KEYWORD] ([PLANET] in [HOUSE]).

Ruler of 11th House (Friendship)
[PLANET] (Ruler of 11th House) in [SIGN] in [HOUSE];
[PLANET] also Rules/Almuten [HOUSE(s)]

His/her friendships (11th House) involve being able to [PLANET KEYWORDS] ([PLANET]) in a manner that is [SIGN KEYWORDS] ([SIGN]), WITH [HOUSE KEYWORD FOR ADDITIONAL HOUSES RULED] ([PLANET] also rules [HOUSE]). He/she is most likely to meet these partners IN [HOUSE WHERE KEYWORD] ([PLANET] in [HOUSE]).

CHAPTER 19

Sally Ride: Relationship Wants

Descendant in Capricorn
Vertex in Scorpio

Notes

Remember that it's difficult for Ride to feel safe or validated under any circumstances. Her partners can meet her needs only to the degree that her needs can be met at all.

Ride's Descendant is in Capricorn, so she is consciously attracted to partners who are responsible, reserved, stable, practical, grounded, and emotionally distant. Ride is drawn to age and maturity. Capricorn partners have an excellent shot at threading the needle of Ride's relationship needs. With her Moon in Aquarius, Ride needs boundaries. A Capricorn partner won't give in to Ride's attempts to forge emotional connections. Her Venus in Cancer will find this frustrating, but her Moon in Aquarius will find it reassuring. More importantly, Capricorn partners will be compatible with her Mercury in Taurus (and Saturn in Virgo). Mercury is the key to receiving deposits in both her Safety and Validation Need Accounts, and Saturn, the ruler of Ride's Moon in Aquarius, has significant influence over Ride's Safety Need Account. That Saturn (the ruler of Capricorn and Ride's Descendant) is in the 4th house conjunct the IC might suggest the cliché that Ride is attracted to men who remind her of her father. Regardless, these partners have an excellent chance of meeting Ride's relationship needs.

On an unconscious level, Ride is attracted to partners who resonate with her Vertex in Scorpio. These partners are eager for intense, prolonged, deep emotional connections, and they'll meet Ride's Venus in Cancer Validation Needs in a big way for a short time. Ride may get swept away with passion, but these partners will cause such severe problems for her Moon in Aquarius that she'll have to break emotional ties with them.

Marriage Blueprint

Ride's Marriage Blueprint is shown in Figure 28.

Notes

We've already noted how important Mercury is in Ride's chart: it rules her Sun and Mars in Gemini and it's the key to meeting her Safety and Validation Needs. That Mercury represents Ride's father suggests that he played a key role in her life. Mercury has dignity by Term and Face, giving it a score of +3. Not only is it the most dignified planet in Ride's chart, but it's also the *only* planet with Essential Dignity. Mercury in Taurus is stable, grounded, traditional, and practical, and Ride may have perceived these qualities in her father.

Father

4th HOUSE	Ruler (+5)	Exaltation (+4)	Triplicity (+3)	Term (+2)	Face (+1)
☿ ♉	♀ ♋	☽ ♒	♀ ♋	☿ ♉	☿ ♉
House Place	House Place	House Place	House Place	House Place	House Place
11th	1st	8th	1st	11th	11th

Mother

10th HOUSE	Ruler (+5)	Exaltation (+4)	Triplicity (+3)	Term (+2)	Face (+1)
♃ ♈	♂ ♊	☉ ♊	☉ ♊	♀ ♋	♂ ♊
House Place	House Place	House Place	House Place	House Place	House Place
10th	11th	11th	11th	1st	11th

Figure 28: Sally Ride's Marriage Blueprint

Sally Ride: Relationship Wants

Jupiter in Aries in the 10th house represents Ride's mother. Jupiter both rules the 10th and occupies the 10th, so Ride's mother is in her own place, which, in 1950s California, was the home. However, Jupiter in Aries is extremely independent, so Ride's mother may not have been a traditional housewife.

There are no connections between Mercury and Jupiter in Ride's chart. They are in adjacent signs and can't see each other. This suggests that Ride may have experienced her parents as leading independent lives. Venus in Cancer is the only factor that links Mercury and Jupiter: Venus has 8 votes on Mercury's Board of Directors and 2 votes on Jupiter's Board of Directors. Ride probably saw that her parents loved each other, but they may not have demonstrated it much.

Ride's Marriage Blueprint carries the expectation of freedom and independence in her romantic partnerships. There aren't any restrictions or ties, and given Ride's need for objectivity and boundaries in her relationships, this would serve her quite well.

Friends, Lovers, Spouses

Sally Ride's relationship houses are shown in Figure 29.

11th House: Friendships
Venus in Cancer in the 1st

Sally Ride is likely to become friends (11th house) with people who align with her need to experience love and appreciation and align with her Core Values (Venus) in a manner that is codependent, reserved, sensitive, and caring (Cancer). She is most likely to meet these partners **IN** her self-expression and pursuit of her desires, personal interests, and happiness (Venus in 1st).

Notes

As we've noted several times before, Ride's friendships are the most important relationships in her life. With Venus (the ruler of the 11th) in her 1st house, she identifies with her friends, and they are a source of happiness for her.

5th House: Love Affairs
Mars in Gemini in the 11th House
(Mars Also Almuten 10th)

Sally Ride looks for casual romantic partners (5th house) who align with her need to take action and expend energy (Mars) in a manner that is two-faced, gossiping, objective, and

RELATIONSHIP HOUSES

5th HOUSE	Ruler (+5)	Exaltation (+4)	Triplicity (+3)	Term (+2)	Face (+1)
♂ ♊	☿ ♉		♄ ♍	☿ ♉	♃ ♈
House Place	House Place	House Place	House Place	House Place	House Place
11th	11th		4th	11th	10th
House Rule	House Rule	House Rule	House Rule	House Rule	House Rule
5th, 10th (alm)	4th, 12th		7th, 8th, 9th	4th, 12th	6th, 10th, 1st (alm)
7th HOUSE	Ruler (+5)	Exaltation (+4)	Triplicity (+3)	Term (+2)	Face (+1)
♄ ♍	☿ ♉	☿ ♉	♀ ♋	♂ ♊	☿ ♉
House Place	House Place	House Place	House Place	House Place	House Place
4th	11th	11th	1st	11th	11th
House Rule	House Rule	House Rule	House Rule	House Rule	House Rule
7th, 8th, 9th	4th, 12th	4th, 12th	11th	5th, 10th (alm)	4th, 12th
11th HOUSE	Ruler (+5)	Exaltation (+4)	Triplicity (+3)	Term (+2)	Face (+1)
♀ ♋	☽ ♒	♃ ♈	♂ ♊	☿ ♉	☿ ♉
House Place	House Place	House Place	House Place	House Place	House Place
1st	8th	10th	11th	11th	11th
House Rule	House Rule	House Rule	House Rule	House Rule	House Rule
11th	1st	6th, 10th, 1st (alm)	5th, 10th (alm)	4th, 12th	4th, 12th

Figure 29: Sally Ride's Relationship Houses

versatile (Gemini) **WITH** her career, life path, and public reputation (Mars almuten 10th). She is most likely to meet these partners **IN** her personal ambition, friendships, and relationships with her peers (Mars in 11th).

Notes

Mars is combust the Sun in the 11th house. A combust planet is invisible, which suggests that Ride's 5th house isn't prominent or much of a priority for her. She'd prefer a friend over a casual romantic partner, although she might be open to a friendship becoming something more. Most of her 5th house creative energies are probably directed toward her 10th house career.

7th House: Marriage

Saturn in Virgo in the 4th House
(Saturn Also Rules 8th, 9th)

Sally Ride's marriage and relationships with other individuals (7th house) involve being able to accept responsibility and establish boundaries and limits (Saturn) in a manner that is critical, shrewd, healing, and perceptive (Virgo), **WITH** her debts, shared resources, and involvement with other people's values and opinions (Saturn rules 8th), and her beliefs, higher education, religion, and foreign experiences (Saturn rules 9th). She is most likely to meet these partners **IN** her home environment, family relationships, and private life (Saturn in 4th).

Notes

We've already considered Saturn briefly in the context of her Descendent in Capricorn. Ride's Saturn is in her 4th house, conjunct her IC, and this suggests that she expects her 7th house partners to provide a stable foundation for her. It also suggests that Ride prefers to keep these relationships private.

Connections Between 11th, 5th, and 7th Houses

Ride will have an easy time moving between the different relationship houses. Even though there are no aspects between the rulers of the 5th,

7th, or 11th, there are some strong connections between the houses. As we already noted, Mars, the ruler of her 5th house of love affairs is in her 11th house of friendship. This suggests that her 5th house romantic partners may end up in the 11th house "friend zone." Both Mars, the ruler of the 5th and Saturn, the ruler of the 7th, are ruled by Mercury in Taurus in the 11th. This emphasizes the importance of friendship as the foundation of any relationship for Ride, but also makes it possible for a casual, 5th house relationship to move to a serious, 7th house partnership.

CHAPTER 20

Interpreting Career, Job, and Money

Career questions involve three distinct areas of life: what you are called to do, or your life path (10th house); your job or routine employment (6th house); and your money, resources, and salary (2nd house and the **Part of Fortune**).

Career, Life Path, and Public Image: 10th House

In traditional astrology, the 10th house relates to honors, awards, and reputation. In modern astrology, the 10th house relates to your career, a concept that didn't exist until the 20th century. In today's culture, where it's so common to base your self-worth and even your identity on your job title, we place great value on having a 10th house career. And yet, what most people call a career is actually a job—and there's nothing wrong with that. The work you do to pay the bills doesn't define or limit who you are.

It's helpful to view the 10th house from a broader perspective. I use the vague term "life path" because it doesn't carry the same professional baggage that "career" does. The ruler of the 10th house describes how you want to contribute to society. The 10th house is an expression of who you are, not of what you do. Avoid the gravitational pull of material solutions. If the ruler of the 10th is in the 3rd, it doesn't mean you need to become a professional writer; it suggests that writing and communication may be an important component of how you embody your life path.

Job and Service: 6th House

In traditional astrology, the 6th house is the house of service. It's work you do for someone else, because you have to do it. This is only demeaning if you base your identity and sense of self-worth on what you do to make a living. You can look to the ruler of the 6th house, as well as the Board of Directors for the 6th house ruler, to learn what you need to be happy in a workplace environment.

Money: 2nd House and Part of Fortune

When it comes to money, you have two areas to consider. The 2nd house relates to your money and resources, and specifically to your salary. The ruler of the 2nd house and its Board of Directors describe your attitude toward money, and how you earn, manage, and spend it.

The Part of Fortune (⊗), known in Hellenistic Astrology as the Lot of Fortune, is a sensitive point in the chart. It's the same distance from the Ascendant as the Sun is from the Moon, and most astrology programs will include it in the chart for you. The sign and house of the Part of Fortune show how and where you experience financial gains. The planet that rules the Part of Fortune represents your money in the same way the ruler of the 2nd house does.

Career, Job, and Money Connections

After considering each category individually, you can look for any connections between the houses. You use the same tools that you used to evaluate connections between the relationship houses, considering aspects between the house rulers, Board of Directors connections, and emplacement.

First, consider the relationship between the 6th house job and 10th house life path. If there is a strong connection between the two houses (for example, because they're ruled by the same planet), then the work you do can also provide personal fulfillment and professional advancement. If there is no connection between these houses, or conflict between the ruler of the 6th and the ruler of the 10th, you will need to keep these parts of your life separate, at least in your mind. There's nothing wrong with holding down a 6th house job and exchanging 40 hours a week for the freedom to pursue the things that matter to you on evenings and weekends.

Next, consider how money relates to your 6th house job and/or 10th house career. Any supportive connection between the 2nd house or the Part of Fortune with either the 6th or 10th house means you can make money with those activities. For some people, money comes easily, because of flowing connections that tie the 2nd house with both the 6th and 10th houses. For others, there's a clear indication that financial gains will come through either a 6th house job, or a 10th house situation where you have greater autonomy and independence.

Blueprint Template Sentences for Career, Job, and Money

These blueprint template sentences will help you to explore the rulers of the 10th, 6th, and 2nd houses, the members of the Board of Directors (BOD) for each house, and the Part of Fortune.

Ruler of the 10th House (Career)
[PLANET] (Ruler of 10th House) in [SIGN] in [HOUSE];
[PLANET] Rules/Almuten [HOUSE(s)]

His/her career and life path (10th House) involves being able to [PLANET BOD WANTS/NEEDS] ([PLANET]) **in a manner that is** [SIGN/ELEMENT/MODALITY KEYWORDS] ([SIGN/ELEMENT/MODALITY]), **WITH** [HOUSE KEYWORD FOR ADDITIONAL HOUSES RULED] ([PLANET] **also rules** [HOUSE]). **He/she encounters these needs particularly IN** [HOUSE WHERE KEYWORD] ([PLANET] **in** [HOUSE]).

Board of Directors for 10th House Ruler
[PLANET] in [SIGN] in [HOUSE] ([#] Votes);
[PLANET] Rules/Almuten [HOUSE(s)]

His/her career and life path (10th House Ruler BOD) also involves being able to [PLANET BOD WANTS/NEEDS] ([PLANET]) **in a manner that is** [SIGN/ELEMENT/MODALITY KEYWORDS] ([SIGN/ELEMENT/MODALITY]), **WITH** [HOUSE KEYWORD FOR ADDITIONAL HOUSES RULED] ([PLANET] **also rules** [HOUSE]). **He/she encounters these needs particularly IN** [HOUSE WHERE KEYWORD] ([PLANET] **in** [HOUSE]).

Ruler of the 6th House (Job)
[PLANET] (Ruler of 6th House) in [SIGN] in [HOUSE];
[PLANET] Rules/Almuten [HOUSE(s)]

His/her job (6th House) involves being able to [PLANET BOD WANTS/NEEDS] ([PLANET]) in a manner that is [SIGN/ELEMENT/MODALITY KEYWORDS] ([SIGN/ELEMENT/MODALITY]), WITH [HOUSE KEYWORD FOR ADDITIONAL HOUSES RULED] ([PLANET] also rules [HOUSE]). He/she encounters these needs particularly IN [HOUSE WHERE KEYWORD] ([PLANET] in [HOUSE]).

Board of Directors for 6th House Ruler
[PLANET] in [SIGN] in [HOUSE] ([#] Votes);
[PLANET] Rules/Almuten [HOUSE(s)]

His/her job (6th House Ruler BOD) also involves being able to [PLANET BOD WANTS/NEEDS] ([PLANET]) in a manner that is [SIGN/ELEMENT/MODALITY KEYWORDS] ([SIGN/ELEMENT/MODALITY]), WITH [HOUSE KEYWORD FOR ADDITIONAL HOUSES RULED] ([PLANET] also rules [HOUSE]). He/she encounters these needs particularly IN [HOUSE WHERE KEYWORD] ([PLANET] in [HOUSE]).

Ruler of the 2nd House (Money)
[PLANET] (Ruler of 2nd House) in [SIGN] in [HOUSE];
[PLANET] Rules/Almuten [HOUSE(s)]

The way he/she earns money and resources (2nd House) involves being able to [PLANET BOD WANTS/NEEDS] ([PLANET]) in a manner that is [SIGN/ELEMENT/MODALITY KEYWORDS] ([SIGN/ELEMENT/MODALITY]), WITH [HOUSE KEYWORD FOR ADDITIONAL HOUSES RULED] ([PLANET] also rules [HOUSE]). He/she encounters these needs particularly IN [HOUSE WHERE KEYWORD] ([PLANET] in [HOUSE]).

Board of Directors for 2nd House Ruler
[PLANET] in [SIGN] in [HOUSE] ([#] Votes);
[PLANET] Rules/Almuten [HOUSE(s)]

His/her money and resources (2nd House Ruler BOD) also involve being able to [PLANET BOD WANTS/NEEDS] ([PLANET]) in a manner that is [SIGN/ELEMENT/MODALITY KEYWORDS] ([SIGN/ELEMENT/MODALITY]), WITH [HOUSE KEYWORD FOR ADDITIONAL HOUSES RULED] ([PLANET] also rules [HOUSE]). He/she encounters these needs particularly IN [HOUSE WHERE KEYWORD] ([PLANET] in [HOUSE]).

Part of Fortune
Part of Fortune in [SIGN] in [HOUSE]

He/she will experience the greatest amount of prosperity and success (Part of Fortune) by being [SIGN/ELEMENT/MODALITY KEYWORDS] ([SIGN/ELEMENT/MODALITY]), particularly IN [HOUSE WHERE KEYWORD] (Part of Fortune in [HOUSE]).

Ruler of the Part of Fortune
[PLANET] in [SIGN] in [HOUSE] ([#] Votes);
[PLANET] Rules/Almuten [HOUSE(s)]

To experience prosperity and success (Ruler of Part of Fortune), he/she needs to [PLANET BOD WANTS/NEEDS] ([PLANET]) in a manner that is [SIGN/ELEMENT/MODALITY KEYWORDS] ([SIGN/ELEMENT/MODALITY]), WITH [HOUSE KEYWORD FOR ADDITIONAL HOUSES RULED] ([PLANET] also rules [HOUSE]). He/she encounters these needs particularly IN [HOUSE WHERE KEYWORD] ([PLANET] in [HOUSE]).

CHAPTER 21

Sally Ride: Career, Job, and Money

To consider Sally Ride's career, we'll look at the 10th house (career), 6th house (job) and 2nd house (money). These houses, the house rulers, and the planets on the Board of Directors are shown in Figure 30.

10th House: Career
Jupiter in Aries in the 10th
(Jupiter Also Rules 6th, Almuten 1st)

Sally Ride's career and life path (10th house) involve her need to grow, expand, and experience faith (Jupiter) in a manner that is explosive, pushy, initiating, and determined (Aries), **WITH** her job, service, and workplace relationships (Jupiter rules 6th) and her personality, self-image, and pursuit of happiness (Jupiter almuten 1st). She encounters these needs particularly **IN** her career, life path, and public reputation (Jupiter in 10th).

Notes

The cause, action, and effect of Jupiter in Aries have been addressed already.

With Jupiter in Aries ruling her career, life path, and public reputation, Ride embodies the energy of a pioneer, a leader, and a trailblazer. Jupiter in Aries seeks to expand identity and chart new territory. As noted many times before, Ride's identity, personality, and sense of self express through her career. That Jupiter is also the almuten of her 1st house means that her reputation and professional accomplishments are personal, and specific to her. This kind of connection between the ruler of the 10th and the ruler of the 1st often suggests a career built around the individual, as opposed to a position that could be filled by just anyone.

Jupiter represents growth, faith, and optimism. Ride will be drawn to a career that pushes the boundaries and adds to what we know and understand about the universe. She will not be happy in an office job, performing the same routine tasks until retirement. She needs a career that allows for innovation and expansion, even if it's only personal.

CAREER HOUSES

2nd HOUSE	Ruler (+5)	Exaltation (+4)	Triplicity (+3)	Term (+2)	Face (+1)
☉ ♊	☿ ♉		♄ ♍	☿ ♉	♃ ♈
House Place	House Place	House Place	House Place	House Place	House Place
11th	11th		4th	11th	10th
House Rule	House Rule	House Rule	House Rule	House Rule	House Rule
2nd, 3rd	4th, 12th		7th, 8th, 9th	4th, 12th	6th, 10th, 1st (alm)
6th HOUSE	Ruler (+5)	Exaltation (+4)	Triplicity (+3)	Term (+2)	Face (+1)
♃ ♈	♂ ♊	☉ ♊	☉ ♊	♀ ♋	♂ ♊
House Place	House Place	House Place	House Place	House Place	House Place
10th	11th	11th	11th	1st	11th
House Rule	House Rule	House Rule	House Rule	House Rule	House Rule
6th, 10th, 1st (alm)	5th, 10th (alm)	2nd, 3rd	2nd, 3rd	11th	5th, 10th (alm)
10th HOUSE	Ruler (+5)	Exaltation (+4)	Triplicity (+3)	Term (+2)	Face (+1)
♃ ♈	♂ ♊	☉ ♊	☉ ♊	♀ ♋	♂ ♊
House Place	House Place	House Place	House Place	House Place	House Place
10th	11th	11th	11th	1st	11th
House Rule	House Rule	House Rule	House Rule	House Rule	House Rule
6th, 10th, 1st (alm)	5th, 10th (alm)	2nd, 3rd	2nd, 3rd	11th	5th, 10th (alm)

Figure 30: Sally Ride's Career Houses

10th House Ruler (Jupiter in Aries)
Board of Directors
Mars in Gemini in the 11th House (6 Votes, Rulership + Face)
Mars Rules 5th, Almuten 10th

Sally Ride's career and life path (10th house Ruler Board of Directors) also involves her need to take action and expend energy (Mars) in a manner that is two-faced, gossiping, objective, and versatile (Gemini), **WITH** her personal creativity, pursuit of entertainment, tolerance for risk, and children (Mars rules 5th), and her career, life path, and public reputation (Mars almuten 10th). She encounters these needs particularly **IN** her personal ambition, friendships, and relationships with peers (Mars in 11th).

Notes

Cause comes from her 5th house of amusement, entertainment, and risk, and from her 10th house of career, life path, and public reputation. Gemini is playful, flexible, clever, skillful, and easily bored—it's also very quick to act, change, and adapt. Ride will accept any challenge, especially if it provides an opportunity for her to demonstrate her intelligence, wit, and dexterity. The biggest stick for Gemini is the word "No." The quickest way to motivate Ride's Mars in Gemini to act is to tell her she can't do something. And if you tell her she can't do something in a professional context (which brings in the 10th house), it's guaranteed to light a fire under her. Ride's Mars in Gemini won't stop until she proves you wrong.

Action is Mars in Gemini. Because Gemini is an Air sign, Ride will use her intelligence to go after the things she wants. She will rely on reason, logic, and abstract concepts, but she will also excel at making new connections, breaking the rules, and finding creative ways to exploit any loopholes in the law. Speed is vital. If she moves fast enough, she can get what she wants and reach her goals before anyone has a chance to object.

Effect is in the 11th house of shared creativity. Ride needs the help and support of other people to reach her objectives. She needs to earn a place on the team, but she doesn't care about leading the team. Ride needs other people to share and explore ideas and solve problems.

As already noted, Ride's Mars in Gemini is combust the Sun, which means it's invisible. All of Ride's "little s" self desires serve the expression of her authentic "Big S" Self, which, as we're about to see, has an even greater influence over Ride's career and life path.

Sun in Gemini in the 11th House (7 Votes, Exaltation + Triplicity) Sun Rules 2nd, 3rd

Sally Ride's career and life path (10th house Ruler Board of Directors) also involves aligning with her Personal Standards of Integrity and expressing her authentic "Big S" Self (Sun) in a manner that is unsettled, distracted, amusing, and informative (Gemini), **WITH** her money and resources (Sun rules 2nd) and her writing, communication, and familiar environment (Sun rules 3rd). She encounters these needs particularly **IN** her personal aspirations, friendships, and relationships with her peers (Sun in 11th).

Notes

Ride's Sun is the almuten of her Jupiter in Aries, with 7 votes on the Board of Directors, giving it more influence than Mars, who has only 6 votes.

Ride discovers and expresses her authentic "Big S" Self through her 10th house career, life path, and public reputation. The fact that Mars, her "little s" self, is united with the Sun, her "Big S" Self, gives her a single focus (or as single a focus as planets in Gemini can manage).

Ride's happiness and success depend on her finding an appropriate career. Until she finds her path, she will be unfocused and restless, and uncertain of her identity. Once she finds a path that inspires her, however, her life will come into focus. As she connects with her authentic "Big S" Self, she will advance in her career. The more she advances in her career, the more connected she becomes to her true Self.

Sally Ride: Career, Job, and Money

6th House: Job
Jupiter in Aries in the 10th
(Jupiter Also Rules 10th, Almuten 1st)

Sally Ride's job (6th house) involves her need to grow, expand, and experience faith (Jupiter) in a manner that is explosive, pushy, initiating, and determined (Aries), **WITH** her career, life path, and public reputation (Jupiter rules 10th) and her personality, self-image, and pursuit of happiness (Jupiter almuten 1st). She encounters these needs particularly **IN** her career, life path, and public reputation (Jupiter in 10th).

Notes

Because Jupiter rules both the 6th and 10th houses, everything that relates to Ride's 10th house also applies to her 6th house job and service.

2nd House: Money
Sun in Gemini in the 11th
(Sun Also Rules 3rd)

The way that Sally Ride earns money (2nd house) involves aligning with her Personal Standards of Integrity and expressing her authentic "Big S" Self (Sun) in a manner that is unsettled, distracted, amusing, and informative (Gemini), **WITH** her writing, communication, and familiar environment (Sun rules 3rd). She encounters these needs particularly **IN** her personal aspirations, friendships, and relationships with her peers (Sun in 11th).

Notes

In this context, because the Sun rules the 2nd house, Ride's ability to earn money is based on her ability to embody her authentic "Big S" Self and align with her Personal Standards of Integrity. She will never be successful if she puts money ahead of principles, but when she puts her principles and integrity first, money will follow.

This also suggests that money is how Ride expresses and aligns with her authentic "Big S" Self.

2nd House Ruler (Sun in Gemini) Board of Directors

Mercury in Taurus in the 11th House (7 Votes, Rulership + Term)
Mercury Rules 4th, 12th

Sally Ride's money and resources (2nd House Ruler's Board of Directors) also involve her need to understand and communicate (Mercury) in a manner that is possessive, sluggish, rugged, and benevolent (Taurus), **WITH** her home environment, family relationships, and private life (Mercury rules 4th) and her personal unconscious, shadow self, and self-sabotage (Mercury rules 12th). She encounters these needs particularly **IN** her personal aspirations, friendships, and relationships with her peers (Mercury in 11th).

Saturn in Virgo in the 4th House (3 Votes, Triplicity)
Saturn Rules 7th, 8th, 9th

Sally Ride's money and resources (2nd House Ruler's Board of Directors) also involve her need to accept responsibility and establish boundaries and limits (Saturn) in a manner that is critical, shrewd, healing, and perceptive (Virgo), **WITH** her marriage, partnerships, and one-to-one relationships (Saturn rules 7th), her debts, shared resources, and involvement with other people's values and opinions (Saturn rules 8th), and her beliefs, higher education, religion, and foreign experiences (Saturn rules 9th). She encounters these needs particularly **IN** her home environment, family relationships, and private life (Saturn in 4th).

Notes

We've explored Mercury and Saturn in great detail already. There's no practical value to exploring them again in the context of Ride's money.

Part of Fortune in Pisces in the 10th House

Ride will experience the greatest amount of prosperity and success (Part of Fortune) by being caring, receptive, healing, and intuitive (Pisces), particularly **IN** her career, life path, and public reputation (Part of Fortune in 10th).

Notes

That Ride's Part of Fortune is in her 10th house suggests she will make money from her career, life path, and public reputation. Because it's in

Pisces, it suggests that Ride will benefit from emotional, spiritual, and subjective energies. Once again we see the need to balance her head and her heart.

Part of Fortune Ruler (Jupiter in Aries)

To experience prosperity and success (Ruler of the Part of Fortune), she needs to grow, expand, and experience faith (Jupiter) in a manner that is explosive, pushy, initiating, and determined (Aries), **WITH** her job, service, and workplace relationships (Jupiter rules 6th), career, life path, and public reputation (Jupiter rules 10th) and her personality, self-image, and pursuit of happiness (Jupiter almuten 1st). She encounters these needs particularly **IN** her career, life path, and public reputation (Jupiter in 10th).

Notes

Not only does Jupiter represent Ride's 10th house career and her 6th house job, but it also represents her money. We've explored Jupiter in detail already.

Connections Between Career Houses

Notes

Jupiter rules both Ride's 6th and 10th houses, which means there's no difference between her job and her career/life path. Jupiter is sextile Ride's Sun, the ruler of her 2nd house, and the Sun has 7 votes on Jupiter's Board of Directors, which shows a strong connection between her money and her job and career. This is reinforced by the fact that her Part of Fortune is in the 10th house (conjunct her Midheaven), and ruled by Jupiter, the ruler of her 6th and 10th houses, which also occupies the 10th house. Any way you slice it, Ride will make her money from her career.

I've included my final astrological portrait of Sally Ride, which I created from these notes and sketches, as one of the Bonus Gifts in Appendix B.

The Spice Rack

CHAPTER 22
A Pinch of Spice

In cooking, you use spices to enhance the natural flavor of food, not to disguise the flavor of it. You add spice at the end. It's optional, and a little goes a long way. Too much spice, or the wrong combination of spices, can ruin a dish.

The same principles apply to astrology. A pinch of spice can improve an interpretation. A pound of spice will ruin it.

The meat of your natal chart interpretation is your analysis of the planets, signs, houses, and aspects. You can enhance your interpretation with a variety of astrological spices. You can include fixed stars, asteroids, **Arabic Parts**, and hypothetical planets in your chart. You can introduce traditional astrology techniques that evaluate the relative dignity or debility of a planet. You can even view the chart on a dial and explore midpoints and planetary pictures. But just as no amount of spice can mask the taste of spoiled meat, your interpretation must be able to hold up on its own, without any extra spice.

If a pattern is truly important, it will show up multiple times in the chart. You can use spice to highlight a pattern and make it stand out, but you can't build an argument with spice alone. If the only way you can illustrate a point is with a minor aspect between two asteroids, you're using far too much spice. No one will swallow it.

Different styles of cooking use different combinations of spices. Italian cooking uses oregano, basil, and parsley, but Chinese cuisine uses cloves, fennel, anise, ginger, and chilies. Different styles of astrology use different combinations of techniques. When learning a particular type of astrology, master the spices associated with it before you experiment with new combinations.

Most of the traditional astrology spices work best in the context of predictive astrology. They don't add much to a natal chart interpretation. In the next few chapters, I'll share some of the spices from my personal spice rack. In small doses, these spices can enhance a practical natal chart interpretation.

CHAPTER 23

Sensitive Points in the Chart

Planets are physical bodies. Planets radiate light and can both make and receive aspects. The angles and house cusps are not physical bodies: they're **sensitive points**. Sensitive points do not radiate light, and they can receive aspects only from physical bodies. If Saturn squares your Moon, the aspect flows in both directions and has an effect on both planets. If Saturn squares your Ascendant, it affects your Ascendant, but does not affect Saturn.

The chart examples in this book include a few additional sensitive points: the Moon's Nodes, the Part of Fortune, and the Vertex. In the right contexts, each of these can add practical value to your interpretations.

The Moon's Nodes

The **Moon's Nodes** are the points that the orbit of the Moon around the Earth intersects the plane of the **ecliptic** (the path of the Earth around the Sun). The North, or Ascending Node is the point where the Moon's orbit rises above the ecliptic, and the South, or Descending Node is the point where the Moon's orbit sets below the ecliptic (Figure 31). The Moon's Nodes have an average retrograde motion of about 3 minutes or arc per day, and complete a cycle of the zodiac every 18 years.

The Moon's Nodes are the transiting eclipse points. When a new moon (Moon conjunct Sun) occurs within 18°31 of one of the Moon's Nodes, it is a solar eclipse. When a full moon (Moon opposite Sun) occurs within 12°15 of one of the Moon's Nodes, it is a lunar eclipse (Figure 32).

Principles of Practical Natal Astrology

In traditional astrology, the **North Node** (*Caput Draconis*, which means "dragon's head") is a **benefic**, similar to Venus and Jupiter, and is associated with good fortune and success. The **South Node** (*Cauda Draconis*, which means "dragon's tail") is a **malefic**, similar to Mars and Saturn, and is associated with what you would expect to come out of the tail end of a dragon. The traditional interpretation of the Moon's Nodes boils down to "North Node good; South Node bad."

The Moon's Nodes are a big part of karmic astrology because they relate to the evolution of your soul. The South Node is thought to relate to past-life experiences that you're bringing forth in this lifetime, and the North Node shows how you're meant to integrate those experiences. This is fascinating, but

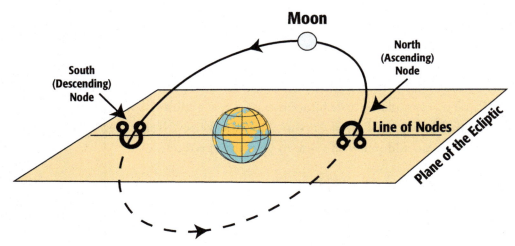

Figure 31: The Moon's Nodes

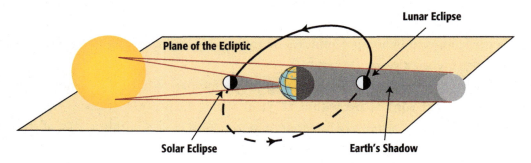

Figure 32: Solar and Lunar Eclipses

it's not practical. Your soul will have the experiences it needs to have regardless of the choices you make on the physical plane. You don't need to avoid the qualities of your South Node or embrace the qualities of your North Node.

The Moon's Nodes have limited practical value in the context of a natal chart interpretation. You can view the house occupied by the North Node as a place of increase, and the house occupied by the South Node as an area of life where you need to let go.

The Moon's Nodes play a role in the Accidental Dignity or Debility of a planet. A planet in a partile conjunction with the North Node is has **Accidental Dignity** with a positive effect on **performance**. A planet in a partile conjunction with the South Node has **Accidental Debility** with a negative effect on performance. And a planet square the nodal axis ("at the bendings") has Accidental Dignity with a positive effect on **prominence** We'll explore these concepts in detail in Chapter 25.

The Part of Fortune

The **Arabic Parts** or **Greek Lots** are sensitive points in the chart that are calculated based on the relative positions of three points in the chart — usually two planets and the Ascendant. The most important of these in the context of natal astrology is the Part of Fortune.

The formula for the Part of Fortune in a Day Chart is **Ascendant + Moon − Sun**. You begin with the Sun, and measure the arc from the Sun to the Moon. You then start at the Ascendant, and follow the same arc to find the Part of Fortune. In a Night Chart, the formula is reversed: it's **Ascendant + Sun − Moon**, and you take the arc from the Moon to the Sun (Figure 33).

The ruler of the Part of Fortune represents your money, and the power, prominence, and performance[1] of that planet can show your potential for wealth in this lifetime.

There are well over 100 different parts to choose from. The default Arabic Parts report in Solar Fire, the software program I use to calculate my charts, gives you the positions of 40 Arabic Parts, including the Part of Treachery, The Part of Land Journeys, and the Part of Sudden Advancement. They have

---

[1] See Chapter 25.

limited practical value in certain types of predictive astrology, and no practical value in natal chart interpretation.

If you choose to work with additional Arabic Parts, keep these guidelines in mind. First, the planet that rules the part is more important than the part itself. Second, only partile conjunctions to a part count, although you could also consider a conjunction with an orb of less than 1°, even if it's not partile.

The Vertex

The Vertex is an angle in the chart, just like the Ascendant or the Midheaven. To be specific, the Vertex is the western point of intersection of the Prime Vertical and the Ecliptic. Unless you're a serious math geek (or are planning to take the Level II NCGR-PAA Certification Exam), all you need to know is that most astrology programs will calculate the Vertex for you. The Vertex doesn't have a glyph; it's usually shown in the chart as "Vx".

The Vertex is a western angle. This means it will always be in the 5th through the 9th house, although it tends to stay close to the Descendant.

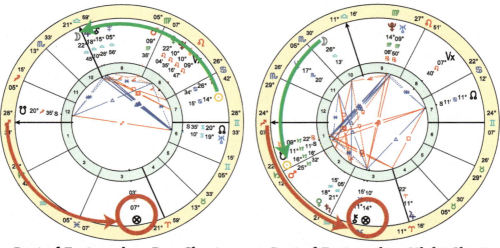

Part of Fortune in a Day Chart: Ascendant + Moon − Sun
Arc from Sun to Moon: 98°30′
Arc from Ascendant to Part of Fortune: 98°30′

Part of Fortune in a Night Chart: Ascendant + Sun − Moon
Arc from Moon to Sun: 80°03′
Arc from Ascendant to Part of Fortune: 80°03′

Figure 33: Calculating the Part of Fortune

Sensitive Points in the Chart

In natal astrology, the Vertex is important when you consider relationship wants. On a conscious level, you're attracted to partners who match the energy of your Descendant. But on an unconscious level, you're drawn to partners who match the energy of your Vertex.

Your Vertex relationships have an unavoidable pull. Even when you know they'll be nothing but trouble, you can't stop yourself. Call it destiny or fate or karma, there's something about the Vertex that sucks you in, almost against your will.

When your Vertex partners don't speak your Safety or Validation Need Language, these relationships are disastrous. Even when these partners do meet your needs, there's an intensity to these relationships that makes them especially volatile.

In the natal chart, you can make note of any planets in tight aspect to the Vertex. You may find that when something blows up in your life, these planets—and the houses they rule—are often involved.

CHAPTER 24
Dispositor Trees

A dispositor tree is a diagram of a chart that shows the hierarchy of rulerships. It literally maps out who reports to whom, and functions as an astrological organization chart. I used to rely on dispositor trees, but I stopped using them when I developed the Board of Directors approach to the Essential Dignities and the Chart Interpretation Worksheet.

Dispositor trees have limited practical value (which is why they're now part of the Spice Rack). **You can't interpret a dispositor tree.** It can contribute to the context of the interpretation by suggesting structure or connections that might not be obvious when you consider the worksheet, but that's as far as it goes. The position of a planet in a dispositor tree does not suggest the importance of the planet in the chart.

Step 1: Find any planets in rulership

Each planet in rulership will be at the top of its own tree. It's possible for a single chart to have multiple dispositor trees.

For the first example, we'll consider **Liza Minnelli** (Figure 34):

- ✦ Minnelli has one planet in rulership, the Moon in Cancer, so this goes at the top of a tree.

- ✦ The Moon rules all planets in Cancer. Minnelli has Mars and Saturn in Cancer, so Mars and Saturn go on the second tier of the tree, reporting directly to the Moon.

- ✦ Saturn rules all planets in Capricorn or Aquarius. Minnelli has no planets in these signs, so this branch is complete.

Principles of Practical Natal Astrology

- ✦ Mars rules all planets in Aries and Scorpio. Minnelli has Mercury in Aries and Venus in Aries, so Mercury and Venus go on the third tier of the tree, reporting directly to Mars.

- ✦ Mercury rules all planets in Gemini and Virgo. Minnelli has Uranus in Gemini, so Uranus goes on the fourth tier of the tree, reporting directly to Mercury.

- ✦ Venus rules all planets in Taurus and Libra. Minnelli has Chiron, Neptune, and Jupiter in Libra, so these planets go on the fourth tier of the tree, reporting directly to Venus.

- ✦ Uranus, Chiron and Neptune don't rule anything, so they represent the ends of their respective branches.

- ✦ Jupiter rules all planets in Sagittarius and Pisces. Minnelli has the Sun in Pisces, which goes on the fifth tier, reporting directly to Jupiter.

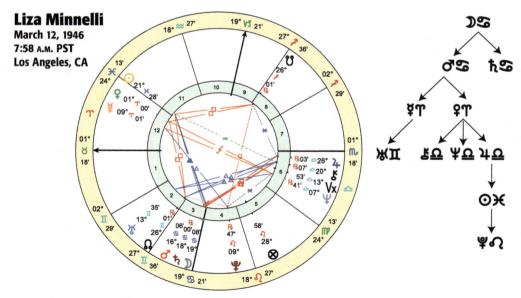

Figure 34: Liza Minnelli's Dispositor Tree
Source: Astro-Databank; Rodden Rating: AA, Quoted BC/BR.

Dispositor Trees

- The Sun rules all planets in Leo. Minnelli has Pluto in Leo, which goes on the sixth tier, reporting directly to the Sun.

- Pluto doesn't rule anything, so this branch ends here, and now all eleven of the planets in Minnelli's chart are accounted for.

The chain of command for every planet in Minnelli's chart leads to the Moon in Cancer. Because Minnelli's Moon rules, or disposes, her entire chart, it's called the **sole dispositor** or **final dispositor**. From this, we can see that Minnelli's feelings, emotions, and Safety Needs (Moon) motivate everything in her life. This could define the context of Minnelli's chart. You might emphasize the emotional, fluid, and intuitive qualities when you create her astrological portrait.

Let's look at another example, **Paul Newman** (Figure 35).

- Newman has one planet in rulership, Mars in Aries, which goes at the top of a tree.

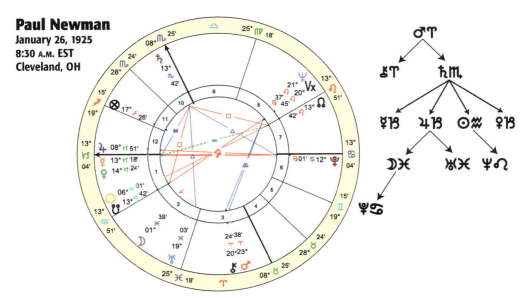

Figure 35: Paul Newman's Dispositor Tree
Source: Astro-Databank; Rodden Rating: AA, BC/BR in hand.

- Mars rules all planets in Aries and in Scorpio. Newman has Chiron in Aries and Saturn in Scorpio, and these go in the second tier, reporting directly to Mars. Chiron doesn't rule anything, so that branch is complete.

- Saturn rules all planets in Capricorn and Aquarius. Newman has Jupiter, Mercury, and Venus in Capricorn and the Sun in Aquarius, so all four planets go on the third tier, reporting to Saturn.

- Jupiter rules all planets in Sagittarius and Pisces. The Moon in Pisces and Uranus in Pisces go on the fourth tier, reporting to Jupiter. Uranus doesn't rule anything, so that branch ends here.

- The Moon rules all planets in Cancer, and Pluto in Cancer goes on the fifth tier, reporting to the Moon. Pluto doesn't rule anything.

- Mercury rules all planets in Gemini and Virgo; Newman has none.

- Venus rules all planets in Taurus and Libra; Newman has none.

- The Sun rules all planets in Leo. Neptune in Leo goes on the fourth tier, reporting to the Sun.

Paul Newman also has a sole dispositor in his chart, Mars in Aries. One would think that this would make him aggressive and impulsive in all things. However, a closer look at his dispositor tree shows that while Mars in Aries is the final dispositor, the only planet that reports directly to Mars in Aries (other than Chiron) is Saturn in Scorpio. Every other planet has to go through Saturn to get to Mars. Mars in Aries is the General ready to order his troops into battle. However, this General has a cautious and responsible Lieutenant, Saturn in Scorpio, who screens the intelligence reports before Mars gets them. This means Newman was less likely to take rash, impulsive action.

Saturn's influence is clear when you review the Chart Interpretation Worksheet, but without the dispositor tree, Saturn's role as a gatekeeper to Mars

Dispositor Trees

is not as obvious. This dynamic could shape the context of your interpretation of Newman's chart in important ways.

Step 2: Find any planets in mutual reception by Rulership

Any pair of planets in mutual reception by rulership, such as Mars in Taurus and Venus in Scorpio, will be at the top of a tree.

Considering **Meryl Streep** (Figure 36), we begin with Step 1 and look for planets in Rulership.

- ✦ Streep has Mercury in Gemini, which goes at the top of a tree.

- ✦ Mercury in Gemini rules all planets in Gemini and Virgo. Streep has Mars in Gemini and Saturn in Virgo, so Mars and Saturn go on the second tier, reporting directly to Mercury.

- ✦ Mars rules all planets in Aries and Scorpio. Streep has no planets in these signs, so this branch is complete.

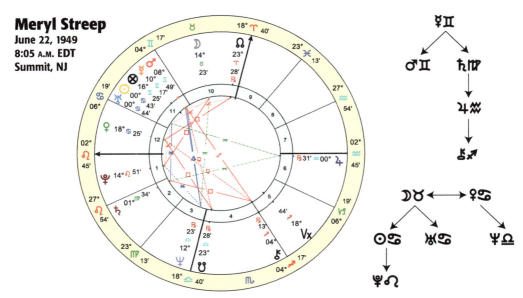

Figure 36: Meryl Streep's Dispositor Tree

Source: Astro-Databank; Rodden Rating: AA, BC/BR in hand.

- Saturn rules all planets in Capricorn and Aquarius. Streep has Jupiter in Aquarius, so Jupiter goes on the third tier, reporting directly to Saturn.

- Jupiter rules all planets in Sagittarius and Pisces. Streep has Chiron in Sagittarius, which goes on the fourth tier, reporting directly to Jupiter. Chiron doesn't rule anything, so that completes this branch.

We've finished Mercury's dispositor tree for Streep's chart, but we're still missing planets. Because she has no other planets in Rulership, we move to Step 2 and look for pairs of planets in mutual reception.

- Streep's Moon in Taurus is in mutual reception with her Venus in Cancer. They go on the top of a new tree, with a double-headed arrow to indicate that they receive each other.

- The Moon rules all planets in Cancer. In addition to Venus, Streep has the Sun and Uranus in Cancer. The Sun and Uranus go on the second tier, reporting directly to the Moon. Uranus doesn't rule anything, so that branch is complete.

- The Sun rules all planets in Leo. Streep has Pluto in Leo, which goes on the third tier, reporting directly to the Sun. Pluto doesn't rule anything, so that branch is complete.

- Venus rules all planets in Taurus and Libra. Streep has Neptune in Libra, which goes on the second tier, reporting directly to Venus. Neptune doesn't rule anything, so this branch is complete.

Between the two trees—the Mercury tree and the Moon–Venus tree—all eleven planets are accounted for.

Notice that Streep's chart is split between the planets that report to her Mercury in Gemini and the planets that report to her Moon–Venus mutual reception. This suggests that Streep might have a split between her emotions

Dispositor Trees

and her intellect. You can't tell this definitively by looking at the dispositor tree, but the dispositor tree raises the question, which might not be as obvious if you consider only the worksheet.

Step 3: Look for a committee of rulers

It's possible to have a committee of three or more planets at the top (or more accurately, the center) of a dispositor tree. To find the committee, you work your way back through the dispositor relationships in the chart until you end up in a loop. Consider **Sylvester Stallone** (Figure 37). He has no planets in Rulership, and no planets in mutual reception, so his chart must have a committee of rulers.

Pick a planet at random to start, such as Jupiter in Leo. Jupiter in Leo reports to the Sun (which rules all planets in Leo). Stallone's Sun is in Cancer, and it reports to the Moon. Stallone's Moon is in Libra, and it reports to Venus. Stallone's Venus is in Leo, and it reports to the Sun. This closes the loop. Venus in Leo reports to the Sun in Cancer; the Sun in Cancer reports to the Moon in

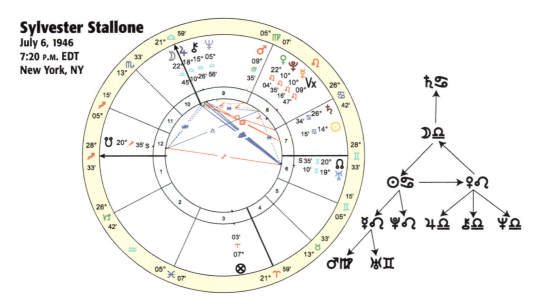

Figure 37: Sylvester Stallone's Dispositor Tree

Source: Astro-Databank; Rodden Rating: AA, BC/BR in hand.

263

Libra; the Moon in Libra reports to Venus in Leo. The Sun, Moon, and Venus are the three members of the committee.

This works no matter what planet you start with. For example, let's try again with Mars in Virgo. Mars in Virgo reports to Mercury in Leo. Mercury in Leo reports to the Sun in Cancer. The Sun in Cancer reports to the Moon in Libra. The Moon in Libra reports to Venus in Leo. Venus in Leo reports to the Sun in Cancer, and you're back to a closed loop.

It's possible to consider the dynamic of the committee in more detail, noting the connections between the planets themselves, and the houses associated with the planets, but personally I don't find this worth the effort.

Once you learn how to create a dispositor tree, it takes only a minute to draw one. If you see something useful that might change the context of your interpretation, such as a sole dispositor, a gatekeeper, or a possible division in the chart, these might be worth further consideration. If you don't see anything useful, which is often the case, then move on.

Remember, you cannot interpret a dispositor tree. Use the Board of Directors for detailed analysis of the dynamic of a chart.

CHAPTER 25
Dignity and Debility

For thousands of years, astrology was predictive. You used astrology to gaze into the future and get practical answers to important questions. To get a clear, unambiguous, definitive answer to a question, you need a two-dimensional approach to astrological interpretation. The two dimensions are planets and signs, and in this system, planets are "good" or "bad," and they can be "strong" or "weak" based on their dignity or debility. This approach is mainly practical in the context of predictive astrology, but it does have limited value in the context of natal astrology.

Most astrologers find the concept of dignity and debility confusing, and with good reason. The terms "dignified" and "debilitated" or "strong" and "weak" are tossed around willy-nilly in traditional astrology, and depending on the context, they could refer to either **Essential Dignity** or **Accidental Dignity**, and evaluate **power**, **prominence**, or **performance**.

Essential Dignity is *essential*. It's determined by the position of the planet at a specific degree of the zodiac. Essential Dignity establishes the context for interpreting the condition of the planet. When evaluating the Essential Dignity of a planet, you consider how many votes a planet has on its own Board of Directors. Accidental Dignity is circumstantial. It's based on external conditions, not the essential qualities of the planet itself. Essential Dignity is more important than Accidental Dignity, and no amount of Accidental Dignity can compensate for a lack of Essential Dignity.

Power

The Essential Dignity of a planet determines how much power the planet has. Consider the planets as actors and the signs are roles they play. Certain actors are better suited to certain roles, and when they get to play those roles, they give award-winning performances and receive great acclaim. In astrology, there are only twelve possible roles, and each planet must play every role at some point in its career, no matter how uncomfortable it may be for the planet (not to mention for the audience). When you evaluate the Essential Dignity of a planet at a particular degree of a sign, you review how effective the actor is in that particular role. If a planet is strongly dignified, it's like Meryl Streep in *Sophie's Choice*. If a planet is strongly debilitated, it's like Sylvester Stallone in *Romeo and Juliet*... playing Juliet.

Each planet has its own agenda. The more power a planet has, the greater its ability to pursue its own agenda and express in the ways that it wants to express. This is a key consideration in horary astrology, because if the planetary significators aren't strong enough to get what they want and overcome any obstacles along the way, you won't get the result you're hoping for. In natal astrology, the relative power of a planet is important only when considering how persuasive that planet will be when arguing its case on a Board of Directors.

The descriptions of each of the Essential Dignities and Debilities applies when a planet holds that position on its own Board of Directors. Remember, these are relative evaluations of the power of a planet, and they have limited and specific application in natal interpretation. A dignified or powerful planet is not "good," and a debilitated planet is not "bad."

Essential Dignity
Rulership

A planet in a sign that it rules gets to set its own agenda. It's an "A-List" actor in the role that made it a star, like Sylvester Stallone in *Rocky*. The planet is very powerful, which is good for the planet, but not necessarily good for the individual. Because a planet in Rulership is its own boss, it doesn't have to play well with the other planets in the chart. Planets in Rulership have enough power to overcome obstacles and achieve their goals.

Dignity and Debility

Exaltation
A planet in the sign of its Exaltation is very powerful; however, it doesn't get to set its own agenda. Planets in Exaltation are treated as honored guests, and other planets make an effort to do things for them on their behalf. Because a planet in Exaltation is a guest in someone else's home, the planet is usually on its best behavior. Planets in Exaltation have enough power to overcome obstacles and achieve their goals.

Triplicity
A planet in its own Triplicity is powerful, but that power has more to do with luck than with inherent skill or ability. Because Triplicity depends on the sect of a chart, like luck, dignity by Triplicity is fickle. When a planet has in-sect Triplicity, it has enough power to overcome or avoid most obstacles and achieve its goals. When a planet has out-of-sect Triplicity, its luck has run out, at least for the moment. It lacks the power to pursue its agenda, but the *potential* power still exists.

Term
A planet with dignity by Term is weak. William Lilly described planets in Term as being in declining fortunes, barely able to avoid being turned out on the street. A planet with dignity by Term does not have enough power to overcome obstacles or impediments. The only way it can achieve its goals is if the goals are downhill and the path is clear.

Face
A planet that has dignity only by Face is *extremely* weak. The planet has no say in its own agenda, but it has a seat on the Board of Directors, so it has to witness the other planets deciding how it will express. Because a planet with dignity by Face has an interest in the matter but no ability to influence the outcome, these planets often exhibit *fear*. Dignity by Face prevents a planet from being classified as **peregrine**, but that's not much of a consolation.

Essential Debility

The Essential Debilities are separate from the Essential Dignities and the Board of Directors. It's possible for a planet to have both Essential Dignity and Essential Debility. The negative scores associated with the Essential Debilities are misleading, because Essential Debility, such as being in **Detriment** or **Fall**, does not cancel out Essential Dignity. Mars in Cancer gets +3 for Triplicity, but −4 for Fall, giving it a final "score" of −1; however, Mars still has 3 votes on its own Board of Directors. The final dignity "score" of a planet has very limited practical value. It's best to consider Essential Dignity and Essential Debility individually.

Detriment

A planet in a sign opposite a sign it rules is in Detriment. Planets in Detriment are very strong; however, they use their strength in ways that get them into trouble. A planet in Detriment is like Sylvester Stallone playing Juliet in a Broadway production of *Romeo and Juliet* because he's convinced it's the role of a lifetime. He's still Sylvester Stallone, so he can do what he likes. No one can stop him, even if it's obvious that he won't be happy with the outcome. Planets in Detriment operate on the mental and emotional planes, and tend to *worry*. A planet in Detriment gets a score of −5.

Fall

A planet in the sign opposite the sign of its Exaltation is in Fall. A planet in Fall, through no fault of its own, is in a situation where its inherent strength is of no use. You may have the skills to knit a perfect sweater, but those skills won't help you if you're drowning. Planets in Fall operate on the physical plane. This has limited practical value, although I have noticed that people with the Moon in Scorpio often experience stomach discomfort when they don't express their feelings. A planet in Fall gets a score of −4.

Peregrine

A planet that has no Essential Dignity (i.e., no votes on its own Board of Directors), is peregrine. Peregrine means "wandering," and a planet without

Essential Dignity wanders because it has no influence over its own agenda. In the context of certain types of predictive astrology, being peregrine is a severe debility. In the context of a natal chart, a lack of Essential Dignity is not a challenge. A peregrine planet gets an *additional* score of −5, which may be added to any other negative score the planet receives for being in Detriment and/or Fall. Mercury in Pisces often receives a score of −14 for being in Detriment, Fall, and peregrine. This has no practical value in the context of a natal chart interpretation.

Prominence

Prominence measures how visible a planet is, and how easily it can interact with the outside world. It's an Accidental Dignity, because it's based on external conditions, such as house placement or proximity to the Sun.

Prominence doesn't make a planet "strong" and a lack of prominence doesn't make a planet "weak." More importantly, prominence does not compensate for a lack of power. Being in the spotlight doesn't make you talented. If a planet has Accidental Dignity (prominence) but no Essential Dignity (power), not only won't it succeed, but everyone will see it fail.

House Placement

Planets in the 1st or 10th house, or within a few degrees of the Ascendant and Midheaven in the 12th or 9th house, have strong Accidental Dignity that makes them very prominent. The next most prominent houses are the 4th, 7th, and 11th. A planet in the 2nd, 5th, or 9th house receives a slight boost of prominence.

Planets in the 12th, 6th, or 8th house have strong Accidental Debility that has a negative effect on their prominence. Planets in these houses are hidden. This does not mean these planets are weak. It means you can't see them, and you're not always aware of how they behave.

At the Bendings

A planet that is square the Moon's Nodes is "at the bendings." This is an Accidental Dignity that increases the prominence of the planet. Because the Moon's Nodes are sensitive points, not physical bodies, you must use a very small orb for this aspect: I recommend less than 2°. The more exact the square to the Nodes, the greater the boost to the prominence of the planet.

Proximity to the Sun

Proximity to the Sun is an Accidental Debility that makes a planet less prominent, because planets that are close to the Sun are invisible. They occupy the same part of the sky as the Sun, so they're in the sky during the day, when the Sun is out, and you can't see them.

Under the Sun's Beams

When a planet is between 8°30 and 17° of the Sun, it is **under the Sun's beams**. The planet rises and sets with the Sun, so it's invisible; however, it's far enough from the Sun that it isn't burned. This is a moderately strong Accidental Debility that affects prominence, because no matter where the planet is in the chart, it's still hidden by the Sun. The planet can fly under the radar and act without interference.

Combust

A planet within 8°30 of the Sun is **combust**. In addition to being hidden by the Sun, a combust planet is also burned by the heat of the Sun. This is a very strong Accidental Debility. It eliminates all prominence. Nothing the planet does will be noticed because the Sun will take all the credit.

Cazimi

A planet within 17 minutes of the Sun is **cazimi**, an Arabic term that means "in the heart of the Sun." This is a very strong Accidental Dignity. During the brief window of opportunity when a planet moves from combust to cazimi, the Sun lends all of its light and power to the planet. This boosts the prominence of the planet as well as its performance.

Performance

Accidental Dignity can also measure the performance of a planet. Performance evaluates how helpful a planet is inclined to be. This has practical value only in the context of predictive astrology. It does not apply to natal chart interpretation.

Benefics and Malefics

In traditional astrology the **benefics**, or "good" planets, are Jupiter, Venus, and the North Node; and the **malefics**, or "evil" planets, are Saturn, Mars, and the South Node. Context is especially important here. The benefics are good and the malefics are bad only when they interact with other planets and create Accidental Dignity or Debility.

A planet in a partile conjunction, trine, or sextile to Jupiter or Venus, or a partile conjunction to the North Node is Accidentally Dignified and receives a boost to its performance. A planet **besieged** by Jupiter and Venus (between them and aspecting them both) is especially dignified. These planets will be inclined to help you reach your goals, and will go out of their way to support you. How effective they are depends on how much power and prominence they have.

A planet in a partile conjunction, opposition, or square to Mars or Saturn, or a partile conjunction to the South Node is Accidentally Debilitated. These planets are having a bad day and are not inclined to help you. A planet besieged by Mars and Saturn is extremely debilitated, and looking to cause trouble.

Retrograde Planets

In astrology, with the exception of the Sun and Moon, all of the planets change direction and move backward, in retrograde motion, through the signs for various amounts of time. From an astronomical perspective, this is silly. The planets never move backward. The reason they change direction in astrology is that astrology views the Earth as the center of the Universe.

The apparent retrograde movement of the planets is an illusion caused by the fact that we observe the planets, which orbit the Sun, from the Earth, which also orbits the Sun. The Sun doesn't turn retrograde because the Earth orbits it, and the Moon doesn't turn retrograde because the Moon orbits the Earth.

Principles of Practical Natal Astrology

Figure 38 shows how we view the **inferior planets** (Mercury and Venus) and the **superior planets** in direct and retrograde motion, from the vantage point of the Earth (⊕).

In the context of predictive astrology, when you take a two-dimensional approach to chart interpretation, a retrograde planet is severely debilitated. In many cases, a retrograde planet is actively working against your best interest. When a benefic planet is retrograde, it's not helpful, and when a malefic planet is retrograde, it's intentionally destructive.

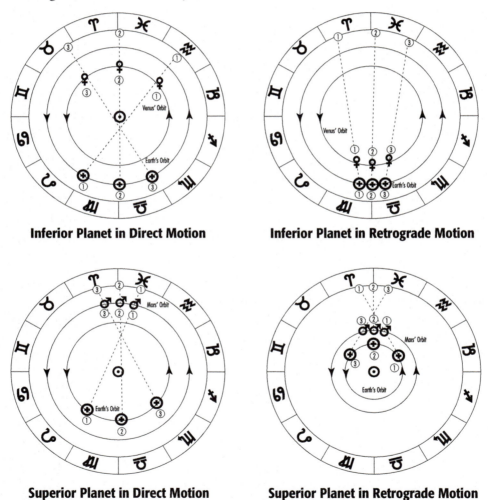

Figure 38: Retrograde Planets

Dignity and Debility

None of this applies in the context of natal chart interpretation.

Interpreting retrograde planets in the natal chart is not practical. You'll find books devoted to theories about the nuances of how a person with Mercury retrograde experiences it differently from a person with Mercury in direct motion, but there's no way to test these theories because your experience of reality is subjective.

Retrograde planets in the natal chart become important in predictive natal astrology. When a planet in your natal chart changes direction by progression, it's significant. And when you interpret a classical solar return chart for the year, it has to be viewed in the context of the natal chart. A retrograde planet in the solar return is a good thing, if that planet is also retrograde in your natal chart.

If you have a **stationary planet** in your natal chart—one that is about to change direction, either direct or retrograde, you can make note of this in your interpretation. A stationary planet may have greater focus and intensity, and this pinch of spice might add something to your interpretation. You can even spot a stationary (or slow-moving) planet in the chart, if you know what to look for.

Mercury and Venus always stay in close proximity to the Sun in the chart. Mercury will never be more than 28° from the Sun, and Venus will never be more than 46° from the Sun. When Mercury or Venus approaches their maximum distance from the Sun, they're about to change direction. When the Sun forms a trine to one of the superior planets, that planet has either just changed direction, or is getting ready to change direction.

Synthesized Natal Chart Interpretation Example

CHAPTER 26

George Lucas Interpretation Notes

An American director, writer, and film producer, **George Lucas** was born on May 14, 1944, at 5:40 A.M., in Modesto, California (Figure 39). Lucas created the epic movie *Star Wars*, first released in 1977, which forever changed the landscape of film, not to mention popular culture. Lucas' companies, including Industrial Light & Magic and LucasArts Entertainment, have pioneered special effects and defined the cutting-edge of computer-generated imagery for visual media.

This chapter includes the analysis, blueprints, notes, and sketch sentences for George Lucas' chart. Chapter 27 contains the finished astrological portrait of George Lucas, created from these notes and sketches.

Part 1: Personality

Elements and Modalities

George Lucas' Elements and Modalities are shown in Figure 40.

Notes

Elements: Emphasis on Earth (3 planets), and Air (2 planets) suggests Lucas is both practical and grounded (Earth) and able to work with abstract concepts (Air). Only one planet in Water suggests he may put a great emphasis on feelings and emotions to compensate for a self-perceived lack. Only one planet in Fire suggests he needs to supplement this energy with daily physical exercise to maintain balance.

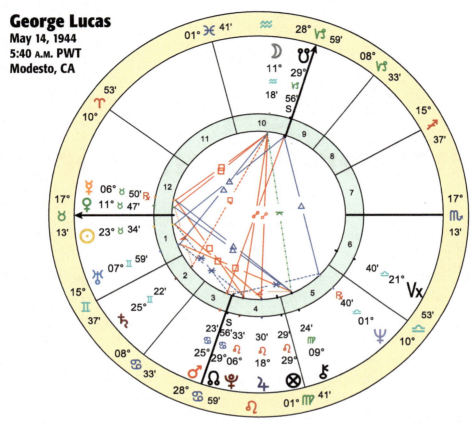

Figure 39: George Lucas' Natal Chart

Source: Astro-Databank; Rodden Rating: AA, BC/BR in hand.

George Lucas Interpretation Notes

Elements	INNER PLANETS	ANGLES	OUTER PLANETS
FIRE	♃	⊗	♇
EARTH	☉ ☿ ♀	AS MC ☋	⚷
AIR	☽ ♄	Vx	♅ ♆
WATER	♂	☊	
Modalities	INNER PLANETS	ANGLES	OUTER PLANETS
CARDINAL	♂	MC ☊ ☋ Vx	♆
FIXED	☉ ☽ ☿ ♀ ♃	AS ⊗	♇
MUTABLE	♄		⚷ ♅

Figure 40: George Lucas' Elements and Modalities

Modalities: Five planets in Fixed signs is extremely telling. Lucas will always look for routine, preferring long-term projects with little change. Only one planet in Cardinal suggests he is not inclined to initiate new projects, and only one planet in Mutable suggests he lacks flexibility, and the desire to complete things.

Lucas will be extremely resistant to change, and is likely to be defensive when other people comment, criticize, or suggest that he alter his routine or his behavior in any way. All impetus to change must come from within him.

Five planets in Fixed suggests a strong emphasis on issues of self-worth and self-esteem. Lucas' core false belief is that he is "not enough," and this underlying lack consciousness will be a major driving force in his life and behavior. Everything he creates, on some level, is an attempt to prove his self-worth and value as an individual.

Lucas will have tremendous endurance, strength, and loyalty because of such a strong emphasis in Fixed signs.

The Sun

The considerations that apply to George Lucas' Sun are shown in Figure 41.

Sun in Taurus in the 1st House
Sun Almuten 12th House

Lucas seeks to express his authentic "Big S" Self (Sun) by being materialistic, sluggish, peaceful and composed (Taurus), **WITH** his personal unconscious, shadow self, and relationship with hidden enemies (Sun almuten 12th). He encounters these needs particularly **IN** his personality, self-image, personal power, and self-expression (Sun in 1st).

Notes

Cause comes from his 12th house unconscious, shadow self, sorrows, and adversity. He won't always be conscious of the triggers, and the behaviors

Planet	Ruler	Exaltation	Triplicity	Term	Face
☉ ♉	♀ ♉	☽ ♒	☽ ♒	♄ ♊	♄ ♊
	5 Votes	4 Votes	3 Votes	2 Votes	1 Vote
Condition	Total Votes	Total Votes	Total Votes	Total Votes	Total Votes
Peregrine	5	7		3	
House Place	House Place	House Place	House Place	House Place	House Place
1st	12th	10th	10th	2nd	2nd
House Rule	House Rule	House Rule	House Rule	House Rule	House Rule
12th (alm)	1st, 6th, 11th (alm)	3rd, 4th, 1st (alm)	3rd, 4th, 1st (alm)	9th, 10th	9th, 10th
Dignity Score	Aspect	Aspect	Aspect	Aspect	Aspect
-5p	♀	☽	☽	♄	♄

♅ Aspect	♆ Aspect	♇ Aspect	⚷ Aspect	Other Aspect	Other Aspect
♅	♆	♇	⚷	⚹ ♂	□ ♃
				1a49	5s03
House Place	House Place	House Place	House Place	House Place	House Place
				3rd	4th
				House Rule	House Rule
				7th, 12th	8th, 11th

Figure 41: George Lucas' Sun

that result from these triggers may create additional resentment, adversity, and challenges. He will be more aware of the Taurus stick: change, disruption, abstract, or impractical ideas. A key trigger for Lucas may be an unconscious need to change.

Action is Sun in Taurus. He needs to align with his Personal Standards of Integrity. For Lucas, loyalty, practicality, and stability are very important. He won't see himself as being stubborn or intractable; he'll see himself as being loyal and dependable. He may resist change because it may feel that it violates his Personal Standards of Integrity. He needs to express his identity (Sun) in a tangible, practical, measured, considered (Taurus) way.

Effect is in the 1st house. He will take everything personally. It's all about him—his personal power, his appearance, his identity, who he is in relationship to other people. He will resist change because it goes against the concept he has of his own identity. He may adopt a "take it or leave it" attitude, which will create resentment, hidden enemies, and build up the internal unconscious pressure to change (Sun almuten 12th). When he finally does change, he will believe it was his idea all along.

Sketch Sentences

Lucas may not be conscious (Sun almuten 12th) of his Personal Standards of Integrity (Sun), and his unconscious definitions of loyalty, harmony, security, and industry (Taurus), which he expresses in his personal power, and self-image (Sun in 1st), may rub people the wrong way, creating hidden enemies (Sun almuten 12th).

Lucas wants to be a hero (Sun) by being artistic, patient, and dependable (Taurus) in his self-expression, personality, and physical appearance (Sun in 1st), but when he falls short of these standards, or doesn't experience enough of them (Fixed), he experiences sorrow and adversity (Sun almuten 12th).

When Lucas experiences adversity (Sun almuten 12th), he takes it personally (Fixed, Sun in 1st), and resolves to work harder and more efficiently (Taurus) to find happiness (Sun in 1st). However, he may become too focused on the physical, material, tangible, and sensual (Earth/Taurus) experiences, choosing comfort and luxury (Taurus) over the higher-consciousness expressions of his authentic "Big S" Self (Sun), which will only create more adversity, sorrow, and self-sabotage (Sun almuten 12th).

It's very important to Lucas that other people see him for who he truly is as an individual (Sun in 1st house), and that he is recognized for his Personal Standards of Integrity (Sun), which embody qualities of beauty, tranquility, generosity, and loyalty (Taurus). Lucas may not be conscious (Sun almuten 12th) of the fact that he may also appear insensitive, stubborn, indulgent, and unrelenting (Taurus), which may create hidden enemies, and result in self-sabotage (Sun almuten 12th).

Board of Directors for the Sun
Venus in Taurus in the 12th House (5 Votes, Rulership)
Venus Rules 1st, 6th, Almuten 11th

To express his authentic "Big S" Self (Sun's Board of Directors), he needs to feel validated, loved, and appreciated, and align with his Core Values (Venus) in a manner that is obstinate, dull, tolerant, and sensuous (Taurus), **WITH** his personality, personal power, self-image, and self-expression (Venus rules 1st), his job, service, and workplace relationships (Venus rules 6th), and his hopes, personal aspirations, and friendships (Venus almuten 11th). He encounters these needs particularly **IN** his personal unconscious, shadow self, and relationships with hidden enemies (Venus in 12th).

Notes

Another iteration of the 12th house and the 1st house, this time Lucas is unconscious of how Venus expresses because it's in his 12th house.

George Lucas Interpretation Notes

Venus is in Rulership and is the sole dispositor of Lucas' chart. It's extremely important and influential: it rules both Lucas' Sun and his Ascendant. It plays a key role in his personality, and needs to be explored in this context, as well as later in the context of his Validation Needs. But it's clear that meeting his Validation Needs and feeling loved and appreciated is a big part of Lucas' personality and a driving force in his identity.

Cause is in his personality, sense of self, personal power, and identity (Venus rules 1st), his job, service, and workplace relationships (Venus rules 6th), and/or his personal ambition, friendships, shared creativity, and acquisition (Venus almuten 11th). Taurus wants sensual pleasure, comfort, stability, practicality, routine, and loyalty; any disruption in the routine in any of these houses will trigger Venus to take action.

Action is Venus in Taurus. The primary goal is to meet his Validation Needs by experiencing or expressing love and appreciation. The secondary goal is to align with his Core Values, which, because Venus is in Taurus, are likely to involve beauty. Lucas will probably look for validation through creativity and artistic expression of some kind.

Effect is in the 12th house, so Lucas is unconscious of his actions and behaviors, although they're obvious to everyone else. Lucas' behaviors (appearance) that result from the action (essence) will create sorrow, adversity, resentment, and hidden enemies. The more he tries to meet his Validation Needs, the less successful he's likely to be.

Sketch Sentences

Lucas is not fully conscious (Venus in 12th) of how important it is to his health, vitality, and happiness (Sun's Board of Directors) that he experience love, appreciation, and validation (Venus) for his diligent, stable, loyal, and practical (Taurus) service, and work that he performs on a daily basis (Venus rules 6th).

Lucas' Core Values (Venus), which are heavily influenced by the qualities of beauty and aesthetics (Taurus), are closely aligned with his Personal Standards of Integrity (Sun's Board of Directors), and these values and standards form the basis of his personal power, and shape his self-image (Venus rules 1st house), although he is not always conscious of how they express (Venus in 12th).

Lucas' overall health and happiness (Sun's Board of Directors) are greatly enhanced when he can experience all forms of pleasure and affection (Venus), although he particularly enjoys physical pleasure, comfort, and luxury (Taurus/Earth). His personal ambitions and aspirations (Venus almuten 11th) may focus on building security through making money and indulging in creature comforts (Earth/Taurus), and he may tend towards hedonism (Taurus) because he's not conscious (Venus in 12th) of his fear that he will never have enough (Fixed). The more he focuses on the material realm, the less happy he will be.

It's important that Lucas be able to express love and appreciation for others (Venus), because that's part of his essential, authentic nature (Sun's Board of Directors). He primarily expresses appreciation on the physical and material planes (Earth/Taurus), but it's also important when he expresses love and appreciation that it's personal (Venus rules 1st). He may not be consciously aware (Venus in 12th) of how important it is that other people know how much he personally appreciates them, but it ties in to his Personal Standards of Integrity (Sun's Board of Directors).

Moon in Aquarius in the 10th House (7 Votes, Exaltation + Triplicity) Moon Rules 3rd, 4th, Almuten 1st

To express his authentic "Big S" Self (Sun's Board of Directors), he needs to feel safe, and express his feelings and emotions (Moon) in a manner that is rebellious, irritable, democratic, and objective (Aquarius), **WITH** his familiar environment, writing, and communication (Moon rules 3rd), his private life, home, and family relationships (Moon rules 4th), and his personality, personal power, self-image, and self-expression (Moon

George Lucas Interpretation Notes

almuten 1st). He encounters these needs particularly **IN** his career, public image, and reputation (Moon in 10th).

Notes

Lucas' Moon has more influence over his Sun than Venus does. Safety is more important to him than validation, although Lucas' Moon and Venus are in a partile Fixed square, so that's a pretty big issue. The difficulties he has feeling safe and validated will be a dominant theme in his chart.

Cause comes from his 3rd house familiar environment and communication, his 4th house private life and family relationships, or his 1st house personality, personal power, and sense of self. The Aquarius carrot is freedom and equality, so anything Lucas judges as unfair will make him feel unsafe and trigger his Moon to take action.

Action is the Moon in Aquarius, so the sole intention is to restore the minimum balance in his Safety Need Account. He will do this in the mental, social, intellectual realm (Air), and will look for greater levels of freedom and social acceptance (Aquarius).

Effect is in the 10th house, so it's public. This is an interesting contradiction, because Lucas will try to address issues in his 4th house private life by taking action in his 10th house public life. This suggests that Lucas' public reputation (10th house) is extremely important to him. His primary concern is that his personal life doesn't have a negative impact on his public persona or his career.

Sketch Sentences

When Lucas experiences his familiar environment (Moon rules 3rd) as being unfair, subjective, or restrictive (Aquarius stick), he is driven to express his authentic, "Big S" Self (Sun's Board of Directors) by defending his views (Fixed/Aquarius) in a public manner (Moon in 10th).

Lucas embodies his Personal Standards of Integrity (Sun's Board of Directors) by publicly and professionally (Moon in 10th) expressing his feelings (Moon) about freedom and unique personal expression (Aquarius) with his private life and family relationships (Moon rules 4th).

The need to feel safe (Moon) is a significant part of both Lucas' self-expression (Moon almuten 1st) and his ability to embody his authentic "Big S" Self (Sun's Board of Directors). He needs to be able to communicate (Moon rules 3rd) freely, and without restriction (Aquarius), and he will take criticism about his ideas personally, viewing it as a personal attack and judgment about his individual worth (Fixed). When he feels attacked or unsafe (Moon), he will need to express his identity (Sun's Board of Directors) and defend his public image and reputation (Moon in 10th).

His private life and family relationships (Moon rules 4th) shape his identity and how he wants to express it in the world (Sun's Board of Directors), although he may tend to be defensive and stubborn (Fixed) and feel the need to justify the abstract and unconventional behavior (Aquarius) of his family to the world (Moon in 10th).

Saturn in Gemini in the 2nd House (3 Votes, Term + Face)
Saturn Rules 9th, 10th Houses

To express his authentic "Big S" Self (Sun's Board of Directors), he needs to establish boundaries, accept responsibility, and respect authority (Saturn) in a manner that is diffuse, restless, articulate, and rational (Gemini), **WITH** his beliefs, philosophies, higher education, cross-cultural experiences, and unfamiliar environments (Saturn rules 9th) and his career, life path, and public reputation (Saturn rules 10th). He encounters these needs particularly **IN** his money and resources (Saturn in 2nd).

George Lucas Interpretation Notes

Notes

Saturn in Gemini has 3 official votes, but because Saturn rules the Moon in Aquarius, Saturn actually controls a total of 10 votes, making Saturn in Gemini the most significant influence over Lucas' Sun in Taurus.

Saturn is the only planet in a Mutable sign in Lucas' chart. Planets in Fixed signs control the rest of the votes on the Sun's Board of Directors, and the Sun itself is in a Fixed sign. However, because Saturn in Gemini rules the Moon in Aquarius, Lucas will not be as stubborn or inflexible as expected. He can be persuaded by clever, objective, communication (Gemini), and is inherently willing to consider both sides of any issue (Gemini), so long as he feels that he's being treated with respect (Saturn).

Cause comes from his 9th house beliefs, higher education, foreign or unfamiliar experiences, religion, law, or from his 10th house public reputation, life path, and career. Gemini carrot is playful, sociable, quick. Gemini stick is old, inflexible, responsible, focused, or practical.

Action is Saturn in Gemini. He needs to enforce and obey the letter of the law (Saturn), but also be able to take advantage of loopholes and speed to avoid having to be held accountable or restricted too much (Gemini). He will use words and ideas to establish authority, responsibility, and boundaries.

Effect is in his 2nd house of money and resources. There's a suggestion here that the more money he has, the less he'll have to obey authority. The person with the most money has the last word. He may use his money and resources to limit, restrict, create structure, or impose boundaries and limitations. He may also believe that when he has enough money, he can make his own laws.

Principles of Practical Natal Astrology

Aspects to the Sun

Mars in the 3rd House (Ruler of 7th and 12th) Sextile Sun in the 1st House (Almuten 12th House) [1a49]
(Mars has no votes on the Sun's Board of Directors)

There is an opportunity for support (sextile) **BETWEEN** his need to take action, expend energy, and pursue the things that he wants (Mars), **WITH** his marriage, partnerships, and one-to-one relationships (Mars rules 7th) and his personal unconscious, shadow-self, and hidden enemies (Mars rules 12th), **COMING FROM** his familiar environment, daily routine and habits, writing and communication (Mars in 3rd) **AND** his need to express his authentic "Big S" Self (Sun) **WITH** his personal unconscious, shadow self, and sorrows (Sun almuten 12th) **IN** his personality, physical appearance, self-image, and self-expression (Sun in 1st).

Notes

Mars is in Cancer, the only planet in a Cardinal sign in Lucas' chart.

Because Mars is in the 3rd house, Lucas encounters this energy as part of his daily routine in his familiar environment; as the ruler of the 7th house, Mars encourages Lucas to engage with other people (7th house), perhaps collaborating with writing or communication (Mars in 3rd house). There's an opportunity to energize himself through these collaborations, and they can help him to become more confident in his self-expression (Sun in 1st).

Because this is a sextile, it's a passive, potential energy. The option to collaborate with a partner is always present, but Lucas will have to make a conscious choice to do so.

Jupiter in the 4th House (Ruler of 8th and 11th) Square Sun in the 1st House (Almuten 12th House) [5s03]
(Jupiter has no votes on the Sun's Board of Directors; Sun has 5 votes on Jupiter's Board of Directors)

There is a friction, tension, stress, and conflict (square) **BETWEEN** his need to grow, expand, and experience faith (Jupiter), **WITH** his debts, shared resources, and other people's values and opinions (Jupiter rules 8th) and his hopes, personal ambitions, friendships, and shared creativity (Jupiter rules 11th), **COMING FROM** his home, personal life, and family relationships (Jupiter in 4th) **AND** his need to express his authentic "Big S" Self (Sun) **WITH** his personal unconscious, shadow self, and sorrows (Sun almuten 12th) **IN** his personality, physical appearance, self-image, and self-expression (Sun in 1st).

Notes

This aspect is not very significant because it's both wide and separating, and because Jupiter has no influence on the Sun's Board of Directors.

The Sun rules Jupiter in Leo, so the aspect has more importance for Jupiter, in the context of how Lucas grows, expands, and experiences faith, than it does in the context of the Sun, his authentic "Big S" Self.

The aspect suggests a slight tendency to be too big, or too much. Lucas may tend to brag about his ambitions and aspirations (Jupiter rules 11th), or he may carry more debt than he can easily handle (Jupiter rules 8th). This aspect does reinforce the "not enough" fears and patterns that come from having so many planets in Fixed signs. Because Jupiter is in the 4th house, the source of the lack consciousness (and the overcompensation by being too much) comes from his family, his personal life, and his relationship with his father.

Ascendant

The considerations that apply to George Lucas' Ascendant are shown in Figure 42.

Ascendant in Taurus

When he interacts with the world and other individuals (Ascendant), he appears to be lavish, adamant, artistic, and affectionate (Taurus).

Notes

Because the Sun is in the same sign as the Ascendant, the mask that Lucas wears to interact with the world (Ascendant) is very like his authentic, "Big S" Self (Sun). What you see is what you get with Lucas.

Ascendant's Board of Directors
Venus in Taurus in the 12th House (5 Votes, Rulership)
Venus Rules 1st, 6th, Almuten 11th

Other people perceive (Ascendant) his need to feel validated, loved, and appreciated, and align with his Core Values (Venus) in a manner that is decadent, insensitive, faithful, and serene (Taurus), **WITH** his personality, personal power, self-image, and self-expression

Planet	Ruler	Exaltation	Triplicity	Term	Face
AS ♉	♀ ♉	☽ ♒	☽ ♒	♃ ♌	☽ ♒
	5 Votes	4 Votes	3 Votes	2 Votes	1 Vote
	Total Votes	Total Votes	Total Votes	Total Votes	Total Votes
	5	8		2	
	House Place	House Place	House Place	House Place	House Place
	12th	10th	10th	4th	10th
	House Rule	House Rule	House Rule	House Rule	House Rule
	1st, 6th, 11th (alm)	3rd, 4th, 1st (alm)	3rd, 4th, 1st (alm)	8th, 11th	3rd, 4th, 1st (alm)
	Aspect	Aspect	Aspect	Aspect	Aspect
	♂ ♀	□ ☽		☽	□ ♃	☽
	5s25	5s55		1a17	

♅ Aspect	♆ Aspect	♇ Aspect	⚷ Aspect	Other Aspect	Other Aspect
♅	⚷ ♆	♇	⚷	♂ ☉	
	0s32			6a20	
House Place	House Place	House Place	House Place	House Place	House Place
	5th			1st	
				House Rule	House Rule
				12th (alm)	

Figure 42: George Lucas' Ascendant

George Lucas Interpretation Notes

(Venus rules 1st), his job, service, and workplace relationships (Venus rules 6th), and his hopes, personal aspirations, and friendships (Venus almuten 11th).

Notes

Venus also rules Lucas' Sun.

Everything about how Venus shows up in Lucas' authentic "Big S" Self (Sun's Board of Directors) is clearly visible to other people (Ascendant's Board of Directors).

Other people are clearly aware of Lucas' Validation Needs (Venus).

Moon in Aquarius in the 10th House
(8 Votes, Exaltation + Triplicity + Face)
Moon Rules 3rd, 4th, Almuten 1st

Other people perceive (Ascendant) his need to feel safe, and express his feelings and emotions (Moon) in a manner that is unrealistic, impractical, social, and analytical (Aquarius), **WITH** his familiar environment, writing, and communication (Moon rules 3rd), his private life, home, and family relationships (Moon rules 4th), and his personality, personal power, self-image, and self-expression (Moon almuten 1st).

Notes

The Moon also has 7 votes (Exaltation and Triplicity) on the Sun's Board of Directors, so everything about how the Moon shows up in Lucas' authentic "Big S" Self is clearly visible to other people (Ascendant's Board of Directors).

Other people are clearly aware of Lucas' Safety Needs (Moon).

Planets in the Ascendant

Lucas has three planets in the Ascendant: the Sun, Venus, and Mercury in Taurus. The Sun and Venus have already been explored in this context, which leaves only Mercury.

Mercury in Taurus in the 12th House
Mercury Rules 2nd and 5th Houses

Other people perceive (Ascendant) his need to understand and communicate (Mercury) in a manner that is self-indulgent, callous, loving, and robust (Taurus) **WITH** his money and resources (Mercury rules 2nd) and his pursuit of fun, tolerance for risk, personal creativity, and children (Mercury rules 5th).

Notes

Mercury brings another 12th house, unconscious element to Lucas' personality.

Cause is from his 2nd house money and resources and/or his 5th house creativity, risk, fun, and children.

Action is Mercury in Taurus. He will communicate (Mercury) in a very practical, tangible, stable, steady, consistent (Taurus) way.

Effect is unconscious because it's in his 12th house. Again, this suggests that Lucas is not conscious of how stubborn and intractable he seems, and this creates resentments and hidden enemies, sorrow and adversity (12th house).

Sketches

His need to communicate (Mercury) with his personal creativity (Mercury rules 5th), in a grounded, tangible, sensual, practical (Taurus) manner, is a noticeable part of his personality (Mercury in Ascendant), although he may not be fully conscious of what he is specifically trying to communicate (Mercury in 12th).

George Lucas Interpretation Notes

His talent (Mercury rules 2nd) for questioning and understanding (Mercury) his unconscious and subconscious (Mercury in 12th) in a patient, persistent, gentle, conservative manner (Taurus) is one of the qualities other people notice in him (Mercury in Ascendant).

Aspects to Ascendant

Jupiter in Leo the 4th House (Ruler of 8th and 11th) Square Ascendant [1a17, PARTILE]

There is friction, tension, stress, and conflict (square) caused by his need to grow, expand, and experience faith (Jupiter), **WITH** his debts, shared resources, and other people's values and opinions (Jupiter rules 8th) and his hopes, personal ambitions, friendships, and shared creativity (Jupiter rules 11th), **COMING FROM** his home, family relationships, and private life (Jupiter in 4th) and affecting how he interacts with the world and appears to other individuals (Ascendant).

Notes

Jupiter in Leo now becomes important in the context of Lucas' personality. The wide, separating square to his Sun, on its own, wasn't significant; however, an applying, partile square to the Ascendant makes Jupiter worth considering in more detail.

A square from Jupiter, especially in Fixed signs, emphasizes the underlying fear of "not enough" and overcompensates by being "too much."

Although Lucas has only one planet in a Cardinal sign (Mars in Cancer) and one planet in a Fire sign (Jupiter in Leo), squares can also create action. We seek to resolve the tension of squares by creating something tangible in the outside world. Lucas' Jupiter in Leo combines self-confidence, power, and expansive faith with an awareness of other people's values and opinions (Jupiter rules 8th) and a need to express his dreams and ambitions through teamwork and shared creativity (Jupiter rules 11th). This creates tension and the need for action, both in how Lucas approaches the world (Jupiter square Ascendant) and, to a lesser degree, in how Lucas embodies and expresses his authentic, "Big S" Self (Jupiter square Sun).

Sketch Sentences

He has big (Jupiter), extravagant, and dramatic (Leo) ambitions, personal aspirations, and dreams (Jupiter rules 11th) that come from his private life and form the foundation of his personality (Jupiter in 4th); however, when they express through his personality and in his interactions with others (Ascendant), they can cause conflict and tension (square).

A very powerful engine (square) of expansive, enthusiastic (Leo) faith and expansion (Jupiter) drives Lucas' personality and feeds his need to express his identity and create things of beauty and lasting value in the world of form (Sun, Venus, Mercury, Ascendant in Taurus).

Neptune in the 5th House Sesquisquare Ascendant [0s32]

There is a minor annoyance or irritation (sesquisquare) caused by dissolving boundaries, fantasy, glamor, and illusion (Neptune) **COMING FROM** his pursuit of fun, tolerance for risk, personal creativity, and children (Neptune in 5th), affecting how he interacts with the world and appears to other individuals (Ascendant).

Notes

This is a minor aspect, but it does suggest that Lucas' 5th house creative expression may cloud how other people perceive him. The boundary between Lucas' identity as an individual and the things that he creates may be blurry at times.

Because Lucas' Sun is in the same sign as the Ascendant, the aspect from Neptune is not likely to be an issue for him. For the most part, people see Lucas for who he is, and the minor glamor or deception that Neptune sesquisquare the Ascendant may bring from time to time barely registers.

George Lucas Interpretation Notes

Summary of Lucas' Personality

Strong unity of purpose because his Sun and Ascendant are both in Taurus. People see him for who he truly is.

He has a clear sense of his identity because the Sun is in the 1st house.

Mercury and Venus both occupy the 12th house, so much of his motivation is unconscious.

His Safety and Validation Needs (relationship needs) are extremely prominent in his personality and his individual identity.

The vast majority of the energies in his personality come from planets in Fixed signs. However, Saturn in Gemini has a surprising amount of influence over the Moon in Aquarius, and by extension over the Sun. Lucas will have some interesting contradictions in his personality: he is capable of being extremely stubborn and extremely flexible. Change, for Lucas, is either a slow laborious process, or so fast that other people may not be able to keep up.

Part 2: Relationship Needs

The Moon: Safety Needs
The considerations that apply to George Lucas' Moon are shown in Figure 43.

Moon in Aquarius in the 10th House
Moon Rules 3rd, 4th, Almuten 1st

To feel safe (Moon), he needs to feel reforming, inflexible, objective, and humanistic (Aquarius) **WITH** his familiar environment, writing, and communication (Moon rules 3rd), his private life, home, and family relationships (Moon rules 4th), and his personality, personal power, self-image, and self-expression (Moon almuten 1st). He encounters these needs particularly **IN** his career, life path, and public reputation (Moon in 10th).

Planet	Ruler	Exaltation	Triplicity	Term	Face
☽ ♒	♄ ♊		☿ ♉	☿ ♉	☿ ♉
	5 Votes	4 Votes	3 Votes	2 Votes	1 Vote
Condition	Total Votes	Total Votes	Total Votes	Total Votes	Total Votes
Peregrine	5		6		
House Place	House Place	House Place	House Place	House Place	House Place
10th	2nd		12th	12th	12th
House Rule	House Rule	House Rule	House Rule	House Rule	House Rule
3rd, 4th, 1st (alm)	9th, 10th		2nd, 5th	2nd, 5th	2nd, 5th
Dignity Score	Aspect	Aspect	Aspect	Aspect	Aspect
-5p	⚼ ♄		□ ☿	☿	☿
	0s55		4s27		

⛢ Aspect	♆ Aspect	♇ Aspect	⚷ Aspect	Other Aspect	Other Aspect
△ ⛢	♆	☍ ♇	⚻ ⚷	□ ♀	☍ ♃
3s18		4s45	1s53	0a29 (Partile)	7a12
House Place	House Place	House Place	House Place	House Place	House Place
1st		4th	5th	12th	4th
				House Rule	House Rule
				1st, 6th, 11th (alm)	8th, 11th

Figure 43: George Lucas' Moon

George Lucas Interpretation Notes

Notes

The Moon has already been explored in the context of Lucas' personality because it has significant influence over his Sun and Ascendant.

Lucas' Safety Needs (Moon) are a significant part of how he expresses his authentic, "Big S" Self (Sun's Board of Directors) and they are visible in his personality and how he presents to the outside world (Ascendant's Board of Directors).

Moon in Aquarius has an Air Safety Checklist. He looks for safety in the mental, social, intellectual, and abstract realms. He needs an intellectual understanding of the situation to feel safe.

Air Safety Checklist means he is not comfortable with emotions, feelings, or anything that is entirely subjective; Air prefers to move across the surface, not to explore the depths.

Aquarius is a Fixed Air sign, concerned with social (Air) self-worth (Fixed). To feel safe, he needs to know that he's in the right group, that he's surrounded by other people who share his beliefs, ideals, and perceptions.

Moon in Aquarius has a great love of humanity, but often has difficulty connecting to individual humans. He's more comfortable with expressing his feelings and compassion on a grand, public, group-oriented scale than he is on a personal, intimate level.

Sketch Sentences

Lucas needs to experience objective, intellectual freedom (Aquarius) in his familiar environment and daily routines (Moon rules 3rd), to feel safe (Moon). He will feel threatened (Moon) by too much emotional subjectivity (Aquarius stick), and will react by becoming inflexible, irritable, and impractical (Aquarius) in his career (Moon in 10th).

Lucas needs to be able to express his feelings and emotions (Moon) in a collaborative, analytical, and articulate (Aquarius) manner, especially with his family and in his private, personal life (Moon rules 4th). However, when he is forced to be practical or to consider the needs or feelings of any one individual on a personal level (Aquarius stick), he will feel unsafe (Moon) and react by taking his private issues (Moon rules 4th) and airing his grievances in a very public manner (Moon in 10th).

Lucas has a very public, professional need (Moon in 10th) to be seen as an individual (Moon almuten 1st) who expresses his feelings and emotions (Moon) in a unique, visionary, objective, and humanitarian (Aquarius) manner.

Lucas seeks to nurture and protect (Moon) his immediate family (Moon rules 4th), as well as his extended family, including his neighbors and people he encounters frequently (Moon rules 3rd) in a very public manner (Moon in 10th) by being funny, gregarious, and innovative (Aquarius). The ideas and innovations (Aquarius) that he explores in his career (Moon in 10th) are meant to nurture and support (Moon) his family (Moon rules 4th).

Board of Directors for the Moon
Saturn in Gemini in the 2nd House (5 Votes, Rulership)
Saturn Rules 9th, 10th Houses

To feel safe (Moon's Board of Directors), he needs to establish boundaries, limits, and structures, accept responsibility, and respect authority (Saturn) in a manner that is prying, variable, talented, and communicative (Gemini), **WITH** his beliefs, philosophies, higher education, cross-cultural experiences, and unfamiliar environments (Saturn rules 9th) and his career, life path, and public reputation (Saturn rules 10th). He encounters these needs particularly **IN** his money and resources (Saturn in 2nd).

George Lucas Interpretation Notes

Notes
The Moon and Saturn are the only two planets in Air signs in Lucas' chart.

Although Saturn in Gemini rules the Moon in Aquarius, Saturn reports to Mercury in Taurus (Triplicity, Term, Face on Moon's Board of Directors), giving Mercury complete control over the Moon's Board of Directors.

Lucas needs boundaries, structure, and responsibility (Saturn) to feel safe (Moon's Board of Directors), but he also needs the boundaries and responsibilities to be flexible and changeable (Gemini). It's almost as if he needs rules, but he also needs those rules to have loopholes so he can avoid following them unless it serves him.

Sketch Sentences
To feel safe (Moon's Board of Directors), Lucas expects the rules, regulations, and boundaries (Saturn) to be objective, flexible, and responsive (Gemini), especially when they relate to beliefs, philosophy, and higher education (Saturn rules 9th). This allows him to be flexible and adaptable (Gemini) in his values (Saturn in 2nd).

To feel safe (Moon's Board of Directors), Lucas needs to know that the laws (Saturn) are public (Saturn rules 10th) and therefore apply to everyone. It's still possible to take advantage of the fact that the laws are often tricky, erratic, and conflicting (Gemini) without ever violating the laws in his money and resources (Saturn in 2nd).

Lucas feels safe (Moon's Board of Directors) when he's being held accountable (Saturn) for being curious, versatile, reasoning, and responsive (Gemini) with his beliefs, higher learning, and philosophies (Saturn rules 9th) and with his life path and public reputation (Saturn rules 10th); however, he will feel threatened and unsafe when he is held accountable for being distracted, unthinking, undependable, and inconstant (Gemini). This will have a direct impact on how Lucas manages his money and resources (Saturn in 2nd).

Mercury in Taurus in the 12th House (6 Votes, Triplicity + Term + Face) Mercury Rules 2nd and 5th Houses

To feel safe (Moon's Board of Directors), he needs to understand and communicate (Mercury) in a manner that is grasping, slothful, robust, and enduring (Taurus), **WITH** his money and resources (Mercury rules 2nd) and his pursuit of fun, tolerance for risk, personal creativity, and children (Mercury rules 5th). He encounters these needs particularly **IN** his personal unconscious, shadow self, sorrows, and self-sabotage (Mercury in 12th).

Notes

Mercury in Taurus rules Saturn in Gemini, so Mercury controls virtually all of the votes on the Moon's Board of Directors. However, the Moon has 7 votes (Exaltation and Triplicity) on Mercury's Board of Directors, so there's a lot of give-and-take between the Moon and Mercury.

With Saturn in the 2nd and Mercury ruling the 2nd, money may play a significant role for Lucas in terms of his Safety Needs. He may have an attachment to money, or to maintaining a certain level of resources or savings.

Sketch Sentences

Lucas may not be conscious (Mercury in 12th) that to feel safe (Moon's Board of Directors), he needs to understand (Mercury) how his money and resources (Mercury rules 2nd) are stable, secure, and dependable (Taurus). Any disruptions in the slow, steady, constant growth (Taurus) of his money (Mercury rules 2nd) will create unconscious anxiety (Mercury in 12th), which will make him feel unsafe (Moon's Board of Directors).

Lucas' stubborn, inflexible, self-indulgent, and tiresome (Taurus) approach to communicating (Mercury) his creative and artistic impulses (Mercury

George Lucas Interpretation Notes

rules 5th) may result in sorrow and self-sabotage (Mercury in 12th) which will make him feel unsafe (Moon's Board of Directors).

To feel safe (Moon's Board of Directors), Lucas needs to be able to understand and communicate (Mercury) in a patient, loyal, peaceful, and practical (Taurus) way, expressing his values and talents (Mercury rules 2nd) and having fun by being creative or playing games (Mercury rules 5th); but because he is unconscious of this need, it might cause resentment and create hidden enemies (Mercury in 12th).

Aspects to the Moon
Saturn in the 2nd House (Rules 9th, 10th Houses) Sesquisquare Moon in 10th House (Rules 3rd, 4th, Almuten 1st) [0s55]
(Saturn has 5 votes on the Moon's Board of Directors)

There is a minor annoyance or irritation (sesquisquare) **BETWEEN** his need to establish boundaries, accept responsibility, and respect authority (Saturn), **WITH** his beliefs, philosophies, higher education, cross-cultural experiences, and unfamiliar environments (Saturn rules 9th) and his career, life path, and public reputation (Saturn rules 10th), **COMING FROM** his money and resources (Saturn in 2nd) **AND** his need to feel safe (Moon) **WITH** his familiar environment, writing, and communication (Moon rules 3rd), his private life, home, and family relationships (Moon rules 4th), and his personality, personal power, self-image, and self-expression (Moon almuten 1st). This could cause him to feel unsafe **IN** his career, public image, and reputation (Moon in 10th).

Notes

Saturn–Moon aspects suggest Checklists From Hell. The expectations and requirements for Lucas to feel safe (and receive deposits in his Safety Need Account) may be unreasonable.

Saturn has significant influence on Moon's Board of Directors and has already been explored in this context.

The sesquisquare is a minor aspect; it tends to be mental, and the tension is often resolved through humor.

This seems to reinforce the idea that Lucas has contradictory needs when it comes to rules and responsibilities, and how they make him feel safe. As noted earlier, he needs the rules to be public (Saturn rules 10th) so they apply to everyone; however, he also needs the rules to be flexible (Gemini), or have built-in loopholes so when he doesn't want the rules to apply to him, personally, he can circumvent them without violating them, by being clever, skillful, and tricky (Gemini). But there's a fine line between a rule that's got just enough of a loophole that he can exploit and a rule that is so diffuse and scattered that it doesn't provide any stability at all.

Uranus in the 1st House Trine Moon in 10th House (Rules 3rd, 4th, Almuten 1st) [0s55]

There is an easy, constant, effortless flow of energy (trine) caused by disruptions and unexpected events (Uranus) **COMING FROM** his personality, self-image, self-expression, and personal power (Uranus in 1st) **AND** affecting his need to feel safe (Moon), **WITH** his familiar environment, writing, and communication (Moon rules 3rd), his private life, home, and family relationships (Moon rules 4th), and his personality, personal power, self-image, and self-expression (Moon almuten 1st). This could cause him to feel unsafe **IN** his career, public image, and reputation (Moon in 10th).

Notes

Uranus–Moon aspects usually suggest, "Safe doesn't feel safe." The trine means the disruptive flow from Uranus is constant and never-ending. It's familiar to Lucas, and he knows how to handle it, so the changes and disruptions don't drain his Safety Need Account; however, they may create problems for other people who aren't comfortable with such unpredictable behavior.

This is yet another indication (along with Saturn in Gemini/Mutable ruling the Moon in Aquarius/Fixed) that as much as Lucas needs structure and stability to feel safe (Moon in Aquarius = Fixed), he also needs to be able to break out of the box.

Uranus is in the 1st house, so the disruptive impulse comes from within Lucas, his personality, and his sense of self. Because the Moon is in the 10th, the disruptions are public, and this may make Lucas feel unsafe. He wants to be able to outsmart the rules because he's so clever, but Saturn rules his 10th house, so he doesn't want a public reputation as someone who is deceptive, duplicitous, or unreliable (Gemini).

Pluto in the 4th House Opposite Moon in 10th House (Rules 3rd, 4th, Almuten 1st) [4s45]

There is a need for balance and compromise (opposition) caused by issues of power, control, and manipulation (Pluto) **COMING FROM** his home, family relationships, and private life (Pluto in 4th) **AND** affecting his need to feel safe (Moon), **WITH** his familiar environment, writing, and communication (Moon rules 3rd), his private life, home, and family relationships (Moon rules 4th), and his personality, personal power, self-image, and self-expression (Moon almuten 1st). This could cause him to feel unsafe **IN** his career, public image, and reputation (Moon in 10th).

Notes

Moon–Pluto aspects suggest issues involving power, control, and manipulation. Lucas is likely to be sensitive to the power dynamic (Pluto) in relationships (opposition). Because Pluto is in his 4th house, he encounters issues of power and control in his personal, private life, and his family dynamics, and may also have ties back to his relationship with and experience of his father. Lucas reacts to these issues in a public manner (Moon in 10th house). The aspect is separating and somewhat wide, so it's probably not a dominant theme for Lucas.

Chiron in the 5th House Quincunx Moon in 10th House (Rules 3rd, 4th, Almuten 1st) [1s53]

There are random, unexpected disruptions (quincunx) caused by his core wound (Chiron) **COMING FROM** his personal creativity, pursuit of fun, tolerance for risk, and children (Chiron in 5th) **AND** affecting his need to feel safe (Moon), **WITH** his familiar environment, writing, and communication (Moon rules 3rd), his private life, home, and family relationships (Moon rules 4th), and his personality, personal power, self-image, and self-expression (Moon almuten 1st). This could cause him to feel unsafe **IN** his career, public image, and reputation (Moon in 10th).

Notes

Lucas has Chiron in Virgo, so his core wound has to do with healing and completing (Mutable) on the physical and material plane (Earth). Planets in Virgo become focused on analyzing the details, and often have issues with perfection (or the perceived lack of it). Chiron in Virgo in the 5th house suggests he encounters this wound when he expresses his creativity, takes risks, and pursues fun and entertainment (Chiron in 5th), and because the Moon is in the 10th house, this wound has a direct impact on his career, life path, and public reputation. At random, unexpected times (quincunx), Lucas may encounter his core wound (Chiron) where he finds flaws and imperfections (Virgo) in his art (5th house), which makes him feel unsafe (Moon) in his career (Moon in 10th).

Mercury in the 12th House (Rules 2nd, 5th Houses) Square Moon in 10th House (Rules 3rd, 4th, Almuten 1st) [4s27] (Mercury has 6 votes on the Moon's Board of Directors, Moon has 7 votes on Mercury's Board of Directors)

There is friction, tension, stress, and conflict (square) **BETWEEN** his need to understand and communicate (Mercury) **WITH** his money and resources (Mercury rules 2nd) and his pursuit of fun, tolerance for risk, personal creativity, and children (Mercury rules 5th) **COMING FROM** his personal unconscious, shadow self, sorrows, and self-sabotage (Mercury in 12th) **AND** his need to feel safe (Moon), **WITH** his familiar environment, writing, and communication (Moon rules 3rd), his private life, home, and family relationships

George Lucas Interpretation Notes

(Moon rules 4th), and his personality, personal power, self-image, and self-expression (Moon almuten 1st). This could cause him to feel unsafe **IN** his career, public image, and reputation (Moon in 10th).

Notes

This is a particularly important aspect, because the Moon and Mercury are so closely connected: The Moon is the almuten of Mercury (7 votes) and Mercury is the almuten of the Moon (6 votes). They are effectively in charge of each other, and at the same time, they are at cross purposes, creating a great deal of tension.

The aspect is wide and separating; however, it is still important because it's a part of the larger, more important square between the Moon and Venus, which will be addressed later.

Squares create stress and tension that can be resolved only by taking action. They're uncomfortable, but squares can be the engines that drive a person to succeed. A square between two planets in Fixed signs is particularly difficult, and it requires sustained, steady action to relieve the tension.

Lucas needs to tell stories (Mercury) that explore feelings and emotions (Moon). Because both Mercury and the Moon are in Fixed signs, the stories must endure, and have weight to them. This drive integrates his 5th house creativity with his 10th house career, and draws on his 2nd house resources, skills, and talents, and his 3rd house writing, communication, early education, and childhood experiences. It taps into his personal unconscious (Mercury in the 12th) and expresses in a public and professional manner (Moon in 10th).

Summary George Lucas' Safety Needs

The most prominent theme with regards to Lucas' Safety Needs is that he needs to balance his need for structure, rules, routine, and stability with his need for freedom, flexibility, and an exception to every rule.

The inherent conflict between Saturn in Gemini and Mercury in Taurus, and that they both make hard aspects to Lucas' Moon make this a difficult path to navigate. The loopholes in the rules have to be small and specific enough that only someone extremely clever could exploit them.

Venus: Validation Needs

The considerations that apply to George Lucas' Venus are shown in Figure 44.

Venus in Taurus in the 12th House
Venus Rules 1st, 6th, Almuten 11th

To feel validated (Venus), he needs to be materialistic, unoriginal, resolute, and patient (Taurus) **WITH** his personality, personal power, self-image, and self-expression (Venus rules 1st), his

Planet	Ruler	Exaltation	Triplicity	Term	Face
♀ ♉	♀ ♉	☽ ♒	☽ ♒	☿ ♉	☽ ♒
	5 Votes	4 Votes	3 Votes	2 Votes	1 Vote
Condition	Total Votes	Total Votes	Total Votes	Total Votes	Total Votes
Rulership	5	8		2	
House Place	House Place	House Place	House Place	House Place	House Place
12th	12th	10th	10th	12th	10th
House Rule	House Rule	House Rule	House Rule	House Rule	House Rule
1st, 6th, 11th (alm)	1st, 6th, 11th (alm)	3rd, 4th, 1st (alm)	3rd, 4th, 1st (alm)	2nd, 5th	3rd, 4th, 1st (alm)
Dignity Score	Aspect	Aspect	Aspect	Aspect	Aspect
5	♀	□ ☽	☽	☌ ☿	☽
		0a29 (Partile)		1s25	

♅ Aspect	♆ Aspect	♇ Aspect	⚷ Aspect	Other Aspect	Other Aspect
♅	♆	♇	△ ⚷	∠ ♄	
			2s23	1s25	
House Place	House Place	House Place	House Place	House Place	House Place
			5th	2nd	
				House Rule	House Rule
				9th, 10th	

Figure 44: George Lucas' Venus

George Lucas Interpretation Notes

job, service, and workplace relationships (Venus rules 6th), and his hopes, personal aspirations, and friendships (Venus almuten 11th). He encounters these needs particularly **IN** his personal unconscious, shadow self, sorrows, and self-sabotage (Venus in 12th).

Notes

Venus has already been explored in detail in the context of Lucas' personality. His need to be loved and appreciated (Venus) is one of the defining elements of both his authentic "Big S" Self (Sun's Board of Directors) and how he appears to others and interacts with the world (Ascendant's Board of Directors).

Venus is also the sole dispositor of Lucas' chart.

Venus in Taurus has an Earth Validation Checklist. He expresses and seeks love and appreciation on the physical, material, tangible plane. He needs sensual, durable expressions of affection and esteem. Words will never be enough to convey love, appreciation, or validation.

Taurus is Fixed Earth, the slowest, most physical energy. Validation is closely tied to his issues of self-worth and self-esteem (Fixed). He needs tangible, enduring evidence that he is worthy and loved—e.g., awards, gifts, presents. Money, luxury, and creature comforts can become how he measures his self-worth, and may also become the default way that he shows appreciation for others. This will be successful only with people who also have Earth Validation Checklists.

Sketch Sentences

He may not be conscious (Venus in 12th) that he loves, appreciates, and values (Venus) individuals who have the same personality traits and appearance that he does (Venus rules 1st), and embody the same values (Venus) of loyalty, patience, tolerance, and competence (Taurus).

He wants to be validated and appreciated (Venus) for being efficient, diligent, warm-hearted, and stable (Taurus) in his job, service, and workplace relationships (Venus rules 6th); however, because he is unconscious of these needs (Venus in 12th), others may experience him as being obstinate, materialistic, and callous (Taurus), which will make him feel invalidated (Venus), and create sorrow and adversity (Venus in 12th).

He wants to be validated and appreciated (Venus) for how grounded, artistic, benevolent, and enduring (Taurus) his hopes, dreams, and personal ambitions are (Venus almuten 11th), but because he is not conscious of this need (Venus in 12th), it may create resentment among his friends (Venus almuten 11th) who may perceive him to be self-indulgent, vulgar, and dull (Taurus).

Board of Directors for Venus
Venus in Taurus in the 12th House (5 Votes, Rulership)
Venus Rules 1st, 6th, Almuten 11th

He wants to be validated (Venus' Board of Directors) **FOR** his ability to align with his Core Values (Venus) in a manner that is dull, insensitive, comfortable, and serene (Taurus), **WITH** his personality, personal power, self-image, and self-expression (Venus rules 1st), his job, service, and workplace relationships (Venus rules 6th), and his hopes, personal aspirations, and friendships (Venus almuten 11th). He encounters these needs particularly **IN** his personal unconscious, shadow self, sorrows, and self-sabotage (Venus in 12th).

Moon in Aquarius in the 10th House
(8 Votes, Exaltation + Triplicity + Face)
Moon Rules 3rd, 4th, Almuten 1st

He wants to be validated (Venus' Board of Directors) **FOR** his ability to feel safe, and express his feelings and emotions (Moon) in a manner that is superficial, contrary, funny, and avant-garde (Aquarius), **WITH** his familiar environment, writing, and communication (Moon rules 3rd), his private life, home, and family relationships (Moon rules 4th), and his personality, personal power, self-image, and self-expression (Moon almuten 1st). He encounters these needs particularly **IN** his career, life path, and public reputation (Moon in 10th).

Mercury in Taurus in the 12th House (2 Votes, Term)
Mercury Rules 2nd, 5th Houses

He wants to be validated (Venus' Board of Directors) **FOR** his ability to understand and communicate (Mercury) in a manner that is jealous, lazy, persistent, and industrious (Taurus), **WITH** his money and resources (Mercury rules 2nd) and his pursuit of fun, tolerance for risk, personal creativity, and children (Mercury rules 5th). He encounters these needs particularly **IN** his personal unconscious, shadow self, sorrows, and self-sabotage (Mercury in 12th).

Notes

All three planets on Venus' Board of Directors have been explored in detail already.

Aspects to Venus
Saturn in the 2nd House (Rules 9th, 10th Houses) Semi-Square Venus in 12th House (Rules 1st, 6th, Almuten 11th) [1s25]
(Saturn has no votes on Venus' Board of Directors)

There is a minor internal tension or friction (semi-square) **BETWEEN** his need to establish boundaries, accept responsibility, and respect authority (Saturn), **WITH** his beliefs, philosophies, higher education, cross-cultural experiences, and unfamiliar environments (Saturn rules 9th) and his career, life path, and public reputation (Saturn rules 10th), **COMING FROM** his money and resources (Saturn in 2nd) **AND** his need to feel validated (Venus), **WITH** his personality, personal power, self-image, and self-expression (Venus rules 1st), his job, service, and workplace relationships (Venus rules 6th), and his hopes, personal aspirations, and friendships (Venus almuten 11th). This could cause him to feel invalidated **IN** his personal unconscious, shadow self, and relationships with hidden enemies (Venus in 12th).

Notes

Saturn–Venus aspects indicate Checklists From Hell that make it difficult for him to receive deposits in his Validation Need Account. This is a minor aspect (semi-square), and it's separating, so the influence is negligible.

Because Venus is in the 12th house, Lucas will tend to be unconscious of everything associated with his Validation Needs. This aspect is far too subtle to register.

Chiron in the 5th House Trine Venus in 12th House (Rules 1st, 6th, Almuten 11th) [1s25]

There is an easy, constant, effortless flow of energy (trine) **CAUSED BY** his core wound (Chiron), **COMING FROM** his pursuit of fun, tolerance for risk, personal creativity, and children (Chiron in 5th) and affecting his need to feel validated (Venus) **WITH** his personality, personal power, self-image, and self-expression (Venus rules 1st), his job, service, and workplace relationships (Venus rules 6th), and his hopes, personal aspirations, and friendships (Venus almuten 11th). This could cause him to feel invalidated **IN** his personal unconscious, shadow self, and relationships with hidden enemies (Venus in 12th).

Notes

Lucas will notice this aspect; however, it will show up more via the quincunx between Chiron and the Moon (i.e., in his Safety Needs) than it will in his Validation Needs. As Lucas must meet his Safety Needs before he can begin to feel validated (Moon almuten of Venus), the Chiron–Venus aspect reinforces one of the big safety challenges for Lucas.

Chiron in Virgo in the 5th house suggests a core wound involving perfectionism with his creativity. The trine to Venus means that the moment Lucas notices some flaw in his creations or some detail he overlooked, he will no longer be able to accept praise, recognition, or validation for that creation. This may drive him to constantly improve his creations so he can feel worthy (Venus in Taurus/Fixed) of the approval and attention they receive.

George Lucas Interpretation Notes

If he experiences this from lower levels of consciousness (i.e., First Kingdom/Victim Consciousness) it will create significant problems for him. He will not be able to accept praise or validation for anything, because nothing is ever as good as he believes it should be. This will trigger his core issues around self-worth and self-esteem (5 planets in Fixed signs), creating adversity, sorrow, and self-sabotage (Venus in 12th).

If he experiences this from higher levels of consciousness, and embraces the truth that perfection is a process, not a destination, this aspect can inspire him to greater self-expression, encouraging him to innovate and move beyond what has been done before, in pursuit of the next level of improvement. He will be able to accept praise and validation for what he has accomplished even as he looks ahead to how he can improve his next creation.

Mercury in the 12th House (Rules 2nd, 5th Houses) Conjunct Venus in 12th House (Rules 1st, 6th, Almuten 11th) [1s25] (Mercury has 2 votes on Venus' Board of Directors)

There is a unity of purpose (conjunction) **BETWEEN** his need to understand and communicate (Mercury) **WITH** his money and resources (Mercury rules 2nd) and his pursuit of fun, tolerance for risk, personal creativity, and children (Mercury rules 5th), **COMING FROM** his personal unconscious, shadow self, sorrows, and self-sabotage (Mercury in 12th) **AND** his need to feel validated (Venus) **WITH** his personality, personal power, self-image, and self-expression (Venus rules 1st), his job, service, and workplace relationships (Venus rules 6th), and his hopes, personal aspirations, and friendships (Venus almuten 11th). This could cause him to feel invalidated **IN** his personal unconscious, shadow self, and relationships with hidden enemies (Venus in 12th).

Notes

The main significance of this aspect is that it reinforces the connection between Lucas' Validation Needs (Venus) and his money and creativity (Mercury rules 2nd and 5th). We've already noted in several instances that Lucas has the potential to become attached to money, luxury, and creature comforts.

Summary of Relationship Needs: Connection Between Moon and Venus
Moon in the 10th House (Rules 3rd, 4th, Almuten 1st) Square
Venus in 12th House (Rules 1st, 6th, Almuten 11th) [0a29, PARTILE]
(Moon has 8 votes on Venus' Board of Directors;
Venus has no votes on the Moon's Board of Directors)

There is friction, tension, stress, and conflict (square) **BETWEEN** his need to feel safe (Moon) **WITH** his familiar environment, writing, and communication (Moon rules 3rd), his private life, home, and family relationships (Moon rules 4th), and his personality, personal power, self-image, and self-expression (Moon almuten 1st), **AND** his need to feel validated (Venus), **WITH** his personality, personal power, self-image, and self-expression (Venus rules 1st), his job, service, and workplace relationships (Venus rules 6th), and his hopes, personal aspirations, and friendships (Venus almuten 11th). This could cause him to feel unsafe **IN** his career, public image, and reputation (Moon in 10th house) and invalidated **IN** his personal unconscious, shadow self, and relationships with hidden enemies (Venus in 12th).

Notes

This is a tremendously significant aspect for Lucas, and the energy of this square drives virtually every facet of his personality, because the Moon and Venus are so influential in his chart.

The Moon's needs are far more important than Venus' needs. The Moon has 8 votes on Venus' Board of Directors, while Venus has no influence over the Moon, plus objectively, Safety Needs are more important than Validation Needs. The Moon in Aquarius means that Lucas is less likely to become attached to the physical and material plane, at least not on a personal level. The square drives Lucas to take action; he needs to create as an expression of his 1st house identity, and he needs to do so in a public and professional way (Moon in 10th house). But the Moon in Aquarius sets the context for this attention, and Aquarius cares about the good of the group, not the good of the individual. Lucas can meet his Safety and Validation Needs only when he is receiving appreciation for having created something that speaks to a wide audience. The benefit to humanity must come first, and he must see that there is objective value and worth in his creations before he can derive any personal benefit from them. Lucas will happily cash the checks from his creative expressions because he knows they're about something bigger than his own personality.

Part 3: Relationship Wants
Descendant in Scorpio/Vertex in Libra
Notes

On a conscious level, Lucas is drawn to partners who embody the emotional depth and intensity of his Descendant in Scorpio. These partners will come into direct conflict with his Moon in Aquarius Safety Needs, because Scorpio and Aquarius are square by sign. Scorpio partners care about emotional depth, and Lucas' Moon in Aquarius is uncomfortable with deep, personal emotions. There will be an initial attraction and an energizing spark, but in the long run, Scorpio partners will create serious safety issues for Lucas.

Lucas will also find these partners attractive because Scorpio opposes his Venus in Taurus, and opposites attract. However, oppositions are challenging when it comes to meeting each other's needs. It's possible for Scorpio partners to meet Lucas' Validation Needs, but it's not likely, because of the conflict between Scorpio and the Moon in Aquarius, and the Moon in Aquarius is more important in the context of Lucas' relationships than Venus in Taurus.

On an unconscious level, Lucas is attracted to partners who embody the objective, harmonious, balanced, diplomatic energy of his Vertex in Libra. Libra is trine Aquarius by sign, and they're both in the element of Air. These partners will do an excellent job of meeting Lucas' Moon in Aquarius Safety Needs. They, too, prefer to operate on the surface, they mean exactly what they say, and they are uncomfortable with deep emotions.

Vertex in Libra partners may have a difficult time meeting Lucas' Venus in Taurus Validation Needs, because Taurus and Libra are quincunx by sign. However, Venus rules both Taurus and Libra, so this may make it easier for Lucas. The biggest challenge is that Vertex in Libra partners will use words, and words alone are not sufficient to meet Lucas' Venus in Taurus Validation Needs. Again, because the most important needs for Lucas are his Moon in Aquarius Safety Needs, and Vertex in Libra partners will meet those extremely well, there's a better than expected chance that these partners will also meet his Validation Needs.

Marriage Blueprint

George Lucas' Marriage Blueprint is shown in Figure 45.

Notes

Both the Moon and Saturn are peregrine in Lucas' chart, so at first glance, his parents were on equal footing.

Saturn (mother) rules the Moon (father). Saturn has 5 votes (Rulership) on Moon's Board of Directors; the Moon has no influence on Saturn's Board of Directors. Plus, Lucas' father (Moon) is in the house of his mother

Father

4th HOUSE	Ruler (+5)	Exaltation (+4)	Triplicity (+3)	Term (+2)	Face (+1)
☽ ♒	♄ ♊		☿ ♉	☿ ♉	☿ ♉
House Place	House Place	House Place	House Place	House Place	House Place
10th	2nd		12th	12th	12th

Mother

10th HOUSE	Ruler (+5)	Exaltation (+4)	Triplicity (+3)	Term (+2)	Face (+1)
♄ ♊	☿ ♉		☿ ♉	♂ ♋	☉ ♉
House Place	House Place	House Place	House Place	House Place	House Place
2nd	12th		12th	3rd	1st

Figure 45: George Lucas' Marriage Blueprint

(10th house). This suggests that Lucas perceived even though his parents appeared to be equal, his mother called the shots in his parents' marriage.

Saturn (mother) in 2nd house suggests that Lucas' mother controlled the family finances.

Saturn and Moon are trine by sign, but sesquisquare by aspect. This suggests that there was some friction between his parents—perhaps his father wasn't entirely happy with the power dynamic—but the conflict was not severe and was probably resolved through humor.

Lucas' Marriage Blueprint supports his Safety Needs extremely well. Lucas will identify with the Moon (his father), which will be a familiar energy for him.

Friends, Lovers, Spouses

George Lucas' relationship houses are shown in Figure 46.

11th House: Friendships
Jupiter in Leo in the 4th House
(Jupiter also Rules 8th House)

George Lucas is likely to become friends (11th house) with people who align with his need to grow, expand, and experience faith (Jupiter) in a manner that is uppity, vain, forthcoming, and charismatic (Leo), **WITH** his debts, shared resources, and other people's values and opinions (Jupiter rules 8th). He is most likely to meet these partners **IN** his private life, family relationships, and home environment (Jupiter in 4th).

Notes

Of the three relationship houses, Jupiter in Leo has the most Essential Dignity, suggesting that Lucas may value his friendships above all other relationships.

Jupiter (ruler of 11th) in the 4th house = his friends, peers, and teammates are his family.

5th House: Love Affairs
Mercury in Taurus in the 12th House
(Mercury also Rules 2nd House)

George Lucas looks for casual romantic partners (5th house) who align with his need to understand and communicate (Mercury) in a manner that is acquisitive, envious, secure, and tranquil (Taurus), **WITH** his money and resources (Mercury rules 2nd). He is most likely to meet these partners **IN** institutions, or spiritual retreats (Mercury in 12th).

5th HOUSE ☿ ♉	Ruler (+5) ♀ ♉	Exaltation (+4) ☽ ♒	Triplicity (+3) ☽ ♒	Term (+2) ♀ ♉	Face (+1) ♀ ♉
House Place 12th	House Place 12th	House Place 10th	House Place 10th	House Place 12th	House Place 12th
House Rule 2nd, 5th	House Rule 1st, 6th, 11th (alm)	House Rule 3rd, 4th, 1st (alm)	House Rule 3rd, 4th, 1st (alm)	House Rule 1st, 6th, 11th (alm)	House Rule 2nd, 5th
7th HOUSE ♂ ♋	Ruler (+5) ☽ ♒	Exaltation (+4) ♃ ☊	Triplicity (+3) ♂ ♋	Term (+2) ♀ ♉	Face (+1) ☽ ♒
House Place 3rd	House Place 10th	House Place 4th	House Place 3rd	House Place 12th	House Place 10th
House Rule 7th, 12th	House Rule 3rd, 4th, 1st (alm)	House Rule 8th, 11th	House Rule 7th, 12th	House Rule 1st, 6th, 11th (alm)	House Rule 3rd, 4th, 1st (alm)
11th HOUSE ♃ ☊	Ruler (+5) ☉ ♉	Exaltation (+4)	Triplicity (+3) ♃ ☊	Term (+2) ♀ ♉	Face (+1) ♂ ♋
House Place 4th	House Place 1st	House Place	House Place 4th	House Place 12th	House Place 3rd
House Rule 8th, 11th	House Rule 12th (alm)	House Rule	House Rule 8th, 11th	House Rule 1st, 6th, 11th (alm)	House Rule 7th, 12th

Figure 46: George Lucas' Relationship Houses

George Lucas Interpretation Notes

Notes

Mercury is not in very good shape in Lucas' chart. It's retrograde, in the 12th house, has dignity only by Face (= fear), and is in a partile square to Pluto, while also separating from a trine to Chiron. Casual dating will not hold much attraction for Lucas—particularly because of the control and manipulation elements introduced by Pluto. The Moon–Pluto opposition means Lucas is already sensitive to this dynamic, and it won't appeal to him.

7th House: Marriage
Mars in Cancer in the 3rd House
(Mars also Rules 12th House)

George Lucas' marriage and relationships with other individuals (7th house) involve being able to expend energy, take action, and pursue the things that he wants (Mars) in a manner that is glum, reactive, intuitive, and sensitive (Cancer), **WITH** his personal unconscious, shadow-self, sorrows, and self-sabotage (Mars rules 12th). He is most likely to meet these partners **IN** his familiar environment, and daily routines and habits (Mars in 3rd).

Notes

Mars, by comparison with Mercury, is in much better shape. Even though Mars in Cancer is in Fall, Mars has dignity by Triplicity, and is sextile the Sun.

Mars is in the 3rd house but conjunct the IC; Lucas views his spouse as part of the foundation of his life.

Mars is conjunct the North Node on the IC: his marriage partner supports him on his soul evolution.

That Mars also rules the 12th house suggests that his marriage may also be where he experiences self-sabotage and adversity. He needs to be careful not to turn his spouse into a hidden enemy.

Connections Between 11th, 5th, and 7th Houses

The strongest connections are between the 7th and 11th houses. Jupiter (ruler of 11th) has 4 votes on Mars' Board of Directors (Exaltation); Mars has 1 vote on Jupiter's Board of Directors (Face). This suggests that friendship is an important foundation of Lucas' marriage.

There are some connections between the 5th and 7th houses, but they're all indirect, via the Moon and Venus. The Moon has 7 votes (Exaltation, Triplicity) on Mercury's Board of Directors, and 6 votes (Rulership, Face) on Mars' Board of Directors. It's possible for a casual, 5th house relationship to turn into something serious, but it's not very likely.

There are no connections at all between the 5th and 11th houses, so Lucas would never consider a casual romantic partner to be a friend (or an equal).

Part 4: Career

George Lucas' career houses are shown in Figure 47.

10th House: Career
Saturn in Gemini in the 2nd House
(Saturn also Rules 9th House)

George Lucas' career and life path (10th house) involve being able to establish boundaries, limits, and structures, accept responsibility, and respect authority (Saturn) in a manner that is restless, volatile, quick-witted, and curious (Gemini), **WITH** his beliefs, philosophies, cross-cultural experiences, and foreign travel (Saturn rules 9th). He encounters these needs particularly **IN** his money and resources (Saturn in 2nd).

Notes

Saturn has been explored already in other contexts.

Ruler of the 10th in the 2nd connects his life path and career with his money.

George Lucas Interpretation Notes

That Saturn rules both the 9th and the 10th suggests his professional life may involve 9th house matters, including philosophy, higher education, foreign travel, law, publishing, or advertising.

Saturn is the only Mutable planet in Lucas' chart, and his career, life path, and public reputation are the areas of life where Lucas will experience the greatest amount of flexibility, adaptability, and speed. Gemini's influence also suggests a great deal of curiosity and a desire to explore and to gather new information.

2nd HOUSE	Ruler (+5)	Exaltation (+4)	Triplicity (+3)	Term (+2)	Face (+1)
☿ ♉	♀ ♉	☽ ♒	☽ ♒	♀ ♉	☿ ♉
House Place	House Place	House Place	House Place	House Place	House Place
12th	12th	10th	10th	12th	12th
House Rule	House Rule	House Rule	House Rule	House Rule	House Rule
2nd, 5th	1st, 6th, 11th (alm)	3rd, 4th, 1st (alm)	3rd, 4th, 1st (alm)	1st, 6th, 11th (alm)	2nd, 5th

6th HOUSE	Ruler (+5)	Exaltation (+4)	Triplicity (+3)	Term (+2)	Face (+1)
♀ ♉	♀ ♉	☽ ♒	☽ ♒	☿ ♉	☽ ♒
House Place	House Place	House Place	House Place	House Place	House Place
12th	12th	10th	10th	12th	10th
House Rule	House Rule	House Rule	House Rule	House Rule	House Rule
1st, 6th, 11th (alm)	1st, 6th, 11th (alm)	3rd, 4th, 1st (alm)	3rd, 4th, 1st (alm)	2nd, 5th	3rd, 4th, 1st (alm)

10th HOUSE	Ruler (+5)	Exaltation (+4)	Triplicity (+3)	Term (+2)	Face (+1)
♄ ♊	☿ ♉		☿ ♉	♂ ♋	☉ ♉
House Place	House Place	House Place	House Place	House Place	House Place
2nd	12th		12th	3rd	1st
House Rule	House Rule	House Rule	House Rule	House Rule	House Rule
9th, 10th	2nd, 5th		2nd, 5th	7th, 12th	12th (alm)

Figure 47: George Lucas' Career Houses

10th House Ruler (Saturn in Gemini) Board of Directors
Mercury in Taurus in the 12th House (8 Votes, Rulership, Triplicity)
Mercury Rules 2nd, 5th Houses

George Lucas' career and life path (10th House Ruler's Board of Directors) also involve being able to understand and communicate (Mercury) in a manner that is dull, overcautious, generous, and practical (Taurus), **WITH** his money and resources (Mercury rules 2nd) and his pursuit of fun, tolerance for risk, personal creativity, and children (Mercury rules 5th). He encounters these needs particularly **IN** his personal unconscious, shadow-self, sorrows, and self-sabotage (Mercury in 12th).

Notes

Mercury has been explored in detail.

Mercury's influence not only connects money (again) with his career, but also risk, entertainment, and personal creativity (5th house). It also reiterates the 12th house challenges because Lucas is unconscious of Mercury's motivation and actions.

Mars in Cancer in the 3rd House (2 Votes, Term)
Mars Rules 7th, 12th Houses

George Lucas' career and life path (10th House Ruler's Board of Directors) also involve being able to take action, expend energy, and go after the things he wants (Mars) in a manner that is manipulative, inhibited, kind, and loving (Cancer), **WITH** his marriage, partnerships, and one-to-one relationships (Mars rules 7th), and his personal unconscious, shadow-self, sorrows, self-sabotage, and hidden enemies (Mars rules 12th). He encounters these needs particularly **IN** his familiar environment, daily routines and habits, writing, and communication (Mars in 3rd).

Notes

With only 2 votes on Saturn's Board of Directors, Mars has nominal influence over Lucas' Saturn and 10th house affairs. It's mostly significant because Mars rules the 12th house, so Mars is the agent of Lucas' self-sabotage and adversity, and it acts in his 3rd house familiar environment, and in his communication.

6th House: Job
Venus in Taurus in the 12th house
(Venus also Rules 1st, Almuten 11th)

George Lucas' job (6th house) involves feeling loved, appreciated, and validated, and aligning with his Core Values (Venus) in a manner that is adamant, sedate, robust, and artistic (Taurus), **WITH** his personality, self-image, personal power, and pursuit of happiness (Venus rules 1st) and his friendships, personal hopes and ambitions, and shared creativity (Venus almuten 11th). He encounters these needs particularly **IN** his personal unconscious, shadow-self, sorrows, self-sabotage, and relationships with hidden enemies (Venus in 12th).

Notes
Venus and Venus' Board of Directors have already been explored.

2nd House: Money
Mercury in Taurus in the 12th House
(Mercury also Rules 5th House)

The way that George Lucas earns money (2nd house) involves understanding and communicating (Mercury) in a manner that is inflexible, lustful, collected, and tender (Taurus), **WITH** his pursuit of fun, tolerance for risk, personal creativity, and children (Mercury rules 5th). He encounters these needs particularly **IN** his personal unconscious, shadow-self, sorrows, and self-sabotage (Mercury in 12th).

Notes
Mercury has been explored already in detail.

2nd House Ruler (Mercury in Taurus) Board of Directors

Venus in Taurus in the 12th House (8 Votes, Rulership, Term, Face)
Venus Rules 1st, 6th, Almuten 11th

George Lucas' money and resources (2nd House Ruler's Board of Directors) also involve being able to experience love, appreciation, and validation, and align with his Core Values (Venus) in a manner that is overindulgent, tough, tranquil, and competent (Taurus), **WITH** his personality, personal power, self-image, and self-expression (Venus rules 1st), his job, service, and workplace relationships (Venus rules 6th), and his hopes, personal aspirations, and friendships (Venus almuten 11th). He encounters these needs particularly **IN** his personal unconscious, shadow self, sorrows, and self-sabotage (Venus in 12th).

Moon in Aquarius in the 10th House (7 Votes, Exaltation, Triplicity)
Moon Rules 3rd, 4th, Almuten 1st

George Lucas' money and resources (2nd House Ruler's Board of Directors) also involve being able to feel safe, and express his feelings and emotions (Moon) in a manner that is elitist, fanatical, democratic, and selfless (Aquarius), **WITH** his familiar environment, writing, and communication (Moon rules 3rd), his private life, home, and family relationships (Moon rules 4th), and his personality, personal power, self-image, and self-expression (Moon almuten 1st). He encounters these needs particularly **IN** his career, life path, and public reputation (Moon in 10th).

Notes

The Moon and Venus have been explored in detail.

Part of Fortune in Leo in the 4th House

George Lucas will experience the greatest amount of prosperity and success (Part of Fortune) by being splashy, infantile, forthright, and magnanimous (Leo), particularly **IN** his home, family, private life, and real estate (Part of Fortune in 4th).

Notes

Lucas' Part of Fortune is very close to his 5th house in every sense. It's at the end of the 4th house in his chart, and it's in the last degree of the 4th whole-sign house in his chart.

George Lucas Interpretation Notes

The Part of Fortune in Leo suggests that Lucas will prosper from being in the spotlight. The 4th house placement suggests money comes from real estate or from his home, family, or personal life.

Part of Fortune Ruler: Sun in Taurus in the 1st House
Sun Almuten 12th House

To experience prosperity and success (Ruler of Part of Fortune) he needs to express his authentic, "Big S" Self, and align with his Personal Standards of Integrity (Sun) in a manner that is bourgeois, materialistic, grounded, and hardworking (Taurus), **WITH** his personal unconscious, shadow self, and relationship with hidden enemies (Sun almuten 12th). He encounters these needs particularly **IN** his personality, self-image, personal power, and self-expression (Sun in 1st).

Notes

Another indication that Lucas is a self-made man. He is his fortune. The more he aligns with and embodies his authentic "Big S" Self, the more he will prosper.

Connections Between Career Houses

Saturn (Ruler of 10th) in the 2nd House; Mercury (Ruler of 2nd) has 8 votes (Rulership, Exaltation) on Saturn's Board of Directors = very strong link between career and money.

Saturn sextile Part of Fortune = another link between career and money.

Venus (Ruler of 6th) is conjunct Mercury (Ruler of 2nd), and has 7 votes (Rulership, Term) on Mercury's Board of Directors = very strong link between job and money.

No direct connection between Saturn (Ruler of 10th) and Venus (Ruler of 6th), so his job may be different from his life path, but no matter what he does, he will be able to make money at it.

CHAPTER 27

George Lucas: An Astrological Portrait

Part 1: Personality

George Lucas has three planets in Earth signs (Sun, Mercury, and Venus), and two planets in Air signs (Moon and Saturn). He has one planet in Fire (Jupiter) and one planet in Water (Mars). Lucas has a slight emphasis on Earth, which suggests he will be the most comfortable operating in the physical and material world, although with his Moon and Saturn in Air signs, he will also be comfortable operating in the mental, social, and intellectual realms. From a temperamental standpoint, this is significant because Earth and Air are stable and objective, while Fire and Water are emotional and passionate.

Having only one planet in Water suggests that Lucas may be uncomfortable operating in the emotional and spiritual realms. Because of this, he may place great value on emotions and feelings. He may find them attractive in other people, and he may have spent much of his life trying to develop these abilities in himself. There's a danger of overcompensation in these situations. Lucas may need to recognize that he's developed his emotional awareness over the years, so it no longer requires extra effort or attention.

Lucas also has only one planet in Fire: Jupiter in Leo. It's important that Lucas supplement the Fire in his chart through daily physical activity. Lucas may be conscious that he feels better when he's physically active, but maintaining a consistent physical routine might be a challenge.

Of greater significance is the fact that Lucas has five personal planets in Fixed signs (Sun, Moon, Mercury, Venus, and Jupiter). Planets in Fixed signs seek to sustain and maintain. They like routine, stability, consistency, and slow, steady progress. Planets in Fixed signs suffer a crisis of self-worth. The driving force behind this is a core false belief in lack. Lucas has an unconscious fear that he is not enough. He is motivated to demonstrate his worth and value at all times.

With five planets in Fixed signs, Lucas will be extremely averse to change. It's easy to write this off as being inherently stubborn, and he will probably seem that way to other people, but it goes deeper than that. Planets in Fixed signs take everything personally. They express to demonstrate worth and value, so any external criticism or stimulus to change calls Lucas' self-worth into question. When Fixed planets feel attacked, they dig trenches, build walls, and prepare for a siege. On the positive side, they give Lucas great strength, stamina, and endurance.

If Lucas learns to work with this energy from higher levels of consciousness, he can keep his process internal and not involve other people. Rather than treating suggestions as personal criticisms and reacting with an automatic veto, he can postpone his response until he has had time to consider the suggestion.

Sun in Taurus

Lucas' Sun is in Taurus, a Fixed Earth sign, so the dominant qualities of Lucas' temperament show up in his authentic, "Big S" Self. Loyalty will be a key Personal Standard of Integrity for Lucas; however, because his Sun is the almuten of his 12th house, Lucas may not be conscious of what loyalty means to him. Lucas' definition of loyalty may be different from other people's. Lucas will see himself as loyal and dependable, but other people may see him as stubborn and intractable.

Lucas' Sun is in the 1st house, which further emphasizes that he will take everything personally. He experiences his life through the lens of his identity. At lower levels of consciousness, this could make him self-involved and narcissistic, but when he operates from integrity, it makes him secure of his identity. He may resist change because it violates his Personal Standards of Integrity and it goes against his self-image. It's important to Lucas that other people see his authentic Self. He wants to be recognized for embodying his Personal

George Lucas: An Astrological Portrait

Standards of Integrity and for expressing beauty, tranquility, generosity, and loyalty, the higher-consciousness qualities associated with Taurus.

Venus and the Moon have the greatest influence over Lucas' Sun: Venus has 5 votes on the Sun's Board of Directors, and the Moon has 7 votes. Lucas' Safety (Moon) and Validation Needs (Venus) are an integral part of his authentic Self. The dynamic between Lucas' Moon and Venus is perhaps the most important theme in his chart. We'll explore the implications of the square between the Moon and Venus in the context of Lucas' relationship needs. What matters here is that the Moon–Venus square is what drives Lucas to create. Because the planets are in Fixed signs, Lucas needs to create things that endure, and because the Moon and Venus are so ingrained in Lucas' personality, everything that he creates is both an expression of his authentic Self and a demonstration of his worth.

Venus in Taurus in the 12th house rules Lucas' Sun. It's the ruler of his 1st house of personality and self-image and his 6th house of job and service, and also the almuten of the 11th house, giving Venus influence over Lucas' ambitions, aspirations, friendships, and collaborative creativity. Venus is arguably the most important planet in Lucas' chart. Not only does it rule both his Sun and Ascendant, but it's also the sole dispositor of the chart: every planet in Lucas' chart reports to his Venus in Taurus, either directly or indirectly. In addition to Validation Needs, which we'll explore in the next section, Venus represents the need to enter into relationship with the Beloved. Venus invites us to discover the Divine not only through human relationships, but also through beauty and artistic expression. Because Lucas' Venus is in Taurus, a Fixed Earth sign, Lucas will look for the Beloved in the material world. He will seek to create tangible, physical, and sensual expressions of beauty.

Venus unites Lucas' Sun (authentic Self) and his personality (1st house) with his 6th house job and service. Lucas can connect with and express his authentic Self through his work, in service, without needing to be the center of attention. Venus also brings Lucas' 11th house into the picture, and suggests that Lucas will seek out other people for collaboration.

Lucas' Moon in Aquarius in the 10th house has more influence over his Sun than Venus does, with a total of 7 votes on the Sun's Board of Directors.

Feeling safe (Moon) is more important to Lucas than meeting his Validation Needs (Venus), although because of the square between the Moon and Venus, this distinction is academic. He won't be able to prioritize one need over the other. Although Lucas' Safety Needs conflict with and challenge the needs of his Venus in Taurus, they also provide valuable balance and contrast.

Lucas' Moon in Aquarius means he's less likely to be narcissistic. He looks for approval and validation for his identity, but the Moon in Aquarius is not comfortable being the center of attention. Lucas needs to feel that he's earned a place as an equal member of the group. Lucas doesn't create tangible and enduring expressions of beauty for personal gain or attention. He wants to prove his worth by making a lasting contribution to humanity. His Moon is in the 10th house, so these needs are public, and he encounters them in his career, but it's important to Lucas that his work stand on its own.

Lucas' Moon rules his 3rd house of writing, communication, and his familiar environment, and his 4th house of his private life and family relationships. Since the Moon is also the almuten of the 1st house, Lucas will be personally invested in these areas of his life. The Moon occupies his 10th house, so on some level Lucas will judge his 3rd house routine and his 4th house personal life based on how they affect his 10th house public image and reputation. Plus, the Moon is in Aquarius, an Air sign, so it's mainly concerned with how things appear on the surface.

The final member of the Sun's Board of Directors is Saturn in Gemini, with 3 votes for Term and Face. Because Saturn rules the Moon in Aquarius, Saturn actually controls 10 votes on the Sun's Board of Directors, which makes Saturn in Gemini the most significant influence over Lucas' Sun in Taurus.

Saturn is the only planet in Lucas' chart in a Mutable sign. Planets in Fixed signs control the rest of the votes on the Sun's Board of Directors, and the Sun itself is in a Fixed sign. But because Saturn in Gemini rules the Moon in Aquarius, Lucas won't be nearly as stubborn or inflexible as we might expect. Lucas can be persuaded by clever, objective communication (Gemini). As long as he feels that he's being treated with respect (Saturn), he will always be willing to consider both sides of an issue (Gemini).

George Lucas: An Astrological Portrait

Ascendant in Taurus

Lucas' Ascendant is in Taurus. Because Lucas' Sun is in the same sign as his Ascendant, the mask that he wears to interact with the world (Ascendant) closely resembles his authentic Self. With Lucas, what you see is what you get.

Lucas also has Mercury in Taurus in the 12th house, which brings more unconscious energy to Lucas' personality. Communication will be important to Lucas, although he may be surprised when other people find his slow, thoughtful, practical ideas to be stubborn, intractable, and dull.

Jupiter in Leo squares Lucas' Ascendant. Squares create tension and stress, and result in action. Jupiter makes all things bigger, and in Lucas' case Jupiter may expand his fear of "not enough." This may cause Lucas to overcompensate by becoming "too much." Jupiter in Leo combines self-confidence, power, and expansive faith with an awareness of other people's values and opinions (Jupiter rules the 8th house) and a need to express his dreams and ambitions through teamwork and shared creativity (Jupiter rules 11th).

Part 2: Relationship Needs

Lucas' Moon and Venus influence virtually every aspect of his life. His Safety Needs (Moon) and Validation Needs (Venus) dominate his personality. As we will see, Lucas faces some challenges in meeting these needs, and it's particularly difficult for him to meet both needs at the same time. But this is the engine that drives Lucas' life, creativity, and career.

Safety Needs: Moon in Aquarius

With the Moon in Aquarius, Lucas has an Air Safety Checklist. He operates in the mental, intellectual, objective, and abstract realms, and to feel safe, he needs to understand the situation. Aquarius is a Fixed Air sign, and planets in Aquarius care about sustaining and maintaining their social and intellectual worth. Lucas will not be comfortable with emotions, feelings, or anything subjective or personal. With regard to his safety, he cares about how things appear on the surface, not how they're experienced below the surface.

The Moon in Aquarius rules the 3rd and 4th houses, so Lucas needs to experience objective, intellectual freedom in his familiar environment, habits, and daily routine, and in his family relationships and private life. Freedom requires rules and boundaries. Lucas needs to believe that everyone in his 3rd house environment and 4th house personal life understands and accepts the agreements that define the standards of acceptable behavior. These agreements make the free exchange of ideas possible. More importantly, they allow Lucas to feel that he is an equal, accepted member of the group. When someone violates an agreement, it makes Lucas feel unsafe. It brings up the unconscious fear that he may be the one who misunderstood the rules, and that he may not be worthy of being an accepted member of the group.

Because Lucas' Moon is in his 10th house, when he feels unsafe, he will take public action to address the issue. All disagreements must be settled in the court of public opinion. Lucas will be concerned with how his private life appears in public, and how it reflects on his career, life path, and public reputation.

Saturn in Gemini and Mercury in Taurus make up the Board of Directors for Lucas' Moon in Aquarius. Even though Saturn rules the Moon in Aquarius, Mercury in Taurus has the most influence over Lucas' Safety Needs. Saturn occupies the 2nd house of money and resources, and Mercury rules the 2nd house. This suggests that money may represent safety for Lucas. He may also believe that if you throw enough money at a "No," you can turn it into a "Yes." Mercury is in the 12th house, so Lucas may not be conscious of these beliefs or of his attachment to money. He's used this pattern in his professional life to push past the technological limits of film and pioneer new options for special effects. But when the unconscious belief that "he who signs the checks makes the laws" shows up in other areas of his life, it will cause problems and interfere with his ability to feel safe.

Mercury is square Lucas' Moon. Squares create tension that can be resolved only by taking action. Because both the Moon and Mercury are in Fixed signs, this square requires sustained, steady action. We could say that Lucas needs to tell stories (Mercury) that explore feelings and emotions (Moon), and these stories must endure and be substantial. The square between the Moon and Mercury integrates Lucas' 5th house creativity with his 10th house career, while drawing on his 2nd house resources, skills, and talents, and his 3rd house writing and communication skills. It taps into this personal unconscious because

Mercury is in the 12th house, and it expresses publicly through his career because the Moon is in the 10th house.

Lucas has a love–hate relationship with rules, authority, and expectations because of the conflicting dynamic between the Moon and Saturn. Because it rules his Moon in Aquarius, Saturn in Gemini sets the agenda for what Lucas needs to feel safe; however, Saturn and the Moon are sesquisquare each other, which makes things a bit complicated. Lucas needs the rules and expectations to be public, because Saturn rules his 10th house. But Lucas' Saturn in Gemini also expects the rules to be flexible, and to have enough loopholes that he can avoid being limited if he's quick and clever enough.

Lucas has aspects from Uranus and Pluto to his Moon, and these further trigger his issues with authority. Lucas is sensitive to dynamics of power and control because Pluto in the 4th house opposes his Moon in the 10th house. The roots of this pattern go back to Lucas' relationship with his father. Until Lucas feels that he is free from the control of his father, he will not be able to feel safe. This is one of many factors that drives Lucas to prove his worth.

The trine from Uranus in the 1st to the Moon in the 10th also fuels Lucas' need for freedom and conflicts with Saturn. Lucas has a fundamentally disruptive quality in his personality (Uranus in the 1st) that means he needs to understand the rules to learn how to break them. However, he wants to avoid being seen as deceptive, duplicitous, or unreliable because of Saturn's influence. It's okay if he outsmarts the rules because he's clever, but to feel safe, he needs to maintain the appearance of responsibility and compliance with the rules.

Validation Needs: Venus in Taurus

Lucas' Validation Needs are quite prominent in his personality, because Venus rules his Sun and Ascendant, and is the sole dispositor of his chart. With Venus in Taurus, Lucas has an Earth Validation Checklist. He expresses affection and wants to experience love and appreciation on the physical and material planes. He needs tangible and durable expressions of esteem. Words will never be enough to convey love, appreciation, or validation for Lucas.

Venus rules Lucas 1st house of his personality and self-image, and his 6th house of work and service, and it's the almuten of his 11th house of aspirations and group creativity. These are the areas of Lucas' life where he most needs approval and recognition. We've noted before that because Venus is in the 12th house, Lucas is not conscious of his need to be loved and appreciated, and this may create challenges for him.

Because Lucas has so many planets in Fixed signs, including the Moon, Mercury, and Venus (the three planets on Venus' Board of Directors), validation is how he measures his self-worth. If he feels loved and appreciated, then he may be able to accept that he is enough.

The Moon in Aquarius has the most influence over Lucas' Venus in Taurus, with a total of 8 votes for Exaltation, Triplicity, and Face. Before Lucas can feel validated, he must first feel safe. This also suggests that Lucas needs to be validated and recognized for his Moon in Aquarius ability to be emotionally objective, and his attachments to humanitarian ideals. Lucas' Moon in Aquarius is not comfortable being the center of attention. It's easier for Lucas to be appreciated for his ideas than for his identity.

Summary of Relationship Needs

Lucas' Safety and Validation Needs play a prominent role in every facet of his life. The challenge for Lucas is that the Moon and Venus are in a partile square to each other, which means that his Moon in Aquarius Safety Needs conflict with his Venus in Taurus Validation Needs. Lucas can never escape this conflict because his Moon and Venus are inexorably linked.

Venus rules Lucas' 1st house, but the Moon is the almuten of his 1st house, so the conflict between his Safety and Validation Needs is personal and a defining quality of his self-image and appearance. The Moon has 8 votes on Venus' Board of Directors, while Venus has no direct influence over the Moon, which suggests that his Safety Needs will take precedence. However, Venus is in rulership, and the sole dispositor of Lucas' chart, so his Validation Needs are extremely important. Lucas has no options; he must figure out how to address both his Safety and Validation Needs at the same time.

Fortunately for Lucas, the conflict and tension inherent in a square can be resolved by taking action. Squares are a 4th harmonic aspect, so they involve creating and manifesting in the world of form. Both the Moon and Venus influence his 1st house, so Lucas needs to express his identity in the world. The actions he takes will involve his 3rd house of writing and communication, his 4th house of his family and private life, his 6th house of work and service, and his 11th house of hopes and ambitions. The effects of his actions will show up in his 10th house of career, public reputation, and life path, and his 12th house of his personal unconscious and adversity.

In many ways, Lucas' Moon in Aquarius is his saving grace. His Venus in Taurus Validation Needs so dominate his chart that it could make him narcissistic and self-indulgent. However, the Moon in Aquarius is uncomfortable with individual attention. As much as Lucas needs to create a public and professional expression of his 1st house identity (because his Moon occupies the 10th house), the Moon in Aquarius cares about the good of the group, not the good of the individual. This means Lucas can meet his Safety and Validation Needs only when he receives appreciation for having created something that speaks to a wide audience. The benefit to humanity must take precedence over personal benefit. Lucas has to know that his creations have objective worth to others before he can feel validated. Lucas can enjoy the vast profits from his creative expression because even though he is personally invested in his work, he knows his work is about more than his own personality.

Part 3: Relationship Wants

On a conscious level, Lucas is drawn to partners who embody the emotional depth and intensity of his Descendant in Scorpio. These partners will conflict with his Moon in Aquarius Safety Needs because the Moon in Aquarius is threatened by deep emotions. The appeal of these partners is quite strong, however, because Scorpio opposes his Venus in Taurus, and opposites attract. It's possible for Scorpio partners to meet Lucas' Venus in Taurus Validation Needs, but it's not likely. After the initial attraction, the lack of safety in the relationship will become too big to ignore.

On an unconscious level, Lucas is attracted to partners who embody the objective, harmonious, balanced, and diplomatic energy of his Vertex in Libra. Libra is trine Aquarius by sign, and they're both Air signs. Vertex in Libra partners will operate on the mental, intellectual, social, and objective planes.

They prefer to stay on the surface, they mean exactly what they say, and they're uncomfortable with deep emotions. These partners will do an excellent job of meeting Lucas' Moon in Aquarius Safety Needs.

Vertex in Libra partners may have more difficulties meeting Lucas' Venus in Taurus Validation Needs because Taurus and Libra are quincunx by sign. However, Venus rules both Taurus and Libra, so there's a way to thread the needle. The main challenge is that Vertex in Libra partners will use words, and words alone aren't enough to meet Lucas' Venus in Taurus Validation Needs. However, Lucas needs to feel safe before he can feel validated, and Vertex in Libra partners will do such a good job of meeting his Moon in Aquarius Safety Needs that they may also meet his Venus in Taurus Validation Needs.

Marriage Blueprint

Saturn in Gemini in the 2nd house represents Lucas' experience of his mother, and the Moon in Aquarius in the 10th house represents Lucas' experience of his father. Saturn rules the Moon, and the Moon (father) is in the 10th house of the mother. This suggests that Lucas' mother had all of the power in his parent's relationship. In particular, because Saturn occupies the 2nd house, it suggests that his mother was the one who controlled the finances for the family. As noted before, Lucas may equate money with power.

Saturn and the Moon are trine by sign, but sesquisquare by aspect. This suggests there was some friction between his parents—perhaps his father wasn't happy with the dynamic of power in the relationship—but the conflict was not severe. The tension of a sesquisquare is often resolved with humor.

In general, Lucas' Marriage Blueprint supports his ability to feel safe, although he may need to address his unconscious expectations about money and financial responsibility in his marriage.

Friends, Lovers, Spouses

Jupiter in Leo rules Lucas' 11th house of friendships, Mercury in Taurus rules his 5th house of love affairs, and Mars in Cancer rules his 7th house of marriage. Of the three relationship house rulers, Jupiter in Leo has the most Essential Dignity (Triplicity), which suggests that Lucas may value his friendships above all other relationships. Jupiter, the ruler of the 11th house, is in his 4th house, which suggests that Lucas views his friends, peers, and teammates as family.

Lucas may find his 5th house relationships less appealing. Mercury in Taurus is retrograde, in the 12th house, has dignity only by Face (which means it's afraid), and it's in a partile square to Pluto. Lucas' Moon–Pluto opposition makes him extremely sensitive to issues of power, control, and manipulation. Because he will encounter these issues in his 5th house relationships, casual dating will not appeal to him.

His 7th house marriage is another story. Mars, the ruler of Lucas' 7th house, occupies his 3rd house, but is conjunct the IC, the cusp of the 4th house. This suggests that Lucas views his spouse as an integral part of the foundation of his life. Mars is conjunct the North Node, so his marriage partner supports him in his soul's evolution. Mars in Cancer has mixed dignity; it's lucky because it has Triplicity, but it's also out of its depth because it's in Fall. Lucas' Mars is sextile his Sun, so he has a personal connection to it. Finding the right spouse can help him to embody his authentic Self. The main challenge is that Mars rules his 12th house, so it's the vehicle of Lucas' self-sabotage and adversity. He needs to be careful not to turn his spouse into a hidden enemy.

Jupiter, the ruler of the 11th house, has 4 votes on Mars' Board of Directors, and Mars has 1 vote on Jupiter's Board of Directors. This connects his 7th house of marriage with his 11th house of friendship and suggests that friendship is an important foundation of Lucas' marriage. Some minor connections link his 5th and 7th houses, so it's possible for a casual relationship to become serious, but given Lucas' general aversion to 5th house relationships, he's unlikely to initiate a 5th house relationship in the first place. The lack of connections between Lucas' 5th and 11th house further supports this idea. Friendship is too important to him, and he would never view a 5th house partner as a friend or an equal.

Part 4: Career

Saturn in Gemini rules Lucas' 10th house of career; Venus in Taurus rules his 6th house of work; Mercury in Taurus rules his 2nd house of money, and the Sun in Taurus rules his Part of Fortune in Leo.

Saturn is the only planet in a Mutable sign in Lucas' chart, so his career, life path, and public reputation are the areas of life where Lucas will experience the most flexibility, adaptability, and speed. That Saturn also rules his 9th house suggests Lucas' career may incorporate elements of philosophy, higher education, foreign travel, law, publishing, religion, or advertising. Saturn occupies Lucas' 2nd house, so money is important in his career, and he will always keep an eye on the bottom line.

Mercury in Taurus has the most influence over Saturn in Gemini, with 8 votes on Saturn's Board of Directors, which strengthens the connection between Lucas' 10th house career and his 2nd house resources, as Mercury also rules his 2nd house. We know that Lucas is unlikely to engage in 5th house romantic relationships, so he will probably channel his 5th house creativity and fun into his career.

Venus in Taurus represents Lucas' 6th house job, workplace relationships, co-workers and employees. Because Venus also rules Lucas' 1st house, the work he does will be personal. This also indicates that Lucas' job and service are connected to his identity and personality. He's the only one who can do what he does.

Lucas' Part of Fortune in Leo suggests he will prosper from being in the spotlight, and the 4th house placement indicates that his money may come from real estate, his home, family, or his personal life. The Sun rules Lucas' Part of Fortune, which further emphasizes that he will be a self-made man. The more he aligns with and embodies his authentic Self, the more he will prosper.

With so many connections between Lucas' career houses, he will easily make money at whatever he does professionally. And in every case, he will use his career, job, and professional life to explore and express his identity.

Appendices and Resources

APPENDIX A
Spiritual Practices

When you know how to interpret a natal chart, you can identify the precise nature of the patterns and challenges in your life or the life of your clients. This is impressive and fascinating, but it's not practical. Identifying a problem doesn't address the problem. The precise, specific information you've obtained from your natal chart interpretation isn't practical until you do something with it. Nothing changes at the level of the chart.

Happiness isn't the result of circumstances in the outside world. Happiness is the consequence of your level of consciousness. The higher you raise your vibration, the happier you feel. The improvements in the conditions in your "little r" reality are the effect of your happiness, not the cause of it.

Albert Einstein said, "You cannot solve a problem from the level of consciousness that created it. You must learn to see the world anew." This means that no action you can take from within your current "little r" reality will improve the situation or make you happier. The only way to solve the problem is to raise your vibration, expand your consciousness, and tune to a different "little r" reality where the situation is no longer a problem.

The simple, yet immensely powerful spiritual practices in this chapter will help you to move into right relationship with each of the Astrological Archetypes. These spiritual practices will help you to step out of Victim Consciousness and into integrity. All of these spiritual practices operate from the nonlinear Spiritual Realities of Third Kingdom, which means they are *true*, but not necessarily *real*.

The effect of these spiritual practices is subtle and cumulative. You will need to follow a spiritual practice consistently for at least a month before you can evaluate the changes in your "little r" reality.

Choose the Best-Feeling Thought Currently Available to You
Right Relationship with the Sun

The first spiritual practice is simple: **choose the best-feeling thought currently available to you.** This is how you raise your vibration and tune to the higher levels of consciousness. *Simple* isn't the same thing as *easy*, however. You can choose the best-feeling thought currently available to you only if you're

in the present moment, and conscious of what you're feeling. The other spiritual practices support you by developing your core spiritual muscles. As you master the other spiritual practices, it becomes easier for you to choose the best-feeling thought currently available to you.

Present Moment Awareness Safety Meditation
Right Relationship with the Moon and Sun

Meeting your Safety Needs is simple because the truth is that you're usually safe. Unless you're in a life-threatening situation (such as being stalked by a serial killer or robbed at gunpoint), you are safe. All you need to experience this is to become aware of it. When

you step into Victim Consciousness, you step out of "My Business," and either dwell on the past, or worry about the future. The past and the future are none of your business. My Business is the present moment.

The way to meet your Safety Needs is to become aware of the present moment. You do this with the **Present Moment Awareness Safety Meditation**.

Spiritual Practices

The Present Moment Awareness Safety Meditation

- Stop whatever you are doing, and take a few deep, cleansing breaths.

- If possible, find somewhere to sit or lie down, and then let yourself feel supported by the chair, floor, bed, or sofa.

- As you become aware of your body and aware of your breathing, feel your mind begin to quiet.

- Gently release your attachments to any thoughts, and simply observe any activity of your mind.

- As you observe your thoughts, notice how they naturally, easily, and effortlessly circle around, gently spiraling inward until they settle in the present moment.

- When you are fully present, consider the truth that **right here, right now, in this moment, you are completely safe.** If any thoughts come up, observe them without attachment. They will settle back into the present moment.

- Consider the truth that **right here, right now, in this moment, every one of your needs is met.** In this moment, **you are enough, and you have enough.** You are completely, easily and effortlessly supported.

- Let your awareness rest on your breath. Let your mind quiet. For a few moments, simply be. Allow yourself to notice how it feels to be completely safe and completely supported.

You can download six MP3 versions of this guided meditation as part of the Bonus Gifts in Appendix B.

Whose Business Is It?
Right Relationship with Mercury and Saturn

Byron Katie is an author and speaker who created a powerful process called "The Work." In her first book, *Loving What Is,* Katie suggests that there are three types of business in the world: "My Business," "Your Business" ("Other People's Business"), and "God's Business."

She points out that anytime you find yourself in Other People's Business or God's Business, you feel stressed. Why? Because you don't have any business in Other People's Business or God's Business. When you're in Other People's Business, or God's Business, you have no control and no influence. In fact, when you're in Other People's Business or God's Business, you are powerless.[1]

Put another way, when you're in Other People's Business or God's Business, you're in Victim Consciousness, so any action you take will only make things worse.

Just because you're involved in something doesn't make it your business. You spend far less time in My Business, than you think. In fact, you probably spend most of your time in Other People's Business. This isn't necessarily a bad thing, as long as you can recognize when you're in Other People's Business, and know how to step back into My Business.

My Business consists exclusively of things that **directly affect you**, which are **your responsibility**, and that you have the **ability to influence or change**. If it doesn't directly affect you, isn't your responsibility, and/or you can't do anything about it, it's not your business.

Does It Affect You, Personally?

This is the most important question, and it has to be applied with absolute precision. For something to be My Business it must affect you, personally, *right now*. Just because something could, hypothetically, affect you at some

---

[1] Katie, Byron, and Stephen Mitchell. *Loving What Is: Four Questions That Can Change Your Life*. New York: Harmony Books, 2002. 3.

point in the future doesn't make it your business. If and when it actually begins to affect you, it *might be* your business, as long as it's also your responsibility and you can do something about it. Until then, it's none of your business.

Even if something does affect you, personally right now, it doesn't have to be My Business. Consider applying the "ignore it and see if it goes away" test. If you ignore a situation and it goes away without causing you any harm, it's none of your business.

Is It Really Your Responsibility?

I struggle with this one the most. My ego believes that it is my responsibility to make sure everyone I encounter follows the rules. If anyone breaks the rules, he or she must face the wrath of my ego. I've come to terms with the fact that my ego is a cross between Superman and Serpico. Smoke in a nonsmoking area, park in a random, illegal manner, or just walk into the sauna at the gym while wearing shoes (ignoring the sign that clearly states that shoes are not allowed in the sauna), and my ego jumps to attention. Rules are being broken and justice must be done!

There's only one catch: it's not my responsibility to dole out justice in these situations. I didn't make the rules. I don't even understand some of the rules. (Why can't you wear shoes in the sauna? Are they going to melt?) And when I see other people ignoring the rules, it truly pisses me off. What it doesn't do, however, is make it my responsibility. I'm not an officer of the law. I'm not even a mall cop. I don't work at the gym. What other people do, even when it's rude, inconsiderate, and in direct violation of the rules, is not my business, because enforcing the rules is not my responsibility.

You know what else isn't my responsibility? Other people's lives. It's not my responsibility to stop my friends or family from making what I know will be stupid, unfortunate, painful choices. It's not my responsibility to take care of anyone but myself. And it's not my responsibility to make anyone else happy.

And just in case I'm being too subtle here, it's not *your* responsibility, either.

There are a few exceptions to this. Parents *are* responsible for their children, at least until those children are old enough to be responsible for themselves. For your grown children to be your business, they need to be your responsibility *and* you have to be able to influence their behavior. Good luck with that.

Do I Have Any Power or Influence to Change It?

If you encounter a situation that affects you personally right now, and is actually your responsibility, the last thing you need to ask is if you have any power or influence over the situation. Are you able to change, adjust, modify, or alter the circumstances in any way? If changing, adjusting, modifying, or altering the circumstances requires that you get other people to change *their* behavior, then the answer is no. There's nothing you can do to get anyone else to behave the way you would like them to behave.[2]

If you can accept that you have no power to change anyone else's behavior, you'll save yourself a tremendous amount of suffering and significantly reduce the amount of time you spend in Victim Consciousness. Once you move out of Victim Consciousness, you'll discover that there are other options. Instead of using force to try to control others (which creates a lose/lose scenario), you can use power to create a win/win scenario, in which everyone is happy. But you can do that only from within My Business.

How to Play *Whose Business Is It?*

I filmed a pilot episode of the game show *Whose Business Is It?* that demonstrates how to play the game. I've included this video in the Bonus Gifts in Appendix B.

The List Exercise

Right Relationship with Saturn and Mars

The List Exercise is a spiritual practice that develops your accountability muscles. It helps you to stay out of Victim Consciousness and within the boundaries of My Business. You will need a small notebook or day planner

---

[2] If you don't believe me, ask my father.

for this exercise. At night, before you go to bed, turn to a new page in the notebook, put tomorrow's date at the top of the page, and then number the lines from 1 to 10. You will be making a list of 10 things you intend to do the next day.

Number 10 on the list is "Make list for the following day." Numbers 1 through 9 are *things you would do anyway*. Nothing on the list should be any kind of a stretch except for number 10, the commitment to do The List for the next day. The other items might include things like "make the bed," "eat breakfast," "walk the dog," or "go to work." **This is not a "to do" list.**

At the end of the day, sit down and review each item on your list. If you did what you said you were going to do, check the item off the list and say to yourself, "I said I was going to do [item on the list] and I did it."

If you did not fulfill your intention, take a moment and acknowledge this to yourself. Say to yourself, "I said I was going to do [item on the list], and I didn't do it." Resist the urge to blame yourself, or to rationalize why you didn't do what you said you were going to do.

It doesn't matter if you do the things on your list or not. **What matters is that you hold yourself accountable.** This means there are absolutely no excuses.

For example, say that one of the items on your list is "brush my teeth." You wake up in the morning, and on your way to the bathroom, you are abducted by aliens and taken on a whirlwind tour of the solar system. Your hosts are charming sentient beings; however, they're telepathic and they don't have mouths, so there's no toothpaste anywhere on the ship. When they drop you back home a week later, you sit down with your list and say, "I said I was going to brush my teeth, and I didn't."

Keep the list simple enough that it's easy for you to do the things you say you are going to do. **Originality does not count.** It is perfectly acceptable for you to have the same list every day. If you notice that you are not completing items on your list, choose different, easier items.

When you begin this process, you will be (metaphorically) working out with 2-pound weights. The challenge is to make sure you are using correct form so that you target the correct group of muscles. Few people are used to exercising their accountability muscles, so using even 2-pound weights can create resistance. **Keep the list simple and do not add any additional weight for at least the first**

three weeks of this spiritual practice. After three weeks of successfully completing every item on your list and holding yourself accountable, you may add *one* item to the list that is a little more of a stretch. If at any time you find that you are not accomplishing all of the items on your list, simplify the items on the list again.

Troubleshooting The List

For such a simple spiritual practice, The List can bring up a remarkable amount of resistance. The List often exemplifies that *simple* is not the same thing as *easy*. Some of the most common difficulties with The List are addressed below.

I'm forgetting to do The List

This is perhaps the most common obstacle during the first 30 days of The List. The entire purpose of The List exercise is to develop your accountability muscles, and if you forget to do The List, it's an indication that these muscles need attention. It can be very difficult to hold yourself accountable, especially if you're not used to it. You may find it easier if you engage the help of a partner to hold you accountable for doing The List exercise. If you're exploring this process on your own, you can ask a friend to hold you accountable for doing The List each day for 30 days. This can be as simple as a daily email check-in to confirm that you're on track.

This is too easy... I can't be doing it right

As powerful as this spiritual practice is, The List does not have to be a struggle. As long as you go through The List each night and hold yourself accountable for each item by either saying "I said I was going to do this, and I did it," or "I said I was going to do this, and I didn't do it," you are doing the exercise perfectly. You can have the same list every day. It's not about reaching goals or accomplishing the items on the list— it's about setting intentions and holding yourself accountable for the commitments you make to yourself.

I'm not getting everything done on my list

Remember, this exercise is about *accountability*. It doesn't matter if you accomplish the items on your list or not. What matters is that you hold

Spiritual Practices

A Good List
1. Eat breakfast
2. Feed cat
3. Go to work
4. Pick up dry cleaning
5. Eat lunch
6. Make dinner
7. Brush teeth
8. Answer emails
9. Take out trash
10. List for August 15th

A Not-So-Good List
1. Eat breakfast
2. Feed cat
3. Quit smoking
4. Cure cancer
5. Universal health care
6. Peace in Middle East
7. Brush teeth
8. Go to gym and work out
9. Make my father proud
10. List for August 15th

yourself accountable for either doing or not doing the things you said you would do. Because the items on your list don't matter, it's a more supportive experience when you make your list items easy and effortless and you can check off all of them at the end of the day. This gives you an extra boost of positive reinforcement. Although saying "I said I was going to do this and I didn't do it," fulfils the objective of developing your accountability muscles, it can also bring up issues of judgment, guilt, and shame, which can create resistance to continuing with The List.

If you're not getting everything done on your list, simplify your list. It's very common to begin the exercise and find it too easy and then sabotage your success because you add too much weight and make your list too difficult. It's not possible for your List to contain intentions that are too simple, because The List is not a list of goals, chores, or resolutions. Three items on your list every single day can be "Eat breakfast," "Eat lunch," and "Eat dinner." The work of The List isn't doing the things on The List; it's being willing to be present with whatever stories and judgments come up for you, while you hold yourself accountable for your intentions.

Gratitude and Core Values

Right Relationship with Venus

These spiritual practices will help you to move into Right Relationship with Venus. For the best results, begin by listening to the **Present Moment Awareness Safety Meditation**. This will ensure that you're starting from a place where you're safe enough to let yourself feel anything, which in turn makes it easier for you to experience the good feelings.

Gratitude ("I Love and Appreciate _____")

This exercise (obviously) targets your gratitude muscles. In this exercise, you will find a minimum of 100 things for which you are grateful. You may find it helpful to use a strand of prayer beads or a stack of pennies to help you keep count. As with The List Exercise, originality doesn't matter. You may find that you include many of the same things each day. Say "**I love and appreciate _____**" and then fill in the blank. Just let yourself ramble and speak whatever comes to mind. "I love and appreciate chocolate. I love and appreciate my cats. I love and appreciate sunshine." The objective is to keep talking continuously.

To get the full benefit of this spiritual practice, **you must speak these affirmations out loud**. Saying them to yourself or writing them down will not have the same impact. If you find it too challenging to come up with 100 statements, work up to it over the course of a few days.

You do not need to feel an emotional investment in these statements. You can literally look around the room and say, "I love and appreciate this pillow. I love and appreciate this book. I love and appreciate this photo." As you practice this exercise, your heart will open. It's not possible to get up from this exercise feeling worse than you did when you started it.

Core Value Affirmation Meditation

The Core Value Affirmation Meditation is a self-guided meditation experience. You begin by selecting one of the Core Values that you wish to experience (Abundance, Balance, Beauty, Freedom, Harmony, Joy, Love, Order, Peace, Power, Unity or Wisdom). Sit comfortably, and allow your eyes to close, as you become aware of your breath. As you inhale, think "I am…" As you exhale, think the name of the Core Value. For example, "I am … Free," "I am … Powerful," or "I am … Love." Begin by practicing this for a minimum of 5 minutes, and then gradually work up to 10 to 20 minutes (or longer).

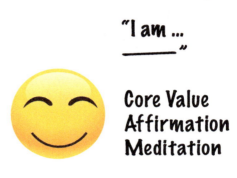

Core Value Affirmation Meditation

Be advised—this is an extremely powerful spiritual practice. It will bring up everything in your life that appears to embody the lack of the Core Value so it can be healed.

Tithing
Right Relationship with Jupiter

Tithing is an expression of appreciation and gratitude in the form of 10% of your income each month, given to the people and places that nourish and feed you spiritually. A tithe does not need to go to the same place each month, and it can be distributed among more than one recipient, so long as the total is 10%. When these two criteria are met—the 10% amount and the heart connection to the recipient—Tithing is a spiritual practice.

Give 10% to people and places where you experience a heart connection.

Tithing is not charity. Charity is a very noble and worthwhile act. However, charity is giving from Second Kingdom. Charity is given to people and organizations that you perceive as lacking. You give charity when you feel that you have enough (sufficiency) that you can help those who do not have enough (lack). Charity on its own will not transform your experiences of prosperity.

When you give charity, you affirm your own sufficiency, but you are also affirm the illusion of lack.

Tithing, on the other hand, is giving from Third Kingdom. Tithing does not come from a place of "I have enough." Tithing comes from the Truth that "I am infinite!" When you tithe, you open the floodgates and claim your infinite abundance and prosperity.

Tithing is a spiritual practice and it requires a leap of faith. Because Tithing comes from Third Kingdom, it is not possible to understand it logically or rationally. Logic and reason are tools of the Second Kingdom (calibrating in the 400s). Tithing calibrates at 540 and above. The only way to understand the greater truths of the Third Kingdom (and beyond) is personal experience.

It is not possible to "work up" to a tithe by giving less than 10%. It's more difficult (and not just for the math impaired) to give 5% than it is to give 10%. Consider the consciousness around the belief that you need to work up to a tithe: it's deeply rooted in First Kingdom and Victim/Lack Consciousness. If you give only 5%, you affirm that you do not have enough, and this is the "little r" reality that the Law of Attraction will create for you. You are certain to feel financially strapped at the end of the month.

When you tithe, however, you affirm the truth of your abundance, and this is what you experience. When you give 10%, you will discover that you have more than you expect left over at the end of the month. This makes no logical or rational sense, but logic and reason are not powerful enough tools to understand Tithing.

If you are new to Tithing, you will need to prepare for it. Spend at least a month practicing the Present Moment Awareness Safety Meditation and the Gratitude ("I Love and Appreciate _____") exercises. These spiritual practices will develop the necessary spiritual muscles to prepare you to take the leap of faith and begin to tithe.

When you begin to tithe, commit to a minimum of three consecutive months. This is long enough for you to have a subjective, personal experience of how Tithing shows up for you. The worst that can happen is that you get a bigger tax refund at the end of the year. The best that can happen is that you open yourself to receiving an endless and infinite flow of prosperity in your life.

Spiritual Practices

When you sit down to write your tithe checks, don't worry if you feel less than grateful. It's common for feelings of fear and lack to come up to be healed when writing a tithe check. Let the feelings come up and be present with them. As long as you're giving 10%, and it's going to people and places that feed you spiritually, you are engaged in the spiritual practice of Tithing, and the consciousness of Tithing is significantly more powerful than the vibrations of your fears. If you surrender and allow these feelings to move through you, they will be instantly healed. Bear in mind, though, that you may have a substantial reserve of these lack-based thoughts, so it will probably take more than two or three tithe checks to clear all of them out of your consciousness. However, the longer you stay aligned with the consciousness of Tithing, the less these thoughts will be able to interfere with your ability to be happy.

APPENDIX B

Bonus Gifts

This book comes bundled with a number of bonus gifts, resources, and special features. You can access and download the bonus gifts by registering online at the following link:

http://TalentedAstrologer.com/PPNABonus

Soon after you register, I'll send you an email confirmation and instructions on how to access your bonus gifts. The bonus gifts include:

- ✦ The Real Astrology Academy's Chart Interpretation Worksheet.

- ✦ Additional examples of celebrity natal chart interpretations, including the astrological portrait of Sally Ride.

- ✦ Six MP3 versions of the Present Moment Awareness Safety Meditation.

- ✦ The complete *Introduction to Archetypal Astrology: The Hero's Journey* presentation.

- ✦ Meet the Planets: MP3s of guided meditations to meet each of the Astrological Archetypes.

- ✦ The pilot episode of the game show, *Whose Business Is It?*

- ✦ A free class on Natal Chart Interpretation and a special discount when you register for the Online Natal Astrology Class.

- ✦ The complete *Astrology, Prosperity & The Law of Attraction* presentation.

And this is just a partial list of the bonus gifts included with this book. I'll keep in touch via email so you'll always know when I've added a new bonus.

APPENDIX C

The Real Astrology Academy

The Real Astrology Academy provides astrological information, education, and training to astrologers and astrology students around the world. The course curriculum of The Real Astrology Academy includes classes on Natal Chart Interpretation, Relationship Astrology, and Predictive Astrology, as well as workshops on classical astrology techniques, and astrological counseling. And for students who are serious about mastering the art of astrology, The Real Astrology Academy offers the opportunity to become a **Certified Talented Astrologer**.

When you complete the **Talented Astrologer Certification Program**, you will be able to write a detailed, specific, practical interpretation of any natal chart on your own, and answer questions relating to personality, relationships, money, job, and life path. You will be able to analyze and interpret the key dynamics between two individuals in any kind of relationship, and describe the connections and challenges the couple may experience. You will be able to use predictive astrology to gain insight into past experiences, and to prepare for upcoming energies.

A Certified Talented Astrologer can do all of this, because a Certified Talented Astrologer has already done all of this. The only way to become a Certified Talented Astrologer is to do the work. It's not enough to view the class lectures. There are no certification exams to test your ability to memorize random facts and figures. At the end of the Talented Astrologer Certification Program, you will have completed written interpretations of dozens of charts on your own. You will have developed advanced astrological interpretation skills and you'll have the confidence to use them. The certification is just a formal recognition of what you have accomplished.

The Real Astrology Academy's Talented Astrologer Certification Program consists of the **Online Natal Astrology Class**, the **Natal Interpretation Training Intensive**, the **Online Relationship Astrology Class**, and the **Online Predictive Astrology Class**.

Online Natal Astrology Class

The **Online Natal Astrology Class** comprises the education component of the information in this book. In fact, this book is the recommended textbook for the class. By now, you're familiar with the grammar and syntax of the language of astrology,

the Essential Dignities and the Board of Directors, and the three-dimensional approach to natal chart interpretation. Experiencing this information through an interactive class experience will help you to understand it better.

During the Online Natal Astrology Class, you'll receive chapters of the *Natal Chart Interpretation Workbook*. The workbook provides you with expanded lists of keywords for the elements, modalities, signs, and houses, and blueprint template sentences for every component of the natal chart. These make your deep practice and skill development much easier.

The Online Natal Astrology Class is offered live once a year, beginning in January, but you can begin the class at any time. All of the classes are recorded, and I'm always available to answer your questions about the class material. Plus, with a Season Pass, you get to take the course again, so you'll be able to participate in the live classes the following year.

Natal Interpretation Training Intensive

The **Natal Interpretation Training Intensive** is the second component of the Talented Astrologer Certification. It's offered once a year, in February, and space is limited.

Everything you need to know about how to analyze and interpret

any natal chart is included in this book and in the Online Natal Astrology Class. All you need to develop your chart interpretation skills is to do the work.

The real challenge of developing skills on your own is that you're developing skills on your own. Your initial enthusiasm will keep you motivated for only a short time. Deep practice is about hard work and delayed gratification. If you follow this training program, you will be able to interpret any natal chart in 12 weeks — but you may not notice any results for the first 8 weeks, and that can be discouraging.

If you're serious about becoming talented, you need to work with a coach. Master coaching is one of the most important components of developing talent. A coach keeps you motivated, holds you accountable, and supports you so you can overcome your resistance and reach your goals. More than that, a coach provides feedback and guidance, helping you to identify your mistakes so you can correct them, improve, and get the most benefit from your deep practice.

I created The Real Astrology Academy's Natal Interpretation Training Intensive to provide the master coaching and support you need to reach your goal of being able to interpret any natal chart on your own.

The Natal Interpretation Training Intensive takes place entirely in The Real Astrology Academy forum, a private online bulletin board. Because all of the education and information you need is included in the Online Natal Astrology Class, there are no additional video classes.

During the first few weeks of the training program, you will work through the exercises in the *Natal Chart Interpretation Workbook*. You will complete the fill-in-the-blank blueprint template sentences for planets in signs, selecting a random variety of high- and low-consciousness keywords for the element, modality, and signs. You will write a total of 336 of these basic interpretation drills.

A first glance, this may seem to be very simple. But as you work your way through the assignments, you'll discover it's also tedious, repetitive, and frustrating.

And it's not about what you think it's about.

Remember, deep practice requires a struggle, and these simple, tedious, repetitive exercises provide that struggle — just not in the way you expect. The neural pathways you will create and strengthen during these first few weeks are essential. They make it possible for you to experience such rapid skill development later in the training program. But building those fundamental connections takes time, and there's no shortcut.

What the first few weeks are really about is overcoming your inner fear and resistance. It's not just my support and coaching that makes this possible, it's also the connections you will create with your fellow students around the world.

In the next phase of your training, you will practice creating notes and sketch sentences from a complete blueprint template sentence. The blueprint template sentences contain a great deal of condensed information. The sketch sentences help you to explore precise and specific ways the astrological signature could express.

Once you're comfortable with how to create sketch sentences from blueprint template sentences, you'll move on to building the main "chairs" of a natal chart. You'll practice with actual celebrity charts, focusing on the different components that make up the personality, Safety Needs, Validation Needs, relationship wants, and career, creating notes and sketches, and working from these to write your final interpretations.

At the end of this training intensive, you will have written a total of four complete natal chart interpretations, on your own.

Online Relationship Astrology Class

The **Online Relationship Astrology Class** is the third component of the Talented Astrologer Certification Program.

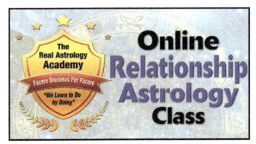

When you complete the Online Natal Astrology Class and the Natal Interpretation Training Intensive, you have the knowledge and the skill to create a synthesized interpretation of any natal chart. You know how to paint an astrological portrait of your subject, and capture a good likeness. In the Online Relationship Astrology Class, you will refine your technique as you explore the hidden patterns and lessons in the natal chart.

Every pattern contains a lesson: an opportunity to expand your level of consciousness, connect with a higher level of truth, and experience greater happiness. In theory, the pain of the negative patterns will drive you to address the issues head-on, learn the lesson, advance in consciousness, and become happier. In practice, you look for a loophole, so you can escape the pain and avoid the process. Loopholes help you cope in the short term, but in the long term, they make everything worse.

In the Online Relationship Astrology Class, you will deepen your chart analysis and interpretation skills as you identify and explore the patterns, lessons, and loopholes contained in the natal chart. Once you understand how these patterns operate for an individual, you'll be ready to explore how they show up in relationship.

You will learn how to use astrology to analyze the dynamic of any relationship. You'll identify the attraction and connection between the two individuals, as well as the most significant challenges they're likely to face. You'll evaluate how safe and validated each person is likely to feel in the relationship. And you'll consider how one person's patterns may trigger or aggravate the other person's patterns.

The skills you will develop as you interpret the connections between two different charts form the basis of the skills you'll need to consider transits, progressions, and directions in the Online Predictive Astrology Class.

Online Predictive Astrology Class

Broadly speaking, predictive astrology is concerned with understanding, and occasionally forecasting, events. Events can be objective (something happened) or subjective (something happened *to me*), and each type of event uses different predictive tools, and has different sets of expectations.

Certain branches of predictive astrology, such as horary and electional astrology, work with objective events. You have only a single chart to consider in your interpretation. For horary, it's the chart of the moment the question was asked, and for electional, it's a future chart that describes the specific outcome you would like to experience. You can evaluate these charts using an objective, two-dimensional approach, and come up with precise and specific answers to your question.

When you want to explore subjective events — what happened to me — this approach doesn't work. You're not analyzing a two-dimensional chart of a specific event; you're analyzing how multiple factors affect a three-dimensional natal chart.

I've created a new category to describe astrology that explores subjective events from the perspective of the birth chart: **Predictive Natal Astrology**.

The foundation of Predictive Natal Astrology is the idea that the potential of your natal chart unfolds over the course of your lifetime. A transit, progression, or direction activates a planet or house in your chart for a period of time, and that part of your life takes center stage. What makes Predictive Natal Astrology so challenging is that you have to interpret every predictive trigger in the context of the natal chart. **The Cardinal Rule of Predictive Natal Astrology** states, "If it's not in the natal chart, it won't ever happen."

In the Online Predictive Astrology Class, you will analyze both the inner experience and the outer event. You will consider significant events for celebrity subjects, using transits, secondary progressions, and primary directions. You will also learn to write a classical solar return interpretation.

The Online Predictive Astrology Class is open only to students who have successfully completed the Natal Interpretation Training Intensive and the Online Relationship Astrology Class. Provided you complete all of the written assignments in the Online Predictive Astrology Class, including the final project, at the end of the class you will be a Certified Talented Astrologer.

Visit http://TheRealAstrology.com/certification to see the entire course catalog of The Real Astrology Academy and learn how you can become a Certified Talented Astrologer.

APPENDIX D
Glossary of Terms

Accidental Debility A condition that has nothing to do with the position of the planet in the zodiac and has a negative effect on the performance or prominence of a planet. Accidental Debilities include placement in a cadent house (prominence), being combust or under the Sun's beams (prominence), being retrograde (performance), or in a partile conjunction, square, or opposition to a malefic (performance). Accidental Debility has limited application in the context of a natal chart interpretation.

Accidental Dignity A condition that has nothing to do with the position of the planet in the zodiac and has a positive effect on the performance or prominence of a planet. Accidental Dignities include placement in an angular house (prominence), being square the Moon's Nodes (prominence), cazimi (performance), or in a partile conjunction, trine, or sextile to a benefic (performance). Accidental Dignity has limited application in the context of a natal chart interpretation.

Air One of the four elements. The Air signs are Gemini, Libra, and Aquarius. The element of Air represents the mental, social, and intellectual realms. Planets in Air signs move horizontally across the surface and form connections.

almuten The planet that has the greatest Essential Dignity for a specific degree of a sign. This is usually, but not always, the planet that rules the sign. In the context of a natal chart interpretation, a planet that is the almuten of a house will express with the affairs of that house, and disruptions in that house will cause the planet to act.

angles The four angles of the chart are the Ascendant, Imum Coeli, Descendant, and Midheaven. They represent the cardinal points in the apparent daily motion of the planets. Planets rise at the Ascendant; they culminate at the

Midheaven; they set at the Descendant; and the Imum Coeli represents the lowest point. The angles are the doors that connect your inner experience of the natal chart to the outside world.

angular A house that contains or is defined by an angle, such as the 1st house (Ascendant), the 4th house (IC), the 7th house (Descendant), or the 10th house (Midheaven).

applying An aspect is applying when the planets are moving toward each other and have yet to form the exact angular relationship of the aspect.

Aquarius A Fixed Air sign and the 11th sign of the zodiac. Planets in Aquarius seek to sustain and maintain a sense of social self-worth.

Arabic Parts Also known as Greek Lots, these are sensitive points in the chart that are calculated based on the relative positions of three points in the chart, usually two planets and the Ascendant. In the context of natal astrology, the most important is the Part of Fortune.

Archetypal Astrology A system of astrology developed by Kevin B. Burk. The seven personal planets live within you as astrological archetypes. You can move into right relationship with each of these archetypes through targeted spiritual practices. The term "archetypal astrology" is used by other astrologers, but these astrologers work with nonastrological archetypes.

Aries A Cardinal Fire sign, and the 1st sign of the zodiac. Planets in Aries seek to express individual identity.

Ascendant The Ascendant, also known as the horoscope, is the degree on the Eastern horizon for the specific time and location of the chart. It's the Eastern angle of the chart, and usually defines the cusp of the 1st house. The Ascendant is the mask that you wear when you go out into the world. It's how you appear to others, and who other people think you are.

aspect In the grammar of astrology, aspects are conjunctions: they connect two phrases or clauses, and link the planets (or a planet and a point) in some kind of relationship. Aspects not only define a relationship between the two planets, but they also define a relationship between the houses ruled by those planets. The two major types of aspects are receptions, where one planet is on the Board of Directors of the other planet, and zodiacal

Glossary of Terms

aspects, which measure the angular relationship between two points along the ecliptic.

Astrological Alphabet The Astrological Alphabet is a system invented by Zip Dobbins that attempts to simplify astrology by combining the meanings of the planets, signs, and houses into a single set of twelve "letters." Letter 1 combines Mars, Aries, and the 1st house; Letter 2 combines Venus, Taurus, and the 2nd house, and so on. This system makes it impossible to interpret a natal chart correctly, because it ignores the fundamental differences between planets, signs, and houses, and disregards the rules of grammar and syntax of the language of astrology.

Astrological Archetypes The seven personal planets as they live inside you and operate as archetypal energies. The Sun is the archetype of the Hero; the Moon is the archetype of the Reflection; Mercury is the archetype of the Storyteller; Venus is the archetype of the Beloved; Mars is the archetype of the Warrior; Jupiter is the archetype of the Dreamer; and Saturn is the archetype of the Judge. You can move into right relationship with each of the astrological archetypes through targeted spiritual practices.

attachment The false belief that you can't survive without getting something that you want. Your ego creates attachments in an attempt to meet your Safety Needs, but the more attachments you create, the less safe you feel.

averse Planets that occupy signs which have nothing in common by element, modality, or polarity (one or five signs apart).

Belongingness and Love Needs One of the original categories of human needs proposed by Abraham Maslow. Belongingness and Love Needs involve being loved and appreciated by other people. They're included in the broader category of Validation Needs.

benefic In traditional astrology, the benefics are Jupiter (greater benefiic), Venus (lesser benefic), and the North Node. The benefics were considered fortunate, and when they form a favorable connection with another planet, that planet gains performance via Accidental Dignity. The concept of benefics has no practical use in natal astrology.

besieged A planet is besieged when it is placed between two other planets, within orb and aspecting them both. It generally refers to being placed between the benefics, Jupiter and Venus, or the malefics, Mars and Saturn.

bi-quintile A minor, 5th harmonic aspect formed when planets are 144° apart.

Board of Directors The planets that have Essential Dignity for a specific degree of a sign. Each dignity gives the planet that holds it a fixed number of votes: 5 for Rulership, 4 for Exaltation, 3 for Triplicity, 2 for Term, and 1 for Face. The planet with the most votes is the almuten for that degree. The planets on the Board of Directors are the actual planets in the chart, and their behavior is influenced by their relative power and degree of autonomy. For example, if Mars in Gemini is a member of a Board of Directors and Mercury (the ruler of Gemini) also serves on that Board of Directors, Mars will always vote with Mercury. However, if Mars in Gemini is on a Board of Directors and Mercury is not on the Board of Directors, Mars is free to pursue its own agenda.

cadent A house that follows a succedent house and precedes an angular house, such as the 3rd, 6th, 9th, or 12th house.

Cancer A Cardinal Water sign, and the 4th sign of the zodiac. Planets in Cancer seek to express emotional identity.

Capricorn A Cardinal Earth sign, and the 10th sign of the zodiac. Planets in Capricorn seek to express identity in the material world.

Cardinal One of the three modalities. The Cardinal signs are Aries, Cancer, Libra, and Capricorn. Planets in Cardinal signs initiate, and always seek something new; they lose interest the moment something becomes routine. Planets in Cardinal signs experience a crisis of identity. The core false belief is, "I'm bad."

cazimi An Arabic term that means "in the heart of the Sun," a planet is cazimi when it is conjunct the Sun with an orb of 17 minutes or less. Cazimi is a strong Accidental Dignity that improves both the performance and prominence of a planet.

checklist An unconscious list of expectations of experiences that will make a deposit in one of your Need Bank Accounts.

combust A planet is combust the Sun when it is within 8°30 of the Sun. Because combust planets rise and set with the Sun, they are invisible. Combust is a significant Accidental Debility that affects the prominence of the planet.

Glossary of Terms

consciousness The vibrational frequency of your thoughts. Your level of consciousness determines your subjective, "little r" reality.

conjunction A whole-sign, 1st harmonic aspect formed when two planets occupy the same degree of the same sign. Planets in conjunction share "A unity of purpose ..." because they are governed by the same Board of Directors.

Core Values A list of twelve qualities of the Divine, including Abundance, Balance, Beauty, Freedom, Harmony, Joy, Love, Order, Peace, Power, Unity, and Wisdom. You designed your human experience to know one or more of these qualities more deeply.

cusp The imaginary line that separates one house from the next, or one sign from the next.

decanate A term that describes the divisions of a sign into 10° segments. The Essential Dignity of Face is based on the decanates or decans of each sign.

deep practice As described by Daniel Coyle in *The Talent Code*, deep practice is how you develop skills and grow talent. Deep practice is slow, focused, precise, meticulous, and always requires reaching beyond your comfort zone. The struggle of deep practice causes the brain to wrap myelin around the neurons associated with the skill. This insulates and upgrades the circuit, allowing the impulses to travel with greater speed and efficiency.

Descendant The Descendant is the degree on the western horizon for the specific time and location of the chart. The Descendant is opposite the Ascendant. It's the western angle in the chart, and usually defines the cusp of the 7th house. The Descendant filters what you expect to see in other individuals, and influences what you find attractive in other people.

Detriment A planet which occupies a sign opposite a sign that it rules is in Detriment. Detriment is an Essential Debility that has a negative effect on the power of a planet. Planets in Detriment are very strong, but they use their strength in unfortunate ways that get them into trouble.

direct motion A planet in direct motion is moving forward through the signs.

diurnal A term that refers to the day, the diurnal sect is ruled by the Sun. A chart is diurnal when the Sun is above the horizon in houses 7 through 12.

Earth One of the four elements. The Earth signs are Taurus, Virgo, and Capricorn. The element of Earth represents the physical and material realm. Planets in Earth signs stay centered and grounded.

ecliptic The Sun's apparent orbital path around the Earth (actually the orbital path of the Earth around the Sun).

electional astrology A branch of predictive astrology in which you choose an advantageous time to begin an important event.

element One of the four fundamental natures, representing one of the four planes of existence: Fire (life/spirit), Earth (physical/material), Air (mental/social), and Water (emotional/spiritual).

emotion An emotion is a feeling with a story attached to it. The story reinforces the false belief that the feeling is the result of conditions in your "little r" reality, when in fact the feeling is the cause of those conditions.

Emotional Guidance System A term coined in the Abraham-Hicks Law of Attraction program to describe how to activate the Law of Attraction by turning toward better-feeling thoughts.

emplacement A term that describes the ruler of a house occupying a different house. It shows a connection between the two houses.

Essential Debility A condition resulting from the position of the planet at a specific degree of the zodiac, which has a negative effect on the power of a planet. The Essential Debilities include Detriment (a planet in a sign opposite a sign it rules), Fall (a planet in a sign opposite the sign of its Exaltation), and Peregrine (a planet with no Essential Dignity). Essential Debility is significant in the context of predictive astrology, but has limited practical value in natal astrology.

Essential Dignity A condition resulting from the position of the planet at a specific degree of the zodiac, which has a positive effect on the power of a planet. The system of Essential Dignity and Debility differentiates traditional astrology from "modern" astrology. The five Essential Dignities include Rulership, Exaltation, Triplicity, Term, and Face. In predictive astrology, the relative power or "strength" of a planet is significant, but this has limited practical value in natal astrology. In natal astrology, rather than

Glossary of Terms

evaluating the condition of a planet, you focus on the planets that receive it by Essential Dignity, known collectively as the Board of Directors.

Esteem Needs One of the original categories of human needs proposed by Abraham Maslow. Esteem Needs involve loving and appreciating yourself. They're included in the broader category of Validation Needs.

Exaltation A very strong sign-based Essential Dignity. The planet with Exaltation receives 4 votes on the Board of Directors. A planet in its own Exaltation is treated as an honored guest; it doesn't set its own agenda, but other planets do things for it on its behalf.

Face A very weak Essential Dignity. The planet with Face receives 1 vote on the Board of Directors. A planet that has dignity only by Face has an interest in the matter but lacks sufficient power to have any influence. Planets with dignity only by Face are afraid.

Fall A planet that occupies a sign opposite a sign of its Exaltation is in Fall. Fall is an Essential Debility that has a negative effect on the power of a planet. Planets in Fall are strong, but their particular skills are not useful in their current circumstances.

feeling Denotes the way you perceive and experience the vibrational frequency of a level of consciousness. Feelings arise spontaneously, and are the cause of experiences in your "little r" reality. If you tune to the frequency of Anger, your "little r" reality will be filled with experiences that are a match to that vibration. Ideally, feelings should be experienced without resistance or judgment. If a feeling is unpleasant, you need only turn your attention away from it, and choose a better-feeling thought.

final dispositor See sole dispositor.

Fire One of the four elements. The Fire signs are Aries, Leo, and Sagittarius. The element of Fire represents the realm of life and Spirit. Planets in Fire signs rise, and always seek greater expression.

First Kingdom One of the four Kingdoms of Consciousness, also known as Victim Consciousness. In First Kingdom, things are done "to me." First Kingdom is the domain of the ego/body and is governed by Mars. The levels of consciousness in First Kingdom calibrate below 200, the critical level of integrity, and use force rather than power. Everything at these levels of consciousness is *real*, but none of it is *true*.

Fixed One of the three modalities. The Fixed signs are Taurus, Leo, Scorpio, and Aquarius. Planets in Fixed signs sustain and maintain. They seek routine and stability, and resist change. Planets in Fixed signs experience a crisis of self-worth. Their core false belief is, "I'm not enough."

force (v. power) Any action taken from a consciousness level below 200 (e.g., from First Kingdom/Victim Consciousness) uses force, rather than power. Force is inherently weak; it can't sustain itself and must consume energy. Force moves in a negative direction, toward lower levels of consciousness with even less available energy. Force always creates a counter-force. Any action taken from First Kingdom is inherently counterproductive.

Fourth Kingdom One of the four Kingdoms of Consciousness. In Fourth Kingdom, things are done "as me," although technically, in Fourth Kingdom, there is no longer a *me* for things to be done *as*. The levels of consciousness in Fourth Kingdom calibrate at 600 and above, and represent the enlightened and transcendent states.

Gemini A Mutable Air sign, and the 3rd sign of the zodiac. Planets in Gemini seek to heal and complete the intellect.

Greek Lots See Arabic Parts.

hard skills As described by Daniel Coyle in *The Little Book of Talent*, hard skills require precision and consistency. They are objective and have a specific, repeatable target. The hard skills in astrology include the Phase 1 skills when you read the chart, and the Phase 2 skills when you assemble the information from the chart in sentences that follow the rules of grammar and syntax.

harmonic aspect The theory of harmonic aspects was developed by Johannes Kepler, who rejected the traditional sign-based theory of aspects described by Ptolemy. Harmonic aspects rely on precise mathematical relationships between the planets. The harmonic aspects are also known as the "minor" aspects, and include the semi-square and the sesquisquare.

Hellenistic Astrology Astrology practiced in Greece and Rome from the 1st century BC to the 6th century AD.

Glossary of Terms

horary astrology A type of predictive astrology in which the chart for the moment a question was asked contains the answer to the question.

house system The boundaries between the houses are hypothetical, not observable. You can't look in the sky and see the cusp of the 2nd house. The choice of a house system is personal, but once you choose one, you need to be consistent. A number of different house systems are in use today, and they fall into one of four categories: Equal, Time, Space, or Quadrant. Most of these systems use at least one of the angles, either the Ascendant or the Midheaven, as a reference point and house cusp, and the most significant differences between the house systems are the locations and sizes of the succedent and cadent houses.

Imum Coeli The Imum Coeli (latin for "bottom of the sky") or the IC, as it is usually known, is the northern angle in the chart. It is directly opposite the Midheaven, and usually defines the cusp of the 4th house. It's the most private and hidden point in the chart, but also the point of greatest connection to the universe. It symbolizes beginnings and endings, and it's the point where the soul enters the body.

inconjunct Ptolemy used the term "inconjunct" to describe planets in signs that have nothing in common by element, modality, or polarity. The planets cannot "see" each other and have no connection. Although Ptolemy used this term to emphasize the lack of an aspect between two planets, in present day astrology, inconjunct usually refers to the semi-sextile aspect and/or the quincunx aspect.

inferior planet A planet with an orbit closer to the Sun than the Earth (e.g., Mercury and Venus).

inner planets Also known as the personal planets, the inner planets are the seven planets visible to the naked eye and used in traditional astrology: Sun, Moon, Mercury, Venus, Mars, Jupiter, and Saturn.

intercepted sign A sign that is entirely contained within a house, such that it does not appear on the cusp of a house. Interceptions are possible only in nonequal house systems.

Kingdoms of Consciousness A model of reality developed by Dr. Homer Johnson, and popularized by Rev. Michael Beckwith. First Kingdom is the domain of the ego; it's known as Victim Consciousness, and things are done "to me." Second Kingdom is the domain of the linear mind, and things are done "by me." Third Kingdom is the domain of spiritual realities, and things are done "through me." Fourth Kingdom is the realm of enlightenment. Beckwith says that in Fourth Kingdom, things are done "as me," but because the ego and the "little s" self no longer exist at these levels of consciousness, there's technically not a *me* for things to be done *as*.

Law of Attraction A Universal Law that states everything in the Universe vibrates at a specific frequency, and like energies attract each other. The Law of Attraction is the highest Law of Third Kingdom, and supersedes the Law of Cause and Effect.

Law of Cause and Effect A Universal Law that states every cause has an effect, and every effect becomes the cause of something else. The Law of Cause and Effect is the highest Law of First and Second Kingdom.

Leo A Fixed Fire sign, and the 5th sign of the zodiac. Planets in Leo seek to sustain and maintain a sense of individual identity.

Libra A Cardinal Air sign, and the 7th sign of the zodiac. Planets in Libra seek to initiate a social and intellectual identity.

malefic In traditional astrology, the malefics are Saturn (greater malefic), Mars (lesser malefic), and the South Node. The malefics are considered unfortunate, and when they form a challenging connection with another planet, that planet loses performance via Accidental Debility. The concept of malefics has no practical use in natal astrology.

Marriage Blueprint A relationship blueprint based on your perception of your parents' relationship that is template for all of your romantic relationships.

Midheaven The Midheaven, also known as the Medium Coeli or MC, is the southern angle in the chart, and it usually defines the cusp of the 10th house. The Midheaven is the most public point in the chart, and relates to your public life, accomplishments, and reputation.

modality The three modalities are Cardinal, Fixed, and Mutable. The modalities determine how planets in a sign express.

moiety Half of the orb of a planet. To determine if an aspect between two planets is valid, you add the degrees of moiety for the two planets.

Glossary of Terms

Moon's Nodes The points where the orbit of the Moon around the Earth intersect the plane of the ecliptic. The North Node (☊) is the point where the Moon rises above the ecliptic, and the South Node (☋) is the point where the Moon sets below the ecliptic. When a new moon (Moon conjunct Sun) occurs within 18°31 of one of the Moon's Nodes, it is a solar eclipse. When a full moon (Moon opposite Sun) occurs within 12°15 of one of the Moon's Nodes, it is a lunar eclipse.

mundane astrology The branch of astrology that deals with world events.

Mutable One of the three modalities. The Mutable signs are Gemini, Virgo, Sagittarius, and Pisces. Planets in Mutable signs heal and complete. They are motivated to complete the current cycle and prepare for the next by adapting and changing. Planets in Mutable signs experience a crisis of completion. Their core false belief is, "I'm incomplete."

mutual reception A situation in which two planets receive each other by the same Essential Dignity.

natal astrology The branch of astrology that is based on an individual's unique birth chart, calculated for the date, time, and location of birth.

natal chart Also known as a birth chart, the chart of the moment a person was born, calculated for the specific date, time, and location of birth.

nocturnal A term that refers to the night, the nocturnal sect is ruled by the Moon. A chart is nocturnal when the Sun is below the horizon in houses 1 through 6.

North Node The point at which the orbit of the Moon rises above the plane of the ecliptic. In traditional astrology, the North Node is considered a benefic; however, because it is a sensitive point and not a physical body, it can receive aspects but not make them. A conjunction to the North Node is an Accidental Dignity that improves performance.

opposition A whole-sign, 2nd harmonic aspect formed when planets are 180° apart, in signs that share the same polarity and modality, but have different elements. Planets in opposition experience "A need for balance and compromise …" that always plays out in the context of relationships. In traditional astrology, the opposition is the most challenging aspect because it can point to direct confrontation and open aggression.

orb The sphere of influence of a planet. The planet occupies the center of the orb, which describes the range of the light, or influence of the planet. Each planet "looks ahead" a certain number of degrees, as its light extends forward in the zodiac, and "hurls rays" the same number of degrees backward. An aspect between to planets is "in orb" if the planets are close enough for their light to intersect. In modern astrology, the orb of an aspect describes the difference between the actual angle between the planets and the exact angle of the aspect.

outer planet A category that includes all planets beyond the orbit of Saturn. The outer planets include Uranus, Neptune, Pluto, and Chiron.

Part of Fortune Also known as the Lot of Fortune in Hellenistic astrology, the Part of Fortune (⊗) is an Arabic Part/Greek Lot that defines a relationship between the Sun, Moon, and Ascendant. The Part of Fortune is a point of increase and represents money. The planet that rules the Part of Fortune symbolizes your wealth, and can be considered in concert with the ruler of the 2nd house. Because it is a sensitive point and not a physical body, it can receive aspects, but not make them.

partile In traditional astrology, where aspects between planets are based on the signs, a partile aspect occurs between two planets at the same whole degree. Partile aspects are more significant than platick aspects, which occur between planets at different degrees. An aspect can be exact and yet not be partile. A planet at 1°59 Aries and a planet at 2°01 Leo are in an exact trine with an orb of 0°02, but the aspect is not partile. However, the trine between a planet at 2°01 Aries and a planet at 2°59 Leo is partile, even though the orb of the aspect is 0°58.

peregrine A planet with no Essential Dignity (no votes on its own Board of Directors) is peregrine. Peregrine means "wandering," which is appropriate because a peregrine planet has no control over its own agenda. Peregrine has no practical application in the context of natal astrology. In the context of horary astrology, a peregrine planet is severely damaged, but in natal astrology, a peregrine planet is not hindered in any way.

perfected An aspect between two planets is perfected when it becomes exact.

performance In the context of Accidental Dignity or Debility and predictive astrology, performance evaluates how helpful a planet intends to be. Whether

Glossary of Terms

the planet can achieve its intentions depends on the power (Essential Dignity) of the planet, as well as its prominence (Accidental Dignity).

personal planets See inner planets.

Physiological Needs The first and most basic category of human needs defined by Abraham Maslow. Physiological Needs include everything you require for physical survival, including air, food, sleep, and shelter. Mars is in charge of your Physiological Need Bank Account.

Pisces A Mutable Water sign, and the 12th sign of the zodiac. Planets in Pisces seek to heal and complete on the emotional and spiritual planes.

platick In traditional astrology, where aspects between planets are based on the signs, a platick aspect occurs between two planets at different degrees. Platick aspects are less significant than partile aspects, which occur between planets at the same whole degree.

polarity A division of the signs into opposing categories of masculine (expressive, yang) and feminine (receptive, yin). The Fire and Air signs are masculine, while the Earth and Water signs are feminine.

power (Essential Dignity) A measure of how successful a planet will be when it pursues its agenda. The more Essential Dignity a planet has (i.e., the more votes it has on its own Board of Directors), the more powerful it is. This has limited practical value in natal astrology, but it's extremely important in horary astrology.

power (vs. force) Any action taken from a consciousness level above 200 (e.g., from Second Kingdom or higher) uses power. Power is inherently strong and self-sustaining. Power creates energy and moves in a positive direction toward higher levels of consciousness. Power has no opposite and creates no obstacles to expression.

prominence In the context of Accidental Dignity or Debility and predictive astrology, prominence evaluates how visible a planet and its expression will be. Prominence is independent of performance (whether the planet intends to be helpful or not) or power (whether the planet has the strength to achieve its intentions).

Ptolemaic aspect A term that describes the traditional, whole-sign aspects included in the *Tetrabiblos*, by Claudius Ptolemy. These aspects include the conjunction, opposition, square, trine, and sextile. They are also referred to as the "major" aspects.

Ptolemy Claudius Ptolemy was a scholar (not a practicing astrologer) who lived in Greece during the 2nd century AD He is best known for the *Tetrabiblos*, which documented the science of astrology at the time. The Latin translation of the *Tetrabiblos* was one of the fundamental astrological textbooks for centuries.

quincunx A whole-sign, 12th harmonic aspect formed when two planets are 150° apart, in signs that have different elements, modalities, and polarities. Ptolemy emphasized that planets five signs apart are not, in fact, in aspect to each other, calling them inconjunct. Even though the quincunx is a whole-sign aspect, it functions as a minor, harmonic aspect and is valid only with very precise orbs. Two inner planets quincunx each other experience "A fundamental incompatibility …" while an outer planet quincunx an inner planet represents "Random, unexpected disruptions …".

quintile A minor, 5th harmonic aspect formed when two planets are 72° apart.

reception An aspect that links two planets via the Essential Dignities and the Board of Directors.

relationship blueprint An unconscious template based on your perceptions of key relationships, used to build those relationships in your life. The most important relationship blueprints are the Marriage Blueprint (based on your perception of your parents' relationship and used to create your romantic relationships) and the Authority Blueprints (based on your relationship with each of your parents, used to create your relationships with authority).

Relationship Needs Safety Needs and Validation Needs, the only needs that can be met by other people. You need to feel safe and validated in every relationship, although how you expect to meet these needs depends on the nature of the relationship.

retrograde motion A planet in retrograde motion moves backward through the signs.

rising sign The sign of the Ascendant in a natal chart.

Glossary of Terms

Rodden Rating A system created by Lois Rodden to classify the reliability of birth data. The highest rating is AA (accurate accurate), which is reserved for data as recorded by the family or state. This includes BC (birth certificate) and BR (birth record). A (accurate) data is quoted from memory by the person, kin, friend, or associate. B (biography) is data from either a biography or autobiography. Data rated AA, A, or B are the only data that should be used in astrological studies. Data rated C (caution), DD (dirty data), X (no time of birth), or XX (unconfirmed data) is highly speculative.

ruler The ruler (of a planet, sign, or house) is the planet that has Essential Dignity by Rulership for the sign.

Rulership The strongest (and most important) of the five Essential Dignities. Rulership is a sign-based dignity. The ruler of a sign receives 5 votes on the Board of Directors and is the CEO of the sign; it sets the agenda. It manages all planets that occupy the sign, and is responsible for the affairs of all houses with that sign on the cusp. A planet in the sign of its own Rulership sets its own agenda, and has the power to accomplish it. This is good for the planet, but not always good for the individual.

Safety Needs The second category of human needs defined by Abraham Maslow. Safety Needs help you to believe that your Physiological Needs will continue to be met. Safety Needs relate to the things that you believe you need to survive. The Moon is in charge of your Safety Need Account. The moment the balance in your Safety Need Account drops below the minimum level, you step into First Kingdom and Victim Consciousness. When you maintain a healthy balance in your Safety Need Account, you operate from integrity, and all of your other needs are met automatically. Safety Needs, along with Validation Needs, make up your Relationship Needs, because Safety and Validation Needs are the only needs that can be met by other people.

Sagittarius A Mutable Fire sign, and the 9th sign of the zodiac. Planets in Sagittarius seek to heal and complete their individual identity.

Scorpio A Fixed Water sign, and the 8th sign of the zodiac. Planets in Scorpio seek to sustain and maintain emotional and spiritual connections.

Second Kingdom One of the four Kingdoms of Consciousness. In Second Kingdom, things are done "by me." Second Kingdom is the domain of the linear mind, and is governed by Saturn. The levels of consciousness in Second Kingdom calibrate from 200, the critical level of integrity through 499, the highest level of reason and logic.

sect Sect is a word that comes from the Latin word *seco*, which means "to cut" or "to divide." In astrology, sect refers to the division between diurnal (day) planets and nocturnal (night) planets. Each of the seven visible planets was classified as either diurnal or nocturnal by nature. The planet's condition in the overall chart was evaluated based on the position and sect of the chart. The diurnal planets are the Sun (most diurnal), Jupiter, and Saturn (least diurnal). The nocturnal planets are the Moon (most nocturnal), Mars, and Venus (least nocturnal). Mercury is "bisectual" and can align with either the diurnal or nocturnal sect. The position of the Sun in the chart determines the sect of the chart. If the Sun is above the horizon in houses 7 through 12, it's a diurnal or day chart. If the Sun is below the horizon in houses 1 through 6, it's a nocturnal or night chart. The sect of the chart determines which planets have Triplicity in the chart.

Self-Actualization Needs The highest category of human needs defined by Abraham Maslow. Self-Actualization Needs are things you do for yourself to reach your highest potential as an individual. The Sun is in charge of your Self-Actualization Need Bank Account.

semi-sextile A whole-sign, 12th harmonic aspect formed when two planets are 30° apart in adjacent signs, and have nothing in common by element, modality, or polarity.

semi-square An 8th harmonic aspect formed when two planets are 45° apart. The semi-square represents "A minor internal tension or friction …".

sensitive point Any nonphysical, mathematical point in the chart, including the angles, the house cusps, the Moon's Nodes, Arabic Parts, and midpoints.

separating An aspect is separating when the planets are moving away from each other and have already formed the exact angular relationship of the aspect.

sesquisquare An 8th harmonic aspect formed when two planets are 135° apart. The sesquisquare or sesquiquadrate, as it's sometimes known, represents

Glossary of Terms

"A minor annoyance or irritation …". Sesquisquares tend to play out in relationships, and often resolve the tension verbally, using humor.

sextile A whole-sign, 6th harmonic aspect formed when planets are 60° apart, in signs that share the same polarity, but have different elements and modalities. A sextile represents "An opportunity for support …".

Sidereal Zodiac A system of measuring the longitudinal position of the planets along the ecliptic used primarily in traditional Hindu, Vedic, and Jyotish Astrology. The Sidereal Zodiac accounts for the precession of the equinoxes, and attempts to align 0° Aries with the fixed stars (sidereal = star) of the constellation of Aries. In the year 2015, the positions in the Sidereal Zodiac are approximately 24° behind the positions in the Tropical Zodiac. The difference between the two systems grows by approximately 50 seconds of arc each year.

soft skills As described by Daniel Coyle in *The Little Book of Talent*, soft skills involve pattern recognition, and require flexibility and adaptability. There is not a single path to a good result. You rely on soft skills when you work with a client, and look for how the "chairs" of the natal chart show up for them.

sole dispositor A planet in Rulership in the chart that directly or indirectly disposes (receives by Rulership) every other planet in the chart.

South Node The point at which the orbit of the Moon sinks below the plane of the ecliptic. In traditional astrology, the South Node is considered a malefic; however, because it is a sensitive point and not a physical body, it can receive aspects but not make them. A conjunction to the South Node is an Accidental Debility that negatively impacts performance.

square A whole-sign, 4th harmonic aspect formed when planets are 90° apart, in signs that share the same modality but different elements and polarities. Squares represent "Friction, tension, stress, and conflict …" and are classified as a "hard" aspect. The tension of a square always can be resolved through action.

stationary planet A planet that appears to be motionless because it is preparing to change direction, either turning retrograde or direct.

succedent A house that follows or succeeds an angular house, such as the 2nd, 5th, 8th, or 11th house.

superior planet A planet with an orbit beyond that of the Earth (e.g., Mars, Jupiter, Saturn, Chiron, Uranus, Neptune, or Pluto).

Taurus A Fixed Earth sign, and the 2nd sign of the zodiac. Planets in Taurus seek to sustain and maintain on the physical and material plane.

Term A weak Essential Dignity. The planet with Term receives 2 votes on the Board of Directors. A planet with dignity only by Term is in declining fortunes. It may be able to accomplish its goals, but only if it encounters no obstacles.

Third Kingdom One of the Four Kingdoms of Consciousness. In Third Kingdom, things are done "through me." Third Kingdom is the domain of spiritual realities, and is governed by Venus. The Law of Attraction is the highest law in Third Kingdom. It includes the levels of consciousness of Love, which calibrate from 500 through 599. This is the level of consciousness associated with spiritual practices and the Astrological Archetypes. Everything at these levels of consciousness is *true*, but it may not be *real*.

top-level planet A term that refers to the main planet under consideration for a particular section of an interpretation. The top-level planet sets the context for that section of the interpretation, and everything else in the section must be considered in this context, including the planets on the Board of Directors for the top-level planet and aspects to the top-level planet. For example, when considering Safety Needs, the Moon is the top-level planet.

trine A whole-sign, 3rd harmonic aspect formed when planets are 120° apart, in signs that share the same element. Trines represent "An easy, constant, effortless flow of energy …". The energy of a trine is always active, and represents a lack of obstacles. This is not always a good thing.

Triplicity A moderately strong, sign-based Essential Dignity. The planet with Triplicity receives 3 votes on the Board of Directors. For the Fire, Earth, and Air signs, the sect of the chart determines which planet has dignity by Triplicity. A planet with dignity by Triplicity is lucky. It generally has enough power to accomplish its goals.

Glossary of Terms

Tropical Zodiac A system of measuring the longitudinal position of the planets along the ecliptic, used in western astrology. The year begins at the moment of the spring equinox in the northern hemisphere, which is designated as 0° Aries.

under the beams A planet is under the beams of the Sun when it is within 8°30 and 17° of the Sun. Planets under the Sun's beams rise and set with the Sun, which renders them invisible; however, they are far enough from the Sun to avoid being burned by it. Under the beams is a moderate Accidental Debility that affects the prominence of the planet.

Universal Law of Relationships Your partners in relationship are your mirrors: they reflect your own issues back to you. It's *never* about the other person.

Validation Needs A category of needs introduced in *The Relationship Handbook: How to Understand and Improve Every Relationship in Your Life*. Validation Needs combine Maslow's Belongingness and Love Needs and Esteem Needs into a single category. Validation Needs relate to how you experience and express love and appreciation. Venus is in charge of your Validation Need Account. Validation Needs, along with Safety Needs, make up your Relationship Needs, because Safety and Validation Needs are the only needs that can be met by other people.

Vertex An angle in the chart that represents the intersection of the Prime Vertical and the ecliptic in the West. The Vertex functions as an unconscious Descendant, showing qualities you find attractive in other people.

Victim Consciousness See First Kingdom.

Virgo A Mutable Earth sign, and the 6th sign of the zodiac. Planets in Virgo seek to heal and complete the physical and material realm.

watchlist An unconscious list of expectations of experiences that will make a withdrawal from one of your Need Bank Accounts.

Water One of the four elements. The Water signs are Cancer, Scorpio, and Pisces. The element of Water represents the emotional and spiritual realm. Planets in Water signs sink, seeking the deepest level.

whole-sign aspect A term that describes the "major" or Ptolemaic aspects that are based on whole-sign relationships, including the conjunction, opposition, trine, square, and sextile.

whole-sign houses An equal house system used in traditional astrology, especially in Hellenistic astrology. The signs are the houses, and the sign of the Ascendant marks the 1st house. The angles do not define the house cusps.

William Lilly An English astrologer who lived and published in the 17th century, Lilly was one of the first astrologers to write in English. He is best known for his book, *Christian Astrology*, which remains a definitive work on horary astrology.

zodiacal aspect An aspect in longitude formed because of the relative positions of two bodies in the zodiac.